TEMPTED

"I am decent now," said Stephen.

His hands drew Arielle's away from her face. Her cheeks drained of color when she saw he wore only a towel wrapped around his waist. Never had she been so close to such an expanse of proudly displayed, naked male virility. She could not move. She could barely breathe.

He put one fingertip under her collar. "The dressing gown looks lovely on you."

"I appreciate you getting this for me," she said stiffly. She took a step back toward the bedroom door.

"Get dressed," he said. "I am ready for some supper and an early night."

With his gaze stroking her back, she went into the bedroom. She closed the door and leaned against it, panting. How much longer could she ignore the longings of her body, which yearned for his caresses—and her heart, which yearned for his love?

Love? She edged away from the door. She must be mad.

Stephen's voice echoed in her head: *Nicaragua changes people.*

"Not that much," she whispered, knowing her protests were futile. She was falling in love with the wrong man.

HER ONLY HERO

JO ANN FERGUSON

Zebra Books
Kensington Publishing Corp.

http://www.zebrabooks.com

ZEBRA BOOKS are published by

Kensington Publishing Corp.
850 Third Avenue
New York, NY 10022

First Printing: January, 2000
10 9 8 7 6 5 4 3 2 1

Printed in the United States of America

For Claudia Yates—
Thanks for keeping me on my toes
and on the straight and narrow, policy guru

CHAPTER ONE

The summer breeze, crisp from the bay, snapped the flag hanging at the end of a pier. Thirty-one stars announced the recent admission of California into the Union. Salt filled the air, hinting at distant lands, and hard voyages ending in wealth or ruin. Rowdy music and laughter stretched invisible, enticing fingers out to invite patrons into the grog shops lining the streets along the piers. Other establishments waited sailors newly ashore, some hidden behind façades of respectability, others blatantly advertising their female wares.

No one paid attention as Arielle Gardiner walked alone along the pathway. She hoped that was because she carried herself with assurance. She did not want any passerby to guess that she never had been in this part of Boston before. The wind teased her cloak to reveal her flounced blue merino skirt. Her dark hair was smoothed back to cluster in ringlets at her nape beneath her fashionably small bonnet of blue muslin and pink rosebuds.

She paused by a tavern door. Looking at the paper in

her gloved hand, she sighed. This was the correct address. She should be grateful Captain Lightenfield had not chosen a worse place for their meeting.

Taking a deep breath, she pushed against the pine door that was studded with iron. It protested, but she exerted all her strength to open it. The reek of rum and the stench of unwashed bodies swarmed out of the dark tavern to buffet her as she stepped inside, warning her to leave. The thick door bumped into her, pushing her forward a few reluctant steps.

Long tables blackened with smoke cluttered the tavern. A few men sat mumbling into their drinks and the afternoon dusk. A barmaid stood in a distant corner, talking with lively gestures to a man who stroked her eagerly. Ignoring all of them, she pulled her cloak more tightly around her. She should go to the bar at the back of the room. She skirted a puddle in a depression in the stone floor.

"What do you want?"

She whirled at the impatient male voice. One look at his soiled apron worn over his bare chest urged her to flee. When she saw the tattoo of a monstrous creature crawling in many colors up his right arm, she clenched her hands on the silk tassels of her reticule. She forced herself to remain calm. This meeting was too important. She must not let her squeamish fears ruin it.

"I am meeting someone here," she answered with quiet dignity. "A man. I trust I may wait for him here."

The barkeeper smiled and flung a towel over his massive shoulder. When he spoke, the odor of onions billowed from his mouth, threatening to gag her. "Usually, darlin'," he said as his gaze roamed along her and his smile broadened, "I don't allow your type of business transactions in m'place."

"Sir, I assure you—"

He held up a single finger. "Just this once, darlin'. A

woman like you gives the place a bit of class, but if you do your business here again, you pay me a share. One quarter of what ye get from the lads, same as her over there.'' He shrugged toward the woman in the corner.

Arielle looked hastily at the barmaid and the man, who were now entwined in an intimate embrace.

"Do you understand?" the man in the apron asked.

Arielle almost retorted that she was not a harlot. She swallowed her answer. It did not matter what the tavern keeper thought of her. She did not intend to return here. She nodded.

"Then sit over there." He pointed to a table in the opposite corner. "Don't bother any of my customers. The girls here got claims on 'em."

"I understand," she said tightly. She gasped as he slapped her buttocks. Her face seared with embarrassment as she rushed away from his laughter.

Arielle sat at the shadowed table. The barkeeper set a glass of some dark liquid on the table. With a knowing grin he winked and walked away. Cautiously she lifted the glass and sniffed. It was just sarsaparilla, but she set it back on the table. She had no intentions of drinking anything in the filthy place.

She checked the small pendant watch she wore pinned to the short coat over her chemisette. Captain Lightenfield was late. She tried not to be irritated. It was impossible. When she had sent a note to his ship, she had emphasized her need to speak with him immediately. *He* had set the time for this meeting. So why was he late?

When the tavern door opened, allowing in a welcome breath of clean air, she looked up in anticipation. A tall silhouette entered. The door crashed shut, and she lowered her gaze to the glass. She should not be staring at the customers as boldly as one of the prostitutes.

Self-assured footsteps came toward her. With them came

the aroma of saltwater. A shiver raced along her back, but she had come too far to turn back.

A man slid onto the opposite bench without speaking or waiting for an invitation. When she raised her eyes to meet his, she could not hide her astonishment. She had known that supplying the filibusters in Central America was a young man's game, but she had not guessed Captain Lightenfield would have thunderhead-gray eyes that swept over her with cool disdain. Under his navy wool cap, his pale hair had been bleached by the fierce glare of sunlight on the waves to a shade lighter than his mustache. The square line of his jaw was as roughly carved as the tavern's door. As he leaned forward to fold his arms on the table, his muscles moved smoothly beneath his open pea jacket.

"You're Arielle Gardiner?" he asked in a voice as deep as the rumble of a storm punishing the beach.

"I am. You're Captain Lightenfield?"

"Stephen Lightenfield," he answered in an easy drawl.

"That is a fancy name for a sea captain," she said before she could halt herself. Her gaze dropped from his sudden smile to the table. The smile, which glittered in his eyes and eased the angles of his hard face, sent a shiver along her spine.

"It's the only name I have that I can repeat in a lady's company." He put his finger under her chin. When she gasped and started to pull away from his presumptuous touch, he tightened his hold. "Now, tell me why a lovely lady like you wants to go to a horrible place like Nicaragua. This should be interesting."

She batted his hand away, and his eyes crinkled with amusement. This was no joke. She must make him realize she was serious. "Do you ask all your passengers that? I thought filibusters liked keeping things secret."

"I leave gun running and revolution to those fools who think they can conquer Central America. I prefer to be just a merchantman."

In her lap, Arielle clutched the strings of her purse. She did not want him to see her anxiety at being in this horrible place with this disturbingly handsome man. Squaring her shoulders, she raised her eyes to meet his. Merriment continued to twinkle there. How was she going to convince him she was serious? There was no way but with the truth. "Captain, I am here solely to discuss business. May we do so?"

He smiled as he sat back, letting his salt-stained sleeve drape over the upper part of the crude wooden bench. She guessed his nonchalance was a well-practiced pose. Stephen Lightenfield was a coiled spring ready to explode if she said the wrong thing. She just did not know what that wrong thing might be. He had earned a reputation for caring only about his ship and his cargo. She had heard it whispered along the docks that many otherwise brave men refused to sign aboard his ship, which he could make fly before the wind. Speed was all that she cared about when she needed to get to Nicaragua right away.

When Captain Lightenfield snapped his fingers, the barmaid appeared out of the dusk. He offered her a practiced smile as she preened before him. "What do you have that is tasty today, sweetheart?"

"Depends on what you are hungry for, Cap'n." She slanted toward him, her full breasts thrusting against the low neckline of her gown. "Why don't you tell me what you want?"

"Rum."

"Just rum?"

Arielle looked from the barmaid's disappointed pout to Captain Lightenfield's grin. She never had wanted to be somewhere else more than she did now. This was madness! She should be home in Concord, getting ready for another year of teaching school, instead of sitting in this appalling grog shop while a crude sea captain flirted with a tavern whore.

Captain Lightenfield's gaze caught hers. Again she saw his amusement, and uneasiness rippled through her in a cold wave. He was enjoying her discomfort. If he could gauge her thoughts so easily, she could be risking more than she should with this meeting.

Fiercely she ripped her gaze away. She could not let him intimidate her with a mere smile. Forcing one on her taut lips, she dared him with his own cruel game. He simply cocked an eyebrow in her direction before turning back to the barmaid.

"Just rum," he said. "For now."

The barmaid ruffled his blond hair and aimed a venomous glare at Arielle, who kept her chin high. She would not be humiliated by a jealous barmaid.

Captain Lightenfield chuckled as the woman swayed away. He surveyed Arielle so boldly, she lowered her eyes, again frightened. This captain was no romantic hero waiting to rescue a woman in distress. He had the morals of a dockside harlot. If only she did not need his help to get to Nicaragua . . .

After a bottle and a glass that were stained with dirt were set in front of him, Captain Lightenfield said, "Miss Gardiner, before you go any further, let me tell you that pretty ladies have no place in Nicaragua. If you wish to indulge yourself in an adventure, why don't you find yourself a lover? You should not be playing where the stakes are higher." He swallowed the rum in his glass and refilled it. "Just a bit of advice, of course."

"I do not want your advice!" she retorted. "Captain, I must go to Nicaragua. Will you take me?"

"No."

Arielle stared at him in disbelief. His eyes were like twin stones above the uncompromising line of his lips. "Captain Lightenfield, I'll pay you well."

"No."

"You are going there," she argued, "so why not take me with you?"

"Because I don't want to." He drained the glass with ease. Standing, he smiled down at her. His finger brazenly traced the curve of her cheek, lingering near the corner of her mouth. A lightning-hot shock sped through her. When she turned away with a gasp, he chuckled. "Thanks for the drink. Good luck finding a ship, but you will not be traveling on *The Ladysong*."

"But why did you come here if you never planned to take me on your ship?"

Resting his hands on the table, he bent until his nose was only inches from hers. She wanted to look away, to look anywhere but at his compelling eyes. She could not. Their cool storminess imprisoned her as his voice's low thunder reverberated through her, battering down every defense she had. "You asked me to meet you so we could talk over a drink. We met, and we talked over a drink."

"But you promised—"

"Nothing. Don't waste your virginal outrage on me, Miss Gardiner." He laughed and patted her cheek. "Thanks again for the drink."

Arielle rose, her full skirts whispering as she hurried after him. She grasped his dark sleeve. When he glared at her, she faced him coolly. "Captain, you don't understand. I *must* get to Nicaragua. Right away. Your ship is the next one to leave Boston."

His eyes narrowed as he brushed her hand off his arm. Gripping her chin, he tilted her head back. Her bonnet slid off her hair to slap her shoulder, but she did not notice it as he took a step closer. Overwhelmed by the firm line of his muscular chest, she leaned away from him. She grasped on to a table as she struggled not to become lost in his mesmerizing gaze. She could not let his domineering posture intimidate her into giving up her hopes of reaching

Nicaragua. She must ignore the odd delight spiraling within her as his thumb skimmed along her jaw.

The bronze skin around his eyes crinkled when he chuckled. "You innocent fool, go home, where you belong."

"I can't. I must—"

His curse sent fire along her spine. He released her and strode into the deepest shadows at the far end of the tavern. She heard the door open and close with a thump.

Arielle sat at the table again. Closing her eyes, she rubbed her aching forehead. What would she do now? *The Ladysong* was the only ship bound directly for Nicaragua that week. She could not wait until the next ship sailed. It might be weeks before another sailed from Boston. Blast Captain Lightenfield! He had enjoyed taunting her when he had known that he would not take her with him.

But she must get to Nicaragua. If she did not, disaster might strike her fiancé. Guilt suffused her. Even her desperate need to get to Caleb did not excuse her wanton behavior in coming to this vulgar place and allowing that crass man to touch her as if he were her lover.

"Oh, Caleb," she whispered as she pressed her hands to her face. "Why did you have to go away to that terrible country?"

She would have no answer to that until she reached him in Nicaragua. In her bag was the tattered, scrawled note she had received the week before from Caleb Drummond. It was the first she had heard from him in more than six months. When he first had left Concord to work for Commodore Vanderbilt's Accessory Transit Company in Nicaragua, he had written often. Each letter had been filled with exciting tales of his journey south and of transporting men across Central America on their way to the California gold fields. Then the letters had stopped.

She had waited, pretending nothing was amiss as she taught in the village school each day and read the newspaper every evening, searching for anything to tell her what was happening in the tiny country that had been taken over by American William Walker and his band of filibusters. Only cloying bits of rumors reached her. Rumors of trouble and unrest.

Then this last letter had come. She had memorized its few words while she packed the few things she could bring with her to Nicaragua.

. . . safe. As soon as you can obtain passage, come, Arielle. In the past months, I have learned Nicaragua is much different from what I had thought. It is even more wonderful. We . . . I have found a place of rare beauty, where we can live in peace together. You will like . . . pretty . . . Clippers leave Boston regularly for Greytown. Take one, and I . . . If not, just follow the map I have included with . . .

But there had been no map. Arielle had searched the shredded envelope, but whatever Caleb had put in it was gone. She had to hope that once she reached Greytown on the eastern coast of Nicaragua, she could contact someone with the Accessory Transit Company. Someone who would know where in that godforsaken country Caleb was. Someone who would explain why after letters complaining about the heat, which made New England dog days seem mild, and of the deadly bugs, Caleb had sent no word for six months, then asked her to join him in that trackless jungle.

Something was wrong. She knew that with a sense that had no name. Fear burned in her heart. Caleb needed her as she had needed him when they were children and he helped her with a scratched knee or to fix her doll.

She was so tantalizingly close to being able to get answers to the questions haunting her. If only Captain Lightenfield . . . blast him! There had to be another way for her to get to Nicaragua.

"Arielle Gardiner?"

At the raspy voice Arielle looked up. Her eyes widened as she peered through the clinging shadows at a wizened, grizzled face. The man's grin pierced the murk, but only a few teeth remained to glisten in the low light. The tail of a loose shirt flapped out of his trousers, and she doubted if he had had a bath in the past month.

"I'm Arielle Gardiner." She flinched. This was the same way the conversation had started with Captain Lightenfield. At least, that arrogant man was gone! "Who are you?"

"Jake."

"Are you with one of the ships in the harbor?"

He gestured toward the bench across from her. When she nodded, he dropped onto it. "Call me Cap'n Jake if ye wish. I hear ye be lookin' to get away from Boston. Nicaragua is where ye be bound."

"Yes." She shuddered at the idea of sailing with this foul man, but comfort was not important if she could reach Greytown. "If you are willing to take me—"

His choking laugh grated on her ears. "Takin' ye be no problem."

"Wonderful!" She clapped her gloved hands together, then held them over her mouth to muffle her joyous laughter. This was a miracle! Better than a miracle, because she could thumb her nose at Captain Lightenfield's imperious refusal to give her passage. Let him ridicule her all he wished. She had found another way to Greytown.

The old man picked up the bottle that remained on the table and drank deeply. He wiped the back of his hand across his full lips, then scratched beneath his collar. "So it be a deal?"

"I suppose we should negotiate how much this will cost. We should—" She halted when she heard a muffled laugh. Squinting to see through the dim tavern, she saw the barmaid sitting on the lap of a sailor. She had to escape this lewdness. Taking a deep breath, she added, "Captain, how much?"

"You be a plain talker for such a pretty looker." He tapped his fingers on the table. "Name a fair price."

Arielle hesitated. She had no idea what a fair price for passage to Greytown might be. Knowing how little she had in her bag, she must be careful. "Why don't you tell me what you think would be fair, sir? I have never done anything like this before."

He wheezed and took another drink from the bottle. "Never before?"

"No. I never had cause to before." When he reached for the bottle again, she said, "Sir, I would rather we hurried through these negotiations. I find them distasteful."

"Talk like a real lady, don't ye?"

Arielle frowned at his insult. She had hoped that all captains were not as ill mannered as Captain Lightenfield, but this man was just as vulgar. "Sir, what do you consider a fair price?"

"Why don't I figure that out fer ye, dearie?" With a laugh he reached across the table and wrapped a fetid hand around the back of her head. He pulled her mouth toward his.

She shrieked and leapt to her feet. As her skirt swirled around her in a blue cloud, she gasped, "Are you mad?"

"What's this ado?" demanded the barkeeper as he burst from the shadows. "Are you causin' trouble, woman? I told you to behave yourself in m'place."

"She be sayin' no when she already said yes," Jake grumbled.

"To passage south," Arielle said, her voice quivering as she wished she could scour the memory of his abominable touch from her mind. "Nothing more."

"Passage? To where, woman?" The barkeeper slapped

the old man on the back and roared with laughter. "Ain't nowhere Jake wishes to be takin' ye but to his bed."

"His . . . ?" She choked and shook her head. When she saw Jake's toothless grin, she backed away. She would not let him touch her again. She bumped into a hard body and rocked forward. Another scream burst from her as the barkeeper put out his arms to catch her.

Broad hands clamped on her shoulders and kept her on her feet. "You should keep watch on where you are going, Miss Gardiner."

She whirled to see Captain Lightenfield's smile. "What are you doing here?"

"Public place. I often come in here to have a drink with a few old friends." He lifted his glass in a salute to the men behind her. "And a few laughs."

Comprehension struck Arielle when she saw Jake's wide grin. Fury flashed through her, as searing as lightning. "*You* sent him over to talk to me. *You* told him that I wanted to go to Nicaragua."

"I just told my old friend that you were a lady looking for some adventure."

When he grinned, tears were hot in her eyes as more laughter surrounded her. Everyone in the tavern must have been privy to this cruel prank.

"How could you send him to mock me, when you know how important it is for me to get to Nicaragua?"

"I know how important it is for you to stay the hell out of that hellhole."

She flushed at his crude language as she edged around him. Let Captain Lightenfield enjoy his tomfoolery. She had no time to waste. She must find a ship going to Greytown.

Her arm was caught in a trap with steel fingers as she was jerked back. Shock burst from her as she gasped, "Captain Lightenfield!"

"Save that proper outrage for those who are not immune to it!" His eyes were as cold as his words as he pulled her so close to him that his strong legs pressed through the layers of her petticoats.

Again the peculiar tumult stirred within her when his hands slid slowly from her shoulders to clasp her arms. She had to tilt her head at an awkward angle to meet his gaze. "Release me, sir."

"When you have listened to what I have to say."

"Why should I listen to you?" she fired back. Blinking back tears she must not let him see, she said, "You have had your fun with me. I want nothing more of you."

"Except passage on my ship."

A pinch of satisfaction delighted her as she could say honestly, "You are wrong, Captain. I want nothing of you. I shall find an honorable captain who will take me to Nicaragua."

"Like old Jake?"

A volley of laughter reminded her that every word she spoke was falling on dozens of ears. Wrapping her tattered dignity around her, she asked, "Why do you care?"

"I don't." His smile returned, although it did not reach his eyes. There rage burned like heated embers. "You are the most confounded woman. I thought you would be smart enough to see sense after—"

"After you and your charming cohorts so kindly pointed it out to me? I am sorry to disappoint you, Captain." Jerking her arm away, she continued toward the door. His savage gaze pierced her, but she did not turn around as she struggled to open the door. Another boom of laughter followed her out into the street.

Arielle clenched her hands under her cloak as she hurried along the walkway. It would have been easier to have a respected ally like Captain Lightenfield, but she did not want his help now. She wished she could give him a sample of his own heartless sense of humor. It was impossible. She must think now only about how she would find transportation to Nicaragua, so she could find Caleb. When she was safe with him again, everything would be fine once more.

   She hoped.

CHAPTER TWO

Stephen Lightenfield did not look back as his clipper ship, *The Ladysong*, sailed on the evening tide from Boston. His steady gaze was seaward, as it had been since his earliest memories as a boy in Charleston. Taking a deep breath of the briny air, he rested his hands on the rail. He gauged the rise and fall of the waves with a skilled eye before looking upward to see the wind straining in the sails.

A good wind. They should be clear of Cape Cod ahead of schedule.

He smiled and tipped his cap back. Walking to where his first mate was crossing the deck, Stephen called, "Looks to be the beginning of a good voyage."

Roach Walden must have had another given name, but Stephen had never heard it. The short man had bandy legs and wiry hair on his arms and chin. A dirty cap covered his bald head. With the ease of his years at sea, he anticipated every motion of the ship.

"Fine beginning," he said in his rasping voice. A broad

grin nearly split his thin face in two. "You were right, Cap'n."

"Right? About what?"

"Finding myself something to do so I would not get bored while we are on our way to Greytown. I did, and it should be a good voyage." He chuckled and scratched his ribs through his thin shirt.

"What mischief—?"

A shout came from the quarterdeck. Stephen slapped his first mate companionably on the back and hurried up the steps. Overhead the snap of the canvas was the sweetest melody he knew. It was just as well that Roach had come up with a way to keep himself entertained this trip out. Things were bound to be different this voyage. Stephen did not like it, but the situation in Nicaragua was volatile and constantly changing. They would have to take extra care, which is why he did not need a pretty brunette cluttering up things on the ship.

Arielle Gardiner! Why was he even thinking of her still? A twinge of guilt answered him as he jumped back down to the main deck. He had set up that prank for her own good. When he had received her neatly penned note, he should have ignored it. Something in the precise handwriting and the cool request for passage to Nicaragua had warned him that Miss Gardiner would not be sensible and accept his advice to go back home. Perhaps, after the meeting with him and a taste of Jake's lechery, she would realize what waited for a woman in that half-civilized jungle. Especially a woman as lovely and enticing as Arielle Gardiner with her ebony hair and her eyes as dark, but sparkling like stars reflected in the sea at night. Her slender form had been well-rounded in all the right places.

He smiled. She had not been afraid of him until he chastely touched her, then she had skittered away. His smile faded as his fingers recalled the downy softness of her skin. Her full skirts had hidden little from him when he had drawn her close.

"Damn," he muttered. She was out of his life. He was wasting time thinking about her.

He had no time to think about her as *The Ladysong* steered clear of any shoals before reaching open sea. While his crew worked together with the competence they had perfected over their many trips south, he checked the cargo manifest and noted two cases that had not been identified. Roach was not usually that careless.

Stephen grinned as he folded the top of the page over and closed the manifest. Whatever Roach had found to keep himself occupied in Greytown must have been pretty special to have taken his mind off his responsibilities of loading the ship. Checking the position of the moon, he knew his first mate should be off watch soon. He would go to Roach's cabin and wait for him there. They would complete the manifest and finish a bottle of rum over a few hands of cards.

Opening a door beneath the poop deck, he went to his mate's quarters, which were forward of his. He was astounded to see a bar dropped over the door. Shouldering it aside, he peered inside. His eyes widened as he gasped, "What in hell are *you* doing here?"

Arielle Gardiner's tear-streaked face was pale, but a ruddy flush climbed her cheeks as her dark eyes met his in disbelief. Unlike the prim woman who had met him in the tavern, her hair was tangled and falling onto her shoulders. One flounce on her full skirt was torn. She whispered, "Captain Lightenfield, what are *you* doing here?"

"I asked first." He closed the door, fighting his fury. How had she smuggled herself onto his ship? Roach! No wonder his mate had been grinning so broadly about bringing something—someone—aboard the ship to keep him entertained.

Arielle raised her chin and met Captain Lightenfield's gray gaze. This was too much. It was horrible enough that Mr. Walden had dared to try to renegotiate their deal after the ship sailed. To be on Captain Lightenfield's ship . . . Her dismay became anger. His cruelty had no limits!

"I suppose you think this is amusing," she said as she clasped her hands on her full skirt.

"Not a bit." Malevolence tainted his voice. "I told you I would not take you to Nicaragua. Why are you stowed-away in my first mate's quarters?"

"I arranged passage with Mr. Walden." Quietly she added, "I did not know that he was your first mate."

The Ladysong was the only ship leaving for Nicaragua this week. Did you think Roach could conjure another from thin air for you?"

"Roach?"

His cold laugh lashed her. "Do you always go off with strange men without knowing their names? I might have misjudged you, Miss Gardiner, when I guessed you to be a lady." Placing the manifest on a table, he leaned on his fists. His grin did not match the fury in his eyes. "I am waiting for the truth."

She hurried to answer, for she did not dare falter. Quickly she told him how his first mate had sought her out at a store on Tremont Street, where she had been buying a pair of sturdy boots for her journey into the jungle. Mr. Walden had told her he could arrange passage on his ship and had even helped her bring her things to the ship.

"But it was getting dark, so I never saw the name on the bow," she finished.

With a derisive snort Captain Lightenfield asked, "And I am supposed to believe that story? I cannot think anyone could be so stupid." His eyes narrowed as he took another step toward her, imprisoning her in the small space between the bed and the table. "Is this your idea of revenge, Miss Gardiner?"

"You think too highly of yourself, Captain! I have given you no thought since I left the tavern yesterday." Arielle struggled to keep her face calm. He must not guess she was lying. She had been plagued by endless thoughts of Captain Lightenfield and how she would make him sorry for his prank. "I have been thinking solely about finding a way to Nicaragua."

"Which you have found."

"Yes, but I had no idea this was your ship. If I had, I would—"

"Enough!" He opened the door and shouted, "Send Mr. Walden here on the bounce." He turned back to her, and she was shocked his smile had not disappeared. He sat on the edge of the table and regarded her with amusement. "I was right. You are a fool." Crossing his arms on his chest, he added, "It might help me if you told me why you need to go to Nicaragua."

She started to answer, but the shadow of a man edged along the floor and up her skirts. Her voice vanished in her arid throat as she faced the man who had turned from a friend to a demon. Captain Lightenfield was right. She had been a fool to trust Roach Walden.

Shock blared on the first mate's face, but it vanished when his captain motioned for him to come forward. Arielle shivered as she recalled Mr. Walden's hands groping at her, twisting in her hair, trying to pin her to the bed. That had been the true price of his help. She had fought him, and he had left, locking her in his quarters with a threat to return.

When she moved closer to Captain Lightenfield, the blond man cocked an eyebrow at her. She did not care what he thought. Of the two, he was less wicked. Icy fear cramped on her as she wondered if the captain would protect her from his mate's bestial scheme.

Captain Lightenfield put his hand on her arm, and she flinched. He glared at her but said quietly, "Miss Gardiner has been telling me about a remarkable understanding she says you have with her, Roach."

The slighter man's gaze flitted toward Arielle. A shadowy smile settled on his full lips. "She came begging me to help her, Cap'n. She bought me whiskey till I agreed. Then she took me up to her rooms." He put one foot on the chair next to Arielle and grinned. "I don't want to embarrass her further."

"Captain Lightenfield—"

"Be quiet!" Captain Lightenfield's sarcastic laugh was wintry as he turned to his first mate. "Very funny, Roach, that for once a woman took advantage of *you*. Now, how about the truth? What do you know of her? Why does she want to go to Nicaragua?"

"I'm not sure, Cap'n." He tried to grin but faltered before his captain's rage. "We were too busy to discuss such things, if you understand what I mean."

"He is lying!" cried Arielle. She would not allow this terrible man to twist the truth any longer. Looking at the captain's cool gray eyes, she saw his exasperation. She had to convince him to heed her. "Mr. Walden made a deal with me, Captain Lightenfield. Mr. Walden told me he would arrange for me to be landed in Greytown."

The short man chuckled. "I told her she could come along but said nothing about letting her leave *The Ladysong*. I just did what you told me to, Captain. Found something to help pass the time."

She pressed her hands to her icy face as she cowered away from the blond man and his horrible first mate. This was all Captain Lightenfield's idea! He had tried to hand her over to one of his lascivious friends in the tavern. That had failed, so he had set up this. Now she had no escape.

Captain Lightenfield cursed. Jamming his hands into

the pockets of his pea coat, he said, "Miss Gardiner, let's assume you are telling the truth—"

"Cap'n," Mr. Walden grumbled, "I protest—"

"Shut up, Roach. I said we would assume only. Go ahead, Miss Gardiner. He invited you aboard. Then what?"

Arielle swallowed roughly. She did not want to speak of the unspeakable things the first mate had done. She just wanted to forget them and him and this loathsome ship and its captain.

"Miss Gardiner?"

The captain's brusqueness stung her into saying, "He took all my money, Captain Lightenfield."

The first mate squirmed as his captain's glare riveted him. "Is that true, Roach?"

"I wanted to keep it safe."

"Uh-huh." Ignoring how his mate recoiled, Captain Lightenfield went on. "All right, Miss Gardiner. What did he do with your money?"

"He put it in a drawer in that table." She glared at the first mate, then smiled. The captain was listening to her. Maybe this would not be a disaster after all. "When he locked me in here, I took it back."

Walden pushed past his captain. Yanking open the drawer, he cursed. "She has robbed me, sir. Took everything."

"Dammit!" Captain Lightenfield stood. "I should throw both of you over the rail. Do you have Roach's money, Miss Gardiner?"

"Yes, but only because I wanted to renegotiate—"

"You heard her, Cap'n," Roach crowed. "She admits it." He grinned at her, running his tongue across his lips. "Why don't you let me settle this with her?"

"Captain, no!" she cried, afraid his hesitation meant he would do just that.

"I have heard enough of this. I will tend to this myself, Roach, but I will talk to you on deck in two minutes."

Captain Lightenfield motioned toward the door. "If you please, Miss Gardiner."

Arielle was glad to escape this room even if it meant going with Captain Lightenfield. When she passed Walden, she pulled her skirts tighter to her body. She did not want to let even her clothes come into contact with the disgusting brute.

Roach called after her, "Later, sweetheart?"

"Enough, Roach!" snapped Captain Lightenfield.

When Arielle gave him a tentative smile of gratitude, the captain scowled. Taking her arm, he steered her out of the room and down a dark corridor. She gripped his arm as the floor convulsed beneath her. The ship rocked the other way, and she reeled toward the wall. With a terse laugh he caught her around the waist and hauled her closer to him.

"You will get used to it," he said as she stumbled yet again.

"So you will take me to Greytown?"

He laughed again. She started to pull away, but the motion of the ship brought her back against his iron-hard body. Her breath burst from her as his arm encircled her again, dragging her to his chest. She did not dare take another breath, for any motion would brush her breasts against him. Staring up at his face, which was masked by the shadows, she moaned when he pressed her to the wall. She should have known better than to have any gratitude to this horrible man. Stephen Lightenfield had saved her from his lustful mate only to abuse her himself.

Even as she thought that, turbulence roiled through her, as savage as his anger, as exquisite as a dream. Her fingers clenched on to his rugged arms. Slowly he bent toward her, and she was sure her heart had forgotten how to beat. She could do nothing but stare up into his enticing eyes.

His chuckle shattered the enchantment he had woven around her with such diabolic ease. He grasped her hand.

Setting it on a narrow rail along the wall, he stepped away. "Hold on to this. Use it all the time until you get your sea legs, Miss Gardiner."

Arielle nodded. She could not speak past the lump of shame clogging her throat as she prayed he had no idea what thoughts had been filling her heart. She did not want to endure his scornful laughter again. Oh, she wished she could get off this appalling ship!

Faint light reached out to Arielle as they entered another room. Her eyes widened as she stared at mahogany walls that gleamed from constant care. The benches along the walls were covered with tufted leather. A table surrounded by a half dozen chairs was set in the middle of the floor beneath a pair of skylights, which allowed moonlight to splash across the rocking floor.

"Go through the door at the far end," Captain Lightenfield ordered. "You can put your things there."

"My bag! It is in . . . in his room."

With a resigned sigh he said, "I will retrieve your bag. Go in there and close the door. I do not need you causing more trouble while I talk with Roach."

"I will not, Captain." She paused, then added, "Thank you, Captain. Thank you very much."

When he grumbled something and strode away, she regarded his back with confusion. She had not been effusive, but she could sense Stephen Lightenfield wanted no gratitude. As she lurched across the room and reached for the latch, she feared it would be a very long, extremely uncomfortable voyage for all of them.

Arielle opened the door and discovered what must be Captain Lightenfield's quarters. Nearly as cluttered as his first mate's, the room was slightly larger and boasted a bank of windows along the back wall over the built-in bed. Doors and bookshelves claimed two walls, but to her left hung a lovely oil painting of a ship cutting through the waves. On the desk a lantern was surrounded by papers and unfamiliar tools.

She perched uneasily on the hard chair by the desk. Watching the door, she wondered what Captain Lightenfield would do now. Certainly he would not take her back to Boston. That would cost him time and probably most of his profits for the trip.

When the door opened only moments later, she rose like a guilty child. She started to clasp her hands behind her, then stopped. She was not a child and had certainly done nothing wrong . . . except steal Mr. Walden's money in hopes that he would let her go in exchange for returning it.

Captain Lightenfield dropped her battered bag on the bed. In the soft light from the lantern, his face's stern planes were as hard as the sides of his ship. His sea-gray eyes showed his frustration with the turn of events. She tensed, waiting for an explosion of the fury tightening his lips. What would he do to her?

His broad arms, hardened by work, crossed over his chest as he stared at her. She bit her lower lip when his gaze roved along her. When a smile twisted his lips, she feared what he would say to her.

"Your chemisette is unbuttoned," he said quietly.

"My chemisette?" Prepared for anger, she was baffled by his kind tone. Her hands clenched as she wondered if he was ridiculing her again.

"It is unbuttoned, Miss Gardiner." He stretched a single finger toward her.

Twirling away, Arielle hastily redid the button. It could have revealed little more than the lace at the top of her chemise, but every effort she had made to maintain her bruised dignity in his company had failed. No wonder Captain Lightenfield considered her no better than a fool.

"Will you sit?" he asked to her back.

Facing him, she said, "Captain, I would like—"

"Sit, Miss Gardiner." His wide hand caught her by the shoulder and shoved her onto the chair. Pacing in front of her, his fingers locked behind his back, he said, "Robbery, for whatever reason, is something I will not tolerate on *The Ladysong.*"

Tears of rage blinded her. "If Mr. Walden had not threatened me, I . . ." She hid her face in her hands as a shudder of revulsion ached across her shoulders.

His voice gentled. "I can guess what Roach had planned for you. Clearly you have figured that out as well. You need to be less naive and pick your dashing heroes with a great deal more care."

"I do not want a hero. I want—"

"To go to Nicaragua." Impatience honed his words that sliced into her. "I know. You have never talked about anything else, Miss Gardiner."

"If you will take me there, I will give you the money I promised your first mate."

His eyes narrowed as he bent toward her. "How much did you agree to pay?"

Arielle whispered, "One hundred fifty dollars."

"One hundred fifty dollars? The fare all the way to San Francisco is less than a third of that. So you were willing to give Roach a fortune along with your virginity?" He laughed as he sat on his bed and rested his elbow on the corner of the desk. When she edged away from his arm's firm length, he smiled a challenge at her, daring her to chide him for his coarse manners.

Arielle fought her irritation at his arrogant amusement. Yet, she reminded herself, the situation was not all horrid. Suffering his callous insults was a small price to pay when she was on her way to Nicaragua. Joy leapt in her even as her stomach twisted with fear. Nicaragua! She really was going there. She was going to see Caleb again. Then maybe she could forget the emptiness in her heart where once she had kept her love for him.

"You present me with a problem," Captain Lightenfield continued.

"A problem?"

His mirthless smile was as cold as his voice. "If you were a man, I would order you slapped in irons until we returned to Boston."

"But I am not a man."

"No, you are most certainly not a man."

She hated the heat rushing over her as he boldly studied her. Not just the fire of embarrassment but a tantalizing flame that seared her as his gaze grazed her skin, as his fingers had in the corridor. It was beguiling and ominous, an invitation to forbidden yearnings.

"So what will you do with me?" she whispered.

"To tell you the truth, I am not quite sure. I will not leave a lady to that war down there." When she sputtered, infuriated, he stated more vehemently, "Understand this, Miss Gardiner. After I have completed *my* business there, you will be returning on *The Ladysong* to Boston."

"Captain, be reasonable!" she cried as she jumped to her feet. She searched his face, hoping to find a hint of compassion. As his lips straightened, she rushed to say, "I may be a woman, but I do not need you to watch over me. I can take care of myself."

"After what I have seen in the past few hours, I doubt that. Rest assured that I have no intention of looking after you. My job is captaining this ship, not playing nursemaid to you."

Arielle's nails bit into her palms as she held back her retort. How dare he behave so beastly! Everything she said, everything she did, everything she tried to do, he belittled with malicious glee. "Captain, I am sorry for the inconvenience I have caused you, but, as you must see, we cannot change what has happened. Our only alternative is to be reasonable."

"*I* am being reasonable, Miss Gardiner. *You* aren't."

"But I must go to Nicaragua."

"Why?"

"That is none of your concern, Captain."

Arielle recoiled as he grasped her arms. When he shoved her onto the chair, she gripped it and stared at his face, which was taut with fury.

"The truth, Miss Gardiner." His voice was menacing. "Now!"

"I must go to Nicaragua," she repeated stubbornly.

"Am I supposed to guess why? I have no time for your silly games."

She looked past him so she would not be caught by his stony gaze, which created such a storm within her. "I assure you, Captain, I do not consider this a game. I am looking for my fiancé, Caleb Drummond."

"Caleb Drummond?"

"Do you know him?"

"The name is familiar," he answered slowly. "What is he doing in Nicaragua?"

"He works for the Accessory Transit Company on the Rio San Juan." Once she began, she found it simple to tell him the tale.

Before she was finished, Captain Lightenfield began to laugh. He leaned against the door and laughed until tears glittered at the corners of his eyes.

"Captain, I—"

He waved her to silence as he managed to choke out, "You missed your calling. Why are you wasting your life as a schoolteacher? You should be in the theater. Such a performance! Your forlorn fiancé sends you a torn snippet to lure you to him in an indescribable paradise. Sure he is in trouble, you flee to his side. Come now," he continued in an abruptly angry tone that was matched by a fierce scowl replacing his grin. "If you are not going to tell me the truth, maybe I should let Roach convince you."

"You would not dare to!"

"If you want to find out, continue with your lies. How about the truth?"

Unlatching her bag, she rummaged through it, then upended it. Her things cascaded onto his bed. Her hairbrush fell to the floor, but she ignored it as she reached for a bundle of letters that was held together by a satin ribbon. Carefully she drew out the top one and handed it to him.

He scanned the tattered page. "Either this is a ridiculously elaborate prank you are perpetrating, or you are more stupid than I had thought."

"I am more stupid than either of us thought," she said with a weary smile, "but I must find Caleb. Something is not right about that letter. I am not asking for your help in finding him, only that you do not hinder me in doing what I must."

"What you will do is get yourself killed. Don't you realize there is a war being fought there? Even without that, you could not survive for more than ten seconds alone in that jungle."

She shook her head, not wanting to listen to what she knew might be true. "I must try."

He seized her arms and shook her. "You fool! Have you considered that is exactly what someone expects you to do? Who will be waiting for you? Caleb Drummond or someone else who wants a pretty Yankee lady?"

"You have a lurid imagination!" she retorted, but fright strangled her.

"Do I?" Disgust filled his voice as he released her. "There are more secrets in that rain forest than you or I could imagine. Continue on your path to disaster, Miss Gardiner, and you might become simply another lost legend cloaked in mystery." He brushed past her and opened the door, giving her a cold smile. "Stay here."

The door crashed closed, branding an ache into Arielle's head. She stared at it. Captain Lightenfield was a boorish

jackanapes if he thought she was going to obey his prepos-
terous orders. She was not going back to Boston without
Caleb.

Throwing open the door, she gasped when her nose
nearly struck Captain Lightenfield's broad chest. He
pushed her back into his room. "I told you to stay here.
My orders are law on *The Ladysong*."

"Not to me!"

He smiled so coldly, a chill crawled along her skin. "Miss
Gardiner, I am the captain of this ship. What I decide will
happen happens. If I say you walk the plank, over you go."

"This is 1856!" She would not let him frighten her with
his empty threats. "No one makes anyone walk the plank
nowadays."

When he stepped toward her, she backed away to keep
the distance between them the same. His voice was as low
as a storm wind as he asked, "Would you prefer the lash?"

"You are not serious!"

"No?" His eyebrows lowered as his finger twisted in her
hair. He tugged on the strand, bringing her closer. As his
hand combed through the tangles, she fought to think
only about her anger. It was scorched from her by the gray
fire in his eyes. When his other hand grazed her lips,
she gasped softly, trying to breathe slowly when her heart
throbbed like a steam engine.

In a near whisper he said, "Set one foot out of this room
before I return, and you will discover exactly how serious
I am ... about many things. I trust I shall not have to
repeat myself. You *do* understand me?"

Anger stiffened her voice as she pushed his hand away.
"I understand that you are an insufferable blackguard."

"And you are a foolish woman." His laughter remained
as he slammed the door again, cutting her off in the midst
of her next insult.

With a sigh Arielle sat on the chair. It did not matter
how she argued. He was correct. On his ship Captain Light-

enfield was king. Every word he spoke was an edict his crew had to follow. Anything else was mutiny.

She looked out the window. Starlight kissed the top of the waves, lingering longest on the bits of foam flying skyward when a wave was swallowed by the wake of the ship. If Captain Lightenfield had his way, her dreams would be snatched away from her before she could grasp for them. She must thwart his plans. Nothing must halt her from finding Caleb.

CHAPTER THREE

A cramp climbed the back of Arielle's neck to wake her. She did not open her eyes as she shifted uncomfortably. Something slithered across her left foot. She screamed.

"Dammit! Can't a man get some sleep without your caterwauling?"

She stared at Captain Lightenfield as he sat up in his bed. The thin sheet slid down to reveal the expanse of his bare chest with its matting of tawny hair. She watched the sheet fall farther and farther along his firmly muscled body toward the narrow line of his hips. With a moan she covered her eyes and turned away.

His husky chuckle did not convince her to lower her hands. She heard his feet slap the floor, moving away from her, then coming back.

"Is this what caused you to screech?" He dropped something in her lap. It wiggled.

She opened her mouth to scream again, then stared at a black cat. Its yellow eyes regarded her with irritation.

With an ear-shattering yowl, it leapt from her lap and scurried out the door.

"Mephisto has very particular tastes." Captain Lightenfield chuckled as he buttoned his cotton shirt. "He is used to being the only one sharing my quarters."

Arielle stood and winced as pain careened along her back. "Captain, forgive me for falling asleep here. It was kind of you not to wake me. If you are not busy, I would like to ask you—"

"As the captain of this ship, I am always busy."

"Then I shall endeavor to be brief," she returned, irritated anew by his contemptuous answers. "I do not intend to be left in limbo for the rest of the voyage."

"That is understandable."

"What do you intend to do?"

He laughed. "You are an obstinate woman. I told you. We have a cargo to land at Greytown. Then all of us will return to Boston."

"Sir, I insist—"

Turning, he placed his hands over hers on the desk. When she gasped, he leaned forward until each hair of his mustache came into sudden clear focus. It took every bit of her will not to cower, but she would not let him learn how easily his raw masculinity could daunt her.

"You are in no position to insist anything," he said, his breath warm on her face. Emotions flew through his storm-swept eyes, then he glowered at her. "Nor am I in any mood to listen to your trivial gripes. The situation is as it is. I am tired after getting *The Ladysong* to sea. I had hoped to get a full watch's sleep, but I see that will not be possible until I do something about you."

He reached into a drawer under the bed and pulled out a rolled pile of rope. He tossed it on the rumpled covers. As he began to unwind it, Arielle realized that it was a hammock. She started to ask him what he planned, but his sharp answer silenced her. Easily he lifted one end and tied the ropes to a hook she had not noticed. When he crossed the room, she was not surprised to see another hook.

"There," he said as he scooped a pillow and blanket from his bed. Dropping them onto the hammock, he added, "Not luxurious, but I suspect you shall be comfortable enough."

"Me?" she exclaimed. "You expect me to sleep in that? Why shouldn't I sleep in the bunk?"

He sat on the hammock and rocked it slightly to test the security of the knots. With his eyes even with hers he smiled without humor. "Because the bunk is mine, Miss Gardiner. I doubt if you wish to keep me company."

"I cannot stay here in this room with you."

"We have already been sleeping together. I am afraid your previously pristine reputation has already been compromised."

Gulping, she murmured, "That was different. That was accidental. I cannot stay here with you."

"All right." He stood and pointed toward the door. "Find your own place to sleep. Roach would be glad for your company. If you do not want him, you should have no trouble finding someone to let you share his bunk. Either that, or you stay here and use the hammock. Make up your mind, Miss Gardiner, because I do not intend to come to your rescue again." He yawned and stretched out on his bed. "Turn down the lantern before you go to sleep."

Arielle was riveted to the rocking floorboards with despair. "Captain," she whispered, "surely there must be another place where I can sleep."

When he rolled to face her, his scowl accented his straight brows. "If I had a spare room, I would happily stash you in it. I want your company no more than you wish mine." He pulled the blanket over his shoulders. "If you are not going to sleep, have the decency to be quiet.

I have the dawn watch, and I intend to get some sleep before then.''

Arielle stared at his back. When she saw his shoulders were shaking, she grabbed the pillow from the hammock. He was laughing at her again! She flung the pillow at him. It hit him on the head.

He exploded from the bed. She ran for the door. His arm wrapped around her waist. Plucking her from the floor, he dropped her on the hammock. She shrank away as the hammock wobbled. No amusement eased the rigid lines of his face. All the fear she had known before was paled by her terror when he reached for her. She tried to scramble away. Her thick skirts and the hammock betrayed her.

She landed on the floor with a thump. Instead of laughing or helping her to her feet, Captain Lightenfield stamped past her. He grabbed her pillow, threw it onto the hammock, then scooped her up as easily as he had the pillow.

Her fingers locked behind his neck when he shifted her in his arms. When her cheek rested against his shoulder, his heartbeat was as rapid as hers. He placed her in the hammock and bent forward as she drew her hands back from him.

"Decide," he whispered.

"Decide what?" she answered as lowly.

"If you want me to sleep or stay awake with you." His hand settled on her waist, his fingers splaying along the ridges of her corset. They slipped higher in a slow, sinuous path as he murmured, "Decide quickly."

Arielle halted him by putting her hand over his. Seeing regret in his eyes before they hardened to steel again, she watched him duck under the rope. He said nothing as he blew out the lantern to leave them in the darkness that concealed cravings she should see on no man's face but Caleb's.

Listening to his mattress rustle as he made himself comfortable, she stared at the ceiling. She wondered how long she could go without sleep, for she did not dare close her eyes. Then she might dream of Stephen Lightenfield and the treacherous passions he had awakened, passions she had never known with the man she had promised to marry.

Light glared off the water and into the captain's quarters. Arielle rubbed her eyes and turned over. With a strangled cry she clutched the edges of the hammock as it rocked wildly. She held her breath, waiting for the hateful laughter that had haunted her uneasy sleep.

When she heard nothing but the waves slapping the ship and a distant shout, she looked around the room, being careful not to set the hammock to dancing again. Relief was intoxicating when she realized she was alone. That was scant comfort, for she had hoped Stephen Lightenfield and his ship had been just a nightmare.

Rising, she smoothed out the wrinkles pressed into her wool skirt. She found her hairbrush and patiently brushed the snarls from her hair. Binding it in a bun at her nape, she wobbled to a bowl beneath a mirror that was too high for her use. She was a bit steadier on her feet as she washed exhaustion from her burning eyes. She had not slept more than two or three hours, but she must make her mind function. She had to think of a way to flee this ship when they reached Nicaragua. She needed to see more of the ship.

A grumble from her stomach reminded her she had not eaten since breakfast yesterday. First she would get something to eat. She staggered toward the door but paused. Captain Lightenfield had ordered her to stay here, and, after last night, she knew she must not risk flouting his commands.

She smiled when she noticed a plate on the desk. Stumbling to it, she took the plate to her hammock. She settled herself comfortably and picked up the sticky biscuit that must have come from a pastry shop in Boston. She took a bite. It was sweet and sugary and frosted with spices.

"I hope you are enjoying *my* breakfast."

Looking over her shoulder, Arielle saw Captain Lightenfield had changed into clothing suited for rough work. His impressive shoulders threatened the seams of the linen shirt he wore over denim trousers. As her eyes rose over the sturdy curve of his chin, she let her gaze slide along his uncompromising features until it reached his hooded eyes.

He seized her hand and lifted the sticky biscuit to his mouth. His mustache stroked her skin as he took a bite of the biscuit. Unable to keep his gaze from capturing hers, she wondered how such a common motion could seem so intimate. When he turned the biscuit toward her, she nibbled on it. He smiled as he raised the last piece to his mouth. She gasped as he licked the last of the sugar from her fingers. Fire seared her—sharp, potent—consuming her as readily as he had eaten the biscuit.

"Very tasty," he murmured.

Arielle tugged her hand away as he winked at her. How could she be enthralled by him when he treated her no better than he had the barmaid?

With a laugh Captain Lightenfield tossed a piece of paper in Arielle's lap.

"What's this?"

"Your duties for the rest of the voyage."

"My duties?" She swallowed her laughter when she saw that for once he was not teasing her. The too-familiar shiver ran its cold finger along her spine. He might mock her, but never did he let her forget he was her master while she was aboard his ship. "Captain Lightenfield, I have told you that I am quite willing to pay for my passage."

"I do not want your money." He stepped aside as she

surged to her feet. Chuckling as the hammock struck her in the backside, he asked, "Are you afraid to work?"

"I did not come aboard to slave for you."

"Have it your way. Get your things."

"Why?"

His eyes twinkled with cold merriment. "You might as well get comfortable in your new quarters."

"But you said there was no place for me, but . . ."

"If I had an empty one, I could have a storage room rigged as a brig." When her eyes grew wide with horror, he added, "That is the usual sentence for stowaways."

"I am not—" Arguing with the arrogant man was futile. He truly was the master of his ship. Hating him more when he laughed again, she wadded the paper. She flung it at the desk and swayed toward the door.

"Where do you think you are going?" He put out an arm to block her way.

Arielle grasped the railing on the wall. If she let him touch her again—even in anger—she was not sure what might happen. Last night she had had to fight every fiber of her body that wanted to sample his caresses. Now she struggled to keep her voice steady. "If I am to work, I should go to the kitchen. I assume that is where you want me to work. I do not know how to do anything else on a ship."

"The kitchen?" He chuckled as he lounged against the door, filling the opening with his broad shoulders. "If you mean the *galley*, do not bother to try to find it." He picked up the piece of paper and pressed it into her hand. "Read it."

She opened it gingerly and read the single word, which had been written with a flamboyant flourish. Puzzled, she said, "I don't understand."

"What don't you understand?"

"It says *paint*."

He moved closer and looked over her shoulder. The

page shook as his warm breath teased the sensitive skin behind her ear. As he bent forward to outline each letter, she was sure she was enveloped by his strong body. "So it does," he whispered.

Closing her eyes as the soft words whirled along her neck, leaving tingles in their wake, she tried to pretend she was oblivious to his fingers etching an aimless design along her shoulder. "But what do you want me to paint?"

"The ship."

Arielle whirled as he laughed. "Are you crazy?"

Taking her hand, he scowled when she tried to escape him. He tilted her palm upward and ran his finger across it. "I see you are not afraid of work."

"I'm not."

"I wish I had had a teacher like you when I was a lad. Perhaps then I would have spent less time at the Charleston docks." His arm curved around her waist. "Think of all the things you could have taught me."

"I am afraid I am too late to teach you anything, except maybe manners, which you clearly do not wish to learn."

"Then shall I teach you?"

When she put her hands on his arm, she was astonished he released her. "You seem to forget I am betrothed, Captain."

"So do you."

His words stung, because they were true. She had known Caleb all her life, but she readily banished him from her mind when Captain Lightenfield drew her close. Quietly she said, "Then I think we both should make an effort to recall that. If you would tell me where you wish me to paint . . ."

"You will find the paint locker forward of the foremast. McDaniels will assist you."

"And what do you want me to paint?" Glad to talk of anything but the desires she should not be experiencing, she wondered if he found it easier than she did to speak calmly.

"Anything made of wood."

"But the whole ship is made of wood!" Her softening toward him vanished.

He opened the door and smiled. "Then I suggest you start immediately." With a mock bow he ushered her out. The sound of his laughter at her back was already excruciatingly familiar, but somehow she would find a way to get the last laugh.

Arielle soon learned exactly how much of *The Ladysong* was constructed of wood. As she spent day after day painting the railing along the deck, she realized Captain Lightenfield had not devised makeshift labor for her. Scouring by saltwater and the sun's strong glare required constant attention to the wood.

She refused to let Captain Lightenfield discover how she enjoyed her work. Soon she was able to cross the deck, a bucket of varnish in her hand, without holding on to the railing. Although her back and shoulders ached from stooping for hours, and she feared she never would remove the spots of varnish from her skin, she exulted in the brilliant sunshine and the clouds that danced with the rhythm of the sails. Each night she fell asleep in the gentle embrace of her hammock before Captain Lightenfield returned to their quarters. Taking his meals with his officers in the large room she had learned was called the saloon, he seldom spoke to her except to ask how much work she had completed. As she sat alone in the cabin, she listened to the men's voices and counted the days until they would reach Greytown.

How wondrous it would be when she found Caleb! Each night she comforted herself by imagining her joy when she reached his jungle paradise. She wondered if he had changed from the gentle man she had known in Concord. Even if he had, their wedding would be glorious. In his dark suit, with its high collar, his red hair neatly combed, Caleb would wait by the altar. She would wear her best gown when she put her hand in his. He would kiss her with the passion he had restrained while they courted. Certainly everything would come to rights once she found him.

Arielle smiled as she thought of that. Although she had become accustomed to her strange new life by the time the first week at sea had passed, she wanted, more each day, to have it over. Alone in the captain's quarters, she loosened her hair and brushed it before confining it in a single thick braid. She smiled when she saw speckles of varnish on her hands as she loosened her chemisette and set it on the back of the chair.

Captain Lightenfield had never offered her room in his cupboard for her clothes, and she refused to leave them on the floor. Unbuttoning her skirt and the layers of petticoats beneath it, she stepped out of them and strained to reach the laces on her corset. She sighed as she hid it beneath her skirt. She stretched, enjoying the freedom of wearing just her calf-length chemise, which dropped off her shoulders, stockings, and black kid slippers.

Hearing a shout, Arielle gasped. She grabbed her light blue silk wrapper from the hammock but could not get it around her shoulders before the door swung open. Holding it up in front of her, she blanched when Captain Lightenfield entered. Salt spray lathered his shirt to his body. Her nose wrinkled as the aroma of rum wafted from him.

"Good evening, Captain," she said. "I shall be out of your way in just a few moments."

"I am not going to bed." He leaned his elbow on the hook holding the hammock in place. "Not when there is a party going on." Reaching over the hammock, he grabbed her hand and tugged her forward. "Why don't you come, too?"

Awkwardly she slipped one arm into her wrapper. Pulling it over her other shoulder, she held it closed at her chin. When he grinned, she looked down to see it gaped open to reveal the lacy front of her chemise. She jerked her hand out of his and shoved her arm into the sleeve. Hastily she tied the ribbons closed. Icily she answered, "No, thank you, Captain. As you can see, I am not properly attired for a party."

"Hell, you look fine." He reached past the hammock and grasped her by the waist. Lifting her over the hammock, he set her firmly on her feet and pulled her toward the door. "You look better than fine."

"Captain, no!"

His smile became gentler. "We are enjoying ourselves. It is time you did, too."

"Please, Captain Lightenfield . . ."

Her wrapper murmured a soft song as he brought her closer. She closed her eyes while his hand cradled her cheek, tilting her face toward him. When his fingers laced upward through her hair, she slid her hands up his chest. Every firm sinew urged her to explore it, to become more familiar with it than she was with her own body. As her loosened hair cascaded over her shoulders, her gaze settled on his lips, which were tilting in a smile. She wondered how they would taste against hers.

She stiffened. Such thoughts were mad. Stephen Lightenfield was not a man who would be satisfied with a single kiss.

"Captain Lightenfield," she said in a strangled voice, "thank you for the invitation, but I must refuse."

As if she had not spoken, he said, "Arielle. That is a lovely name, you know."

She shivered as his deep, husky voice caressed her name. "Thank you."

"Arielle, tonight we are halfway to Greytown." He backed away half a pace and held out his hand. "At this point we always celebrate with a bottle or two. Join us."

She watched as her fingers were swallowed by his larger hand. He would accept nothing but obedience to what she knew was an order. Guessing that few women had ever denied Stephen Lightenfield his desires, she vowed that she would. Caleb waited for her to come to marry him. She must never forget that.

Arielle let Captain Lightenfield lead her through the saloon but tensed as they walked onto the deck. Every eye turned toward her. Her dishabille and her hand securely in Captain Lightenfield's announced their supposed intimacy.

Captain Lightenfield took a cup of rum and offered it to her. When she shook her head, he shrugged and drank. She gasped when the sea breeze thrust her wrapper back to reveal her bare ankles. Hearing a murmur of appreciation from the men, she tried to keep the wrapper closed.

The Ladysong's second mate, a spare man with thinning hair, emerged like a wraith from the darkness. "Cap'n, if I could have you at the helm for a moment."

"Of course, Mr. Simon." He smiled and pressed his cup in Arielle's hand. "Watch this, honey. I will be right back."

"Do not be in any hurry," she replied, but he was gone into the shadows. She suspected he had not heard her. How dare he call her *honey* in front of his crew! There was no end to the ways he could find to embarrass her.

Leaning against the railing, Arielle watched the clouds scud across the sky. She wanted to return to her hammock, but Captain Lightenfield would drag her back. Instead of listening to the sailors' lewd stories, she looked south, letting the wind sweep away their voices. Perhaps Caleb was watching the stars and thinking of her.

Caleb Drummond loved her. He had told her that the night he asked her to marry him and again before he left.

Everyone in the village assumed they would wed, so Arielle had not been surprised when he proposed. Then he went to Nicaragua, telling her he wanted to see a bit of the world before he spent the rest of his life working in his father's mercantile. With Caleb, things had been so simple. Things would be simple again when she was with him.

A shadow edged over her, and she turned. She froze as she met Roach Walden's smile. Despite the close quarters on the ship, she had managed to avoid the first mate since she came aboard.

"You would not have had to work all day and all night if you had stayed with me," he said with a jeering laugh. "I would have let you sleep during the day instead of painting."

Arielle looked back at the water. Roach was the perfect name for the repulsive man. Maybe if she ignored him, he would go away.

"C'mon, girlie. I have been watching you, and you're aware of every man eyeing you up and down. Oh, you like it, you do."

"You are crazy!" She tried to edge past him, but he kept her imprisoned between his gaunt body and the railing. "I am not interested in any man on this ship."

"Not even the one you sleep with?"

"You don't know what you are talking about."

His cruel laugh cut into her. "I know Stephen Lightenfield, and I know he wouldn't pass up the opportunity to—"

"Opportunity for what, Roach?" Captain Lightenfield stepped out of the shadows. When he put his arm around her shoulders, she did not shy away. She was glad to have him between her and his first mate.

"Uh, nothing, Cap'n," Roach mumbled.

"I thought I made it clear you are not welcome here tonight."

"Hell, Cap'n. I just came out for a breath of air. I wasn't doing anything."

"If you are doing nothing, why not do it elsewhere?"

"Aye, Cap'n." Like the snake he was, he slithered away.

Captain Lightenfield sighed, startling her. For the first time, she wondered what had been said between the two men the night *The Ladysong* sailed out of Boston. The conversation had been short, for the captain had returned to his quarters within minutes. Was it possible they had been friends before this voyage? She did not want to believe that Captain Lightenfield could choose such a beast as a friend.

"I did not expect that you would be here still," he said, intruding on her thoughts.

"Wasn't it an order?"

"But you haven't learned to obey any of my other orders, have you?"

"I am painting the ship."

"I mean the ones to keep you out of trouble." He closed the distance between them until everywhere she looked, his strong form overwhelmed her. He bent so his ashen gaze held hers. "Obey this one, Arielle. Kiss me."

"I beg your pardon?"

His hands clamped over hers on the railing, keeping her prisoner. He slowly slid her hands behind her. Holding them in place with one hand, he raised the other to cup her chin. He pressed closer until she was aware of every angle of his male body, her bulky skirts not there to protect her. Her breath burned, hot and fast in her throat as his mouth descended toward her. His lips brushed her forehead. A gasp burst from her. This could not be the kind of kiss he had meant.

She closed her eyes and sighed with soft delight when his lips touched her cheek, then teased her eyelids and the tip of her nose. The sigh became a breathless moan as his mouth left dazzling sparks in a meandering path along her neck. He released her hands, and she clenched his sleeves as he pulled back her wrapper to taste her bare shoulder.

Drawing away only enough so that his lips did not touch hers, he whispered, "Kiss me, Arielle. That is an order."

"No." Her voice sounded oddly distant in her ears. "I am promised to Caleb. I cannot kiss you."

"Do you know that it is mutiny to refuse my direct order?"

"Don't do this," she whispered.

"Do you love him?"

Arielle did not want to admit that she had no idea how she felt about anything beside her craving to have his lips on hers. With a shudder, she tried to compose herself and ignore his hands stroking her back in a slow circle as she said, "I promised to marry Caleb." Anguish sliced through her at her own words. She *was* promised to Caleb. Quickly she moved out of Captain Lightenfield's arms. "Good night, Captain. I think I should go to bed now."

"Bed?" His voice rose, and she saw the mischievous glitter return to his eyes. "You want to go to bed, honey? That sounds like a good idea to me."

She screamed as he flipped her over his shoulder easily. Pounding her fists on his back, she cried, "Let me go!"

"Not tonight."

His crew hooted catcalls after them. He kicked the door closed to make it clear that they did not want to be disturbed. With a chuckle, he deposited her in the hammock. Cringing, she stared at him. He must be deranged! One moment he was a gentle lover wooing her into insanity with his touch. The next he became a lecherous rogue.

Stooping under the hammock's ropes, he said, "Don't start snoring too soon. It would not be good for my reputation."

"Your reputation? What of mine?"

He took her by the shoulders. Fear strangled her as he

put his face close to hers. When she turned her face aside, he grasped her head and forced her to look into his eyes. The fury there diminished hers. "Don't you know that it was *your* reputation I was trying to protect?"

"By telling everyone that—" She choked on the words she could not say.

"Not a man out there doubts that you are mine and mine alone." He released her so roughly, the hammock rocked. "I cannot watch you every minute, but apparently others have been. If you want to reach Boston in the same virginal state as you left—"

"I am not going back to Boston."

"—you need the protection of this lie."

Arielle realized how much she owed him. He could have left her to Roach Walden or let his men use her as they wished. He could have bedded her himself. Instead, he was safeguarding her. Perversely she argued with herself that the passion behind his kisses had been real, hadn't it?

"Thank you," she said softly.

"Do not flatter yourself. I did not do it for you. I don't want trouble on my ship." Going to his bunk, he kicked off his low shoes. "Just be quiet and go to sleep."

He gave her no chance to answer as he blew out the lantern. She buried her face in her musty pillow as she thought of how much she had wanted his kiss. Tonight she had been ready to betray everything she held dear in exchange for a kiss that had been nothing but a charade. She could not be so stupid again.

CHAPTER FOUR

Roach Walden stamped into the saloon. When he saw the door to his captain's quarters was open, he peeked in. Empty!

He went back to the door to the deck, edging around a bench with a sign marking that it had been recently varnished. His lips peeled back in a feral grin when he saw the woman crouching near the railing. The sun painted her dark hair with reddish lights. Some of the strands had fallen forward along her high cheekbones to accent her lips, but his gaze fastened on the firm line of her breasts and her slim waist.

"Damn woman!" he muttered. He had spent too many sleepless hours thrashing on his rumpled bed as he imagined that lithe form in his bed instead of in the captain's.

That had been unexpected. He had sailed with Stephen Lightenfield for more than ten years, watching the younger man rise through the ranks until he was able to take command of his own ship. Their last four years on *The Ladysong* had been profitable for both of them. Together they had enjoyed the brothels of New Orleans, Boston, and New York. Hundreds of times, they had emptied a bottle together. Dozens of times, they had brawled together, usually leaving their opponents senseless on the tavern floor. They had shared everything.

Until this voyage.

Roach rubbed his bristly chin. Something was different about the way the captain treated this woman. Roach swore viciously. Every other woman had bored his captain after a single night. Yet this one still shared his bed after almost two weeks. A surge of jealous desire brought another curse to his lips. He should have bedded her first.

He frowned as he watched the captain pause to talk to her. Cap'n Lightenfield had his hands locked behind his back, and the woman's movements were taut. They did not have the look of lovers.

Then, what was it about Arielle Gardiner that had driven a wedge between him and the captain?

Roach closed the door to the deck and sprinted across the saloon to the captain's quarters. If someone came in, the click of the latch would warn him to get back to the saloon. He left the door to the cabin open.

A scornful chuckle rumbled in his throat when he saw the hammock in the middle of the room. No, they were not lovers. So why hadn't the captain forgiven him for his prank? When Cap'n Lightenfield had given him a dressing-down that first night, it had been halfhearted. The next day the captain relieved him of all his duties. No explanation. Just "You're relieved, Mr. Walden."

"Why?" he grumbled. "What did she tell you?"

Roach recognized the woman's bag on the floor. He emptied it. Pawing through the soft silk of her clothes, he picked up a bottle. He sniffed its lilac aroma. If it was some sort of voodoo concoction, it was like none he had smelled before. Not that he expected a New England lady would carry a potion with her, but that would have been an easy answer to the captain's peculiarities.

He sat back on his heels as he picked up a stack of letters. Ripping off the velvet ribbon, he scanned the envelopes.

"This is interesting," he said as he noted that all but one had been postmarked from Nicaragua. The first had been mailed from New York, the next few from Greytown on Nicaragua's eastern shore, the topmost from the capital city of Granada.

He pulled out the first and struggled to read the words. Too many big ones. He tossed it aside and grabbed another. He was about to open it, when he saw another envelope under the lace of a chemise.

The tattered envelope nearly fell apart when he pulled it out. Reading the shredded letter, he chuckled. *This* was why she had been so doggedly determined to get to Greytown, but that still did not answer the most important question. What did all this mean to the captain? Turning the envelope over, he swore when he saw the return address.

A creak came from the outer door. Roach leapt to his feet and bumped into the hammock. It banged against the wall before he could halt it.

In the saloon Stephen heard the commotion and strode to his door. It could not be Arielle in his quarters. He had just exchanged some more harsh words with her on deck. Dammit, the woman did not have a lick of sense!

His irritation refocused on Roach when he saw his former first mate standing in the middle of a cloud of white silk, Arielle's bag in his hand. "Do you want to explain, Mr. Walden?"

"Maybe you do, Cap'n."

"Me? These are my quarters."

Roach held up a piece of paper. Stephen took it carefully, then held out his hand for the envelope.

The first mate shook his head. "Answers first, Cap'n.

Why didn't you tell us she's betrothed to one of Commodore Vanderbilt's boys?"

"That is her business." He forced a taut smile. "And mine."

"Caleb Drummond," Roach read off the envelope, then shoved it into his captain's hand. "I know that name. So do you."

"Sure, I know it. Drummond worked the Rio San Juan route for the Accessory Transit Company about six months ago. Quiet type. Worked hard, never got into any trouble that I heard of."

"So now you are taking his fiancée down to meet him?"

Stephen said, "You have heard what I have told her. She is going back to Massachusetts with us. I did not want her along in the first place. *You* brought her on board. I shall put her off in Boston. And you, Mr. Walden."

His first mate's eyes widened. "You cannot be serious, Cap'n. It was just a joke. She was eager."

"And you did not think past the chance to get her in your bed." Shaking his head, he said, "I cannot have someone in my crew I can't depend on. You should be able to get work. Hershey's always looking for men."

"As crew, not as mates."

"You should have thought of that before you brought her aboard." Stephen motioned for Roach to come out into the saloon.

The shorter man hesitated, then kicked aside Arielle's bag. It slammed against the wall as he stamped into the bigger room.

Stephen ignored Roach as he went to the map case on the wall. Withdrawing the rolled maps he wanted, he sighed. He wished he had another choice, but he had to leave Walden shorebound. After all, he had not thrown his first mate into the brig for disobeying him. For almost any crime short of murder, he would have forgiven Roach . . .

and had! But he would never forgive his mate for betraying him with lies.

Stephen spread the map in the center of the large table by the windows. His other officers wandered in and took their usual seats around the table. When they glanced uneasily at his former first mate, Stephen said, "Mr. Walden, I trust you will excuse us while we have our meeting."

The short man's jaw clenched, but he nodded before scurrying out of the room. The second mate got up and closed the door.

"Thank you, Mr. Simon," Stephen said as if he had not seen the uneasy glances between his other officers. "Now, will you report on our position?"

As Simon, who somehow managed to maintain his pasty complexion even in the tropical sun, announced they were less than a day out of Greytown, Stephen eyed each man at the table. All of them had been with him for years. Kany, the bo'sun, was the newest among them, and he was ready to celebrate his first anniversary of sailing on *The Ladysong*.

"Gentlemen," Stephen said as he leaned back in his chair in an unruffled pose, "I do not need to stress the delicacy of the situation in Nicaragua. Reports out of Granada suggest that Walker's hold has deteriorated since our last visit. The Nicaraguans, who had hailed him as a liberator, disagree with his proslavery stance."

"Does that mean shore leaves will be canceled?" Simon asked.

He smiled at their lack of interest in the volatile situation in the small country but had expected the question. His men were not interested in Nicaraguan politics, just in getting some good Jamaica rum in their bellies and a pretty señorita in their arms. "Mr. Simon, tell the men they will have leave, but leaves may be shortened. No one is to depart Greytown without my permission." Waving aside the grumbles, he stated, "That must be understood, or no one shall step foot off the ship. Not even to go to the Haven for a grog."

"And you, Cap'n?" asked Kany.

Again he smiled. "I am not sure. I will have to wait until we get there and see what is waiting there. The *Daniel Webster* and the *Granada* should be there out of New Orleans by now."

"The *Cahawba* was due to sail from New York a few days after we left Boston," the second mate added.

"Maybe you can win back a bit of what you lost to Napier last time we were both in Greytown."

Kany's babyish face lengthened. "But what is our schedule, Cap'n?"

"I don't think we will be spending more than a fortnight in Greytown, but, if the situation warrants it, we will have to stay until everything is completed."

Stephen gauged the uneasy expressions on his men's faces. Not a man among them was ignorant of the potential perils of being anchored in the middle of small war that could become a big one at any moment. He might have to depend on one or all of them to get his ship out of Greytown if things detonated around them.

While his men debated the watch schedule for port, he let his thoughts wander to the woman who was working on deck. She could not have picked a worse time to go off on this quixotic quest! A few months before, things had been quiet in Nicaragua. A few months from now, it should be settled down again. Now . . .

Pyramiding his fingers in front of his face, he tapped the top two together absently. He should be thinking about the watch schedule and not how enticing Arielle looked as she sat, surrounded by her full skirt, by the railing. The sun was giving her skin a healthy sheen that urged him to caress it each time he saw her.

She had been icily polite to him since the celebration on deck. Wishing him good morning or nodding to him when he passed by, she said little else to him. He knew she was stewing over how he had treated her in front of his crew.

Hiding his amusement behind a stern expression as he nodded to Kany's suggestions, he wondered if she had heard any of the comments the next day as his crew jested with him about the prim woman who had become a hellcat when he flung her over his shoulder. No doubt, Arielle had heard most of them. The crew found the whole thing hilarious, nothing more than a joke shared by lovers.

He sighed. If they were lovers, he might be able to keep his thoughts on his work instead of thinking how sweet her hair smelled or how her snapping eyes had gentled when he held her by the railing. It was just as well she intended to remain faithful to Drummond. He did not need her cluttering up his life. There were warm women waiting at the Haven, the seamen's haunt in Greytown. The kind of women he liked—compliant, not sassy, and certainly not interested in anything more than a tumble.

"So what do you think, Cap'n?" asked Kany with the impatience of a man who had had to repeat himself.

Stephen grinned wryly. He had not heard a word anyone had said for the past five minutes, but he trusted his men. "All right. Take the orders to the crew. We should be able to reach landfall by tomorrow night." He grimaced as he folded his arms on his chest and glowered at his toes, which were stretched far beneath the table. "I'll be glad to see Greytown. This surely has been the longest voyage we've ever taken."

Mr. Simon, more eager than ever since he had taken over Roach's duties, hastened to say, "We are making good time, Cap'n."

"Mr. Simon, why don't you get a bottle so we can enjoy a short libation before we get back to work?"

The mate leapt to his feet to collect a bottle of rum and some tin cups from a shelf near the map case. He poured a generous serving in each cup and placed them in the middle of the table.

"Mr. Kany," Stephen continued, "check the capstan before we reach the harbor. I do not want the trouble with the anchor that we had in Boston." Stephen stretched forward to snag a cup. "I suggest . . ."

He frowned as he realized he could not stand. His legs and the chair seemed to be one and the same. In amazement he dropped back so the legs of the chair struck the floor with a resounding crash. Again he tried to stand. Again the seat clung to his thighs.

"What the hell is going on?" he demanded. Shaking his shoulders, he found them glued tightly to the slats along the back.

Muffled laughter brought his head up as he glowered at his officers, who were fighting to restrain their amusement.

"I could use some help, gentlemen," he said stiffly.

Simon and the bo'sun grabbed the chair. The mate pulled back and stared at his sticky fingers. "Varnish, Cap'n. It's covered with varnish." When the officers roared with appreciative laughter, he added, "You never have to worry about standing watch again. You always will have a comfortable seat."

Stephen tapped the side of the chair and lifted his fingers to his nose. Varnish! Recently applied varnish. He snapped an order. Kany raced out. As he crossed his arms on his chest again, Stephen stretched out his legs in the only position that was comfortable and stared at the windows. He smiled tightly while Simon continued to chuckle. They would not find it funny if he had them practicing general quarters drills all night. But his frustration was not aimed at them. It was aimed at—

"Miss Gardiner, Cap'n," said Kany with unnecessary formality.

Arielle gasped as she entered the room. "Captain Lightenfield, you shouldn't be sitting there! You shouldn't—

You—" Laughter swallowed her words. She pointed her brush at him, unable to speak.

Stephen glowered at his men, who were convulsed with laughter. "Gentlemen, you're dismissed!"

He did not watch them leave. Seeing the malicious amusement in Arielle's eyes, he fisted his hands on the table. Not just amusement, but satisfaction. The wench must have been planning this all week. He should have known she would be looking for revenge for her public humiliation.

"Is this your work?" he asked, although he had no doubts.

"Of course. Who else paints everything made of wood on *The Ladysong?*" Her dark skirt swayed as she walked easily across the deck. "I was only obeying your orders, Captain."

"I did not tell you to paint my chair."

"You said everything made of wood on the ship, and your chair is made of wood." Going to the windowsill, she picked up a small piece of paper. "I put up a sign saying there was wet varnish in the room."

He leaned his elbow on the table and heard his shoulder seam rip. When he snarled an oath, she laughed. "And it was simply a coincidence," he asked, "that you chose my chair for your attentions today?"

"I would say it was more a coincidence you chose to sit on it."

"You know I have meetings every day at this time."

Putting her brush on the windowsill where new varnish glistened in the sunlight, she said, "Captain Lightenfield, I have been so busy following your orders that I have had no time to pay attention to your daily life."

"You are lying."

"Am I? I thought I was only following orders." She walked toward the door to the deck.

He half rose, then sat when he realized how ridiculous

he looked bent over the table with the chair attached to his buttocks. "Get back here. This discussion is not over yet!"

A smile played with the corners of her lips, but her eyes lost none of their triumphant glitter. "On the contrary, Captain, this conversation is over *now*. I have to get back to my duties. There is still more than half of the ship waiting to be painted."

She left the door gaping behind her. From where he sat, Stephen could see her strolling toward the bow as if she were the mistress of *The Ladysong*. He let the chair thump viciously on the floor. No man had ever dared to defy him openly. No woman, who was half a head shorter than him, was going to beat him in any contest of wills. How he would like to wipe that insolence from her face!

He pounded his fist on the table as he suddenly realized he wanted only to hold her in his arms and press his mouth over her wine-red lips. Her lips were probably as bitter as the dregs left in the bottom of a bottle, but the image remained to taunt him. Maybe he should let her jump ship in Greytown. Then he would be rid of her and the temptation of letting a woman muddle up his life.

He could not sit here until the chair rotted. Cursing, he raised his right leg as he pressed down on the chair. Varnish caked on his hands as he peeled the denim off the varnish. He did the same with his other leg. As he rose with the chair flapping against his thighs like a cloak frozen with a wintry seawind, he tried to reach over his shoulder to strip his shirt from the back of the chair.

"Would you like some help?"

Stephen whirled and swore when the chair legs smashed against the table.

Arielle laughed as she closed the saloon door. Setting a reeking container and some rags on the table, she said, "If you will sit and be quiet, Captain, I think I can solve your problem."

"As you should, seeing that you are its cause."

Arielle laughed again as he tried to rearrange the chair beneath him without touching its sticky surface. She dipped a rag in the container and handed it to him. "Wipe the turpentine on your hands. It should get the varnish off them." Dunking another rag, she said, "I will work on your shirt. You know, Captain, you should be more careful."

"I am not used to having my own crew sabotaging my chair."

Putting her hand on his shoulder, she ran the rag along the top slat of the chair. She could not stop smiling. She never had guessed her prank would be so successful. When she had planned this, she had guessed nothing more would happen than the tacky surface of the chair would be bothersome and embarrass him in front of his officers.

"You have enjoyed this, didn't you?" he asked.

She wet the cloth again and continued rubbing the fabric with the pungent liquid. Beneath her fingers his strong muscles moved as he tried to pull away. She drew back. She had not imagined having to touch him like this.

"What is wrong?" he asked, looking over his shoulder.

"Nothing," she mumbled, and dabbed at his shirt again.

"Nothing?" He caught her hand. Pulling her forward, he held her so her face was even with his. "Why so quiet, Arielle? Why aren't you exulting over your revenge?"

"Captain," she retorted, glad for her anger that could hide her disquiet, "I do not want to end up stuck to this chair too."

"You?" He twisted at an impossible angle. Arching his eyebrows sardonically, he said, "Interesting. The front of your bodice glued to the back of my chair. That would be a charming situation."

Arielle jerked her hand out of his. "I am sure a barbarian like you would think so." Splashing turpentine on his shirt, she scoured the varnish off it.

"Save some skin, Arielle." He moved forward as the

material loosened. "I guess you think this will make us even."

"I guess." She tried to ignore the firm muscles beneath her fingers as she ran the dripping rag across his back. "Why don't you sit still so I can get this off? I know how busy the captain of the ship is. I would not want to keep you from any of your important duties."

"Are you enjoying the chance to remind me of every insult I have given you?" He reached up to her cheek. Bringing her face closer, he said, "It does not matter. You are right."

"I am?"

"I will sit here and enjoy *this*."

Turpentine puddled on the floor as she stared down into his gray eyes. When she started to move away, frightened by the potent emotions glowing in them, he caught her wrist. His shoulder brushed against her breast, and she gasped as a flame seared her.

She shoved the cloth into his hand. "You should be able to clean off the rest."

"What are you so afraid of?"

"I don't know." When he grinned at her honesty, she said more sharply, "Captain, release my hand. Must I remind you again that I am betrothed?"

"Is that what frightens you? Marrying Drummond?"

Instead of answering, she pushed on his shoulder. The last of the fabric stuck to the chair popped off. Standing, he flexed his arms. She hurried to collect the brush she had left on the windowsill.

"You should dip those clothes in turpentine as well," she said without looking at him. "There is plenty in the paint locker."

"Thank you, if thanks is the right word."

Arielle smiled at his ironic answer. "Anytime, Captain."

"I will remember that." He wiped his hands on a rag and tossed it to her. Coming around the table, he said, "I may just arrange for this again, honey." His damp fingertip traced a curlicue along the back of her hand. "I like these fingers touching me."

His hands moved along her arms, their warmth oozing through her muslin sleeves. He stepped closer as his fingers draped over her back to massage her tired muscles. She closed her eyes as she savored his gentle touch. When he took the turpentine and rags from her and dropped them on the table, she let him seat her on the bench beside him. His thumbs played across her shoulder blades, releasing them from the fatigue cramping them.

His throaty whisper fired the pulse pounding in her ears. "Don't you agree this is very nice, Arielle?"

"It is very nice."

"And this?"

He spun her to face him. Her gasp vanished beneath the firm pressure of his mouth on hers. Her fingers clenched on his shirt, then softened to spread across his chest. Gently, persuasively, his teasing tongue urged her lips to part. When she tasted the rum he had shared with his men, she was sure she would be intoxicated by its sweet fire.

Lifting his mouth from hers, he whispered, "Very nice."

"Yes," she answered breathlessly.

Her fingers sifted up through his golden hair as his mustache grazed her cheek. His lips sprinkled a shower of kisses across her face. A hunger ached within her, and she steered his mouth back to hers.

Leaning her back over his arm, he pressed her against the back of the bench. He delved deeply into her mouth, awakening every slippery pleasure within her. As her fingers splayed across his shoulders, he brushed her hair away from her face.

A soft moan bubbled from her when his mouth crept along her neck. She quivered against him, unable to restrain the desire soaring through her.

When he drew away, Arielle opened her dazed eyes to see his smile. She raised her hand to his cheek, which was as coarse as his fingers. Turning his head, he teased one finger into his mouth. She shivered as his tongue caressed it. She reached for him, and—

"Ouch!" she cried as she tried to move her head. At his triumphant laugh, she groped behind her to discover her hair was stuck to the varnish on the windowsill. "You— you—"

"Bastard?" he supplied with a grin. Standing, he grabbed a damp rag off the table and threw it in her lap. "Now we are no longer even, Arielle." He bent toward her.

She tried to avert her face, but her hair was too securely caught. He kissed her with slow, lingering passion that sent trembles to the tips of her toes.

She whispered, "You are going to be sorry."

"I know." He laughed and walked out of the saloon.

Tears of frustration blinded her as she awkwardly dabbed turpentine on her hair. Somehow she had to get off this blasted ship and find Caleb. Then she would forget all about Stephen Lightenfield's twisted sense of humor. But it would not be as easy to forget the thrill of his lips stroking hers.

CHAPTER FIVE

At anchor, *The Ladysong* rocked gently in the cove at the mouth of the Rio San Juan. The bare-poled ship rested after battling the fickle seas. Lights from the small settlement of Greytown broke the tropical night like diamonds dusting the sky. Stone huts with thatched roofs edged the beach. Most of them needed repair. Around them, tents and garbage littered the sand, left behind by men who had found passage on the Accessory Transit Company packet across the isthmus and to another ship, which would take them to the gold fields of California.

But it was the jungle that drew Arielle's eyes. A giant thicket, black with nightfall, it was severed only by the dirty waters of the Rio San Juan. She had not guessed it would be so primitive or so forbidding.

She shivered as she listened to the ship's creaking. No voices called on deck. No cargo thumped as it was rolled down the long pier alongside *The Ladysong*. The moment she had waited for since they had anchored in the early hours before dawn had come. The ship was guarded by only a few men who grumblingly were waiting their turns for shore leave.

As she closed her bag, she tried to shut away her fears. Shortly after they had reached Greytown, Captain Lightenfield had sent a man into the settlement. Word soon came back that Caleb Drummond was not there. He had not been seen on the river for the past six months. Rumor hinted he was in Granada.

Yet nothing had changed. She must go to Granada if that was where he was. Through that impenetrable jungle. She rubbed her icy hands together as she stared out the window at the trees and undergrowth that reached all the way to the beach. She would be safe on the packet up the river. At least she hoped she would.

Setting her bonnet on the back of her hair, she did not check her appearance in the mirror. She must go now. She could not let fear hold her back, because she might never have this chance again.

Captain Lightenfield had gone into Greytown an hour before to meet the captains of the other ships in the harbor. If she could sneak away while he was gone, she would find the Accessory Transit Company's office and arrange for passage up the Rio San Juan to Lake Nicaragua. Beyond that inland sea was Granada, the capital of the American filibusters. There Caleb might be waiting for her.

Arielle picked up her bag and took a steadying breath. Nothing had gone as she had planned so far on this journey, and she tried not to think what she would say to Caleb when she found him. She was not sure what she would tell him about Stephen Lightenfield.

As she went to the door, she looked back at the cramped room and the hammock swinging to the rhythm of the waves beneath the ship. She had not thought it would be so hard to walk away.

She squared her shoulders and raised her chin. She could not turn back now. Hurrying out the door before she could change her mind, she bumped into a bench in the darkened saloon. She bit back her gasp of pain as she bent to put her hand out to guide her around it.

She saw the motion from the corner of her eye. A man-sized shadow congealing out of the night, a raised hand, something that glittered. Everything vanished into a cacophony of agony as the floor came up to cradle her in darkness.

Torment woke Arielle. Her head ached with the blast of a dozen cannon. A stench surrounded her, strangling her. She coughed, then moaned as the cannon erupted again against her skull. Struggling to breathe slowly and shallowly, she tried to batter back the pain so she could think.

Voices drifted to her. Feminine voices! On *The Ladysong*? She was the only woman on the ship. Then she noticed the floor beneath her was steady. If she was not on the ship, where was she?

She opened her eyes to stare at filthy stone walls. Once they might have been covered with plaster, but only bits of it remained. Slowly she realized she was lying on a thin mattress. Straw rustled under her head as she turned to discover the pallet was on a floor that was even more squalid than the walls.

A shout ricocheted through her head, and she winced. Looking across the room, which was not much bigger than the captain's quarters on *The Ladysong*, she saw five or six women. She was not sure how many, because her eyes still refused to focus.

"*¡Muy hermosa!*" cried one of the women.

Arielle choked back a shout when she saw the dark-haired woman was holding up her best chemisette. Another swirled about in two petticoats, one about her waist, the other draped from her shoulders like a lacy cape. If they had taken her clothes . . .

She gasped. Her legs were naked beneath her thin chemise. Even her shoes had vanished. How dare they steal her clothes and parade before her with them!

"Give me back my clothes!" She started to sit up, then gasped when she heard a metallic clink when pain scraped her right wrist.

Horror paralyzed her as she stared at the manacle around her arm. The other end, only a few links away, was locked on an iron ring in the wall. This must be a nightmare. When she looked from the iron links to the women, they giggled. She did not need to know their language, which she guessed was Spanish, to know they were laughing at her.

Their amusement disappeared as the door opened. A massive woman with thick black braids heaved her bulk into the room. With a snapped order she sent the other women scurrying.

"My clothes!" Arielle called after them, then sagged against the dirty pallet.

"*¡Silencio!*" The fat woman's voice was surprisingly melodic as she continued in Spanish.

Arielle shook her head and sat straighter. "I don't understand you."

"You obey. No need to understand." Her English was thick with her accent.

"I need my clothes."

A rumble came from deep inside her. "No need clothes. Not here. Work. You eat. No work. You no eat."

"Work?" This sounded too familiar. If this was another of Captain Lightenfield's pranks . . . As pain pulsed across her forehead, she knew it could not be. He might embarrass her. He might pretend to want to kiss her so he could stick her hair into varnish, but he would not knock her senseless.

The woman pinched Arielle's cheek. When Arielle tried to push her away, the woman slapped her. As Arielle cringed in pain and astonishment, the woman kneaded her bare shoulder and pressed on Arielle's breast.

"No!" she cried in disgust, backing away as far as the short chain allowed and crossing her arms in front of her. "Don't touch me!"

With a smile the woman muttered, *"¡Virgen!"*

Arielle's eyes widened in horror. That word was close enough to English for her to understand. She could not ignore the truth any longer. A group of half-dressed women and a massive protectress in a filthy hut. She nearly gagged as she realized she must be in a brothel.

"This is a mistake," she said, trying to slow her frantic voice. "I don't belong here. There has been some kind of mistake."

"No mistake."

"But I don't belong here!"

"Man bring. He sell to me. I sell you to men."

Icy terror clawed at Arielle's stomach. "Who brought me here?"

"Man." With a grunt she touched Arielle's leg. When Arielle tugged her chemise down over her bare feet, the woman nodded. "Good. You wait. Men come. Many want *norteamericana*. You see. You work. You eat." She patted her round stomach and laughed. "You work much."

"Come back!" Arielle called when the woman waddled out of the room.

Her only answer was the door slamming shut.

Arielle crouched against the wall. As bugs crawled across the floor, she shuddered. This must be what hell was like. She tugged on the iron ring, but it was secure in the stones. When the first tears cascaded down her face, she could not turn back the tide of terror washing over her. She hid her face in her hands and huddled on the reeking mattress as she sobbed herself into a nightmare that could be no worse than what she would face when she woke.

A foot poked Arielle in the back. She muttered in her sleep. The foot kicked her again harder. With a gasp she sat up and stared at the fat woman. Backing away, Arielle shook her head.

"Work now." The woman's collection of chins wobbled as she chuckled. "Work good. You eat." She called in Spanish as she walked out the door.

Arielle pulled her knees up to her chest and huddled against the stones as she wondered how she would endure this depravity. A shadow crept toward the floor as disgusting as the bugs flitting from stone to stone. Her breath burned in her chest. She could not release it without screaming.

A man appeared in the door. When light glinted gold on his hair, she cried, "Stephen! Oh, thank God, it's you. Help me! Get me out of here! Please."

He grinned as she used his given name for the first time. Closing the door, he crossed the room in two strides. He sat cross-legged in front of her and said, "You have really gotten yourself into a mess this time, Arielle. How did you manage this?"

"I did nothing! I was in the saloon on *The Ladysong*. Then something crashed into my head. I woke up here."

He set her small bag between them. "You apparently were leaving *The Ladysong*."

Grabbing the bag, she opened it. She moaned when she saw it was empty.

"Don't worry," he said tersely. "I have the señora collecting all your things from her *putas*."

"Her what?"

"Her whores." He laughed as she shuddered. "Don't you know where you are?"

"I have a good idea."

"I told you to stay on the ship, but I guess you had to see the more pleasurable parts of Greytown for yourself."

Arielle snapped the bag closed. "If this is your idea of a joke—"

"I don't think there is anything funny about you ignoring the order I gave for your own good." He gripped her elbows and shook her gently. "You fool!"

"I did not come here on my own!" Her headache flared as she fought to focus her eyes again. "I told you someone knocked me on the head. I woke up here." She forgot the pain as she saw the truth in his furious eyes. "Roach Walden! He did this, didn't he? Where is he?"

"Roach is bound for San Francisco on the morning tide. *The Gray Storm* will be continuing around the Cape, and I made arrangements with her captain to take him."

She held up her shackled arm. "He did this to me, and you just let him go?"

"He betrayed *me*, Arielle. *I* decided what his punishment would be." His smile returned. "And now maybe you can understand why I told you to stay on the ship. Greytown is no place for a woman on her own."

As if to second his words, unmistakable sounds oozed past the door. Arielle pressed her hands over her ears, but nothing could silence the lustful grunts. When Stephen put his hands over hers, she leaned her head on his chest.

"Help me get out of here," she whispered.

Seeing the tears in her eyes, Stephen nodded. Damn Roach! He might have been able to forgive his first mate for bringing Arielle aboard but not for disobeying him a second time or for selling her here. By the time *The Gray Storm* reached California, Roach would have learned his lesson. Weeks of working in the bilge was punishment enough for ignoring his orders.

He pulled a thick key from his pocket and slipped it into the manacle around her arm. When it cracked open, she gently rubbed her wrist. He saw rust ground into her soft skin. Damn Roach! He should have keelhauled him before handing him over to Turner on *The Gray Storm*.

"All right," he said. "Let's go."

"I cannot leave looking like this."

He could not halt his gaze from following her curves, which were so enticingly outlined by her thin chemise. How easy it would be to push her down on that straw pallet and teach her the pleasures they could share! With her silky hair draped over his shoulders and her breasts against his chest, he would let her body surround his with the succulent heat of passion until they both were consumed by its maddening fire.

"Stephen, can I at least get a blanket?"

Her frightened voice shattered his fantasy, and he sighed. "Wait here."

"No!" She clutched onto his arm. "If I stay here, someone might come, and . . ."

His laugh was sharper than he intended, but her virginal fears were irritating. If she had any idea how much she risked by pressing her soft body to him, she would be glad to wait alone. He pulled off his frock coat and settled it over her shoulders.

"You do not have to worry," he said as he helped her to her feet. "I bought an hour of your time. You did not come cheap, honey."

Caressing the soft warmth of her flushed cheek, he drew her into his arms. She trembled as she clung to him, but he knew she would regain her normal quarrelsome nature once she was freed from this place. That would not be easy. The señora would be reluctant to lose a woman as lovely as Arielle Gardiner.

Stephen kept his arm around her as they walked down the short hall to the hut's main room. When they stepped over a drunk, Arielle shuddered but said nothing. That surprised him. She must be more frightened than he had thought. Maybe she had learned her lesson about what could happen to her alone in Nicaragua.

"Looking for more fun, handsome?" called one of the whores in Spanish.

He ignored her as he plucked the bag from Arielle's hands and waved it in front of the fat woman's nose. "Where are the rest of her things, señora?"

The huge woman shrugged and pointed to a pile of clothes in the middle of the floor. "That is all she brought."

"She had a bundle of letters with her." He reached up to the shelf over her head. "Tied in this ribbon."

Again she shrugged. "I have no need for papers. I threw them out."

"Where?"

"Out."

Stephen knew it would be a waste of time to try to get anything more out of her. Shoving the clothes into the bag, he handed it to Arielle. She gripped it like a drowning man holding to a bit of flotsam. Quickly he explained what the woman had told her. Arielle nodded, but two tears rolled silently along her pale cheeks.

Damn Roach!

"Go back to the room you were in," he said softly. When she shook her head vehemently, he put his hands on her shoulders. "Arielle, go back and get dressed. I will find your letters."

"If I go back there—"

With a growled curse he pulled some coins from his pocket. He slapped them into the fat woman's hands. He ignored her chuckle as he said, "Satisfied, Arielle? I just bought you for the next hour, too. So do as I tell you and get back in there and get dressed before you cost me my next year's profits."

"You cannot *buy* me!"

"I just did, honey."

"I am not a whore."

"What language for a schoolteacher!" He cupped her chin and whispered, "Can I hope that I have been such a bad influence on you?"

Arielle whirled away. More tears stung her eyes. She was saying all the wrong things. She should be thankful to Stephen—how easily she thought of him that way!— instead of snarling at him. She just wanted to get out of this place and never come back. Why hadn't Caleb warned her? She flinched as she realized Stephen had, but she had not listened. She wanted to run away. She wanted to take a bath for hours until every bit of the scum from this horrible hole was scoured from her skin. She wanted to be home and safe in the world she knew.

Hearing more groans from behind another door, Arielle ran into the room she had just left and slammed the door. She groped in her bag for her clothes. She put Stephen's coat on the pallet and shook out each garment, fearing there would be bugs in it, before she buttoned it in place.

The door opened as she was closing the cuffs on her chemisette. She whirled, then released her terrified breath as she saw Stephen come in with a handful of dirt-covered papers.

"Here." He tossed the envelopes to her. "I do not know if that is all of them, but I am not searching through that dung heap any longer."

Sitting on the pallet, she sorted through them. With a sigh of relief she pressed the last letter she had received to her heart. She looked up to thank Stephen, but her words withered away as she saw his strange expression. His lips were taut, and the merriment in his eyes had been replaced by sadness. Then he laughed, baffling her more.

She could not guess what he was thinking. His mercurial moods changed too fast for her to follow.

Tying the ribbon around the letters, she put them in her bag. She took out the boots she had bought in Boston and set them on the pallet.

"What is missing?" Stephen asked while she pawed through the bag.

She shook her head. "My stockings are gone."

"No one ever sees your legs anyhow." He smiled as he squatted and ran a finger along her bare calf. "That is a shame, too."

Arielle wanted to snarl a rebuke, but his touch kindled the barely quiescent longings she had tried to ignore. Her hand touched the soft hair along his muscular arm as he bent toward her, his fingers drawing her knee closer to the firm line of his legs. Slowly he leaned her back toward the pallet, his face descending toward hers.

"No," she whispered in a desperate voice. "Not here."

Husky craving edged his words. "Why not here? What better place to kiss you than in this *burdel?*"

"Stephen, don't." She smoothed her skirts down over her legs and reached for her boots. Pulling them on, she took the hand he held out to her. She did not meet his eyes as she added, "Let's get out of here."

"Back to *The Ladysong?*" When she hesitated, his lips straightened again. "Let's get out of here first. Then we can argue."

Arielle put her hand on his arm as he led her down the short corridor. Heat scored her face when they entered the room where the fat woman was sitting. The skimpily dressed women were surrounded by a group of men whose clothes stank of cheap rum. She moved closer to Stephen as the men turned to stare at her. Wishing her bonnet hid her face, she lowered her eyes. The fat woman called something in Spanish, and the men laughed. Stephen spat back a retort.

The woman held out her hand, blocking their way to the door. When Stephen dropped more coins into her hand, she poured them into her lap and put up her hand for more. He cursed but placed several bills across her palm.

"Come on," he muttered, tugging on Arielle's arm. "Let's get out of here before she decides you are worth even more."

"You paid her almost fifty dollars!" she exclaimed.

He shoved her out the open door. "Shut up, unless you want to convince her to renegotiate your price."

The eastern sky was tinged with gray, and Arielle realized the whole night had vanished. As she shivered in the cool sand and listened to the lisp of the water whispering to the shore, she said, "I will repay you, Stephen."

"How?"

"I have—"

He put his arm around her and herded her along the shore. "You don't really think they gave you back your money, do you?"

"I had almost two hundred dollars with me."

"That explains why she was willing to let you go for a measly fifty more."

Arielle stepped over some dried seaweed. "I will pay you back."

"How?"

"When I find Caleb, I will ask him for the money. We shall send it to you."

He sniffed with derision. "Do you think Drummond's going to be thrilled to learn that his wife spent a night in a Greytown *burdel?*"

Arielle faltered. Being kidnapped and imprisoned in a brothel was not her worst crime since she had met Stephen Lightenfield. She had let this handsome man tempt her into his arms, teasing her with his feverish kisses, washing all thoughts of her fiancé from her head. Not wanting Stephen to see her shame, she looked across the harbor. She was able to pick out *The Ladysong* at its mooring.

"If you need help finding *The Gray Storm*," Stephen said, taking her bag, "it is the clipper between the two steamships."

"I was not looking for it." Sand sifted over the top of her low boots as she continued along the beach. "If you really want to help me, point out which building holds the Accessory Transit Company."

He gave a low laugh that twirled through her, making her wish for his arms around her. "I should have known better. You still have not learned this is not a place for a woman like you."

"Caleb is not here. I must find him." She tried to make her voice light, but it was heavier than her eyes that burned with the remnants of her tears. "After all, how else will you get your money back?"

"He should have been waiting for you," Stephen grumbled.

"Maybe he could not get here in time."

In the thin light spreading across the sky, his eyes narrowed to silvery slits. "Couldn't? Do you think he is in some sort of trouble?"

She wiped her sweaty palms on her skirt. "I don't know, but he would have been here if he could. Caleb always keeps his promises."

"Nicaragua changes people."

"Not that much."

With a chuckle he grabbed her hands and turned her to look at him. "There is no sense in arguing. I will not let you wander off into the jungle alone."

"I must go." Fear squeezed her breath from her as she

stared at the black jungle where night still ruled. "Caleb needs me. I must find him."

"Agreed, but you cannot go alone."

Jerking away, she demanded, "And whom am I supposed to take? You?"

"Sure. Why not?"

Arielle stared at him, certain he was taunting her again. She could not believe this abrupt change of heart. "Why would you want to cross the isthmus with me?"

His shrug was as indifferent as the fat woman's. "Why not?"

"That is no answer."

"Then how about curiosity? I have been ferrying gold-hungry idiots and their supplies down here for the past year. I have a hankering to see what they have seen." He grinned. "Besides, after a year of following the same path from Boston to Greytown and back, I could use an adventure."

"This is not an adventure. I have to find Caleb."

"But why can't we have fun while we are looking for him?"

Arielle snatched her bag from him and continued along the beach. Fun! Going into the jungle with all this heat and the bugs and only God knew what else lurking in there was not her idea of fun.

A hand on her arm whirled her to face Stephen. Her boots slipped in the sand, but he kept her on her feet. "How about it, Arielle?" When she hesitated, he said, "You need my help. You do not speak Spanish, and you do not have any idea of what is ahead of you."

"I thought you had to return to Boston immediately."

Again he gave her a lazy shrug. "Things changed. *The Ladysong* is going to be here for a while longer, so I might as well enjoy myself watching you make an ass of yourself in the jungle. This way, I can watch as you explain to your exemplary Drummond why his chaste bride needs to repay me fifty dollars. That should be the most fun."

Stung by his mocking words, she put her hands on her waist. "If you think you can keep up with me, come along."

"Keep up with you?" He laughed as he linked his arm with hers. "My dear Arielle, I do not intend to miss a moment of your bumbling across this isthmus."

CHAPTER SIX

Rain splattered fitfully on the windows of the captain's cabin on *The Ladysong* as Arielle brushed her damp hair into the ringlets. Her bath had been quick, but the filth from the brothel was gone. She grimaced as her brush touched the tender spot where Walden had struck her.

She scanned the shore as she buttoned her white chemisette. Stephen should have been back by now. How long did it take to obtain two passages on the Accessory Transit boat?

With a sigh she sat on the chair and brushed dust off her black skirt. She still could not understand why Stephen intended to travel with her to Granada just to collect his fifty dollars.

"And the fifty for your passage south," echoed his deep voice in her mind.

He had arranged for Mr. Simon to take command. If the new first mate had been startled by the orders, there had been no sign of it on his doughy face.

When she heard the outer door open, she recognized

Stephen's assertive footsteps. She smiled and reached for her battered bag.

"Might as well put that away," he growled as he tossed his red-banded panama on the desk. His blond hair was slicked to his head, and rain dripped from his mustache to dot his green brocade vest. She held out a towel while he crossed the room, leaving puddles in his wake. He ripped it from her hands and rubbed it against his face.

"You couldn't get passage?"

"There is a waiting list longer than your arm. We could not go west along the river for at least another month." Putting down the towel, he sighed. "Arielle, I cannot wait that long."

"I understand." She reached for her bag.

His hand closed over her wrist, drawing her hand away from the bag. "Don't even think about going by yourself."

"I have to," she whispered, trying to ignore how much she had looked forward to having his help. Going into that jungle alone terrified her. "Caleb needs me."

"Arielle, I will not let you cross the isthmus alone."

"But—"

"Will you be quiet for once?" Wrapping his arm around her waist, he tugged her against him. His hand tilted her face to the perfect angle beneath his.

She thought of protesting. She should push him away, reminding him, as she had so often, that she was betrothed to another man. Her arms rose to encircle his broad shoulders. Closing her eyes, she welcomed the caress of his warm mouth against her, tenderly persuading her to surrender to him. His arms tightened around her when his tongue stroked hers, daring hers to touch him as boldly.

"Is this the only way to silence you?" he whispered with a chuckle. With his finger against her lips, which were damp where his mustache had brushed them, he asked, "Can I use the same tactics to convince you not to go?"

Arielle picked up her bag and held it between them. "I *am* going, Stephen."

"All right." He sighed. "I will need to find us transportation all the way to Lake Nicaragua."

"Us? You are still going with me?"

"Why not?" A smile peeked from beneath his mustache. He opened his clothes cupboard and took out a leather knapsack. Tossing in a few clothes, he said, "Don't just stand there. We have to be at the river docks within the hour."

Arielle's eyes widened when he chuckled. "You have had passage for us all along?"

"You didn't think I would come back here and tell you that you could not go upriver just because the packet's full, did you?" His smile drifted away from his eyes as he drew open the top drawer of his desk. He lifted out a revolver. When she froze, he arched a single tawny brow at her. "Don't forget, Arielle, that there is a war going on inland. I don't suppose you know how to shoot a gun."

"Not very well." She suppressed a shudder as she held out her hand. "I suppose I could if I needed to."

He put the gun in his belt and closed his sack. "I hope you do not need to. Come on. Let's get this adventure started."

Arielle nodded, afraid to speak, for the immensity of what they were about to attempt was suddenly real. When Stephen glanced back and held out his hand, she pushed her stiff feet forward to put her hand in his. She hoped he did not notice how it trembled as they walked off the ship and through the mist into a world she could not imagine. Nor did she want to.

Arielle followed Stephen as he threaded his way through the crowds on the docks. He stopped in front of a boat that looked like a flimsy balsa raft with built-up sides. A rotund man with a balding pate stood in it. He waved and greeted Stephen with an enthusiastic spurt of Spanish.

When Stephen tossed her bag into it, she asked, "Are we traveling to Lake Nicaragua in that?"

"Either we go with Miguel or wait for the Transit line."

"Maybe we should check into the Transit packet again." She pointed to the brightly painted ship waiting farther along the pier. Only a few men loitered by it. "It does not look too crowded now."

"Trust me, Arielle. This is the only way."

Her eyes widened. "Trust you? Why would I trust you of all people? I will not travel in that leaky tub!"

"Be quiet!" His smile froze her. "Miguel is my friend. He has agreed to take us to his village, which is about twenty miles upriver. From there we may be on foot if we cannot find another ride." His fingers tightened around her arm. "Luckily he does not understand much English."

"But if we sink—"

"We won't. Miguel knows this river better than I know your lips." He swept her closer, but his body was taut with fury. "He is a proud man. Insult his *bungo* again, and we will leave you here on the docks."

"It looks so rickety," she said.

"Does it?"

She shrieked as he grabbed her by the waist and dropped her into the boat. She stumbled, then fell heavily onto the narrow board nailed to the railing. Clutching it, she watched Stephen jump down next to her.

"See?" he asked in the superior tone she despised. "It is sturdy."

At Miguel's laughing comment and Stephen's answer, she flushed. The two men could discuss her without her knowing what they said. She had never felt so out of place. This was crazy. At the same time she was telling Stephen she did not trust him, she was allowing herself to become more dependent on him. Yet she wondered if she had any other choice if she wanted to reach Granada.

With a sputter, a steam engine burst into motion. She looked at the Transit packet, then realized, as the *bungo* quivered, that the sound came from a small roofed shelter at its stern. She was amazed. She had had no idea this primitive craft was powered by a steam engine. Opening her parasol, she hoped the sun would come out.

Greytown vanished as the boat maneuvered against the brown, silty current. Arielle sat stiffly and watched the banks. She saw a few huts among the trees and vines and rampant greenery.

At midmorning the sun burst from the angry mountains of clouds. A silver mist formed. It was nothing like a familiar New England fog. Soon she was soaked with its steamy heat and wishing for a breath of cool air. The engine chugged contentedly. Its erratic beat crawled inside her. She shifted on the narrow seat but could not get comfortable.

Fatigue crushed her, and she swayed with the motion of the boat. When Miguel came forward with a package in brown paper and a tin canister, he put them in her lap and gave her a ragged-tooth grin. Unsure, she smiled back weakly.

"It is your lunch!" called Stephen from the stern. He had rolled up his sleeves. Sweat stuck his shirt to his back. She watched the easy ripple of his muscles as he tossed another stock of wood into the engine's maw, then looked away when he turned to discover her staring at him.

"Eat," Miguel said in a voice as rumbling as the engine. Perspiration coursed down his full face, but his black eyes sparkled with friendship. "Good."

"Thank you," she answered. "I mean *gracías*, Miguel."

The boatman chuckled and lurched back to the stern. As she opened the brown package, Stephen sat opposite her. He said nothing as she looked at a meat-filled patty.

"Tortilla," he explained. "It is like a sandwich."

"What kind of meat is in it?"

"Do you really want me to find out?"

Arielle smiled for the first time since they had left Grey-town. "You are incorrigible." She pointed to the packet he had on his lap. "You try it first."

"I will." He unrolled his meal and took a bite. "How long are you going to wait to see if my toes turn green and fall off?"

Cautiously she sampled the meat roll. Spices burned her tongue, and she coughed. Groping for the tin, she took a drink. Rum metamorphosed into liquid fire in her mouth. Scorching her throat, it left her tongue charred.

"Good?" he mumbled around a mouthful of food.

"Fine," she managed to gulp, then coughed again.

When another tin was held under her nose, she shook her head. She did not want more rum.

"Take it," Stephen ordered, chuckling. "It is juice. We must have mixed up the containers."

Sipping the drink, she glared at him through watery eyes. The cans might have been mixed up but not accidentally. When Miguel shouted a short phrase and Stephen laughed, she clenched her hands on the tin.

"Don't glower at me, Arielle. It is too nice a day for fighting." Leaning back and putting his muddy boots on the board next to her, Stephen added, "We have a long, hard journey ahead of us. We might as well enjoy this part of it."

"The fun part?"

"Exactly."

Screeches from birds and monkeys followed them through the afternoon as the sun raced away like an unob-tainable treasure. Sitting beneath her parasol, Arielle understood why Caleb hated the thick heat.

When she saw Stephen leaning against the bow with his hat pushed over his eyes, she knew he was asleep. His arms were folded on his chest, which rose and fell evenly. It irritated her that he could be so comfortable when she was sweltering and cramped and miserable.

Adjusting her feet, she smiled when her boot's sharp toe struck his shin. He woke with a startled yelp and rubbed his leg. When he glared at her, she smiled sympathetically. "I hope I did not kick you when I moved." She tilted her parasol to shadow her grin.

He knew she was lying. She could see that in his expressive eyes. That would teach him for tossing her into the boat and giving her unwatered rum. When he stood and went back to where Miguel was stoking the engine again, she laughed softly. This might be the fun part after all.

The sun was dropping into the river when the steam engine went silent. Arielle roused from a stupor, hoping the horrible journey was coming to an end. Every bone ached.

"Nice nap?" Stephen asked, and she discovered he was sitting next to her.

She realized, as well, that she must have been leaning her head against his shoulder while she was lost somewhere between sleep and being awake. "Not really." Then, not wanting to insult him when he had been kind enough to offer his shoulder, she added, "That clanking kept me awake."

"It will be pretty quiet here."

"Here? Miguel's village?" She scanned both shores. "Where?"

Laughing, he pointed to several wooden shafts that might have been a pier protruding from the water that might have been a pier. Miguel leapt around the boat like an oversized spider to tie it up to one of the poles. Jumping into the water, he waded ashore and motioned for them to follow. Stephen sloshed through water that was higher than his knees.

Clutching the side of the boat, which rocked wildly, Arielle shook her head when he called to her. "I can't! I am wearing my new boots!"

"I hope you are not waiting for me to tote you to shore."

"If you were a gentleman, you would not have to ask."

Miguel chuckled as he climbed the hill along a path that disappeared among the thick trees. He paused at the top and shouted.

"He says the mosquitoes will eat you alive!" Stephen warned.

"I paid good money for these boots."

"Damn your New England penny-pinching. I paid fifty dollars for you last night, and what did I get for my money? Just more of your complaints."

Arielle hoped no one who understood English was listening. "You did not have to come with me!"

"How else would I be sure I got my money back?" Not waiting for her answer, he waded into the muddy water. It eddied around him like melted chocolate. He held up his hands. When she hesitated, he demanded, "What is wrong now?"

"You won't drop me, will you?"

A laugh as wild as a cataract exploded from him. He pushed on the side of the boat. It tottered crazily. She screamed as she plunged out of it. He caught her. In her ear he growled, "Maybe, one of these days, you will start trusting me, honey."

She held her skirts out of the water. When he walked toward the shore, she breathed a silent sigh of relief. She *was* beginning to trust him, but, if she admitted that, he would do all he could to prove her wrong.

"Here you go." His terse laugh was her only warning before he set her in thick mud. He pressed down on her.

"Stop!" Slime oozed over the top of her boots. She

grappled with her skirts, trying to keep them out of the filth. Trying to free her feet without losing her boots, she cried, "You have ruined my boots! You promised to help me."

He wiped tears of amusement from the corners of his eyes. "I promised only that I would not let your precious boots get wet. You said nothing about mud."

With a frustrated cry she shoved him. His arms wind-milled, and water soared in an impromptu fountain as he fell in the river. He leapt up and spit out dirty water. He stretched to capture his hat that was floating on the gentle current twisting through the cove.

He glared at her, but she scrambled to drier footing. Hearing Miguel's laugh, she climbed the steep trail. She wanted to wash the mud off her legs and clean out her boots. She did not care if Stephen chased his hat all night.

Footsteps beat the path, but she did not turn. An arm snaked around her waist. She tried to shake it off, but it tightened, pulling her back against him.

"You are all wet!" she cried. "Let me go!"

Twirling her to face him, he held her against his soaked clothes. As his gaze moved along her in a slow stroke, he murmured, "And you are all dirty. Do you think we can get a bath here?"

Her nose wrinkled. "You stink. You could use a bath."

"So could you." He smiled as his wet hand moved in a circle across her back, leaving the moist heat of his fingers. "Why don't you wash the sweat off me, and I will wash the mud off you?"

Arielle gasped, "Of course not!"

Releasing her, he tapped her nose. "Let me know if you change your mind." He climbed the hill.

With an exasperated sigh she followed. The hidden vil-lage was nothing more than a few huts arranged haphaz-ardly about a narrow clearing. Dogs barked as they approached, but the animals slunk away when Miguel shouted. Most of the children watching her with large-eyed wonder were naked. Their parents stared as openly.

Miguel pointed to a hut at one end of the clearing. He winked as he spoke to Stephen. With a lecherous laugh he slapped the blond man on the back.

Arielle frowned. Stephen might pretend innocence, but the boatman did not hide that they were discussing her. "Are you going to share the joke?"

"Miguel asked us to join him for supper."

"Thank you, Miguel," she said, although she was sure supper had not been mentioned. *"Gracias."*

Miguel shot another grin at Stephen before walking away. When Stephen held aside the cloth hanging in the doorway of the hut, Arielle entered.

The single room was empty except for a straw mat in the middle of the floor. Despair threatened to overflow in tears. She wanted to be home where her comfortable bed waited in her bedroom with its chintz curtains. Was there no end to this nightmare?

"You've got to admit it is better than where you slept last night," Stephen said as he walked past her.

"If I had known we were going to stay in a sty, I would have waited for the Transit packet."

The curtain swung back. A young man tossed their sacks onto the floor and left without speaking. Her bag came open. She knelt to pick up her other chemise. Dirt stained it.

"Everything I own is going to be ruined," she moaned. "Look at this!"

He set his hat on the floor. "It does look pretty bad."

Amazed that he would agree, she said, "Stephen, maybe we should go back to Greytown."

Running his fingers along the dirty chemise, he mused, "This looks much better when you are inside it, and I can imagine you out of it."

She slapped his hands away. Laughing, he pushed aside

the cloth and left. She did not care where he went as long as he would leave her alone. As she stuffed the chemise into her bag, she could not ignore how his words tempted her to let him draw her into his arms so she could drown once more in the flood of luscious sensations his kisses undammed.

Arielle batted at a mosquito that was whining in her ear and wished that things had remained simple. If Caleb had never left Concord . . . If some other captain had been willing to bring her to Nicaragua . . . If Stephen's merry eyes and enchanting touch did not lure her into madness . . . The door flap fluttered, freeing her from her uneasy thoughts.

Stephen carried in two buckets. He took a bowl and some rags out of one, then poured water into the bowl. He sat on the mat and began cleaning his boots. Raising his eyes, he said, "Help yourself."

Arielle took a rag and dipped it into the water. It was filthy, but it would get the mud off her. She hesitated as she reached for her hem. Asking Stephen to leave while she washed would be a waste of breath. If she scrubbed quickly, she might be finished before he made another snide comment.

She pulled up her petticoats and slipped off her boots. With her back to him, she used her skirts to hide her legs. Not that it mattered after last night, but she wanted to maintain what dignity she could. The mud melted away as she ran the cloth from her knee to her ankle. A few stubborn spots remained. She wet the rag and tried again. They refused to rub off. She touched them. They were not dirt. With a strangled gasp she grabbed the bucket and poured water over her legs. The mounds did not move.

"Stephen! What are these things?"

He put down his boot and knelt beside her. Chuckling, he said, "I guess you have been pretty healthy."

"What's that supposed to mean?"

He poked one of the inch-long pieces of slime. "Bloodsuckers. Leeches, if you are squeamish about calling them bloodsuckers."

"Can you get them off me?"

"Sure."

"Then, do it." When he stood, she begged, "Please, Stephen!"

"So you are my friend again? You always are when you need me to do something for you."

Irritated by his teasing, she snapped, "Go away! I will take care of this myself."

He shrugged and picked up his boot. Whistling, he polished it, but she sensed his gaze on her bare legs as she pulled her skirts over her knees.

She shuddered as she touched a leech. It was damp and slimy. She pulled on it. Her eyes grew wide when it stretched and stretched far beyond its original length without relinquishing its tenacious hold. Releasing it, she watched in horror as it reshaped itself on her leg.

"Like this, honey." Stephen's weathered fingers pinched the creature between them. He pulled until it popped off. "They like your New England blood. Do you want me to remove the rest?"

"Will you?"

A slow smile crinkled the bronze skin around his eyes. "If you will reward me for my chivalry."

"How?"

"You are a suspicious woman! Just a kiss."

"I would rather kiss Miguel!"

Waving his hand toward the door, he said, "I am sure he would like looking at your ankles. Do you want me to help or not?

"If it wasn't for you, I would not have this problem."

"No, you would still be standing in the boat, waiting for Miguel to take you back to Greytown."

With a sigh she extended her legs. A heated flush climbed her cheeks as his fingers brushed her leg, but she winced as he plucked off each of the leeches. When he was finished, he scooped them up and threw them out the door.

"Done," he announced. Putting his finger under her chin, he brought her eyes up to meet his. "Now, pay up."

"All right." Arielle held her breath and closed her eyes. His lips touched her cheek, and she recoiled.

With a laugh he pulled on his boots. "Did you think I intended to throw you down on this floor and ravage you until you gave yourself to me?"

Arielle stood and brushed off her skirt. "You ask the most unseemly questions." When he rose so his head brushed the low rafters, she said, "I should be used to it by now, but I keep hoping you will be a gentleman. At least once."

He tangled his fingers in her hair. Leaning toward her, his mouth brushing her ear, his words were a fiery whirlwind through her whole body. "You don't know a gentleman from a draft horse. If I had not been a gentleman, your stay on *The Ladysong* would have been very, very different. So many times I saw you on the deck and wanted to do this."

He placed his lips lightly on the crook of her neck. As her body swayed against him, conforming to his hard planes, he whispered, "And I wanted to do this." The tip of his tongue traced the downy curve of her ear. Quivers fled across her, and she swept her hands up his back as he spun her to face him. "And, more than anything else, I wanted to do this."

He captured her mouth, demanding it cede every bit of itself to him. Putting one arm under her knees, he lifted her into his arms. She clung to him, not wanting to sever the magic of his kiss as he knelt. Gently he leaned her back on the rough mat. A throaty moan drifted from her lips as he tasted the sensitive skin along her neck. In the curve at its base he nibbled lightly. Her fingers combed upward through his thick hair, holding him tighter to her.

When his mouth claimed hers again, it was gentle, so gentle that she longed for more. He whispered, "That is what I would have done if I had not been a gentleman."

"Oh ..." She could say nothing else as she was enmeshed in his bewitchment.

"Lucky for you, I am a gentleman." When he chuckled and sat, she stared at him.

He was taunting her again! Each time she dared to welcome him into her arms, he poked fun at her as he tempted her to forget a man who never had teased her so cruelly.

Standing, Arielle said with what dignity she had left, "As you are a gentleman, I am sure you will agree when I ask you to put an end to such exhibitions."

"Just like that?" He leaned his elbow on his knee as he looked up at her.

"I must not forget why I am here." She hesitated, wondering how she could say what she must when her lips still burned from his kisses. "I should not be in your arms."

"No, you shouldn't." His pensive expression was a surprise. "Perhaps you are right. If your fiancé refuses to take you in, I shall have to bring you back to Greytown and probably back to Boston." Getting to his feet, he smiled coldly. "He won't pay me my hundred dollars either."

Arielle was torn between relief that he would acknowledge her betrothal and dejection that he had agreed so quickly. "I am glad we understand each other."

He grabbed his panama, swearing as water cascaded over his shoulders. A growl oozed from his lips as she laughed.

A knock on the door frame was followed by a spate of Spanish.

Stephen translated simply, "Supper."

As she put her hand on his, she said, "Thank you."

He raised it to his lips. "Promise me one thing, honey."

"What?"

"You will let me be the first to know when you get tired of a gentleman's company."

CHAPTER SEVEN

Arielle wondered if each day would be more unbelievable than the one before. As she stood on the shore of the Rio San Juan and watched a young man in brilliant red trousers maneuver a raft closer, she could not believe this was how they would be traveling for the next few days.

One corner of the raft banged into the shore and scraped off a layer of mud. The young man, who was dressed only in the ragged trousers, tied the rope connected to his raft around a tree. His lanky legs moved along the steep bank easily.

"Buenos días, mi amigo." Dipping his head in an impromptu bow, he gushed, *"Buenos días, señorita."*

"English, Girolamo," Stephen said. "Miss Gardiner does not speak Spanish."

"Of course, Cap'n," he said, startling Arielle, for his words were accent free.

"Girolamo got his education on the river. He has wisely used the time he has spent with prospectors to learn English." He grinned as he tousled the youngster's raven hair. "You may find that his is not exactly the English you would use in Concord."

"I understand." She greeted the lad with what warmth she could muster, for she had spent another sleepless night. The incessant squeal of mosquitoes and their irritating bites had kept her awake. At dawn Stephen had told her she should have pulled her blanket over her head to keep the bugs away.

She yawned as the two men negotiated what it would cost for Girolamo to take them west. They bargained with mutual respect, their words a queer mixture of English, Spanish, and broad gestures.

"We are all set," Stephen called. Holding out his hand to her, he put one foot on the raft.

Arielle stepped forward cautiously. When she put a hesitant toe on the logs, the raft teetered. She gasped and gripped Stephen's hand tighter. As he held her around the waist, she clutched his shoulders.

"Don't be afraid, honey," he murmured in her ear.

"It is going to capsize!"

"No, it won't." He laughed, and the raft slowed to a stop. "See?"

Infuriated, she watched as he started the raft rocking again. "You think it is fun to scare years off my life?"

Girolamo leapt aboard and picked up a long pole from the pile in the center of the raft. "Cap'n, you should not frighten Señorita Gardiner. If you are not kind to her, another will be."

Unsure whether to thank the young man or to be embarrassed by his assumption that Stephen was her lover, she glowered at Stephen. He chuckled with his usual good humor and told her to sit on a crate nailed to the middle of the raft.

She did, checking clandestinely to be sure nothing horrible waited there. Her boots slid on the logs, but she managed to get to the box without falling. Sitting, she rearranged her skirts. When she saw a thin layer of water coating the logs, she sighed. Nothing could damage her skirt more. Perhaps the water would wash away the mud.

Girolamo pushed the raft from the shore, and Stephen picked up another pole. He went to the rear to shove it upriver against the current. The younger man stood at the opposite corner at the front and steered the raft past any obstructions.

At first Arielle watched the riverbanks but grew fascinated with Girolamo's easy mastery of his craft. With a single well-placed shove he could propel the raft across the current to avoid a rock or tree root.

Stephen removed his shirt and tied it around his waist. His bare chest was as deeply tanned as his face. That told her he had been honest the night before. He had changed his habits while she was aboard *The Ladysong,* as a gentleman should. Despite herself, she stared at his body, which was turned in profile to her. His skin glistened with sweat, but his muscles moved smoothly as he pushed on the pole. The too-familiar flush climbed her cheeks.

How he would laugh at her if he could guess what she was thinking! She had pushed him away, telling him she must remain faithful to Caleb, but Stephen intruded on her thoughts and dreams as she imagined how delicious it would be to find herself in his brawny arms. She wanted to learn more about this enigmatic man who laughed so easily yet seldom revealed what he was thinking. He was comfortable on the deck of his ship or shoving a raft up this river to find a man he did not know so he could get back his one hundred dollars.

"Nicaragua changes people."

She was beginning to believe Stephen was right. The Arielle Gardiner who had left Concord was being replaced by a stranger who craved the caresses of a man she barely knew. Surely Caleb must be as changed by this alien land. She had feared during the months of silence that he had found another woman to replace her in his heart. Not once before she began this journey had she asked herself if she wanted to marry *him*. It always had been assumed that she would.

As they worked against the current, the men could not waste energy on talking, but the morning was not silent. Beneath the raft the waters splashed lightly. Birds and animals called from the trees. Arielle's boots tapped on the logs as she shifted on the low box. She despised doing nothing, but she knew better than to intrude as the men worked in perfect unison.

When Girolamo called for a stop to eat, she stood and stretched. Every muscle recalled the hard ridges of the straw mat. She hoped that she would have a more comfortable bed tonight.

"Move aside!" shouted Stephen.

She nearly fell when a jerk on her arm pulled her back onto another log. Stephen's steering pole dropped right where she had been standing. When she glared at him, he wiped his hands on his trousers and glowered back.

"You have got to keep an eye out," he grumbled.

"I would have if you would give me a minute to get out of the way."

Girolamo chuckled and jumped off the raft with the ease of a cat. After he had anchored them to the shore, he held out his hand to Arielle.

"Thank you," she said as she stepped onto the gently sloping bank. Grass beneath her skirts tickled her bare legs, and the odor of rot rose as she walked across the thickly matted ground.

"The word is *gracías*," Stephen corrected her.

She did not look at him as she said, "*Gracías*, Girolamo, for *your* being a gentleman today."

With a laugh the lad scampered back onto the logs. From beneath the box he pulled out a skillet and several packets. He offered them to her.

"Fix us something tasty. Be quick. We are starved," said Stephen as he untied his shirt. He wiped beads of sweat from his forehead and left his sandy hair spiked across the top of his head. "We will cool off while you make lunch."

"Maybe I would like to cool off too," Arielle protested.

With a calculated smile he reached for the belt of his trousers. "You are welcome to join us for a swim."

"A swim?" She backed away as he kicked off his boots.

Girolamo interjected, "Cap'n, if she wants to swim, we can go to the next cove."

"The more the merrier." Stephen loosened his belt and the top button on his trousers.

Arielle did not stay to see if he would really strip in front of her. His smug laughter followed her through the trees to a small clearing. Glancing swiftly over her shoulder, she saw no sign of the river or the men. Her knees trembled as she knelt to put the skillet on the ground.

She closed her eyes and took a steadying breath to slow her ragged breathing. Just thinking of his slippery skin caressing her was dangerous. Nothing would cool the heat burning them if there was nothing between them but the water.

"Stop!" she moaned. She must not think of such things, but, when she heard the men splashing in the water and shouting to each other, her fantasies taunted her with images of Stephen's slick muscles pressed against her.

Busying her hands would silence her mind. She opened the packets to find they contained tin dishes and food wrapped in muslin. She found dried meat and some sort of beans she did not recognize. Flat circles of dough resembled the tortillas. She could not guess what the green flakes were. Using a cup to dig out a fire pit, she filled it with dried vines and fallen twigs for a fire. She set the skillet on two rocks in the hole. In the pan she placed all the food. She had no idea what she was cooking or how it would taste.

As she stirred it with a stick, the steam made her mouth water. Sampling it, she found it tasted better than it looked. She called to the men and hoped they would come before the food burned, because she refused to go near the river while they were swimming.

"The Old Ones are just nonsense," Stephen said as he pushed through the clinging underbrush. "You know that, Girolamo."

The younger man, who was using a frond to dry his hair, retorted, "Lots of people believe in them."

"Believe in whom?" asked Arielle as she dished the food onto three tin plates.

"Nonsense." Stephen's eyes twinkled as he added, "The water was wonderful, Arielle. You should try going for a swim sometime."

"What makes you think I haven't?"

He laughed as he buttoned his shirt, which clung to him, outlining the breadth of his chest. "Madame Schoolmarm swimming in the nude? Now, there is an intriguing idea."

Again Girolamo came to her rescue. "Cap'n, you should be nice to Señorita Gardiner. After all, she cooked this meal for us."

"That is right," she agreed stoutly. She handed the men the heaped plates and leaned back against a tree. Its scratchy bark jabbed through her sweaty chemisette, so she edged away.

Stephen sat next to her and greedily dug into his food like someone breaking a long fast. When she saw Girolamo staring sadly at his already empty dish, she scraped her untouched food onto his.

"Aren't you hungry?" asked Stephen. "Or did you poison the food?" He screwed up his face as the boy laughed.

"I did not poison anything. I am just not as hungry as Girolamo."

"No one has ever been as hungry as that bottomless pit, but you cannot starve."

"I shall be fine."

He lifted his spoon and held it out to her. "Eat!"

"Don't you want it?"

Instead of answering, he placed the spoon by her lips. She compliantly opened her mouth. Her eyes widened with delight as she chewed on the tough meat. The spices she could not name were delicious.

Taking a bite for himself, Stephen said, "I think I like you better when you are ornery, Arielle. Don't be this nice too often. I might get used to it." He chuckled as he kissed her cheek.

She fought the yearning to press closer as desire flared in his eyes. He waited, silent, for her to decide. If she let him hold her now, there would be no excuse of Caleb to separate them. She drew back. Staring at her tightly clasped hands, she bit her lower lip to mute her despair. *She* had insisted Stephen acknowledge her betrothal to Caleb. *She* had insisted he should stop teasing her with kisses. *She* now ached for those kisses, but she must remember the promises she had made to both men.

When he offered her another spoonful, Arielle forced a smile. "Make sure you have enough for yourself."

"I have plenty." He added to Girolamo, who was chasing the last bit of meat around his dish, "So the river has been quiet?"

"Since President Walker returned from Rivas, he has been keeping everything quiet."

"As he should, after leaving his men to be slaughtered." His bitter tone shocked Arielle. "The Costa Ricans should have chased him all the way back to Granada."

"Back to the United States," asserted Girolamo. "We do not need gringos here." He grinned wryly. "No insult, Cap'n."

"None taken. Not all gringos agree with Walker, remember."

"Gringos?" asked Arielle.

"Us. North Americans." Stephen relaxed against a tree and tossed his plate on the ground near the fire. "Let's just hope things stay nice and quiet until we get back to Greytown."

"Not if the Old Ones have returned," the lad said in a darker tone.

"Don't start that again." Stephen smiled at Arielle as he pulled his hat down over his eyes. "Don't listen to him. The Old Ones are nothing more than a superstition. Like seeing a black cat or breaking a mirror."

Girolamo sat straighter. "It is more than that, Cap'n. They bring trouble when they come. Everyone says that."

"I don't." Folding his arms over his chest, he muttered, "Wake me up when you get the dishes clean, Arielle."

She looked at Girolamo, but he lowered his eyes. The boy believed what he said. She sighed as she collected the dishes. She had enough to worry about without letting some primitive superstition complicate things.

Arielle kicked dirt over the ashes, then pushed her way through the trees. Stephen could have been courteous enough to ask her to do the dishes instead of making it an order. With no cloth and no soap, it would not be easy to get them clean. Perhaps she could find some dry sand to scour the skillet.

Swarms of insects followed her to the river. She swatted them away. It did no good. They returned to buzz in her ears.

She knelt on the bank and rinsed the dishes in the torpid water. When she was finished, she stood rubbing her aching lower back. Tonight she must get a good night's sleep.

Regretfully she regarded her skirt. A dingy pattern showed where her knees had settled in the mud. By the time she reached Granada, she would be a complete ruin. She had no money to buy new clothes, so she would have to find a way to clean these.

Setting the dishes near the raft, she fought the curtain of steamy heat back to the clearing. Only snores greeted her. The thought of taking a nap was seductive, but they must keep going. She put her hand on Stephen's shoulder and shook him gently. "Wake up, Stephen."

"Sure, honey," he mumbled. "Who wants to spend the night sleeping?" His long arm herded her to him. Off balance, she fell across him, her elbow striking his stomach. He yelped as his eyes opened. "What in hell do you think you're doing?"

"Me?" Standing, she stated, "You grabbed me!" It was easier to be angry than to think of his enticing words, especially when she was not certain if he had been dreaming of her. "Come on. I am done. Let's go."

Girolamo muttered an obscenity before he walked off into the trees.

Stephen put his hand on her shoulder. "Don't worry about him," he said through a yawn. "He is used to the slower pace along the river."

"You said to come back when I was finished."

He winced as he raised his arm to loosen stiff muscles. "You did not need to hurry that much."

She put her hands on her waist. "Captain Lightenfield, have you forgotten why we are tramping through this wretched jungle?"

"You are a heartless woman," he declared, a smile spreading across his face. His arm draped companionably over her shoulders. "Come on. I want to get my hundred dollars. I just hope Drummond does not ask *me* to pay him."

"For what?"

He tweaked her nose. "To take you back." Releasing her, he walked away, chuckling.

Arielle sighed. Someday she was going to get the last laugh. She hoped it would be soon.

* * *

"How much farther before the rough water?" asked Stephen.

Girolamo leaned on his pole, pushing lightly, for the current was slow. "Not far. We shall be there before sunset."

"Rough water?" Arielle looked up from where she was struggling to stay awake. Sleeping on the damp ground the past three nights had been only slightly more comfortable than the straw mat, but Girolamo's enthusiastic snores had kept her awake.

Drawing the pole out of the water, Stephen cautiously moved toward the center of the raft and squatted next to her. "Arielle, this is safe. I don't have any intentions of ending my life on a miserable river in the middle of a jungle." His voice lightened. "That would not be fun, honey."

"Do you mean rapids? Caleb wrote there are parts of the river where it is truly dangerous."

He patted her hand and stood. "Did he tell you how Commodore Vanderbilt sailed from Greytown straight through to the lake to prove the Rio San Juan is navigable? If the Commodore could make it in a bulky boat, we should not have much of a problem. After all, the iron-sided packets go through all the time."

Arielle wanted to believe him but heard the turbulent roar before the rapids came into view. She saw tattered leaves and twigs, broken from their fierce ride. Girolamo let out a wordless screech of excitement as they rounded the edge of a sleepy cove to discover what lay before them. Bubbling, frothing like a cauldron at a boil, the water crashed over the rapids.

She had to shout to be heard over the thunder of white foam. "We cannot go through that!"

"Nonsense!" Stephen rolled up his sleeves and flexed

his hands. Gripping the pole, he called, "Let's go, Girolamo!"

Arielle clung to the wildly bucking raft as she listened
to the two men shout to each other. They bobbed and
danced with the crazed currents. Holding out her parasol
to keep the spray from scraping her face, she wondered if
they were making any headway against the rushing waters.

Something wet poked her. "Don't just sit there. Get a
pole and push," Stephen bellowed.

Fear nibbled on her as she tried to stand. The raft
bounced to the right. She collapsed on the hard logs. They
hit a rock and tilted backward. She screamed and grabbed
on to the logs. A pole bounced over her hands, ramming
her fingers. Tears burned on her cheeks, but she gripped
the pole and pushed herself to her feet.

She called over the roar, "Where do you want me to
stand?"

"At the front. Opposite Girolamo," Stephen shouted
back. "Don't try to steer. Just push. Whatever you do, do
not fall in!"

Arielle lurched to the side. When Girolamo gave her a
tight smile, the raft hit another rock.

"Watch where you are going!" Stephen yelled. "Push,
Arielle!"

Gripping a long pole, she stuck it viciously into the water.
She would rather use it to beat some sense into Stephen.
She gasped as the water tried to rip the pole away. The
rough bark cut into her palms, but she tightened her grip
and gritted her teeth. Spray burned her face. A voice cut
through the deafening roar. It was Girolamo chanting to
help her use her pole in rhythm with his. Not able to keep
his pace, she matched every other stroke as she fought to
keep her footing on the raft that leapt like a white-tailed
deer.

"Look out!" called Stephen.

The raft crashed into a boulder. Arielle fell to her knees.

Girolamo's corner ricocheted off another rock. She was knocked flat. The men shouted. She got to her knees as the raft spun nearly out of control.

She managed to rise to her feet. She pushed blindly and hoped Girolamo could guide them through the wild waters. She tried to pull the pole out. It jerked from her hands.

She heard Stephen swear as he stretched to get it. A sudden eddy caught the raft and twisted it.

"Stephen!" she cried as he teetered on the edge.

"*¡Madre de Dios!*" Girolamo shouted.

Stephen's curse was swallowed by a crash as the raft careened off a boulder. The pole snapped with the sound of a gunshot. He tumbled forward and disappeared in the froth. Shrieking his name, she crawled toward where he had been standing.

A hand caught her arm. Girolamo shouted, "Stay here. I will get him, señorita!"

He dove into the maddened waters. Arielle reached for a pole, but another impact tumbled her onto her stomach. She screamed when the raft skipped like a pebble across the foamy water. Over the thunder of her terrified pulse she heard Stephen's shout.

"Jump! Jump before you crash!"

She shook her head. She could not jump!

The two men scrambled onto the rocks as the raft flew toward them. Stephen held out his hand. "Grab hold, Arielle!"

She clawed her way toward him. The raft spun. She saw him dive beneath the water as she passed. She cowered, her arms over her head as the raft raced toward a tangled web of tree roots.

She slammed into the box when the raft crashed. Pain exploded along her ribs as the raft bounced backward. It hit the roots with another teeth-jarring blow. Twisting, it tried to escape, but it was caught.

Leaning her scraped face on the wet logs, Arielle slowly released her convulsive grip on the vines that had held the raft together somehow. She cried out when the raft lurched. Choking as water splashed her, she clung to Stephen when he drew her up to her knees. He stroked her snarled hair, saying nothing.

She did not want to move. With his swift heartbeat against her ear and his strong arms holding her, she wanted to pretend this was where she belonged. She touched the firm muscles of his back and heard his pulse accelerate. With a sigh she slipped out of his arms. Tormenting both of them with something that could never be was more cruel than any of his pranks.

Gently he framed her face with his hands. Her eyes widened when she saw the rage twisting his lips. "You damn fool!" he snapped. "You could have been killed!"

"We all could have been killed." She scanned the river. "Girolamo? Where is he?"

A cheerful voice sounded behind her as Girolamo climbed onto the raft. "Here I am, señorita." He chuckled. "Those damned water devils will not take me today."

Stephen caught her face between his hands again. When she gasped with pain, he tilted her cheek so he could see the scratches. "Dammit, Arielle! You heard me! Why didn't you jump off?"

"I cannot swim!"

His hands dropped to her shoulders. "You don't know how to swim?" Looking at Girolamo, he repeated in disbelief, "She does not know how to swim."

"That is what she says, Cap'n." He sat and wrung water out of his trousers.

His fingers dug into her shoulders. "How could you be so stupid? Why didn't you tell me you do not know how to swim?"

"You never asked!" She wrenched away, dropping back into the mound of her soaked skirts.

"Maybe I should ask a hell of a lot of other things about you."

Stung by his sharp word, she retorted, "Maybe you should grab a pole and get us past those rapids."

He snatched his panama as it floated by. Standing, he caught the pole Girolamo tossed him. He kicked the raft away from the roots. "You ungrateful wench, I should have let you drown." Under his breath he growled, "I know I am going to regret saving you before this is over."

CHAPTER EIGHT

Stephen stormed across the littered clearing to where Arielle sat next to a broken crate. Squatting next to her, he said, "Sorry, honey, but we will be walking from here."

"How far?"

"Just a few days."

Shrinking into herself, she leaned her head on her arms folded on her drawn-up knees. She never had been so exhausted, and, as rough as it had been on the river, traveling on land would be worse. "Can't you convince one of them to take us to the lake?"

"What do you think I have been trying to do?" When she followed his glance toward the crowd of men, one of them shouted in Spanish and shook his hand. "Even money cannot get them to listen."

"Why?"

"No good reason."

She caught his sleeve as he stood. His hooded eyes warned her he was lying. "Stephen, tell me."

"I told you. No good reason." Pulling her to her feet,

he said, "We might as well get going. It is not easy from here." He flung his knapsack over one shoulder and picked up her bag.

Arielle looked back at the men by the thatched huts. She did not need to understand their words to hear the dread in their voices. Something was scaring them. Something that waited between here and the lake. The war! Had the war started in earnest? Caleb could be in the middle of it.

"And so will we!" she whispered with heart-stopping terror. She must know the truth. She stared at the men, then looked at Stephen, who was almost to the trees.

An old man shouted after them, panic tinging his shaky voice. Stephen whirled and grabbed her hand. Tugging her toward the trees, he did not slow when the old man called to them again.

"What is he saying?" Arielle asked, half turning so she could see the village behind them.

"Bon voyage," he stated grimly. "Let's go. If you listen to every superstitious peasant, you will never find your sweetheart."

"Superstitious?" Comprehension sank through her like a rock in the pit of her stomach. "The Old Ones?"

He smiled without humor. "You are a quick study, Arielle. If you want to know, he said the Old Ones are walking."

"What does that mean?"

"How the hell do I know?"

A shiver flowed like ice water along her spine. Stephen's sharp voice warned her that he still was not telling her everything. She wondered what waited in the jungle ahead.

Sweat and rain became the pattern of their days as Arielle followed Stephen through the undergrowth. He searched for the simplest path among the twisted vines. They fol-

lowed the sound of the river until they reached a village
where they could buy food and shelter.

She learned to sleep with goats or a dozen people
crowded into a room no bigger than Stephen's quarters
aboard *The Ladysong*. As exhausted as she was, she did not
care. All she wanted was to sleep deeply. In the morning she
prepared breakfast, sharing a fire with the other women in
the settlement. Stephen went down to the river to shave
while he spoke with the men to discover what he could of
the jungle ahead of them.

She lost track of the days after the first week passed. It
no longer mattered that her clothes were filthy and her
chemisette torn from trying to squeeze past trees. She did
not notice Stephen's ripped shirt as he swung a machete
to clear a path for them. There always were more trees
and the sound of the river beside them. Chattering monkeys and scolding birds reminded her that she was unwelcome.

Sometime during the second week after they had left
Greytown, the jungle reluctantly thinned, but the walking
was no easier. Every night Stephen paused early enough
so they could find a village and trade for a place to sleep.

When she heard the chug of the Transit packet passing
on the river, she paused and shaded her eyes to look into
the morning sun. It was a hint that the civilization she had
left was not just a dream.

"What are you stopping for?" Stephen called.

"Listen!" She watched his face as the sound of the steam
engine became louder. "Why don't we flag down the
packet?"

He laughed. "We do not have passage, remember?"

"I remember!" As sarcastically she added, "I have not
forgotten that one step of the way through this blasted
jungle."

"So let's keep going."

She hesitated as she saw the brightly painted boat through the trees. "Stephen, wait!"

"Why?"

"If we flag them down, surely the captain will have compassion for us." She held out her bedraggled skirt, which hung limply over a single petticoat. She had traded her others for the two threadbare blankets in Stephen's knapsack. "Look at us! They will see we need help. Certainly he will not leave us here."

He scratched one of the insect bites on his neck as he glanced toward the river. "Too late. They are going by."

"We can still catch them." She hefted her bag and ran toward the shore. "Come on!"

When he grasped her arm and held her back, she watched the packet sail around a bend. The echo of its engine vanished, swallowed by the trees.

Shaking his hand off her arm, she cried, "How could you let them sail past? We could have gotten a ride." Tears streamed down her face as she choked more softly, "We could have gotten a ride."

"No, honey. This is not Massachusetts. Gentlemen do not stop to give a pretty lady help." He sighed. "Ask any of the men waiting in Greytown. The company's policy is clear. If you do not have a ticket, you do not ride."

"But it cannot be that far to the lake. If—"

"Come on, Arielle." He walked away into the trees.

She looked at the empty river. She was as empty inside. Closing her eyes, she wiped away the tears on her sweaty face. If walking so close to the river she could hear the packet pass had been Stephen's idea of a joke, it was his most sadistic yet.

Arielle paused at the top of a knoll and watched the sun flee into the river. Overhead, the nightly concert was beginning. Squeals and buzzes surrounded her, but she was too tired to bat the bugs away. There was not anywhere they had not already bitten her.

The moon was rising to wash all color from the jungle and paint shadows where there should be none. They never had walked after moonrise. It was too dangerous. She hoped they would stop soon. She took a step forward and bumped into Stephen. His arm around her kept her from collapsing. When he did not chide her for not watching where she was going, she looked up to see the taut line of his chin.

"What is wrong?" she asked, not really caring. She just wanted to sleep and sleep and sleep until every exhausted bit of her was rested.

"I think we should sleep here."

"Here?" Disbelief heightened her voice.

"It is warm." He shrugged off his knapsack. "We have food left over from what we bought last night. If we rest here, we should be able to reach the lake sometime tomorrow."

"Tomorrow? Lake Nicaragua?" She pressed her hands over her mouth as she fought back tired tears. She had begun to believe that the lake was nothing more than a dream she could never touch.

"If we want to make it there tomorrow, we had better get some sleep now."

"Here?"

"Here, dammit!" He pulled their supplies from his sack and shoved them in her hands. "Make us some supper, woman! I will cut some branches to put on the ground to keep out the dampness while we sleep."

Putting her fingers to her forehead, she bowed deeply. "Yes, master."

"You are especially nasty tonight!"

She put the packages on her bag. "And why not? Don't you think I get tired of your orders, Captain Lightenfield? I am not one of your crew."

"Fortunately for you!"

"Fortunately for me! I do not ever want to sail again with a blackguard like you."

When he hooked an arm around her waist and pulled her to him, she gasped and put out her hands. The warmth of his skin through the shirt plastered to his body scorched her fingers. He bent toward her, whispering in her ear, "You could use a blackguard or two in your life, honey. You need a man to hold you when you are burning with fury and to turn that flame into sweet madness."

"Stephen . . ." She raised her hand to stroke the rough whiskers on his cheek.

As he caught it, his laugh had a barbed edge. "A bargain's a bargain, honey. You are saving yourself for Drummond, right?"

She whirled away from him and his heartless mirth. It was a mirror that reflected her hypocrisy. Clenching her hands, she wished she never had met Stephen Lightenfield or Caleb Drummond.

When she heard the muted whack of the machete, Arielle dragged her leaden feet toward the packages of food. She opened them and turned away from the odor. Only extreme hunger would let them eat this.

Stephen must have shared her distaste, because he took one bite and set the plate aside. "I swear, if a cow walked through here, I would kill and butcher it with my bare hands. I am tired of beans and meat that probably came from the underbelly of a dog."

"Don't!" She tried not to gag. Putting her plate in her lap, she asked, "Isn't it bad enough that we have to eat it to stay alive? Do you have to make it worse?"

"I have told you that I do not have any interest in being your brave hero who suffers in silence, Arielle." A devilish grin lit his eyes as he patted her knee. "I do not do anything in silence."

She decided the best reply was none. If she opened her

mouth, she might not be able to hide how his words freed the dream that obsessed her every night as she slept in her blanket. In them she was closer still to his firm body as he taught her lips again the lilting melody that played within her heart.

When Stephen went to cut more fronds, she swept any crumbs away from their bags. They did not need ants biting them too. She edged down to the river and scraped the food into the water. She backed away as the water boiled with whatever lived under it.

"Let's go to bed, honey," Stephen said as she put the last of their supplies in his knapsack.

So tired she ignored his inappropriate words, she whispered, "All right." Walking to the fronds, she groaned. "Why didn't you separate them?" She bent to pick up a handful.

His hand halted hers. "I did not feel like cutting enough for two beds." Sitting, he drew off his boots. His big toe stuck through a hole in his sock. He leaned back on the fronds. "Take my knife and cut your own bed if you do not want to sleep here. Sleep wherever you want, and let the skeeters feast on you."

"You bought mosquito netting in the village where Girolamo left us," she argued.

"*I* did, and *I* am going to use it." He folded his hands under his head. "Either lie down or go away."

Arielle knew she had no choice. She was too tired to swing the machete even once. As she brushed away a mosquito, she sat gingerly on the edge of the fronds. "Hand me some of the netting."

"Lie down."

"Stephen, just hand it to me."

"Lie down," he repeated firmly. "I will tuck it in around us. The little bastards can sneak through any opening."

She nodded and curled up on the fronds. They rustled

under her head. One jabbed into her waist, and she shoved it aside.

"All set?" he asked.

"Go ahead."

The netting ticked her nose as he drew it over her. His fingers brushed her face when he bent to be sure the netting was wrapped around her. Cautioning her not to move, he stuck the other end of the netting under her boots.

Her fingers fisted under her cheek and her breath caught over her furiously beating heart as his hands slowly edged up her legs. His fingers brushed her thigh, and she shivered with an uncontrollable pulse. She must not surrender to these passions that were for the wrong man. His arm grazed her hip, and she tried to remember how she had hated him for making her walk when they could have taken the packet. He was a horrible man. He taunted her on every turn—

She caught his face between her hands and brought his mouth to hers. She tasted his smile against her in the moment before he pressed her into the fronds. Stealing her breath from her with the storm of kisses across her face, he slipped his arms around her to envelop her in longing.

His fingers found the tatters in her chemisette and embellished her skin with pleasure. Wanting to touch him, she bunched his damp shirt beneath her hands. The sweaty skin beneath it was as rough as his hands. His swift breath against her mouth urged her to be more bold.

His lips played along hers in a teasing, lyrical melody. Each hot touch left a lingering spark of delight on her skin. When his tongue glided beneath the collar of her chemisette, she swayed toward him, wanting every inch of him against her. She shuddered as the skin bared by his ripped shirt brushed against her.

When his thumb brushed her breast, a soft moan fanned

the blaze within her. Gently, slowly, he encircled her breast, climbing along it as wave after wave of succulent rapture swelled over her. Her fingers clenched on his back as he captured her mouth again. She gasped deep into his mouth when his tongue touched hers in rhythm with his fingers. Nothing had ever been so agonizingly sweet, and she wanted more. More until she melted into these passions that were absorbing her.

His mouth caressed her neck before he whispered against her ear, "Sorry, honey. A bargain's a bargain. Seems like one of us is having a difficult time remembering that. Go to sleep." Chuckling, he rolled away from her.

Arielle flinched as the netting fell on her face. Lost in the passion, she did not understand his words for a moment. Then she cried, "To sleep? How could you? You arrogant—"

"Bastard? Go ahead! Say it."

With her back to him, she choked out, "Why don't you just leave me alone?"

"You kissed me." He grasped her shoulder and twisted her to look into his face, which was shadowed by the dim light. She did not need to see to know how taut his mouth was as he spat out, "That was a warning, honey. The next time I will not bother to remember our bargain and the fact that you belong to another man."

He shoved her away. Pulling some of the netting over him, he turned his back on her.

She never had been so alone.

Lake Nicaragua stretched past the horizon. Accented by the caress of the sun, the blue water moved endlessly toward the small collection of buildings next to a pier trying to tame the shore.

Sitting on an inverted *bungo*, Stephen skipped a rock through the water and watched as it sank. He sighed. This trip was not going as he had planned. It should have been fun and given him a needed respite from his work on *The Ladysong*. For so long he had wanted to see the other end of the Rio San Juan and this lake.

"Lightenfield?"

He did not turn as he answered in Spanish, "Yes."

"I thought you would be here two days ago."

"We got delayed."

The low chuckle came around him as a short man sat on the other end of the boat. The gray-headed man pulled a pipe from the pocket of his ragged trousers, then stuck it into his mouth, which was nearly hidden by his hedge of beard. He puffed, then asked through a cloud of noxious smoke, "Has anything changed?"

Stephen looked at him directly for the first time. "I am speaking to you here instead of in Greytown."

"*That* is different." He tapped his bare feet against the boat. "Where is your first mate?"

"Roach?" Stephen was startled to realize he had not given Walden a thought in the past week. "He is on his way to California."

"So you are traveling alone?"

"No." He pointed to the largest building on the shore.

The old man whistled sharply under his breath when Arielle came out to stand on the beach and look at the *Director*. The steamship, which once had belonged to the Accessory Transit Company before being nationalized by President Walker, was surrounded by a bevy of stevedores and passengers waiting to board. "So that is what delayed you. Don't waste all your strength on bedding her."

"I haven't." He smiled at the old man's puzzled expression when he did not react to the crude words. As if the matter were of no more import than the birds screaming overhead, he asked, "You can take us?"

"Yes, for a price."

"The usual?"

"Twice that." He used one long fingernail to pick his teeth.

"Why?"

He laughed again. "Because I think you will pay it to keep that pretty señorita away from them." With his pipe he gestured to a group of prospectors who were looking toward the tattered woman.

One, then a second, then the rest of them surged toward Arielle. Even from where he was sitting, Stephen could see the shock and dismay on her face.

He stood and jammed his hand into his pocket. The bills stuck together, but he loosened several. Slapping them into the old man's hand, he crossed the sand to where Arielle had vanished within a circle of men.

He tapped one on the shoulder. The man glared at him, but Stephen pushed past him. Elbowing another man aside, he ducked when a fist flew at him. His lips grew tight in a vicious grin as he returned the blow, knocking the man back into another. Shouts sent the birds along the shore soaring. He grinned as he dodged another swing. He raised his fists. A scream halted him.

"Arielle! What—?"

A fist slammed into his face, staggering him. He leapt up and grappled his way through the fray. Wiping blood from his mouth, he swore as he saw a tall man advancing on Arielle.

Her face was flushed, and she held her bag in front of her ripped shirt. Her bonnet was crushed on the ground, and her long hair was falling in loose waves along her filthy chemisette. She looked tired and furious and incredibly alluring.

"Cash, sweetheart," the man was saying. "Real, *norteamericano* cash."

Stephen walked over and slapped the huge man on his bulbous arm. "Leave the lady alone, friend. She clearly is not interested in your company."

"Why don't you leave us alone, *friend?*" He turned, a broad smile across his porcine face as he hefted a pocket pistol. "This says I saw her first."

"Stephen, be careful!" Arielle cried.

"Stephen?" The man's lips twisted in fury. "Is she your wife?"

Taking a step closer, Stephen noticed no noise behind him. The fighting must have stopped, so the bored men could watch. As the gun rose to aim at the middle of his gut, he said, "She is mine."

"Back off, *friend,* or she will be your widow. I will—" The man sagged to the ground. Groaning, he pushed himself up to meet Stephen's boot. He fell and did not move.

Stephen stepped over him as Arielle lowered her bag. She would not need to hit the big man again. "Thanks."

"Someone had to be the hero." With a shiver that was so strong he feared she would shatter, she said, "I was not going to let him shoot you."

"I appreciate that." He dabbed at his split lip with the back of his hand. "I think we should get out of here."

She nodded. "They told me we could board the *Director* anytime. I was just waiting for you."

"The *Director?*" His brow furrowed as she pulled two tickets from her pocket. "How did you buy those? I thought the whores stole your money."

"A lady does not carry all her money in her bag if she is smart."

"That still does not explain how you got those tickets. Those men have been waiting for weeks."

Her eyes widened in an innocent expression he knew was totally false. "I just asked, Stephen. The nice man behind the counter was so eager to help me."

"I can imagine." He brushed her hair back over her shoulders. "What did he want in return?"

"Cash," she fired back at him. "Real, *norteamericano* cash.

I did not offer him anything else." Holding out one ticket, she went on. "Let's board. I do not want to have to tramp all the way around Lake Nicaragua."

Stephen did not take the ticket. Surprise flashed in her ebony eyes, then they narrowed with exasperation. She threw the ticket on the ground and walked toward the boat. He scooped up the ticket before striding after her. Ignoring the derisive hoots behind him, he grabbed her arm and spun her so he could look down into her face.

It was not soft with sleep as it had been when he had woken just before dawn to discover Arielle nestled against him. Then her hair had trickled across his arm, inviting him to pull her beneath him. Every time he looked at her, he was astonished anew how enticing she was. He had seen other women who were more classically beautiful, for her nose was a bit too pert and her chin far too stubborn. Other women had longer legs or a more voluptuous figure, but he never had met a woman who could stir his blood as she did. Her sparkling eyes, her honed wit, the way she doggedly dared him to challenge her, it was a combination that would appeal to any man.

"Let me go," she said in a broken voice. "I can get to Granada by myself from here."

"And then what?"

"I shall find Caleb."

"Are you sure of that?"

Fear flickered across her face, and a twinge of guilt pricked him. He ignored it. He was only making her understand what might be waiting ahead of her.

"I have to be," she finally answered. A shrill blast from the steamship stiffened her. "Stephen, I must go."

"I arranged a way across the lake for us."

Bafflement threaded her forehead. "How? The *Director* is the only steamship here."

"Another way." He turned her to look down the shore

to where the gray-haired man waited patiently, smoking his pipe.

"Are you crazy?" she gasped. "You want to go across in a *bungo* when we have tickets on the steamship?"

"Arielle—"

She shook her head, spraying his arms with her silken hair. "If you want to risk your life in another leaky tub, go ahead. I am sailing on the steamship." As if to accent her words, the whistle on the sidewheeler shrieked again. "If this is good-bye, then that is what it must be."

"Is that what you want?"

"I must find Caleb," she whispered as she had so many times. She lifted his fingers one at a time from her sleeve and stepped back. "We will send you your money, Stephen." She hesitated, then kissed him on the cheek. "Good-bye."

Stephen did not follow as she rushed to the pier. The men boarding the boat were too eager to get one step closer to the gold waiting in California to notice the slender woman in their midst.

If he was smart, he would let her go. She was nothing but trouble—for him and everyone she met. If Drummond was not waiting for her in Granada, she would follow any clue to find him. Then the quest could become fatal.

He glanced at the *bungo*. The old man waved to a lad by one of the huts. The boy ran over to the small boat, then raced across the sand to Stephen. Holding out the money Stephen had given the old man, the boy grinned.

Stephen took the money. All but one bill he put in his pocket. He gave that back to the lad, who turned to scamper away.

"Hey!" called Stephen.

The boy paused. "Señor?"

"*Muchas gracias.*" He tossed the child a coin.

Tilting his hat back on his head, Stephen stuck his hands

in his pockets and walked toward the ship. He whistled a merry bawdy tune. Arielle Gardiner was in for a surprise when the ship sailed. He had come too far to miss seeing her grand entrance into President William Walker's city on the shores of Lake Nicaragua. It should be fun.

CHAPTER NINE

Arielle stood on the lower deck of the *Director* and looked in both directions. The smokestack rose between the twin paddlewheels on the sides of the ship. When the whistle blasted, she climbed the stairs to the upper deck.

She pushed her way through the press of men to the stern. Knowing she was foolish, she nevertheless wanted one last chance to see Stephen. With her bag close to her, she ignored the curious glances in her direction. She heard a bellow of laughter and hurried past the men who were pointing at her. If one of them wished to feel the edge of her bag, she would not hesitate to crease his head with it too.

At the rear railing she put the bag on the deck. Her fingers settled on the smooth metal. She pulled them back. It was as hot as the sun that was burning down on her head. She could not remember what she had traded her parasol for or in which village.

The deck lurched beneath her as the steamship left behind its moorings. Another toot cut a wide gash into her. Biting her lower lip so its trembling would not reveal her misery, she searched the beach. So many men crowded there, but she did not see the one she sought.

"Nice day for a lake voyage, isn't it, miss?"

At the oddly pitched voice Arielle frowned. She did not want to be annoyed by another lecherous man. When she remained silent the question was repeated. Hearing muffled laughter, she whirled around.

"Stephen! You're coming with me?"

He tipped his panama to her and offered his ripped sleeve. "It would seem so, wouldn't it? I am not interested in swimming back to shore. There are sharks in this lake."

Not caring how many eyes watched her, she threw her arms around his neck. "I did not think I would ever see you again."

"I try to keep track of my investments."

"Is the sun bothering you?"

"No, why?"

She tapped his turned-up collar that rose nearly to his hat. "You look like a naughty child skulking into school hours late. Is something wrong?"

Instead of answering, he led her to the bow. The breeze carried the scent of mud and the hint of distant surprises. Small waves dashed themselves into oblivion beneath the bow. "It is strange to feel the pulse of an engine on a ship."

"Not like *The Ladysong*, which soars with the wind."

"Nothing is like *The Ladysong*."

For the first time Arielle was sure he was being completely honest with her. Pride filled his voice as he leaned on the railing and stared toward the distant horizon.

With a sigh she sat on a bench by the railing. This was heavenly. Taking a deep breath of the fishy-smelling waters, she tried to imagine what she would say when she found Caleb. She looked at Stephen and then at her folded hands. Maybe it would have been simpler if she had taken the last part of the voyage alone. How could she explain that she and this enigmatic man had traveled the length of the Rio San Juan alone? If she told Caleb the truth ... She sighed. He never would understand. Why should she expect *him* to when she did not understand herself why she was so drawn to this man?

She flinched as Stephen's voice broke into her thoughts. Astonished, she stared into his angry face. Something must have happened, but what?

"I am going to get a drink," he said tersely.

"A drink? It is barely midday."

His chuckle was icy. "After mucking through the mud, I deserve more than one! Meet me here when we reach Granada."

"But, Stephen—"

"Lord, woman, don't you think I deserve some fun after all the temper tantrums I have put up with from you in the past month?"

The sound of her hand striking his face caught the attention of every passenger crowded on the deck. He slowly turned and walked toward the stairs. What was wrong? He had been laughing with her only minutes earlier.

Arielle dropped back to the bench and shook her head when a nearby gentleman asked her if she needed assistance. She had too many men in her life already, and she did not understand either of them.

The deckhand whirled to face Arielle as she asked, "Excuse me? Can you help me?"

In his eyes she saw shock. He tilted the brim of his jaunty cap. "Yes, ma'am."

"I am looking for Caleb Drummond. He works for the Accessory Transit Company. Tall as you. Eyes my color. Red hair. From New England."

"Sounds familiar." He rubbed his chin pensively. "Did he work on the *Director*?"

"He once mentioned the *Sir Henry Bulwer*."

He nodded. "That is on the Rio San Juan. The crews switch off with us occasionally to keep from being bored. Why don't you come with me? I will see if Cap'n Hall will speak to you. If Drummond ever worked on the lake, Cap'n Hall will know him." He flushed when she smiled at him.

Arielle tightened her grip on her bag as she went with the deckhand toward the wheelhouse at the stern. After all this, was it going to be so easy?

Her smile disappeared as they passed the lounge. She was tempted to look in, but she didn't want Stephen to think she was following him. Let him waste his time over rum and cards! She would find Caleb by herself.

At the door of the glass wheelhouse she nodded when the deckhand motioned for her to wait. She understood why when two men glanced at her, identical scowls on their faces.

"What is this?" demanded a man in a navy jacket. "No passengers allowed here. You know that, Smitty."

"Cap'n, this is Miss Arielle Gardiner. She wants to speak to you about . . . something." He crossed the small room and whispered to the captain.

Captain Hall turned to her. His thinning hair and long mustache were the gray of the iron sides of his ship, but his blue eyes appraised her with lively interest. "Excuse me for saying this, Miss Gardiner, but you look as if you have had a mighty rough trip."

"The journey up the Rio San Juan is not easy."

His eyes narrowed. "Did a packet go aground?"

"No."

"I understand," he answered, although his tone made it clear he did not. "Smitty said you wanted to ask me about Caleb Drummond."

"Do you know him?" she asked with sudden fervor.

"Knew him. He disappeared from the Rio San Juan almost six months ago. 'Twas a surprise. He sailed with me for a month or two, and he is the last one I would have expected to jump ship for California."

"But he is here. In Nicaragua." When the man stared at her in disbelief, she continued. "He wrote to ask me to join him here. Do you have any idea where he might be?"

His chin jutted at her in a fearsome scowl. "If I knew, Miss Gardiner, he would be facing his captain's displeasure. Commodore Vanderbilt expected loyalty from his men, and we have maintained the same standards since Walker took over the company. Just because a lad gets a hankering to see the country does not mean he can take off at any time."

She wanted to say that Caleb had never left a job half done but did not. Defending him would only anger the captain. Quietly she said, "Captain, if you hear of Caleb being found, could you let me know?"

"Where, Miss Gardiner?" His mustache twitched.

"In Granada, sir." She let him bow over her hand. "I intend to speak to President Walker himself if necessary."

At a guffaw the captain glared at the man holding the wheel. That did not stop the man from saying, "Walker will be right happy to see the likes of her. He likes them small and dark. Look how he took to tiny Doña Irena!"

"Robinson!" snapped Captain Hall. To Arielle he said more evenly, "I wish you good luck, Miss Gardiner."

"Thank you." She put her hand on the door. "May I ask your crew about Caleb, Captain Hall?"

"Yes, certainly, but do not interfere with their duties."

"Of course not." It was a vow she did not intend to keep. She planned to pester every man on the *Director* until she found a hint as to Caleb's location. The trip across the lake was not a short one, and she intended to use every minute and every feminine wile she had to get the answer she needed.

With her softest smile on her face, her eyes glittered with determination as she saw her first target. By the time the ship reached Granada, she wanted to be able to tell Stephen exactly where Caleb was. How shocked Stephen would be! As she spoke with the crewman, she did not stop to realize she thought more of Stephen's surprise at her success than of Caleb's at her arrival.

Arielle climbed the steps to the upper deck. Around her were excited shouts as the passengers swarmed onto the long pier. Palm fronds rattled in the breeze, which carried the scent of oranges onto the ship.

The deck was deserted except for one man, who was pacing by the bow. She steeled herself for Stephen's fury. The ship had docked almost an hour earlier, and she wondered if he had been stamping across the deck all that time.

"Where in hell have you been?" he exploded.

"Having fun! Isn't that what we are supposed to do on this trip?" She hated the pained sound of her voice, but she was too tired of this journey and too tired of Stephen Lightenfield to dissemble.

When he did not bombard her with more questions, Arielle was suffused with an irrational guilt. Maybe she would not be so miserable if she *had* been having fun.

He took her bag as they walked down the stairs and onto the pier. She was glad when he offered his arm. In the crowd it would be easy to be jostled away from the only person she knew.

As they climbed down from the high pier Stephen asked, "What have you been doing for the last hour?"

"I was asking if anyone aboard the ship knew where Caleb might be."

"And?"

"Nothing."

His large hand was gentle as it stroked her cheek. "Nothing at all?"

"All I have heard is that he vanished about six months ago."

"If anyone can find him, you will, Arielle."

She almost laughed at the platitude she had not expected from Stephen. Maybe the earth had opened up and swallowed Caleb. That would explain why no one knew where he was.

Although carriages waited by the docks, Stephen continued to walk toward the city. The tallest building was no more than two stories high except for the churches. As they walked down a wide street, Arielle was sure she had entered a new world.

Flowering bushes edged the walkway, but their blossoms were no brighter than the garish clothes the women wore. The splash of whitewashed walls was the perfect backdrop for the flowing rainbow of vibrant color. Scents filled the air, luscious spices and perfumes as well as the disgusting ones of a city. From somewhere she heard the honeyed strains of a guitar.

Arielle froze at a sudden shout and a pistol firing. Stephen shoved her back against a wall. Two horses sped by. She stared after them. The two riders were holding hands. As they careened around a corner, one man fell to the stones. She choked back a scream as he rolled to a position impossible for an unbroken body.

"Damn fools!" grumbled Stephen. Picking up the bag he had dropped, he added, "Welcome to Granada and their quaint local customs."

"You mean they were doing that for fun?" She looked back to see a crowd gathering around the injured man.

"Servants are cheap here, so the rich are bored. They work at killing themselves." He cocked an eyebrow at her. "Not my idea of fun, honey."

Arielle did not answer as they entered a central plaza.

A huge cathedral sent its shadow cascading across the merchants who were reopening their shops after the afternoon siesta. Everyone turned to stare at them. She hoped she did not look as dirty as Stephen, but knew she must.

"How about the Hotel Granada?" he asked as they crossed the plaza. His roguish grin returned. "After the lesson I gave the gentlemen on the steamer about the inadvisability of going against the odds, I thought we might as well live in comfort on the money they lost."

She stopped, but Stephen hurried her along. "You cannot be serious!" she gasped. "Staying at a hotel?"

"And where did you plan to stay? In the street?"

"There must be a nice boardinghouse somewhere."

"This is not Boston."

"I know that." Exasperation sharpened her voice. "But there are many Americans here." She looked at the plain walls facing the streets. "They are welcome to keep this place. All I want is to find Caleb and go home."

"Not the paradise you expected?"

Pausing again, she did not move when he tugged on her arm. "Stephen, don't tease me now. I know I cannot leave until I find out what has happened to Caleb. I just want to be sure he is all right before I go home."

"You aren't going to marry him?"

"I do not want to stay here."

"If he goes home with you, will you marry him?"

Arielle wished he would not ask questions she did not have answers for. "I don't know," she said, too tired to lie.

Stephen put his arm around her and steered along a narrow alley. He opened a gate that looked no different from others they had passed. As she stepped past it, she stared about in disbelief. The plain façade hid luxury. Colored tiles created a flowered mosaic that glistened in the light of a single lamp hanging on the wall. A man popped out of the shadows and greeted them profusely in Spanish.

She listened as Stephen answered. The broadening smile on the swarthy man's face revealed he was pleased. He kept looking at her while they talked but did not speak to her. She guessed Stephen had told him she spoke no Spanish.

When the man led them into a garden that was sleeping in the twilight, Stephen said softly, "We are all set, honey. He has room for us."

"This is the hotel?"

"Throw away your prejudices. This is Granada. It is nothing like the rest of Nicaragua."

The innkeeper opened a door and with a wide smile motioned for them to enter. Stephen stepped back to let Arielle go first.

She sighed with delight as her feet sank into white carpeting. She ran her fingers along the wicker and overstuffed furniture that was arranged about the generously portioned room. Through the window, which was edged by dark red drapes, was a view of the garden.

Stephen walked past her and opened a door she had not seen in the shadows. Leaving her muddy bag by the main door, she kicked off her boots. Her bare toes curled in the carpet as she looked through the other door to see a tester bed encased in mosquito netting. French doors led to a small private terrace.

"How lovely!" she said when the hotel owner smiled at her. Searching her mind, which was entangled in cobwebs of exhaustion, she said, *"Muy bueno."*

In excellent English he replied, "I am glad you are pleased, señorita. This is our best room."

When he went to speak to Stephen, Arielle wandered out onto the terrace, which was covered by a green and gold awning. The clatter of wheels on the cobbles did not invade the garden's peace. Bright hibiscus surrounded a fountain. The copper had weathered to blue-green. Water sang as it flowed from a cherub's urn and a fish's mouth to sparkle in the sunshine.

Crossing the terra cotta tiles, which were warm against her bare feet, she reached past a row of clay jars and touched a wrought iron gate. It was locked. The alley beyond was empty except for a scrawny cat.

Hearing her name, she called, "Out here, Stephen."

He smiled broadly as he tossed his hat on a table by the French doors. He pulled a wicker chair out onto the stones. Sitting, he put his feet on one bowl of the fountain. "I do not have to ask you if you like this place," he said as he locked his hands behind his head. "You are all aglow."

"It is lovely." She sat on the low wall by the bushes. "It has walls and a floor, and it does not rock or whistle. It has a real carpet and real furniture and a bed that is not set on top of dirt."

Brushing at the mud stains on her skirt, she wondered how long it would take to have water delivered for a bath. Nothing sounded more deliciously decadent than soaking away the grime. Glancing at Stephen, who was leaning back with his eyes closed, she did not want to be rude, but she needed privacy for her bath.

Quietly she asked, "And where will you be, Stephen?"

"What do you mean?" He yawned and stretched. When his shirt ripped more, he glowered at its tatters.

"I just wondered how I should contact you while we are here. If—"

His laughter silenced her. "You thought this was for you?"

"This is your room?"

"Of course."

Her lips tightened as she asked herself why she had expected him to be a gentleman. He had proven too many times that he had no intention of doing anything but what he wanted. "Then where, pray tell, am I staying?"

"Here."

Her voice squeaked as she repeated, "Here?"

"Why the sudden modesty?" He sat straighter in his chair. "You have been sleeping with me since we left Boston."

"There was no other choice!" Jumping to her feet, she surged across the terrace. She halted when the waistband of her skirt cut into her, and she turned to see Stephen holding the dirty material in his fist.

"Where are you going?" he demanded.

"Anywhere where you aren't!" As he stood, he did not release her skirt. Defiantly she straightened her shoulders. "If you want a cheap doxy, you should be able to find one in the taverns by the lake."

His smile glittered beneath his mustache as he moved until there was no room between them. When he caressed her hair, she jerked her head away. He laughed and caught his fingers in the snarls.

He tilted her mouth beneath his. She refused to capitulate, although she was captivated by the too-familiar desire. Clenching her fists at her sides, she fought the longing to wrap her arms around him and delight in the tempo of his breath racing like wildfire into her mouth. She would not fall prey to his mockery again.

"What makes you think I want a cheap doxy?" He slapped her on the buttocks. "You are costing me enough!"

"How dare you!" Her hand rose, but she lowered it.

"Learning manners, honey?"

"One of us must! Being with you has taught me how important they are."

His arm clamped around her waist and pressed her to the firm strength of his body. "That is not what I wanted to teach you, Arielle," he said lightly, but a flame burned silver in his eyes. He ignored her protest as he put his arm beneath her knees and scooped her into his arms.

Gazing at him, she wanted to tell him to put her down, but no words came from her lips, which ached for his kiss. Her hand rose to bring his mouth to hers. The tantalizing caress of his tongue against her lips lured her closer.

When he stepped through the French doors, she pulled away in horror. His arms tightened around her.

"No, Stephen," she whispered. "I am filthy."

He laughed throatily. "I am as dirty as you. Do you think I care?"

"No, Stephen," she repeated, desperation tainting her voice. She wished he would put her down. It would make this easier. When he took another step toward the bed, she cried, "Stephen, no! The sheets are clean, and . . ." Her voice faded as she heard a knock on the outer door.

With a laugh he set her on her feet. "That probably is the bath I ordered for you. Enjoy it, Arielle."

"A bath? You brought me in for a bath? You were not going to . . . ?" She could not finish, as embarrassment choked her.

He opened the door to the other room. "I like the way you think, honey. If you still feel the same way after you wash the dirt off your nose, let me know."

"I should say thank you." When his grin widened, she hurried to say, "For the bath, I mean."

"I know what you mean." Ignoring another knock, he put his hands on her shoulders. The chaste touch exploded through her body like the most fervent caress. She wanted him to touch her but knew he was right when he said, "Just keep lying to me, honey. It is easier that way for both of us to keep our bargain that way."

Arielle did not answer as he closed the door quietly behind him. Lying was so much simpler than telling him how easily he could have lured her into that bed with one soul-searing kiss. She knew all the reasons she should not complicate her life with Stephen Lightenfield, but she could push aside common sense for those splendid sensations when his fingers danced along her in an invitation to passion.

When a parade of servants entered with bathwater and the tub, she went back out onto the terrace. She did not want to see their veiled curiosity and sly smiles. The peace of the garden offered no answers to her dilemma. It would not be that simple. She could not run away from this as Caleb had run from the wedding neither of them had questioned.

When the noise from the bedroom disappeared, Arielle went back in. She locked both doors. Her fingers hesitated as she tested the door to the other room. How like Stephen it would be to have another key to the bedroom. She glanced at the steaming water. If she delayed, it would grow cold. She smiled wryly. Just then, a bath was worth the chance of compromising what little modesty she had left.

Lighting a candle after she had drawn the drapes on the French doors, she began to peel off her mud-encrusted clothes. Her chemisette fell to the floor when she undid the buttons along the back. She stared at the fabric in astonishment, for the once-white linen was a grayish-brown. Unhooking her merino skirt, she stepped out of it. With a snort of disgust she picked up a length of the black material and wondered if the stains could ever be removed from it.

She untied her remaining petticoat and kicked it aside. The muslin had withstood the rough trip better than her other clothes. Unlacing her corset, she tossed it onto a chair next to a dressing table. She ran her hands along her sides and breathed freely for the first time since they had started the journey up the Rio San Juan.

Arielle glanced once more at the door as she lowered her chemise over her breasts. "Nonsense," she said aloud. Stephen was probably asleep on the settee in the other room by then.

Putting him from her mind, she stepped into the tub. She sighed with absolute delight as she slowly lowered herself into the water so each inch of her skin could savor the anticipation of being released from its layers of dirt. Clean water! She had almost forgotten it existed. The dark bruises along her shins ached, but she leaned back against the metal sides and enjoyed the comfort she would never take for granted again.

Arielle lathered her hair with the bar of soap by the tub and rinsed it again and again until it squeaked between her fingers. She attacked her skin with the same fervor and discovered more cuts and bruises among the insect bites. She looked as battered as one of the huts in Greytown.

A rumble of voices from the other room startled her. She set the soap back onto the floor and stood. Reaching for the towels the servants had left for her, she twisted her hair into one and wrapped another around her. Water collected on the carpet as she gasped. Her bag! She had left it in the other room. Her clean dress was in it, but she could not dash across the room in no more than a towel. Disgust churned in her as she imagined putting those hideously foul clothes over her clean body.

She flinched when she heard a soft rapping at the terrace door. Tiptoeing to the door, she drew back the velvet drapes enough to peek out. She saw a young woman on the terrace. The girl motioned for her to open the door.

Arielle did but only a few inches. "Yes?"

The girl answered in Spanish. When she saw Arielle did not understand, she held out a bundle that was wrapped in brown paper and tied with a gold ribbon.

"For me?"

"¡Sí!" The girl's hoop earrings bounced against her long hair as she nodded enthusiastically. She added more, but all Arielle understood was *Capitán Lightenfield*.

"*Gracias,*" she said as she took the bundle and closed

the door. Going to the bed, she untied the brown paper and took a step backward as she lifted out a chemise that was decorated with a single blue ribbon in the center of the lacy bodice. A gold satin wrapper was folded over a pair of white silk stockings.

As she sat on the bed, tears were heavy in her eyes. Stockings! How had Stephen guessed how horrible it had been to be without a single set of stockings?

With a laugh Arielle slipped them on. She dropped the towel on the floor as she drew the chemise over her head and adjusted the lace that fell off her shoulders to accent the curves of her breasts. Sliding the wrapper on, she buttoned the mother-of-pearl buttons along the front.

She used the comb on the dressing table to force the snarls out of her hair. Pulling it back with ribbon from the package, she looked at her reflection in the mirror. The prim woman who had left Concord had vanished. That woman would not have been so unfashionably tan, nor would she have let her hair cascade along her back in the company of a man.

Arielle hesitated when she gathered up her dirty clothes. They would soil her clean clothes. With a grin she took the damp towels and wrapped them around the pile. She unlocked the door, then picked the huge mound. With her hip she pushed the door open. She listened for the whisper of the well-oiled hinges to tell her the door had opened, because she could not see over the mass of laundry.

Carefully she inched across the room. A whimsical breeze from an open window lifted the lace of her petticoat and wafted it in her face.

"Watch out for the chair," Stephen called.

"Where?" She could see nothing.

"Move to your left."

"Thank you." Glad for assistance, she allowed him to

steer her across the room. With a sigh of relief she dropped the clothes by the door. Bending, she examined the skirt, wondering if anyone could get it clean.

"A problem?" Stephen asked.

She did not look at him as she ran her fingers over the caked wool. "I fear it is ruined."

"We can find another skirt for you here in Granada."

"I hope so." Standing, she dropped the material on the floor. "I—oh, my!"

With his knees drawn up in the tub, only the curve of them and Stephen's broad chest were visible. He held up a bar of soap and smiled. With a horrified moan she covered her eyes. She heard his laugh and bit back her fury. She should have known. Every time he did something nice for her, he ruined it with another callous prank.

She heard vigorous splashing and a cheery whistle. He was continuing his bath as if she did not stand there! Tightly she said, "If you had told me you intended to bathe, I would have been glad to wait in the other room."

He chuckled. "I was hoping you would offer to wash my back, Arielle."

"I would like to drown you."

"Why don't you come over here and try it?" She knew he was grinning but kept her fingers pressed over her eyes as he added, "It could be a lot of fun."

If she tried to maneuver across the room blindly, he would not help. Trapped, she listened as he continued his leisurely bath. "Will you hurry and make yourself decent?"

"I am decent now," said Stephen, surprisingly close.

His hands drew hers away from her face. Her cheeks drained of all color when she saw he wore only a towel wrapped around his waist. A single drop of water inched along his skin, leading her eyes from the sleek skin on his shoulders through the golden hair on his chest, which glittered with dampness, to the narrowing firmness of his stomach. Never had she been so close to such an expanse of proudly displayed, naked male virility. She could not move. She could barely breathe. She could think of nothing but how much she wanted to sift her fingers through each golden strand over his heart before daring to explore farther.

Water struck her nose, and she blinked, torn from the thoughts she must keep secret. When she looked up at his smile, another drop fell from his mustache on her. Exasperation offered an escape from the spell he could cast upon her without speaking. "Why didn't you dry your face?"

"If you want me to use my towel, I can."

"No!"

With a chuckle he asked, "Arielle, have you ever considered that I tease you so much because you are so much fun to tease?" He put one fingertip under her collar. "The dressing gown looks lovely on you."

"I appreciate you getting this for me," she said stiffly. She took a step back toward the bedroom door. Instantly she feared it was a mistake, because her gaze was caught by the sturdy muscles of his bare legs. She had to put an end to this before she went mad with the longing to touch him as he held her to his firm body.

"I will just add its cost to what Drummond owes me."

"Do that," she whispered. She took her bag when he held it out to her. His fingers grazed hers, and she shivered with the intensity of the craving that had made her its captive.

"Get dressed," he said. "I am ready for some supper and an early night."

"Yes."

With his gaze stroking her back, she went into the bedroom. She closed the door and leaned against it, panting as if she had raced across the isthmus. How much longer could she ignore the longings of her body, which yearned for his caresses—and her heart, which yearned for his love?

Love? She edged away from door. She must be mad.

Stephen's voice echoed in her head: *Nicaragua changes people.*

"Not that much," she whispered, knowing her protests were futile. She was falling in love with the wrong man.

CHAPTER TEN

Arielle lifted her petticoats to an unseemly height and knelt to look under the bed. Where could it be? She was sure she had left her corset on the chair when she had undressed the previous night.

With a grumble of frustration, she stood. She patted the rumpled covers on the bed. She could not have slept with it. The sharp edges of the whalebone would have cut into her while she tossed and turned.

She had thought her greatest worry last night would be the discussion of where they would sleep. When they had returned from eating, Stephen kissed her lightly on the cheek and told her to take the bedroom while he slept on the settee in the larger room. It should have been perfect, but the sleep she wanted so desperately evaded her.

Now she could not find her corset!

Arielle slipped her arms into the gold wrapper. Buttoning it, she stormed to the door. Perhaps she had mixed it up with the clothes she wanted cleaned. That could not be, because last night she had worn the corset. She had taken more towels to the pile before breakfast this morning. Maybe it had been with them.

Stephen was still at the table, drinking another cup of coffee and reading the *El Nicaragüense*. The newspaper crackled a complaint as he lowered it to smile at her. "What is wrong?"

"I lost something."

"Do you want help looking?"

She shook her head. His help was the last thing she wanted. If he found her corset, he would display it to add to her embarrassment with this ridiculous situation. She needed more clothes, but, without money, that was impossible. Somehow she would manage with her lone dress until her skirt and chemisette were cleaned and repaired. Her boots were hidden by her full skirt, so she could pretend she wore leather slippers. But she needed her corset!

Her nose wrinkled as she dug into the heap of clothes and found nothing. Pushing aside his knapsack, she peered under the table. She scowled as she straightened and looked around the room. Nothing!

"Are you sure you don't want help?" Stephen asked from behind the newspaper.

"I am sure."

"What are you looking for? Maybe I have seen it."

"Just a piece of clothing."

He folded the newspaper. Putting it on the table, he stood. Arielle could not keep from staring at his fashionable clothes. His high stock was tied perfectly with the ends tucked into his blue vest. Over it he wore a long coat that narrowed at his waist and flared along the taut line of his legs. Beneath plaid trousers she could see his shining black boots. He looked as dashing as one of the rich Granadans they had seen flaunting their wealth on the square the evening before.

"Where are you going?" she asked.

"I have made a few plans for us today. I thought we

would see what fun we could find here." He smiled as he added, "Now, what are you looking for, Arielle?"

"I told you." She did not like the way her stomach fluttered with eager anticipation when she imagined riding about the city, resting her cheek against the satin brocade vest. It would be smoother than his skin but not as beguiling.

"You have told me nothing, so I assume this piece of clothing is an unmentionable."

"Maybe I left it in the bedroom," she said, wishing she had not gone out there. His gaze along her reminded her how little she wore under the silk wrapper.

Stephen watched the disquiet deepen in her ebony eyes as he admired the soft curves of her breasts, which were outlined so tantalizingly against the gold silk, and the smooth length of her shapely legs. The familiar ache of desire pulsed through him. He wanted her in his arms and in the bed they should be sharing. When he stripped away that silk and lace, her satiny skin would quiver when his mouth stroked it. The low moans he had heard as he caressed her beneath the mosquito netting resonated through his tight body.

Her hands rose to him. He took them and brought her a half-step closer. Combing his fingers through her lush hair, he watched her eyes close in delight as she swayed toward him. So easily he could kiss her, but, if he did, the torment would only increase.

"If you are looking for your corset, Arielle," he said, hoping her fury when he told her the truth would irritate him enough so he could forget how he longed to seek deep within her to find the source of that flame that burned in her eyes, "don't bother. I threw it out."

"You threw it out?" she whispered. Her face turned gray beneath the warm color left by their days at sea. "You threw away my corset?"

He frowned. She should be outraged, not staring at him

like a wounded child. "You do not need that garment of torture. My hands could span your waist even without you being pinched into that corset."

Sitting on a wicker chair, she said, "You threw it away." Her words stabbed at him like a dozen knives. "How could you do that when you knew I wanted to speak with some of the Americans here to discover if any of them knew Caleb? I cannot call on them when I am half dressed."

"I will buy you another corset today," he grumbled, wishing she would snarl at him as she usually did.

She continued to stare at the carpet. "I wanted to go to speak with Mr. Childs today."

"Childs?" He gripped the back of her chair as he banked his reaction to having her speak the last name he wanted to hear while he was in Granada. He was glad she was not looking at him as he asked with feigned indifference, "Who is that?"

"He works for President Walker. One of the crewmen on the *Director* suggested I contact Mr. Childs because he was involved in President Walker's revocation of Vanderbilt's charter for the Accessory Transit Company."

"And you think a pompous, bureaucratic thief will help you?"

"Not if I show up half dressed."

Stephen was unprepared for the sharp pain in his gut when he saw tears rolling along her cheeks. He reached to wipe them away, then drew back his hand. Damn woman! He had only wanted to tease her and enjoy the sharp edge of her wit. Jesting with her muted the craving that plagued him on every breath. If she had had any idea how he had burned last night with the need to push through the bedroom door and make his fantasies reality . . .

"Go tomorrow." When she looked up at him, her eyes awash with more tears, he snapped, "*¡Mañana!* What's another day going to matter?"

"I don't know. It may mean the difference between

finding Caleb alive or finding him dead.'' Her voice was so soft, he had to bend forward to hear her. "I know you think I do not care because I have let you treat me like a harlot, but I owe Caleb more than I can ever repay."

"You do not owe him anything. He abandoned you to come here."

Wiping her hand against her cheek, she said, "I owe him my life, Stephen. If Caleb had not been there the day Mr. Patterson's bull went mad and broke out of the barn, I would be dead. He pushed me out of the way. It went after him instead." She shuddered as she wrapped her arms around herself. "It nearly killed him before Papa and Mr. Drummond were able to shoot it. I remember seeing him bleeding in the dirt and praying that I would be able to repay Caleb somehow, someday, for his bravery."

"By marrying him?" he asked, wondering why the words were so hard to say.

"I don't know. But I do know that I must find him. I fear he is in as much danger as I was that day. I must save him." Her voice cracked. "But how can I now?"

Stephen put his hand on her shoulder. She flinched away from him. Anger exploded in him. This had just been a joke. Fiercely he said, "Go and see Childs! Unless you are planning on sleeping with the man to convince him to help you, he will never know that you are not wearing a corset."

She stood and regarded him with more pain than he ever had wanted to see on any face, especially hers. "Someday, Stephen Lightenfield, you are going to discover that life is more than an adventure. More than an endless search for fun."

When the bedroom door closed behind her, he grabbed his panama off the table. He strode out the door, making sure it slammed loudly enough so she would hear it through her tears. Damn woman! The best thing he could do would be to put her out of his mind while he did what he had come to Granada to do.

Arielle stepped from the rented chaise and shook her head when the driver asked her, in heavily accented English, if she wished for him to wait. She had no idea how long she might be, and she must not waste the few dollars she had left on such a luxury. If she could not find another chaise, she would walk back to the hotel, although she had noticed only the poor walked in Granada.

She *was* poor. Except for the blue dress she wore and the paisley silk shawl draped over her shoulders, she had nothing. She was dependent upon Stephen for her food and the roof over their heads.

Blast that man! She was tired of his endless escapades at her expense. She wished he would, just once, have compassion for her as she explained why she must not stop looking for Caleb. And most of all, she longed for his arms around her.

Angrily Arielle shook her head. Stephen had not returned before she left. He might be out of her life. She should put him out of her mind.

She rehearsed what she wanted to say as she walked up the steps in front of her. The house's whitewashed walls were broken by a pair of windows. Lace curtains, like those she would find in any house in Concord, flapped in the breeze off the lake, obscuring the fancy ironwork. A number was nailed into the wall next to the door. It matched the one on the piece of paper she held.

Arielle lifted the heavy brass knocker and let the lion's paw fall back against the door. Instantly the door opened.

A tall man looked down his long nose at her. His eyes had sunk so far into his head, his age-ravaged face looked like a skeletal mask. Dressed in spotless black livery, he spoke in Spanish, then asked in English, "May I help you?"

"I was told this was the home of Rutledge Childs."

"Señor and Señora Childs live here," he said in a dolorous voice.

"May I see Mr. Childs?"

His gaze swept over her blue dress. With obvious disdain he sniffed, "May I say who is calling?"

"Arielle Gardiner," she said, determined not to let the white-haired man irritate her. Her dress was wrinkled, and one of the flounces on her full skirt was ripped, but its jacket was decorated with dark blue velvet to match the ruching on her bell sleeves. It was the best dress she owned, the dress she had planned to wear when she married Caleb. Brushing her hands over the creased ruffles, she said, "I wish to speak to Mr. Childs about a personal matter."

If her words piqued his curiosity, she saw no sign. He said nothing, only stepped aside to allow her into the foyer. He vanished into shadows beyond a curving staircase.

Arielle winced when the heavy heels of her boots echoed on the marble floor. She must be careful if she wanted to make a good impression. Mr. Childs, like most of President Walker's filibusters, was from the southern United States. She had heard that southerners considered themselves the final remnants of chivalry. Such a gentleman would be more willing to help an unblemished lady who appealed to him for assistance in a battle she could not wage alone.

She rubbed her clammy palms together and looked around her, hoping to find some clue to the man who lived in this large house. The foyer went straight to the back of the house, and she could see a garden in a courtyard through the arched door. No portraits hung on the plaster walls, and dark, cumbersome furniture edged the foyer.

The butler returned and mumbled that she was to follow him. His lips were straight in an expression of disapproval, but she could not guess if he objected to her or his master's decision to receive her.

Her boots slipped on the marble steps leading down to a sunken parlor. She gripped the wrought iron railing and kept her face serene, although she had jarred every bone in her tired body.

The room was large and furnished with an odd mixture of furniture from the United States and Nicaragua. A china milkmaid on the wooden mantel over the huge hearth was so similar to one in her house, it could be a twin. A grand piano stood covered by a large scarf in a far corner. Flowering bushes obscured the bottom halves of the tall windows to leave the room in a soft, green light. Beneath Chinese carpets, the marble floors were dull in the faint sunshine.

"Wait here," the butler ordered.

Arielle sat on a red horsehair settee and tried to banish Stephen from her thoughts. She had to concentrate on this meeting, not let her mind drift to the warmth of his smile the moment before his lips stroked hers.

"No, not now!" She must think of something else.

"Miss Gardiner?"

Rising, she said, "Yes." She hoped the woman had not heard her mumbling to herself.

"Welcome to our home. I am Francine Childs." The blonde's soft drawl reminded Arielle of Stephen's. Again she shoved him out of her thoughts as Mrs. Childs gracefully offered her hand and smiled. Her sparkling blue eyes were the perfect accent for the most beautiful face Arielle had ever seen. "My husband is attending President Walker, but he should be home soon. Tadeo said your question for my husband is of a personal nature." Her smile dimmed to polite coolness.

Arielle wondered exactly what the butler had suggested. "Mrs. Childs, I have come to Nicaragua at my fiancé's request. Unfortunately he was unable to meet me in Greytown. I had heard he was in Granada and was told that Mr. Childs might be able to help me in my search."

Mrs. Childs's smile warmed. "Please sit, Miss Gardiner. Our American community in Granada is small. If your intended is here, we shall ferret him out." She snapped her fingers, and a maid appeared with a tray.

Taking the glass of iced tea Mrs. Childs had poured, Arielle said, "I hope my journey ends here."

"You have traveled all the way from Greytown by yourself. You are incredibly brave." She offered Arielle a frosted cake.

"I did not travel alone."

"No?"

Arielle's bruised conscience taunted her. Weeks before, she would have shared Mrs. Childs's astonishment with her tale. Weeks before, she never would have considered sleeping in the same room with a man. Weeks before, she could not have imagined that she would yearn for any opportunity to sample his kisses and the fiery touch of his hands.

"Miss Gardiner?"

She forced a smile as she met Mrs. Childs's eyes. "Excuse me, Mrs. Childs. These cakes are delicious."

"Call me Francine." She selected a pink iced cake. "It is impossible to maintain even the slightest formality in this heathen land. Now, tell me about your journey, Arielle. You did not travel alone?"

She had hoped her hostess would allow her to change the subject, but avoiding it now might cause the scandal she must prevent. "Captain Lightenfield of the clipper *The Ladysong* traveled with me to help with the difficulties of this foreign land."

"How charming that he would offer to help you! He must be a very good friend."

"Without his help I fear I would have faltered before I left Greytown."

Francine waited for her to go on, but Arielle decided to let her hostess draw her own conclusions. Friend? She doubted if she ever would consider Stephen a friend. Nothing that mundane, nothing that tame, would fit their uneven relationship.

"I trust we shall meet Captain Lightenfield during your stay in Granada," the blonde said as she refilled her glass of tea. "We always enjoy meeting the few *norteamericanos* who come here. Why don't you and the captain join us for dinner some evening this week?"

"I do not think Stephen enjoys social calls."

Francine's perfectly arched eyebrows rose, and Arielle realized how much she had revealed by using Stephen's given name. Her hostess's smile broadened as she said, "Then, my dear, you must convince *Stephen* to change his mind. I shall have a small party to introduce you to the others here." Her eyes twinkled as she clapped her hands. "Why, when you find your fiancé, you must allow me to offer this house for your wedding. How romantic that will be!"

Arielle was spared from having to answer when a man walked down the steps. Francine held up her cheek for his kiss, and Arielle struggled to hide her shock. Mr. Childs could have been his wife's father. White hair was sparse across the top of his head, but his peppered mustache remained thick. Bright eyes, as blue as his wife's, smiled as he turned to Arielle.

"Rutledge, darling, this is Arielle Gardiner." Francine rose to slip her arm through his. "Arielle, my husband, Rutledge."

He lifted Arielle's fingers to his lips as he bowed over her hand. "Welcome, Miss Gardiner, to Granada. Are you here for a visit, or do you intend to join our small colony?" His southern accent softened his rumbling voice.

"Only a visit, I regret to say." She smiled and did not add how glad she would be to leave behind the heat and humidity of the country these people had adopted.

"Tadeo tells me you wish to speak to me about an urgent

matter," he said as he sat next to his wife. The smile he gave Francine when she handed him a glass of iced tea seemed too intimate to Arielle. She wondered if they were newly married.

Francine gushed, "Oh, Rutledge, you must hear her tale. It is the saddest one I have ever heard." Taking a lacy handkerchief from the bodice of her stylish gown, she dabbed at her eyes. "I swear it moved me to tears."

Arielle answered Mr. Childs's questions, but she was growing more puzzled. Before he had arrived, Francine Childs had been a gracious hostess. Now she clung to her husband's arm, hanging on each word he spoke as if she had no mind of her own.

She forgot Francine's odd behavior when Mr. Childs asked, "Caleb Drummond? With the Accessory Transit Company?" He sighed and shook his head. "A few months ago it would have been easy to trace him through payroll records, but many of the records have been mislaid in the reorganization."

Her fingers tightened on her glass as she understood what he could not say. The takeover of the company had not been a peaceful one. No one else had ever dared to trifle with Cornelius Vanderbilt's empire. In one of the few articles she had found on Nicaragua while she waited to hear from Caleb, she had read that Commodore Vanderbilt vowed to take his company back and see President Walker crushed. She had not paid much attention to the article at the time, because she had never guessed that only a few months later she would be in the heart of William Walker's kingdom.

"Mr. Childs—"

"Rutledge, if you please." His smile stripped years from his face. "As I am sure my sweet wife has told you, we find it easier to be informal."

She glanced at Francine and saw the young woman regarding her husband with open adoration. A pang of envy rushed through her as she wished she could find a man who would love her as Rutledge Childs did his wife. Not wanting to be distracted by the disturbing thoughts, she asked, "Do you know Caleb?"

"I have not had the honor of making his acquaintance," Rutledge replied formally.

"Do you know if he is in Granada?"

"That I can look into, Arielle. Do you have anything that might help me narrow the search?"

"The last letter I received from Caleb was so tattered, all I could gather was that he wished me to join him here. He wrote he had found a paradise."

"Paradise?" Francine gave a sharp laugh. "In Nicaragua?"

"Now, now, lamb. That is no way to talk about our new homeland." His wife subsided, but Arielle saw a flash of rebellion in her eyes as Rutledge continued. "Do you have the letter with you?"

"It is at the hotel."

When he gasped, "Hotel?" Arielle knew she had said the wrong thing again. He rushed on to ask, "Would it be possible for you to bring the letter for my perusal? If you would be willing to trust me with this treasured missive, I shall show it to some of the president's other advisers. Surely one among us will know of your fiancé. Why don't you call tomorrow afternoon?"

"Tomorrow?" After all this time, it seemed impossible she might find an answer so soon.

Francine squeezed Arielle's hand. "Do come to call. I will be home all afternoon."

"Thank you," Arielle said as she stood. "I cannot tell you how much I appreciate your help."

"Nonsense." Rutledge bowed over her fingers again. "We look forward to your visit. Don't we, Francine?"

"Undoubtedly." She smiled but did not rise. "I think

Arielle and I shall be friends. And, Arielle, if you wish to bring your charming escort, you must feel free to do so."

"Escort?" asked her husband.

"Why, I do believe we have not mentioned Captain Lightenfield's name," Francine purred. She put her hand on her husband's arm. "He has brought Arielle here to find her fiancé. Have you ever heard of anything more romantic?"

Rutledge's eyes narrowed as they met Arielle's. She knew he was reappraising her as he tried to fit all the pieces of her story together. "Very romantic," he said slowly. "Until tomorrow, Arielle."

She hurried up the steps to the foyer, but the memory of Francine's satisfied smile haunted her. As the heat of the afternoon struck her, she shivered with the cold deep within her. Nothing had been as she expected in Nicaragua, and she wondered if she had been a fool to come to this house.

CHAPTER ELEVEN

Stephen shook sand from his boots as he paused in the hotel's garden. He rubbed more sand from his eyes, wondering when he last had slept. Not last night or the night before that or . . . He was not even sure what day it was or how long he had been in Granada. Finding what he wanted in Granada was not hard. The life along the pier was raucous with the fatality of men and women who expected to die soon. Even as they gossiped about the armies that were rumored to be gathering on Nicaragua's borders to oust Walker, they drank and ate and whored.

It was time to get out. So many rumors could not be wrong. This city was doomed if the allied armies threw their strength against the filibusters. He wondered how many Walker would leave dead in his wake this time.

"Dammit!" he snarled when the doorknob refused to turn. Arielle must have locked it. Searching in his pockets, he wondered where he had lost the key. Let it stay lost. He was not interested in returning to the shore and its entertainments until he got a hot bath and a good night's sleep—or two or three.

He pounded on the door. Getting no answer, he slammed his fist against it and grimaced. She was not answering the door if she was in there. He glanced at the thin moon. Wandering about Granada at this hour could be dangerous for her.

With another curse he went out to the alley running along the hotel. Rats skittered away as he entered its black maw. He stepped in something that stank, but he did not slow to wipe off his boots. He had smelled worse in the taverns down by the docks. Reaching the wrought iron gate at its end, he shouted for Arielle to open it.

Again he got no answer.

Stephen's exasperation became icy disquiet. Didn't the woman have a lick of sense? On the short walk back to the hotel he had taught a lesson to two pickpockets who wanted to ease the load in his pockets. He wiped his bloody lip and scowled. Losing her purse was not the worst thing that might happen to Arielle.

Grasping the wrought iron shafts in the gate and putting his feet in the grooves in the stone wall, he climbed over the gate. A pointed shaft jabbed into his leg, and his trousers ripped with a shriek. His boots thumped on the terrace tiles. A candle burned in the bedroom. She must be in there. He had to show the wench how sorry she was going to be for ignoring him.

As he reached for the latch, he heard the muffled sound of weeping. Not from inside, but from the corner of the terrace. He squinted through the darkness to see a slim silhouette by the fountain.

"Arielle?" he called.

Puzzled when she did not answer, Stephen crossed the terrace. He knelt by Arielle and touched her arm. When, with a gut-deep sob, she threw her arms around him, she nearly knocked him to the ground. Her tears burned against his neck as her body shook with the strength of her grief.

Drummond! It had to be Drummond. Stephen's teeth clenched so tightly, his jaw hurt. If he had guessed Childs might come up with something about Caleb Drummond, he would have talked to the man himself.

"Arielle," he whispered against her hair, which smelled of jasmine soap.

He should be thinking of comforting her, not of her slender arms around him and her cheek on his, but it was impossible. His mouth brushed her ear, and another tremble raced through her. Her fingers tightened on him as she murmured his name. Sweeping aside her full skirts, he stroked the slender leg he longed to have entwined with his. So sweet she was. So sweet and vulnerable and, he realized with a reluctant sigh, so naive, for not once had her belief wavered that she would find Drummond in this country where men came to lose themselves.

"Arielle, what is it?" he forced himself to ask. Each word strained past his lips that should be against hers. He had been a fool to come back. He wanted her in that lush bed or on these cool tiles that would heat with the fire of their passion. When his mouth found every pleasure she could provide, she would writhe with the same hunger obsessing him.

"Caleb . . ." she whispered.

Stephen swore silently when her broken voice reminded him of the obligation she held dear. "Arielle, what about him?"

"He is dead."

Stephen sat back on his heels and stared down into her damp face. "Dead?"

"Yes." When she drew away from him, he released her. She said nothing, and he followed her into their rooms.

Arielle picked up a slip of paper from the table in the main room. Brushing tears from her eyes, she held out the page that had been delivered along with Caleb's letter to her by one of the Childs's servants. She waited while he read it. The words blazed from the paper to burn into her heart. This was not the way her quest should have ended— with nothing but the anguish of knowing she had been too late.

Because she had not cried when he gave her the news, Rutledge had called her brave. He had urged her to let him bring her back to the hotel. She had refused, so numb that she wanted to be alone until she could feel something again. Pain had struck her when she returned to find the rooms as empty as they had been since the day after their arrival in Granada.

Now Stephen was back, filthy and smelling of cheap rum and cheaper perfume with his trousers torn and blood on his lip. But she never had been happier to see anyone. He had shared enough of her quest to know how horrifying it was to have it end like this.

"This is what Childs told you?" he asked, his deep voice too loud in the room that was usually so quiet. "That Drummond was killed in the battle against the Costa Ricans in Rivas?"

"Yes."

Laughter exploded from him. Slapping his tattered trousers, he dropped heavily into a wicker chair and leaned his head back and laughed.

Arielle stared at him in disbelief. How could he find her grief so funny? She snatched the letter out of his hand and stamped toward the bedroom. Slamming the door behind her, she reached for the lock.

The door burst open. She leapt back. Stephen gripped her shoulders and pulled her to him. Fury erupted with silver fire in his eyes. "Dammit! Can't you see what is happening?"

"You think it is funny that Caleb is dead!"

When she tried to wrench away, he shoved her onto a

chair. "I think it is hilarious that you believe Childs's lies. Drummond did not die in Rivas."

Arielle opened her mouth, then closed it as shock withered her words. Her hands clenched on the limp flounces of her gown as she stared up at him. Finally she whispered, "He is not dead?"

"He may be dead now but not as it says in that collection of lies." He stabbed at the page she still held. "That battle took place last March. The letter you got from Drummond was postmarked out of Greytown less than three months ago."

"It could have been lost all that time."

"Do you want him dead?"

She flinched as his question flailed her. "I want to know the truth."

"All right." He held out his hand. "Let's go get the truth."

"Where are we going? To Rivas?"

With a sharp laugh he said, "It is more than fifty miles from here along the lake. Even if we managed to get there, we would not get out alive. They have cholera down there. Why do you think all the filibusters have come here to Granada?"

"Then, where are we going?"

Taking her bonnet from the top of the dressing table, he tossed it to her. "To get the truth, if it is still possible to find it in this city."

Arielle held her breath as Stephen handed her out of the hired carriage. The stone hut before them looked like all the others along the shore. Garbage and broken bottles covered the sand in front of it. If there had ever been glass in the single window, she saw no sign of it. Thatch barely covered the rafters. She looked back at the city. It seemed impossible that it was only a short walk to where Rutledge and Francine lived in opulent luxury.

"Go on in," he said impatiently. "I would like to get back and get some sleep before dawn."

"This is horrid."

"If you want to find out the truth about Drummond, your best chance is in here." His low chuckle rumbled in her ear. "After all, you have been in worse places, Arielle."

She did not answer as she followed him into the crowded room. If she had not wanted to know the truth about Caleb so much, she would have turned and fled. Water dripped from the thatch into puddles on the dirt floor. At the few small tables, the click of chips matched the fast pace of the faro games. Everything stank of unwashed bodies and stale liquor and vomit. She pressed her lips together, not wanting to be sick too.

Stephen grabbed a bottle from a shelf and motioned to a dark-haired woman who wore little more than a knee-length chemise. The woman smiled back, then frowned at Arielle. Swaying over to them, she asked, "Want something, señor?"

"I was in here last night."

She walked her fingers boldly up his sleeve. "I remember that. I remember you, señor." Glancing again at Arielle, she asked, "Didn't you think I could satisfy you by myself?"

"I am looking for a man I was talking to last night." He brushed her hand away. "Old codger. Had only one leg."

Her nose wrinkled. "That is Charlie."

"Where is he?" When she shrugged, he stuffed a bill in the cleavage of her full breasts. "Do you remember now?"

"Maybe."

Beneath Arielle's fingers his arm tensed with frustration. Finding this man must be the reason Stephen had brought her to this loathsome place. Although she wanted to urge him to give the prostitute as much money as she wanted so they could talk to this man and leave, she said nothing. She had to trust that Stephen knew what he was doing.

When another bill followed the first, the woman smiled and motioned for them to follow her through the low back door of the tavern. Arielle started to ask a question, but Stephen put his finger to her lips. She nodded, hoping that trusting him was the right thing to do. If this was another of his pranks . . .

The woman stopped in front of a hut and shoved aside a curtain in a door. She shouted something in Spanish. Pinching Stephen's cheek and giving Arielle another glower, she sashayed back to the tavern.

A flurry of curses startled Arielle. They were in English. When a man peered out the door, he held up a candle. Arielle's heart turned over as she stared at his hair, which was the same red as Caleb's. The resemblance ended there because the man's nose had been battered by many fists. His cheeks were covered with rusty whiskers, but she did not see the scar left by the bull the day Caleb saved her life.

The man scratched himself and muttered, "What d'ya want?"

"To talk about the battle down in Rivas, Charlie," Stephen answered in an emotionless tone. "We want to ask you some questions about it."

The old man squinted at them, then, jabbing a wooden crutch under his arm, hobbled out to reveal his left leg had been amputated above his knee. "I have seen ya before, boy."

Stephen chuckled. "I bought you a few rounds last night."

"Yeah. You were the one asking about—"

"We want to know about the battle at Rivas," he interrupted sharply.

"Who is the looker?"

"She is trying to find out if her fiancé was killed at Rivas."

"Fiancé?" The old man gave a vulgar snort. "Who are ya? Her brother? Trying to marry her off? If ya want to get rid of her, they will give ya a good price for her in there." He sat on a rock and pointed to the tavern with his crutch. "Just for tonight."

"I have already paid enough for her."

Arielle's fingers bit into her palms as she clamped her lips closed. She should have known Stephen would take every opportunity to embarrass her.

"Who are ya lookin' for?" The old man smiled slyly. "I hope ya brought something to wet our tongues while we talk."

"Got cups?" Stephen lifted the bottle he carried.

Reaching into the hut, he pulled out a bent tin cup. "One."

"That is enough." Stephen took it and filled it. Handing the cup to Arielle, he said, "It is just wine, honey. You look like you could use it."

As the men passed the bottle between them, Arielle sipped on the wine. She had to admit Stephen was right again. The wine warmed the cold emptiness in her while she listened.

"Horrible, it was." Charlie burped loudly, then took another drink from the bottle. "Those damn Costa Ricans were everywhere. Snuck up on us. We had to get out while we still had breath in our bodies. Those who could not get out died when President Mora arrived with more Costa Ricans. Killed every prisoner, they did. Walker tried to go back and rout the bastards out, but there were too many of them."

Arielle moaned when he gave them a detailed, matter-of-fact description of how the filibusters had been overrun and slain. When Stephen put his arm around her, she moved closer to him. She asked, when Charlie paused to take a breath, "Was there a man named Drummond with you?"

"Drummond?" He tapped absently on the stump of his left leg. "I know that name. Yeah, I remember a Drummond there."

"*Caleb* Drummond?"

"No, his name was Ralph." Scowling, he said, "Caleb Drummond. Isn't he the boy with red hair?"

"Yes." Her fingers dug into Stephen's arm as she gulped the last of the bitter wine in the cup.

"Worked for the Transit Company." The old man held out his hand for the bottle. Tipping it back, he drank deeply. He lowered it. "Wasn't with us in Rivas." Stabbing at his chest, he said, "I was the only redhead there that day."

Arielle put her fingers to her mouth but could not silence her gasp of relief. "Thank you. Oh, thank you." She smiled when Stephen squeezed her, but all she could do was repeat, "Thank you."

The old man grinned as Stephen drew her to her feet. Wanting to spin about and dance with happiness, she laughed lightly. She took Stephen's arm and watched as he handed old Charlie some money. She was sure Stephen would add that and the cash he had given the woman to what he expected Caleb to repay him.

Her feet had an odd tingling, but she hurried with Stephen back to the carriage. She heard him laugh as he sat next to her, and he joined in when she began to sing. She paid no attention to the words, just to the happiness coursing through her.

At the hotel he kept his arm around her while they walked to their rooms. She giggled and undid the ribbons on her bonnet. Dropping it onto the table, she whirled about, letting her skirt bell around her.

"Watch out, honey!" Stephen called with another laugh. "You are going to knock over the candle."

"I do not care. Caleb is alive!"

When he did not answer, she turned to see the peculiar tension on his face. Her foot caught on the rug, and she nearly stumbled, but she put her hands on his arms. "Aren't you glad he is not dead, Stephen?"

"I would feel better if I knew why Childs was lying to you."

"You heard Charlie. There was another man named Drummond at Rivas. It must have been just a mistake." She giggled again and drew his arms around her waist. "You have made mistakes, haven't you, Stephen? Or are you always right?" She cocked her head to one side and smiled. "You know, that is your most tiresome habit. Being right all the time." Slipping her hands up his arms to his wide shoulders, she whispered, "Wouldn't you like to make a mistake just once?"

Her fingers on the back of his head guided his mouth to hers. Stroking his tongue with hers, she tasted the tang of the wine. She moved closer, wanting to feel his strong body against her.

When he stepped away from her, she choked, "No!"

He ignored her protest and held her at arm's length as he asked, "How much did you drink?"

"Just a little wine." She tapped him on the nose as he had her so often. "I am glad you came back tonight. I thought you had abandoned me."

"No, honey."

"Then why did you go away for so long?" She ran her fingers along his chest and smiled when he drew in a breath.

"You know why," he said roughly. "A man can take only so much before he goes mad."

She laughed. "You already are mad, Stephen." Looking up into his quicksilver eyes, she whispered, "Do not go away again. Stay here with me tonight."

"You are drunk, Arielle. You do not know what you are saying."

"I am drunk, but I know what I am saying." The words bubbled from her as she whispered, "Stay with me tonight. I need you tonight."

"You deserve better than me, honey."

She slid his dirty coat from his shoulders. Dropping it to the floor, she whispered, "Don't you think you should let me decide that?" She began to undo the buttons on his shirt. Her eager fingers twisted through the hair across his chest. As she pressed her face to its wiry warmth, her hands swept beneath his shirt up his naked back.

With a moan he tugged her against him. The sound swirled through her when his mouth captured hers. Her breath grew ragged as his hands curved around her waist.

"No corset," she whispered with a soft giggle.

"I told you that you did not need it."

Her laugh faded into a breathless sigh when his tongue teased her ear. Every bone within her melted in the tempest. When she wobbled, he lifted her into his arms. She closed her eyes and leaned her cheek against the firm pillow of his shoulder.

She was startled when he set her on her feet instead of on the bed. Her smile returned when he reached around her. Resting her head on his chest, she spread her fingers across his back as he unhooked her gown. She pulled on his stock to loosen it. Throwing it into a shadowed corner, she whirled out of his arms.

She rested her hands on the bed, but the room continued to twirl wildly. Hearing soft footsteps, she realized Stephen must have taken off his boots. How kind of him when every sound reverberated through her head, which felt so curiously light! He gently turned her into his arms again.

"Let's not argue tonight," she whispered. "Just for

tonight, pretend you are my friend. I need a friend tonight.''

"I do not want to be your friend." His low growl deepened as he went on. "I want to be your lover, Arielle. I want you as I have never wanted any other woman. As I will never want any other woman again."

He gave her no chance to answer as he crushed her lips beneath his. The iron bar of his arm molded her against his hard body. Her dress drooped from her shoulders as he undid the last hooks so slowly that she wanted to cry out with the agonizing longing inside her. He let the dress slither down her arms as her fingers clenched on his back. He lowered the dress over her breasts, every touch a separate spark that was setting her afire with this need she had discovered in his arms. A quick tug on her petticoat untied it, and it fell to the floor like orange blossoms drifting on an indolent breeze.

When she reached for the buttons on his shirt, he batted her fingers away. Against her neck he whispered, "Patience, honey."

"I do not want to be patient. I cannot be patient. Not when I feel like this."

"I like the way you feel." His broad hands pushed her dress down over her hips. As it dropped to her feet, his fingers curved around her, pressing her even closer until she had no doubts that he was as much a captive of passion as she was.

This time when he scooped her into his arms, he placed her on the bed. She held her arms up to him, but, smiling, he said, "I have never bedded a woman who wore boots to bed."

With another cascade of giggles she drew her feet away from his fingers. At his order to cooperate she laughed and eluded his hands. He caught her right ankle and pinned it to the mattress. As he pulled off her boot, she let the pillow cradle her head. Nothing would stay still. Even the top of the bed was revolving like a child's top.

She closed her eyes and concentrated on his fingers moving along her foot as he took off her other boot. She clutched the sheets as he rolled her stockings down her leg. When he teased the back of her ankle with the tip of his tongue, she was sure lightning had seared her with its untamed power.

Reaching past her, he doused the lamp. The room settled into the gray twilight before dawn, but her eyes could not adjust. She blinked, but the darkness continued to whirl madly.

The bed moved, and she gripped it. She did not want to be lost in the darkness that clung to her like a smothering blanket. Suddenly fright tightened its claws around her. The maelstrom swept her into its turbulence.

She had no idea she had spoken until Stephen drew her into his arms and whispered, "Hush. Soon you will feel better, Arielle. Trust me."

She wanted to answer, but his lips settled over hers in a gentle kiss that pulled her into passion's eddy. Down, deeper and deeper, she sank, until she was overwhelmed by the sensations and surrendered herself to the warm darkness of his embrace as all conscious thought faded into ecstasy.

Arielle moaned and forced her eyes open. Every strand of hair ached when she rolled onto her side to stare at the ceiling which was distorted by the mosquito netting swathing the bed. She tried to lift her hand to press against her pulsing forehead, but it was too heavy.

What had happened? Maybe she had been hit by a runaway dray. Maybe she was sick. Maybe she would just die soon and be done with this pain.

The door opened. Its creak resonated through her skull.

She stiffened when Stephen walked in, carrying a tray. She sagged against the pillow. Her modesty did not matter when she was about to die from the agony in her head.

"Good morning," he said softly.

Even his whisper hurt. She moaned when he opened the drapes on the French doors and let sunlight flow across the floor. She squeezed her eyes shut. "Go away. I want to die in peace."

"You are not going to die." He chuckled as he poured a cup of steaming coffee and carried it to the bed. "Even if you want to. Why didn't you tell me that you get pixilated on just one cup of wine?"

Managing to open one eye a slit, Arielle glared at him. As he bent toward her, she was inundated by half-formed memories sending a wave of icy alarm through her. He had leaned over her like this before in this bed. Pixilated? Her?

"Sit up and drink some coffee." He smiled as he sat next to her. "Take it from someone with a great deal more experience than you with the effects of a bottle. This helps." He laughed softly. "A little."

When she struggled to push herself up, she collapsed to the bed with a moan. "I cannot. Just leave me alone."

"Come on, Arielle." He took her hand and helped her sit. Holding to the cup to her lips, he ordered, "Now drink."

She did not listen as she stared at the bits of muslin and lace she was wearing. With a gasp she pulled the blanket up to her chin. His lips twitched as he ran a finger along her bare shoulder.

With the heat of a Nicaraguan afternoon, memory surged through her. The horror of believing Caleb was dead, the truth, and the wine she had gulped. Those memories were clearer in her head than what had happened after. Maybe it was just a dream. So many times she had dreamed that Stephen would take her in his arms and teach her the music of two hearts soaring with love.

She saw the truth in his eyes. It had not been a dream. Looking at the pillow next to hers, she saw the indentations that told her she had not slept alone. Shame twisted in her stomach.

"Stephen . . ."

"Hush," he murmured. "Drink this. It will help your head."

She wanted to tell him that her aching head did not worry her as much as her heart, which had betrayed her into his arms. When he repeated the order, she took the cup in her quivering hands. Steam struck her face, scraping her tender forehead. Sipping the strong coffee, she forced her tight throat to swallow. The flavor washed away the dregs of wine in her mouth. She leaned back and closed her eyes.

"Arielle, you will survive. I promise." Stephen put the cup on the dressing table. His fingers stroked her cheek and smoothed back her loosened hair. "And what a temptress you are when you shed your Yankee puritanism!"

Her skin remembered the textures of his as he held her to this bed. Turning her face away, she begged, "Do not say that."

"Honey, do not cry." She flinched when he put his lips against her hair.

"Just leave me alone, Stephen. Please." Bitterness seeped into her voice. "You did not have any trouble leaving me alone before."

With a sudden growl of frustration he tugged her back to face him. "What is wrong with you, woman? I told you last night why I left. Maybe you did not hear me because you were too interested in your own desires, but I cannot stay here with you and not make love to you. Don't you understand?"

She tried to cover her barely clothed body, but he held

her hands away as he leaned her back on the rumpled sheets. When she squirmed to escape, he pinned her legs to the mattress. She shuddered as his mouth found the most sensitive spot along her neck before he whispered in her ear, "I would never take advantage of a drunk woman, Arielle, but you are not drunk now."

"You did not—? We did not—?" Her face flushed.

Standing, he said, "No, and I came in here to tell you that you do not need to worry about this. I am leaving."

Arielle pulled a blanket around her shoulders as she jumped from the bed to follow him into the other room. "Stephen!" she cried, ignoring the lash of pain in her head.

"I will be back to get my stuff when I find a place to stay." He picked up his hat and brushed sand from it.

"You are going to leave me here alone?" As he walked to the door, she blurted out, "Stephen, you cannot go! I need you to help me."

"You do not need me, honey." He gave her a wry smile, but the line of his jaw remained taut. "You have got new allies now. Once Childs realizes he has made a mistake, he will do anything he can to help you. I will just complicate things if I stay around."

"But I love *you!*"

His back stiffened as his steps faltered. Then he opened the door and disappeared into the glare of morning sunshine.

CHAPTER TWELVE

Arielle jabbed her finger with the needle as a knock on the door intruded on the silence. Her curse would have gained her respect from Stephen if he had been there. More tears oozed into her eyes, and she wondered how long she would have to weep until all her tears were as dried as her soul.

Dragging her heavy body to the door, she opened it to see Francine Childs's smile. The blonde was perfectly attired in a pink gown that was so starched that even the Nicaraguan humidity could not dampen its ruffles. Lovely, poised, and polished, Francine was the perfect wife for Rutledge Childs, who rumor suggested would be appointed as the first ambassador to the United States from President Walker's new government.

"Arielle, I hope you can forgive me for calling unannounced at such an hour."

"Such an hour?" Arielle repeated. She saw the long shadows of sunset in the garden. The whole day had evaporated in the heat of her grief.

Francine brushed dampness from her skirt. "I wanted to deliver our apology in person. When Rutledge told me there had been a mix-up, I had to come immediately to tell you."

"I know Caleb was not killed in Rivas."

"You know? How?"

Arielle explained how the last letter had been posted after the battle but omitted any mention of the other events of the previous evening. She stuttered when she perceived Francine's slightly amused gaze on her wrapper and bare feet. Suddenly she noticed Stephen's shirt hanging over the back of a chair by the table. Picking up her skirt, which she had been repairing, she placed it over his shirt, hoping Francine had not seen it.

"Would you like something cool to drink?" She had to be a good hostess, although the thought of swallowing anything sickened her.

"I cannot linger. Rutledge expects me home within the hour, but I wanted to give you this." She held out a cream-colored card that was closed with sealing wax. "Do say you will come, Arielle! It would be so delightful if you would join us."

She turned the card over to see her name and Stephen's written on the opposite side. "An invitation?"

"You must have heard that there is a ball at the palace on Saturday." Francine turned, sending her full skirts swirling around the chairs and settee. "It will be the perfect opportunity for you to ask the people who matter in this horrible little country about your fiancé's disappearance."

"You are inviting me to a party at President Walker's house?"

"A ball, my dear." Francine peered into a mirror and brushed her golden hair back from her wide eyes. "Merely a show for the Costa Ricans and Guatemalans." With a shrug she said with a disinterest Arielle did not think was feigned, "I do not know why we bother. President Walker's army has beaten them soundly before."

Arielle saw she believed her words, which contradicted the story Charlie had told them last night.

Francine went on. "But I am glad for any excuse for some excitement to come into our dreary lives in this dreary country." She grasped Arielle's arm. "Arielle, you must come to the ball. You *and* Captain Lightenfield must come to the ball."

Francine's fervor was unnerving, but, searching the blonde's face, Arielle saw only a warm smile. With a sigh she held out the invitation. "I cannot come, Francine. This dress," she said, pointing to the blue gown hanging on the door, "is the best I have with me."

"Nonsense!" she retorted. "The ball is a week away. You must come tomorrow and pick out one of my gowns. I shall have it fitted to you, and, if Captain Lightenfield has no interest in serving as your escort, I shall find you one. There will be many men eager for your company. They might consort with the native women, but, for an event of this import, they will be glad for a lady from their home-land."

"Let me think about it."

"Do that." Francine smiled warmly as she went to the door. "I shall be awaiting your call tomorrow. Bring Captain Lightenfield with you. Rutledge and I would so like to meet him."

"Has Rutledge discovered anything else about Caleb?"

"Not yet." Patting Arielle's hand, she said, "Do not lose hope. Perhaps Mr. Drummond will hear that you are in Granada and are searching for him. Just think. It is possible that you shall attend President Walker's ball with your fiancé." She tapped her long finger against her lips. "Hmm, that will cause a bit of a complication. There are so few women here, but I shall try to find Captain Light-enfield an escort if it comes to that."

Arielle was unprepared for the blade of jealousy cutting into her as she imagined another woman in Stephen's arms and watching as they turned to the seductive strains of a waltz. She lowered her eyes, not wanting Francine to see how it hurt to realize that even as they were talking, Stephen might be holding another woman in one of the shoreside brothels.

"Do not be so sad," Francine said again. "I shall implore Rutledge to do what he can to find more information on Mr. Drummond." Her laugh sparkled in the quiet room. "Mr. *Caleb* Drummond. I shall see you and the captain on the morrow."

"I am not sure Stephen can come tomorrow."

With a wave of her hand she smiled. "Then I shall steal him from you for a dance at the ball, my dear Arielle, so I can get to know him better. I have been intrigued by his gallantry. Till tomorrow, then."

The door clicked closed as Arielle picked up the invitation Francine had set on the table. She held it to her breaking heart. Stephen had been right yet again. She did not need his help anymore. But she needed his love.

Stephen opened the door to the light of a nearly glutted candle. Its sickly light splashed over the settee and the gold of Arielle's wrapper. He tiptoed across the room to get his knapsack. This was for the best. He had told himself that all day while he looked for another place to stay. With more filibusters flocking to Walker's banner every day, the city was full. It was time to get back to *The Ladysong* and Boston. Staying longer was stupid.

He saw a folded card on the table. Picking it up, he held it close to the candle to read it. He swore silently as he turned it over to see his name written in a fine hand next to Arielle's. An invitation to Walker's inner circle of confidants. Damn! He should have just taken his knapsack and hightailed it back to Greytown. Now that he had chanced to see this . . . He could not let Arielle face those piranhas alone.

"Stephen?" Her wispy whisper reached across the room to him.

Turning, he saw her rubbing sleep from her eyes. Her tousled hair urged him to grasp a handful and hold its silk to his face before letting it flow along him. Clenching his teeth, he said tightly, "I came to get my things. I found a place closer to the lake."

"Are you leaving Granada?"

"I was."

Her eyes widened, and the sleepiness fell from her face. "You *were?*"

He held up the invitation. "I read this. I thought it might be fun to see how Walker has fun."

"Good." She took the invitation. "Tomorrow when I go over to her house to get a gown, I will let Francine know you will be coming."

"A gown?" He sat on the arm of the settee and looked down at her face, which bore the ravages of the pain she had suffered in the past day. Damn Drummond! Damn Childs! And, he admitted silently, damn himself most of all. If he had done as he had wanted and had her share his bed while they sailed south, surely this endless fascination with the curve of her lips and the touch of her fingers would have turned to boredom by now.

"I cannot wear my blue dress. Even if it were not torn, it is a walking dress, not a ball gown."

He pulled a handful of bills from his pocket. Slapping them into her hand, he said, "Buy yourself a gown. You do not want to go to *El Presidente*'s house in a secondhand gown."

"No, thank you." She held out the money to him. When he did not take it, she dropped it on his leg. "Caleb cannot afford to buy me a dress when he already owes you more than one hundred dollars.''

"This," he argued, pressing the money back into her hand and closing her fingers over it, "is a gift."

"It is too much."

He shook his head. "It is a gift, honey. You cannot give a gift back. Besides, I want to see the prettiest woman there outshine all these bureaucrats' wives.''

He could not halt his fingers from stroking her ebony curls. When she leaned her head against him, he sighed. He had to stay until Walker's party was over.

Arielle jumped to her feet, and he watched, baffled, as she pulled a piece of thread from the pocket of her wrapper. Smiling, she ordered, "Stand up."

"What for?" He crossed one leg over the other and folded his arms in front of him. "If you plan to hang me, Arielle, I must warn you that you need something a bit sturdier."

"You can be sure if I planned to hang you, I would have the noose ready." Her eyes sparkled as she said, "If you are going to President Walker's fete, you cannot do it in tatters. If I want to convince someone to help find Caleb, I cannot do it while appearing on the arm of a man who looks as if he has been loading cargo at the lake."

He tapped the dirt clinging to his sleeve. "I thought I cut a dashing, romantic figure in my rags." Yawning broadly, he said, "I will find something." He picked up his knapsack. "If you need anything, Arielle, send word to old Charlie. He will know how to reach me."

When she blocked his way, she said, "You will understand, I am sure, when I say I do not trust you on this. Let me measure you. Then I can take your measurements to the seamstress. She will make you a new frock coat and trousers."

"You are going to be insistent about this, aren't you?"

When her smile widened, he set the knapsack on the table. "Go ahead."

When she wrapped the string around his neck and marked where the two pieces came together, he teased her again about measuring him for a noose. She laughed, and he knew she did not share his gloomy dread that trouble would come to Granada before the ball.

"Now your arm," she ordered.

He raised his right arm so she could run the string along it. When she had trouble keeping it in place, he chuckled. "Let me hold one end."

"Thank you."

She folded his hand over the thread to secure it. When her fingers touched his, he held them captive. She glanced at him and away, but he saw the barely quiescent fires in their dark depths flash to life. When she placed the string along his sleeve to his shoulder, she looked at him. Her lips parted in a soft invitation. Heat throbbed through him. This had been more stupid than deciding to stay for Walker's fete.

Her voice trembled as she said, "Your chest now."

He wondered how the coat would fit when he was holding his breath the whole time she measured him. Her warm breath caressed his neck as she drew the string around him. As her breasts grazed his chest, his arm went around her waist. He brought her tight to him.

Gently she stepped back. "Stephen, you want to look good for the president's ball, don't you?"

Her husky voice echoed the desire he saw in her eyes. He nodded, because he did not trust himself to answer. When she knelt to measure for his trousers, the brush of her fingertips along his leg was excruciatingly sweet. They climbed higher and higher, past his knee and along his thigh and—

He grabbed her arms and jerked her to her feet. "Is

this your revenge, honey?" he rasped. "To make me insane with desire for you?"

"I want you to stay," she whispered as she encircled his face with her hands. "I want you to stay tonight and for as long as you want."

"What about Caleb?"

Arielle looked up at the silver storm in his eyes. The power of that tempest would consume her in the passions she could no longer control. Softly she said, "I love you, Stephen."

"Honey, I—"

She touched his lips with hers and whispered, "Don't say it. Take my love, Stephen. It is a gift. You cannot give a gift back."

"Are you always going to throw my words back into my face?"

"For as long as I can." Her hands tangled in his hair. It drifted, thick and golden, over her fingers.

She gasped when he swept her up into his arms. More tenderly than he had ever kissed her, he placed his lips against hers before raising his head to smile at her. This was not what she wanted. She wanted— With a laugh he captured her lips, demanding her love. The silk along her legs heated with his touch as he carried her to the bed she would share with him until . . . She did not want to think of that moment, only of this, when she would partake of the quintessence of love.

Kicking the door closed, he set her on the lush bed. He lit a candle and set it on the dressing table. As he sat next to her, he drew the mosquito netting to leave them a gauzy half-light. He put his arms around her and leaned her back into the pillows. A roguish grin transformed him into a lascivious pirate. His lips followed the conservative neckline of her wrapper.

He took her lips again, daring her to admit her own ungovernable passion. As he pinned her between the mattress and the firm line of his body, her fingers inched up his back, holding herself to him, wanting to be a part of his dreams as he was part of hers. Gasping against his mouth when the longing threatened to overwhelm her, she shivered as his tongue delved deep, past her lips, to inflame all of her with its fiery touch. When she tasted the flavors of his mouth, her body disintegrated into the strength of her need for the love that had refused to be repudiated.

"Tell me this is what you want, honey," he murmured as he buried his face in her hair, which flowed across the sheets.

"I want you to love me." Her breathless voice was nearly muted by the pounding of her heart as his hand moved along her side to find her breast. With the gentle, inviting brushes of his fingertip along its curve, he lured her into the mindless rapture . . . into his arms . . . into love.

His fingers sought the buttons holding her wrapper in place, but he did not undo them. She stared up into his eyes as he raised his lips from hers. Knowing that he was offering her a final chance to deny the truth, she wondered if any other man could be so tender and so sacrificing, when she could sense how much he wanted her in his kiss, along his body, in his touch. Her hand slipped along his shoulders to find the top button on his vest. She loosened it to reveal his ripped shirt beneath it. As silently, she released the next and the next until his vest fell open.

When he bent to taste her lips, she held up her hands with a soft smile. He frowned, perplexed, then grinned as she began to undo the buttons along the front of his shirt. That grin became fervent longing when her fingertips swept along the skin bared by his gaping shirt. Taking her lips anew, he moaned as her bold hands explored his chest.

She quivered when the powerful surge of uncontrollable craving washed over her as her fingers twisted in the warm matting across his heart. The firm muscles beneath his skin moved beneath her touch, urging her to discover each delight waiting for her. When he shrugged off his loosened clothes, she gazed at his strong body covered only by his trousers, which outlined every masculine angle of his legs. Her eager fingers refused to be forbidden the chance to touch him and uncover every texture of his skin.

"Let me see you, honey," he whispered against her throat as his lips left heated sparkles of delight on her skin.

"Yes," she murmured. Slowly her fingers reached for the buttons on her wrapper.

He drew her hand away and turned it palm upward. The feverish caress of his mouth on it melted her into a fragrant flame. She wanted his mouth on every inch of her as she surrendered herself to their combined pleasure. As he held her gaze with his, she became the pulse of his heartbeat, which she could sense with every breath. No longer separate but not yet one, she ached for the consummation of the rapture pledged by his eyes.

He loosened her wrapper and threw it to the floor, forgotten, to leave her dressed only in her chemise. A soft cry of astonishment burst from her when he pushed her deeper into the bed. He leaned over her, smiling with devilish desire.

She was sure he would speak and waited for his teasing words. When his hand settled on her knee and crept upward in a lingering serpentine path, she reached up to wrap her arms around his shoulders and draw him down to her. Even as his fingers stroked the sensitive skin along her inner leg, his lips sampled the curves above the drooping neckline of her chemise. Beneath the dual assault she could do nothing but hold tightly to him as she struggled not to drown in the intoxicating potion of passion.

He pulled the straps of her chemise along her arms, lowering it to bare her to his eager eyes. As her hands swept along his back to his lean hips, his lips brushed the

underside of her breast. She could not silence the gasp of
his name when his tongue slid in a meandering journey
up the gentle slope to its very peak. When he drew it into
his mouth to surround her with his impassioned yearning,
she pressed closer to him, wanting to share this incredible
joy.

With a growl of impatience he pulled her chemise over
her head. Lightly his fingers ran along her, leaving a dazzling blaze in its wake. He stood, but she rose to kneel on
the bed before he could remove his torn trousers. A smile
filled his eyes as she drew aside the last of the clothing
separating them. As eagerly as he had touched her, she
stroked him, delighting in the angles of his body, which
were so different from hers.

He pushed her back into the pillows and laughed husk-
ily. When his lips demanded exactly what she longed to
give him, the length of his body against hers urged her to
entangle her legs with his to savor every inch of his strong
form. Unable to halt the quivers racing through her, she
clasped his shoulders when his fingers boldly stroked
upward along her legs to seek the essence of the fire burning deep in her. A low cry burst from her but was muted
by his mouth claiming hers.

A rhythm roiled within her, a rhythm that was of him
and his probing caress, yet was of her and the unrelenting
passion that had exacted its hold over all of her. When he
drew her beneath him and melded her to him, she surrendered all of herself to that engulfing rhythm. Moving
to it, a part of it, a part of him, she tasted his mouth
on hers and his straining breath swirling through her.
Through her, through him, through the need that was the
rhythm as fathomless and potent as the sea until, in a
timeless moment of perfection, she poised on the crested
waves of ecstasy before being flung upon the glorious
shores of paradise.

* * *

Arielle opened her eyes to a symphony of soft kisses against her. Stephen's smile was as bright as the happiness inside her. Still wrapped in rapture, not wanting to shatter it by speaking, she traced the fullness of Stephen's bottom lip with her fingertip. He drew her finger into his mouth, sucking lightly on it, resurrecting the thrill of passion that would never be completely silent again.

"You are wondrous," he whispered.

"It was wonderful, wasn't it?" When he laughed, she could imagine nothing more splendid than lying in the arms of the man she loved. When he leaned her head against his chest, the hard muscles of his body made a wondrous pillow. Her fingers draped across him, but she could move no farther.

"Tonight we shall sleep together again." His voice filtered through her hair to slip along her neck in a gentle caress.

She turned her cheek against the soft hair on his chest. "At first I could not imagine sleeping with you. On *The Ladysong* I wanted to hate you."

"I know. I had hoped you would."

"It would have made things much easier."

With another chuckle he put his hand on her hip and drew her legs closer to him. "But not as much fun." He tapped her wrinkled nose. "Fun is not an obscenity. You have had fun on this trip, haven't you?"

"Sometimes."

"Didn't you enjoy painting *The Ladysong?*"

"Parts of it."

"Like my chair?"

She ran her hand across his chest and up to curve along his jaw. "That was among the best parts."

"Then come back with me to *The Ladysong*."

Bafflement wrinkled her eyebrows. "But, Stephen, I have not found Caleb yet."

As he rose to one elbow, she saw his eyes growing stormy with the dark emotions he had banished while he held her. His voice was as cold as a New England winter night. "You still are willing to risk your life to find him?"

"My obligation to him has not changed just because I love you."

He cursed. "I should knock you on the head, stuff you into a bag, and put you in irons as soon as we reach the ship."

"Stephen, please understand."

"I understand that I am giving you ten more days to find him." When she started to protest, he held up a single finger. "One week until Walker's ball, then a few days to see if anyone is willing to help you. After that, I swear I will tote you back to *The Ladysong* in a bag. I will not leave you here to get killed when Walker's little kingdom blows up in his face."

"You think—?"

With a laugh he stroked her from knee to the curve of her hip. "Honey, I do not want to think. I just want to feel you all around me again."

Her eyes widened at his renewed desire. Even as his mouth was descending toward hers, the answering craving blossomed within her. Many questions needed to be answered, but she pushed them from her mind as she pulled him to her. Tonight was for fun.

Tomorrow . . .

CHAPTER THIRTEEN

Arielle drew her white silk stockings along her legs and smiled. Rising, she reached for her starched petticoats, which rustled as she stepped into them. Tying them in place, she watched with delight as they belled around her. She picked up the hastily made ball gown. The dress slipped over her head as she tried not to disarrange her hair, which hung in ringlets behind her left ear. A fresh flower she had picked on the terrace topped the curls.

Smoothing the pink skirt overlaid with black lace, she convinced the trio of flounces with their generously proportioned black bows to settle over her petticoats. A trail of the thick lace followed her as she turned to check her hair in the mirror. No damage. She had to look perfect tonight on the slight chance that she would have the opportunity to speak to the most powerful man in Nicaragua.

Her smile softened when she looked at the reflection of the bed in the mirror. In the past week Stephen had introduced her to a joy she had not guessed existed, even in his loving arms. A patient teacher, he dared her to experiment and learn with him what brought them both ecstasy.

Yet, not once had he spoken of what would happen after they returned to *The Ladysong* and the United States. She suspected he would let her stay aboard his ship as his mistress. The idea troubled her. Nicaragua had changed her, but not that much.

An impatient knock jolted her out of her thoughts. "Hurry up, Arielle, or we might miss his high-and-mightiness's grand entrance."

"I am still dressing."

The door swung open. Stephen came in with his usual intensity, saying, "I do not know why you women wear all these lacy, frilly things that just get in a man's way."

"Finish hooking me up, will you?" As he deftly handled the small hooks, she glanced over her shoulder to ask, "Did you ever think that we wear them because they do get in a man's way? That we want to slow down your ardor long enough so you will notice us?"

He tipped her face toward him. "You should have no complaints on that, honey. You never have escaped my notice."

Slapping his hand lightly, she said, "Finish hooking me, please, or we *will* be late."

"I would rather unhook you, honey." His fingers stroked her waist. In feigned shock, he said, "What? No corset?"

"No."

"To think you're going to meet the exulted *El Presidente* half dressed. Shameful."

As Arielle drew on her silk slippers that had been dyed to match her dress, she noticed that Stephen's face was taut with emotions he was trying to conceal. "Why do you hate Walker so much?"

"The man is an idiot with dreams of magnificence. Isn't that reason enough?"

"Not for you." Knowing that she was broaching a sensitive subject, she said, "You allowed Roach Walden to stay aboard your ship after he smuggled me aboard."

"I always allow a man one mistake. Roach made his, and so has Walker." He bent to kiss the back of her neck. "I shall be polite this evening, Arielle. Not one insult about his high-and-mightiness will slip past my lips." Handing Arielle her lace mitts, he drew her to her feet and turned her to face him.

Arielle held her hand to the row of delicate lace along the low neckline of her dress as she stared at Stephen. The design of his black formal evening coat suited the trim lines of his muscular body. Cut back sharply to reveal his black satin trousers, the frock coat was as spotless as the white shirt he wore beneath it. His high stock held his head at an uncomfortable angle, but the tie was perfectly arranged at the top of his blue vest.

"I am sorry I did not live *down* to your expectations," he said with a smile. "No rags, I'm afraid."

"When did you get this? I never took your measurements to the modiste." Her eyes narrowed. "*Someone* made off with the thread I used."

"I have my methods, honey."

"So I have noticed." Arielle set her silk shawl over her shoulders and drew on her lace gloves. When his fingertip traced the design that matched the trim on her gown, she longed for him to touch her more sensuously.

Coldness drilled through Arielle as she rode with Stephen in the chaise he had rented for the evening. While he teased her, she had been able to shunt aside her dread of what might wait for her at the party. If no one knew of Caleb's whereabouts, she had no doubts that Stephen would hold her to her promise to leave Granada in three days to return to *The Ladysong*. The rumors about an impending assault by Walker's enemies on the city were growing more panicked.

The carriage halted in front of the ornate entry of the presidential palace. Slowly it turned through the gate and wound up the driveway to the house, which was lit brightly against the velvet darkness of the tropical night. As the carriage came to a stop, Stephen's arm tightened around her. His lips seared into the skin behind her ear as his hand slid up her breast.

"Do not drink too much champagne," he whispered. "I don't want you falling asleep on me tonight."

She leaned back against his arm and smiled as she stroked the smooth skin of his freshly shaven cheek. "That is torture." She laughed when he regarded her in confusion. "Can you imagine a more exquisite torture than spending the evening here, when I would rather be alone with you?"

"We could go back to the hotel." He chuckled as he waved aside the driver and handed her from the carriage. "Don't say it. I know tonight is your chance to speak to Walker."

"This gallantry is an unexpected pleasure."

He grinned. "Don't get too used to it, honey. I do not take my *company* manners out too often." When he offered his arm, she dipped in an insolent curtsy. He drew her to her feet and slapped her on the buttocks.

"Stephen!"

"Don't worry, Madame Schoolmarm. My behavior will be exemplary the rest of the evening." He added so softly only she could hear, "Until we get back to our rooms."

Arielle smiled as they walked toward the double doors. From beyond them came music interwoven with conversation. In the small foyer she allowed a servant to take her shawl. Her eyes widened as they entered the ballroom. Every man was dressed as fancily as Stephen, although several of them wore bright sashes across their chests. The ladies' gowns were a festival of colors, exploding in pastel laces and silk trims.

An orchestra played valiantly but had to contest the voices of the guests who were not dancing. As Stephen steered her beneath one of a trio of crystal chandeliers marching in a column through the center of the room, her full skirts bumped against the gowns of the other women, slowing them. Their impeded progress allowed her more time to eavesdrop.

Only one subject was being discussed: the war and the upcoming confrontation with the forces allied against Walker's filibusters. More men were coming from New Orleans and California to join the valiant effort to keep Nicaragua from falling into the greedy hands of Commodore Vanderbilt or the vengeful armies of Costa Rica and Guatemala.

Stephen's face was blank, but Arielle could not suppress her shiver of fear. *This* must be the true reason he was insisting on their leaving Granada. She stroked his arm. It was as tight as his face, but he was listening intently.

She tried to emulate his cool politeness as he nodded his head toward each lady they passed. She was pleased when they reached a table where red wine was bubbling from a small fountain. She took the glass Stephen handed her and only nodded when he teased her about drinking this one and no more.

"Which one is President Walker?" she asked, looking around at the few guests who were dancing.

Stephen chuckled. "He is not here. Either the situation is more grave than gossip suggests, or he simply wishes to make an entrance grand enough for the newly inaugurated president of Nicaragua. I—"

He was interrupted by a deep voice. "May I believe I have the honor of addressing Captain Stephen Lightenfield?" A dignified young man who appeared uncomfortable in his evening dress bowed to them. Dark hair curled across his forehead, and his smile appeared from beneath a grand mustache waxed in curls at each end. He held out his hand. "I am Calvin O'Neal, in service of President Walker. I had heard you had joined us, Captain."

"You have heard wrong, O'Neal. This is a pleasure trip for me." He smiled at Arielle. "I am escorting Miss Gardiner while she looks for her fiancé here in Nicaragua."

With exaggerated grace O'Neal clicked his boots together and bowed over her hand. "Excuse my forwardness, Miss Gardiner, but I must tell you that the tales I have heard fail to express your beauty. Perhaps it is because our language contains no superlatives grand enough for your loveliness."

Over Mr. O'Neal's bent head Arielle almost laughed as she saw Stephen's smile. So often she berated him for failing to be a gentleman, but she had grown to appreciate his honesty. "You are very kind, Mr. O'Neal."

"Captain Lightenfield mentioned your fiancé?" O'Neal asked, curiosity bright in his eyes.

"Caleb Drummond, sir. He worked for the Accessory Transit Company. He came here about two years ago." Entreaty softened her voice. "Do you know him?"

"The name is familiar. Didn't he work on the side-wheelers?"

"Yes!"

Stephen said smoothly, "Drummond sent Miss Gardiner a message to join him. Unfortunately the part giving his exact location was lost."

"That happens too often. Although President Walker has improved conditions, it may be years before we can convince the natives to work at a level of competence we expect in the United States." He smiled with the graciousness she had been accustomed to in New England. "Let me ask about, Miss Gardiner. All the most powerful people in Nicaragua are in attendance tonight." His tone included himself in that prestigious group.

"Thank you. I look forward to our conversation later."

"As do I." He bowed over her hand again, nodded to Stephen, and disappeared into the swirl of the crowd.

When Stephen chuckled, she struggled not to laugh too. She said, "He was just trying to be nice."

"A pompous idiot." Taking her hand, he placed it on his arm and led her toward the dance floor. "These quixotic fools are so caught up in their fantasy that they cannot believe they are not invulnerable." He pulled her into his arms at the edge of the smoothly polished wooden floor. "Let's leave the battles to the warriors while I have the chance to show every man that you belong to me tonight. We might as well have fun. I doubt if we shall ever see such a display of self-indulgence again."

She put her hand on his shoulder and moved with him into the pattern of the waltz. He twirled her across the floor without regard to the sedate oval traveled by the other dancers.

"Ouch!" she exclaimed when his foot landed on her toes for the fourth time in as many steps. "Stephen, will you watch where you are going?"

He murmured in her ear, "Think how we will move together much more sweetly later. I promise you that you shall find it far more pleasurable than dancing."

Laughing, she retorted, "I would find walking on heated coals more pleasurable." She skipped out of his way as his boot brushed her foot again.

When he did not answer, she discovered he was paying more attention to the guests than to the dance. He spun her toward a group of men standing apart from the others. Dancing her about in a small circle, he boldly eavesdropped. She could not guess why he cared about the war talk.

A short man tapped Stephen on the shoulder and asked his permission to dance with her. Stephen nodded before the man even completed his question; she suspected he had been hoping for this when he brought her to the dance floor. She forced a smile as the man who introduced himself as Christian Foner twirled her around the floor. Twisting her head to follow Stephen, she saw him disappear into the crowd not far from where the men stood.

"Thank you for accepting such a presumptuous offer, Miss Gardiner." Mr. Foner grinned with boyish charm as he spoke so stiffly, she was sure he had practiced his words.

"Mr. Foner, I suspect you are from the South."

"Yes, miss." His freckled cheeks flushed. "I hail from Kentucky."

"Nicaragua is a long way from Kentucky."

He nodded but kept the rhythm of the dance. "When you come from a family with six brothers and more sisters, you find little waits for you. I left as soon as I could. In New Orleans I found work with Mr. Childs. When he decided to come here, he asked me if I wanted to join him. I had nothing better to do, so I did."

She replied politely and listened while he continued to talk about his work. When the dance was finished, she looked for Stephen, but he was nowhere in sight. She was given little chance to rue his absence. One after another the men asked her to dance.

She wasted no time quizzing them about Caleb. Although they were shocked that her fiancé was not the man who had escorted her to the ball, they answered her questions. She learned nothing new. Many knew of Caleb, but no one knew where he might be. When her seventh partner paused in midstep and midword, she looked past him to see Stephen's smile.

"If I may . . ."

Arielle sighed with happiness as familiar arms surrounded her. Relaxing, she allowed Stephen to pull her closer. His fingers roved along her back in a rhythm that was far sweeter than the melody from the violins.

"You have quite a list of admirers, honey."

"They are too accustomed to the same faces. Ours are new and exciting." She slid her hand along his shoulder to tease his nape. "I was wondering if you were going to dance with all the other ladies before you finished our dance."

He laughed. "I had no idea these women would be eager for me to trod on their toes."

"These are courageous women. They are used to peril."

"I wish Walker would appear," he said with sudden fervor.

"You want to see him?" She was shocked by his about-face.

His smile returned but not to his eyes, which were dark with uneasiness. "I just do not like our illustrious hero being absent when a ball in his honor is rife with rumors of war."

"If you think we should leave—"

"And miss your chance to meet his high-and-mightiness?"

"Stephen!" She hoped no one had overheard him.

"Here is someone who will be eager to dance with you. If you will excuse me . . ."

He left her standing in the middle of the dance floor. Hearing her name spoken, she forced a smile as she greeted Rutledge Childs and nodded when he asked her to dance. Blast Stephen! He had promised to behave like a gentleman this evening.

Rutledge swirled her around the floor, and Arielle relaxed to enjoy the dance. Although she loved being in Stephen's arms, he moved about the floor as forcefully as he crossed the deck of *The Ladysong*. It was a pleasure to dance with someone as accomplished in the art as Francine's husband.

She laughed when Rutledge said, "You have adapted

well to the Spanish beat this orchestra gives to a Viennese waltz, Arielle."

"It is easy to dance when the floor is empty."

"True." His face lengthened as he sighed. "Too much talk tonight is not a good thing."

"Is it as bad as they are saying?"

"It may be." He glanced at the others, who seemed to have no cares but how much wine to drink. His dismay was as out of place in the ballroom as his silver hair, which was glowing in the light of the candles suspended in the chandeliers, was among the richly hued locks of his youthful companions. "I think you and Captain Lightenfield would be wise to consider leaving Granada as soon as possible. I know you have not found Drummond, but you shall do no one any good by staying here to die with us."

"Die?" she squeaked. She lowered her voice when the other dancers glared at her. Abruptly she realized everyone in the room feared what Rutledge did but refused to admit it. "If it is so dangerous, why isn't anyone leaving?"

"When you meet President Walker, you will understand. Although this situation appears grim, he has led us through worse ones. I cannot believe it will different this time. Since *El Nicaragüense* named him a 'gray-eyed man of destiny,' he has been invincible."

"Rutledge, you can't be serious. No man is invincible."

The fanatical smile creasing his face was frightening, for she had considered him a sensible man. "I assure you, my dear, I am completely serious. The battle is waiting just past the horizon of tomorrow. It will be a telling one. Even though we shall be victorious, there will be those who shall fall in defense of our ideals." As his blue eyes held hers, she shivered. "Yes, the battle is coming, Arielle, and anyone who is in Granada must be willing to fight for President Walker or die."

* * *

Stephen took another glass of wine and surveyed the room. Never had he seen so many fools in one place. Each of them was willing—no, worse, they were eager—to follow Walker into death. Only the thought of the glory of an honorable death for the cause made their lives worth living. He drank and grimaced. He hungered for the taste of a rough Jamaica rum, not this wine, which had as many affectations as this false court that had sprung up around a false prophet of peace.

"Good evening, Captain Lightenfield."

At the soft purr he nodded absently, not wanting to be distracted from his thoughts. Then his eyes were caught by a stunning beauty, and he enjoyed a second, longer look. The woman's gold dress was molded to the generous curves of her voluptuous body before belling out to allow a man the pleasure of using his imagination. White lace edged with gold drew his gaze to the expanse of flesh escaping the deep neckline.

"You have the better of me," he said as the woman flowed toward him, her motions so graceful she could have been a wave sliding past *The Ladysong*. "You know my name, and I have yet to have the honor of an introduction."

"Forgive my informality, Captain. I am Francine Childs. I feel as if we are friends, for Arielle has spoken of you so often."

He concealed his surprise. *This* was Childs's wife? Arielle's description had not done the woman justice. Not only for her elegance, but Arielle had never mentioned the coolly controlled smile and the calculating glow in Mrs. Childs's eyes as they appraised him.

He bowed over her slender fingers that sparkled with jeweled rings. "My pleasure. You are not dancing, Mrs.

Childs?'' he queried pleasantly, but his gaze returned to the floor, where Arielle moved in perfect harmony with the music.

With Rutledge Childs he noted with a touch of irony. His brows lowered when he saw Arielle's tense expression. Childs had Walker's ear and the president his. When Arielle nodded, every inch of her stiff with apprehension, Stephen wondered if Childs was telling her the details of the danger amassing on the border.

He forced a smile as he realized Mrs. Childs was waiting for his next compliment. "I would have thought you would have many men eager to dance with you.''

She placed her fingers lightly on his arm. "I am afraid Arielle has stolen this old married woman's admirers.''

"I can assure you, few of the men in this room consider you old, Mrs. Childs.'' He gazed at her gown's provocative style and grinned. He could not imagine any man with a bit of life remaining in him ignoring this incredibly gorgeous woman. Glancing back at the dance floor, he almost laughed aloud. If that was so, why was he wishing Mrs. Childs was entertaining someone else so he could concentrate on watching Arielle . . . and listening to the filibusters? With a sigh as silent as his laugh, he recalled his promise to Arielle. He would be a gentleman tonight.

"I think your husband and Arielle are going to dance again,'' Stephen continued. "I will not punish your feet by dancing with you, but may I get you a glass of wine?''

"If you will join me in the garden while I drink it. I find this room close tonight.''

Stephen looked at the stairs he had heard Walker would use, then nodded. If *El Presidente* made an appearance, the uproar would reach into the garden to warn him. He offered Mrs. Childs his arm as they walked into the starlight-dusted garden. Cool fresh air was a relief after the cigar smoke.

As they strolled along the terrace, Stephen said, "Mrs. Childs, I must tell you how much Arielle has appreciated your friendship."

She smiled. "Arielle calls me Francine. Why don't you do the same?"

"I would be honored." He hesitated. They could not linger long. When this waltz was done, he wanted to claim Arielle for the next to find out what Childs had revealed to her. Thinking of holding her lithe form in his arms, he quickened his pace toward the door. It was time to be done with this posturing and return to the ecstasies of their bed: her soft breath against his mouth, her fingers gliding along him, his body hot and sweaty against hers as the passion pulsed between them, weaving them together into a single, undeniable need.

Francine's husky voice interrupted, pulling him away from the thoughts that were an exquisite torment. "It astonishes me that a man like you might be interested in someone like Arielle."

"I do not understand what you mean."

"I think you do, Stephen." Her hand on his arm moved along his sleeve as her lush body brushed against him in a candid invitation. "You and I have seen much of the world. Arielle is an innocent child. How you must long for a true woman!" She took his hand and drew his arm around her waist. "I do not want you to be lonely, Stephen."

Astounded at her offer and his peculiar reluctance to accept it, he moved away from her. "I am not lonely."

"You do not need to lie to me." She ran her fingers along his shirt, and her eyes glittered.

With a laugh he pushed her away far more gently than he really wanted to. "Sorry, Mrs. Childs, but you guessed wrong this time. I am not interested. You will have to find yourself some other sucker."

He ignored the insult she called after him. As he strode back to the house, he thought only of how hurt Arielle would be if she learned of this before they left Granada. He had promised her three more days to search for Drummond, then they would be bound along the river back to *The Ladysong*. He was ready to put these fanatics behind him.

By the time he reached the ballroom Stephen had a fake smile firmly in place. He arrived just as the waltz was ending. He hid his pity for Rutledge Childs as the older man escorted Arielle to him. When she held out her hands, he pulled her close and kissed her soft cheek. Her love offered something a practiced beauty could never give him.

"I am sorry," he whispered.

Arielle was shocked. Stephen never apologized. Something must have happened. Although his smile was warm, she saw dangerous emotions in his eyes. No hint of why trickled into his words as he spoke with Rutledge.

When Rutledge paused, she followed his possessive gaze to Francine. Arielle's smile faded as Francine shot a venomous glare at her. No, not at her. At Stephen. His arm tightened around her. His face was as devoid of emotion as the chandeliers.

Francine slipped her arm around her husband's and pressed her face against his shoulder. Rutledge's face grew long with dread. "My dear, what is wrong?"

Francine sobbed, "How can you treat *him* like a friend after what he did?"

"Him? Captain Lightenfield? What did he do to you, my sweet?"

"He offered me a distasteful proposition in the garden while you were dancing with his mistress." She spat out the last word at Arielle, before adding, "I was so foolish to let him lure me there, but . . ."

Cries sounded as she swooned. Her husband caught her. When Stephen put out his hands to help, Rutledge snarled, "You have done enough, Lightenfield."

"I have done nothing," Stephen replied sharply.

"Are you calling my wife a liar, sir?"

Arielle tried to say something, but her breath was clogged in her throat. Seeing Stephen's eyes grow dark with anger, she whispered, "Rutledge, Francine must have mistaken Captain Lightenfield's jests for sincerity."

"Is *this* a joke?" Rutledge placed his wife on a window seat. Taking a fan from a dowager who was craning her neck to see, he waved it over Francine. His face was colorless.

"There was no joke, Childs." Stephen shook off Arielle's warning hand and ignored the crowd gathering around them. "Your wife seemed completely serious."

Rutledge straightened as Francine opened her eyes and pressed her hand to her head. She took her husband's hand. For a moment Arielle saw a flash of satisfaction in Francine's eyes. This was nothing but an act. But why? None of this made sense.

"Captain," Rutledge said, "you are a guest in our country, so I will allow you one more chance to retract those scurrilous words."

"*You*," he retorted with a sharp laugh, "are the guests in Nicaragua, and unwelcome ones at that."

"Stephen!" Arielle's warning was swallowed by the gasps of outrage.

Stephen took her arm. "Let's go, Arielle. I have had enough of this grand experiment in hypocrisy."

"That is more than a gentleman can listen to without demanding satisfaction." Rutledge's jaw pointed belligerently. "Name your choice of weapons."

Stephen smiled coldly. "I choose words."

"Words?" Rutledge choked.

Arielle put her hand over Stephen's, hoping he knew what he was doing. When his fingers stroked hers, she rested her head on his shoulder.

"What better weapon?" Stephen's glare included all those listening. His voice rose as the orchestra began playing in a vain attempt to defuse the escalating anger in the room. "They are dangerous in the wrong hands." His frigid gaze swept over Francine, who was standing to cling to her husband's arm. "Your wife uses them to make you jealous enough to engage in this idiocy after she used other words to seduce me."

"Rutledge," Francine cried, "I never—"

Stephen continued relentlessly. "You used words, Childs, to convince Arielle that her fiancé was dead. Do you think you would have hurt her less if you had pierced her with a dagger?"

"That was an honest mistake," Rutledge argued.

"As was tonight. It was a mistake for Arielle and me to come here." He tugged on Arielle's hand. "We bid you good night and good-bye."

Hearing Rutledge sputter behind them, Arielle pushed through the crowd with Stephen. She hesitated when he strode toward the door. She could not leave while there was still a chance she might be able to speak with President Walker.

"What is wrong now?" His impatience warned her that his fury hadn't been a joke. She was astonished, for, as much as Stephen relished playing the role of a rogue, she had not thought he would take offense when he was accused of not being a gentleman.

She laughed. She could not halt herself. This was a ludicrous ending to a ridiculous evening. Stephen and she did not belong in this peculiar world of diplomats and words that could be used to twist an ally to help or destroy an enemy. Speaking her mind had become a refreshing pleasure that she did not want to set aside to be part of this *norteamericano* society.

Grinning, Stephen whirled her out into the foyer and into his arms. He held her between his hard body and the cool wall as he whispered against her ear, "Do you want to know every despicable detail of what happened in the garden?"

"No."

He stroked her cheek. When she shivered, he said, "I had hoped you would be a bit jealous, Arielle."

"I trust you."

Amazement stripped away his smile. "You are as much of a fool as Childs."

"It may gall you, Stephen, but you are a man of honor." She stepped away to gesture at the ballroom, where conversation had resumed again. No doubt all of it centered on her and Stephen. "Certainly more than them. I know you would not seduce another woman now."

"Only now?"

"Yes, only now." When she saw him flinch, she put her hand on his arm. "Stephen, what is really bothering you?"

"What did Childs tell you while you were dancing?"

She should have guessed Stephen's keen eyes would not miss their conversation. She began to explain, but he halted her by grabbing her arm and tugging her toward the front door.

"No!" she cried. "I came to see President Walker, and I will not leave until he gets here."

"Then," he said tightly, "I assume you can find your way back to the hotel."

"You are leaving?" She stared at his taut mouth. Moments earlier it had tilted with a smile. "Why?"

"I have had enough of this party." He ran a finger around the inside of his collar. "This is not for me. This place stinks of disaster. I am getting the hell out of here."

"Three more days. That is what you said."

"I am not sticking around that long." His lip curled in a savage smile. "You *are* a fool, honey. When are you going to learn that trusting me is stupid?"

She was left to watch his lean form weave through the colorful crowd. She did not follow. It would be futile. She tried to guess why he was lying to her. She feared she would never know.

CHAPTER FOURTEEN

A cacophony of trumpets blasted across the ballroom. Arielle gasped. Only one man in Granada would be announced with such a triumphant flourish! She entered the big room to see a clump of men descending the stairs. One of them had to be William Walker, but she could not locate him among his crowd of advisers.

The orchestra struck up a cheery tune to greet the president. Her stomach wrenched as she realized the president's entourage would be passing directly by her. Awe soldered her feet to the floor.

The men paused to speak to the guests, but William Walker remained silent as he gazed about the crowded room. The new president of Nicaragua was a slight man. His hair was a lifeless shade, and freckles added the only tint to his skin. He was far from handsome, but when his eyes turned toward her, she forgot his diminutive size.

His eyes reminded her instantly of Stephen. The same shade and as compelling, they hinted at the strength within him as well as the dream that had brought other filibusters to his side. She fought the overwhelming compulsion to curtsy, and she simply held out her hand when he stopped before her.

When he bowed over it, she murmured, "It is an honor to meet you, Mr. President."

"Yes." His eyes appraised her as if he were trying to determine how he could use her to consolidate his hold on his country. The man next to him said in a loud whisper, "Miss Arielle Gardiner, Mr. President. A visitor to our city."

"Gardiner?" Walker seemed to ruminate deeply on the single word. As Arielle fought not to squirm beneath his piercing eyes, he said, "We must speak later, Miss Gardiner."

"Yes, Mr. President." As he moved away, she remembered to add, "Thank you, Mr. President."

The aide who had identified her did not continue with the others. Pulling out a slip of paper, he, with the efficiency of bureaucrats everywhere, made a note on it and stuffed it back under his coat. "Tomorrow morning at ten, Miss Gardiner, the president will grant you an audience for a few minutes."

"Yes. Yes, thank you," she stuttered. How had President Walker discovered she wanted to talk to him? The feeling he was the quasi god his followers considered him suffocated her, but she shook off the uneasy thoughts. Rutledge Childs had told his president. Walker had not divined anything. She loathed the fact that Stephen was right yet again. She was becoming as much of a fool as the ones who had named William Walker their leader.

Her gaze followed the men as they circled the room. As soon as she could, she edged back into the foyer. Her shawl was brought quickly. She hesitated, then asked for her carriage. When it appeared, Arielle smiled sadly. Trust Stephen not to leave a clue as to where he had gone.

She leaned back against the cushions and tried to think of nothing. If she let her mind dwell on Stephen, she might not be able to keep the tears swimming in her eyes from falling. Blast that man! He had some scheme in mind now. She was as sure of that as she had been of anything. He had been looking for something when he came to the ball, and he had a reason for leaving her there. With a shiver she hoped it was not because he was tired of her.

No, she told herself, he was not tired of her. He had proven that last night and this morning when they stayed in bed long after the sun was up. With a tremble she recalled the heated caress of his fingers on her naked skin. His soft growls against her as she touched him, delighting in the hard male angles of his body, had burned on her mouth with the flame that could be quenched only in a fathomless sea of rapture. No, he had left for some other reason.

"Blast!" she grumbled, then added, "Damn!" Nothing helped relieve her frustration with his baffling actions and her need for his body moving with hers to the sumptuous melody of passion.

She had to think about Caleb now and the meeting with President Walker. She had come thousands of miles by sea, crossed hundreds of miles of horrible jungle, and endured that nearly daylong ride on the lake to get to this moment.

But it was not what she had expected. No euphoria, no eager expectations. Just a sense of relief at reaching the end of her quest in Granada . . . and a pulse of sorrow.

She wiped a vagrant tear from her face. Blast Stephen! Why did he have to put his unreasonable hatred of President Walker and his men before anything else? She longed to share the good news with him. Then he would tease her and make her laugh and make her angry and make her gloriously satiated with love, but he would not have let her shiver with dread as she did now. She wished she had some idea what he was up to.

Arielle shoved him from her mind. The best thing would be to get a good night's sleep. She must be prepared for whatever President Walker had to tell her in the morning. Her heart fluttered like a broken-winged bird as she hoped he would have good tidings for her. She could not imagine for what other reason the president wished to speak with her.

She walked slowly through the dimly lit garden of the hotel. Tonight should not have ended with her being so numb, she couldn't feel anything but fatigue.

Not even candlelight welcomed her when she opened the door. The room sprang into life when she lit a lamp. As a moth flitted through an open window to sear itself on the flame, she drew off her shawl. She clutched the silk as she stared at where Stephen's knapsack had been. It was gone!

A sob threatened to strangle her. Even when he had vanished when they first reached Granada, he had left his knapsack to let her know he would return. Now . . . She was not sure what to think. She did not want to feel anything but the consoling numbness.

She collapsed on the bed. When she recalled how she had slept there in Stephen's arms, she rolled on her back and stared at the curtains. Slow tears burned along her cheeks before they washed her into a restless sleep and dreams that had become nightmares.

Arielle stood stiffly in the antechamber of the office of Nicaragua's president. No one had offered her a seat, and she did not dare to pace. With her hands clasped in front of her, she stared out a window that was set deeply into the stucco wall. The fragrance of the flowers swept in on the warm breeze to tickle her nose.

For more than an hour she had been waiting. Before

that she had spent more time in another room beyond this one. The aide who escorted her to this one intimated that President Walker would see her soon. Soon had passed a long time ago.

She did not want to be alone with her thoughts. Rubbing her gloved hands together, she tugged at her gray velvet jacket. *Do not think about Stephen,* she had told herself over and over since she awoke before dawn. She must concentrate on Caleb this morning. Afternoon, she noted silently as she heard church bells toll midday. The chiming that wafted over the city suggested a peace that might vanish at any moment.

The door of the narrow room cracked open, and she recognized Calvin O'Neal, the president's aide who had spoken to her at the ball. "Miss Gardiner, President Walker can spare you a few moments."

Her lips tightened at his condescending tone. The president had asked her to meet with him. Despite that, his aide treated her as if she were the least supplicant to come before the prestigious and benevolent William Walker.

Brushing past him, Arielle entered the office, which resembled her library at home. Books lined the walls and were piled on the windowsills. She recalled William Walker had studied law and worked as a journalist before deciding to obtain himself a kingdom in Central America. Her eyes widened as she saw a map pinned on the wall. It was marked with boundaries that did not really exist. President Walker displayed his scheme to annex all of Central America boldly.

She forgot that as the man sitting in a chair by the window rose. Again she was shocked by his diminutive size, which contrasted with his intense eyes.

"Miss Gardiner, welcome."

"Thank you, Mr. President." As she had the night before, she fought the urge to bow. Fear broke over her. This man was a parasite. He attracted men to him and consumed their strength, will, and ultimately their lives in his unrelenting ride to glory. She must be careful he did not use her in whatever he planned next for his filibusters.

He gestured toward a chair. "Please sit. Tell me why you are visiting my country."

Not surprised he made no apology for her long wait, she perched on the very edge of the seat. Getting comfortable would be the most idiotic thing she could do. "I am here to find my fiancé."

"Caleb Drummond?"

She was astounded, then realized that his assistants had investigated her. Remembering she was in the presence of the most powerful man in Central America, she said, "Yes, sir. He asked me to come here to meet him."

"Here?"

"To Nicaragua. He worked for the Accessory Transit Company, so I have followed that route westward. I have found no sign of him, and I wondered if he might have joined your noble cause." The idea of Caleb becoming a filibuster would have been laughable except that she feared she never would find him if she sought in logical places.

The small man shook his head. "No Caleb Drummond has fought with my men, but his name is not unknown to me. . . ."

Arielle fought the temptation to fidget when his voice trailed away. President Walker's reputation for being taciturn should have warned her that she must pull every word from his mouth.

The silence lasted so long that she flinched when he spoke again. "Drummond is not one of us, and I have heard nothing of him being in Granada."

She nodded. Her lack of reaction to the news that dashed her hopes yet again surprised her more than the announcement. She had known with a sense that came from the heart and not the head that Caleb was not in Granada. Ignoring the truth had allowed her to avoid deciding what to do next. She should return to Greytown, but the same sense that told her Caleb was alive somewhere in this horrible country told her that he needed her help as she had his the day he saved her life.

President Walker said, "I understand you are not traveling alone."

"No, sir."

He leaned forward. "Well?"

"Captain Stephen Lightenfield of *The Ladysong* came with me."

"Why?"

Arielle's forehead wrinkled in bafflement. Stephen had nothing to do with Caleb. A horrid suspicion rankled her. If Stephen was involved in this somehow, that would explain his odd behavior. He had known Caleb was not in Granada. Her gloved fingers clenched. She did not understand any of this. How could she love a man who toyed with her heart so easily?

Quietly she answered, "He told me he wished to see the country beyond Greytown."

Walker nodded, but she wondered why he would ask about Stephen. If he thought he might draft Stephen to become one of his men, he would soon discover that Stephen Lightenfield answered to no master but himself.

"Very well, Miss Gardiner. I—"

The door crashed open. President Walker's lips tightened and his face paled, making his freckles more pronounced. A man raced in, shouting, "Henningsen has arrived! He has brought men and over a thousand Minié rifles. Artillery, Mr. President! He has artillery and ammunition!"

Visibly excited, Walker strode out of the room, shouting for his carriage to take him to the docks. The man followed. Arielle stared after them, unsure if she should stay or leave. She went to the door. The outer chamber was empty, but she heard enthusiastic voices from the corridor. Whoever

Henningsen was, the filibusters were thrilled he had arrived.

The tidings must have been spread through Granada on President Walker's heels. As Arielle returned to the hotel, her carriage was slowed by the press of traffic, all flowing in a human stream toward the lake. She heard excited whispers. Henningsen's name was repeated over and over.

At the hotel the usually jovial innkeeper demanded to know what Arielle had learned about the rumors of more *norteamericanos* arriving to defend the city. Then he asked her for money for the room.

She managed to end the talk of money by giving him what little information she had. Leaving him to translate for his staff, she crossed the garden. Noise battered through the thick walls to chase her to the haven of her room.

When she opened the door, Arielle stared at a shadow on the far wall. "Stephen!" she whispered before she could stop herself.

He wore the rough clothes that were stained from their trip through the jungle. They accented the strong lines of his body, sending another throb of need through her. Pushing his foot into his boot, he straightened. The odor of rum followed him as he went to the table. "I heard you had an audience with Walker this morning. I thought I would come back and get a few things I had forgotten."

"And find out what President Walker said to me." Tossing her shawl onto the settee, she shook her head. She had to dislodge the longings that urged her to forgive him for anything if he would only love her. "Not this time, Stephen Lightenfield. I am tired of being your hound dog, sniffing out information you cannot get on your own."

"What gives you that idea?"

"How did you pay off the sailor to tell me to go to

Rutledge Childs for help? I did not think you had left the saloon the whole time we were on the *Director*."

He shrugged as he stuffed a bottle of wine into the knapsack. "A couple of coins will buy all kinds of cooperation. I sent a lad to tell him what to say and to bribe him just enough so he would do it."

"What are you after?" She drew off her gloves and set them on the table. Sitting in the wicker chair, she repeated her question to his back.

"Isn't it obvious?"

"Not to me."

He chuckled. "Your habit of honesty is becoming tiresome, honey. All right, if you want the truth—"

"It might be a change."

"I wanted to see what was going on here in Granada so I could be sure to keep my ship from getting mixed up in it." With a shrug he tied his knapsack closed. "I thought it was obvious."

"And you have seen all you want to see?" She gestured toward the table. "Don't forget your hat on your way out."

Arielle had planned on a dignified exit, but Stephen caught her arm as she passed. She glared at him. He glared back.

"Don't be more of a fool than you usually are, honey," he growled.

"I was a fool to think you care about anything except your damn ship."

His eyebrows arched. "*Damn?* Such language, Madame Schoolmarm!"

"Just go if you are going."

Stephen searched her face. It was pale, and her eyes glittered with unshed tears. Cursing Walker silently, he released her arm. Arielle would not give up a battle so easily unless something else was disturbing her. He resisted putting his hand against her soft cheek. If he gave in to the craving to touch her, he would not be able to satisfy himself with no more than that gentle caress. He wanted her hair falling around him as their bodies entwined.

"What did Walker say to you?" he asked quietly.

"Nothing to endanger your ship." She picked up his knapsack and shoved it into his arms. "Why, are you worried about anything else?"

"Did he know about Drummond?"

She did not answer. With her eyes narrowing at his persistence, she crossed her arms in front of her. He tried not to think how her mouth would soften beneath his or how her fierce eyes would unfocus with rapture when he drew her into his arms. If he touched her, she would spit at him like the ship's cat.

Grumbling, he swung his knapsack to his shoulder. It was worthless to waste his breath when she was this stubborn. Striding toward the door, he reached for the knob. A pillow struck him in the back.

"Is that your way of saying good-bye?" he asked.

"Go!" Pain scored her voice. "Just go and do not come back this time."

Stephen started to retort, then faltered when a single tear rolled down her cheek. Damn woman! She could not see the truth. Something hit his knapsack and fell to the floor with a crash. He looked back to Arielle. Her upraised hand held her other boot.

"I get the message," he said quietly. He opened the door. A laugh followed him out. Dampness flowed down the back of his trousers. He saw a red stain along his pants leg and across the rug.

"Dammit!" He shrugged off the knapsack and tore it open. Lifting out the bottle of wine, he grimaced when he saw the broken bottom. He pulled out his clothes. They were soaked with red wine. "You do not have to just stand there, laughing."

"What do you expect me to do?" She pointed toward the bedroom. "If my bathwater is still in there, you had better soak those things before they are permanently red."

He pushed past her and threw the whole knapsack into the tub, ignoring the water that splashed on the floor. When he came back out into the main room, he discovered Arielle on her knees, dabbing at the carpet.

"You do not need to do that," he said.

"You won't, and the carpet will be ruined if it is not cleaned up right away. I do not want it to get ruined. I want something to stay nice." Her smile wobbled and fell as she covered her hands with her face. A shudder quaked across her shoulders as she sobbed softly.

Bending, he put his hands under her elbows and drew her to her feet. She hid her face against his shirt, wetting it with a rapid shower of tears. "Honey, are you ready to tell me now what Walker told you about Drummond?"

"Nothing."

"He would not talk to you?"

When she shook her head, her silky hair stroked his neck. An answering hunger surged within him, but he tried to ignore it as she whispered, "He talked to me. He said Caleb was not in Granada. He did not know where he might be."

"I am sorry, Arielle."

She raised her eyes, and he saw her agony glowing in them. Putting his hand against her damp cheek, he wished he could think of something to bring her scintillating smile back. He steered her mouth to his and tasted the salt from her tears on her lips. Against him her shivers of grief lessened as she leaned into his kiss. Her arms swept up his back, and she clung to him. When he raised his head, she moaned a protest.

Stephen fought his own yearning for her touch. "It is

time to leave Granada, honey. You are not going to find Drummond here."

"I know." Her fingers toyed with the button in the middle of his shirt. Another pulse of pleasure riveted him as her fingers traced a meandering pattern across his chest. "But I must keep looking. I will not leave Nicaragua until I find him."

His fingers bit into her shoulders as disbelief combated with his rage. "Are you crazy? Where are you going to look?"

"On the other shore of the lake. If he had been in Rivas, President Walker would have known. Maybe he is in Comolapan. If he is not there, I shall go north to Lake Managua."

"You have no chance of finding him in that damnable jungle."

"I have to try. I owe him that much."

With a curse he released her. He turned to look at the wall so he did not have to see the pleading in her eyes that urged him to forget common sense. "I am starting back tomorrow. Are you coming with me?"

"No."

"You are crazy!"

"Am I?" Her voice was heavy with pain as she asked, "Would you abandon one of your men here if there was a chance he might be alive?"

"I will not leave *you* here to get yourself killed." He sighed as he faced her. "We leave in the morning, honey."

"I will not—"

His arm snaked around her and jerked her against him. "Listen for once, Arielle. We—both of us—are leaving here tomorrow." When she opened her mouth, he covered it with his. She clutched his shoulders as he tasted the luscious flavors within it. Her shallow breath swirled into his mouth and through him. His voice sounded raspy as he said, "We are getting the hell out of here, honey. Walker is planning something. You could not have missed hearing about the hubbub down by the lake."

"Someone named Henningsen has arrived with more men and a lot of weapons," she murmured as she rested her head on his shoulder.

"Then it is even more important that we leave. You know what this means."

"I am not sure what anything means anymore. I do not know why Caleb has disappeared, and I do not know why he came here in the first place. I do not know why the president asked to speak to me, but he seemed more interested in you than in Caleb."

Stephen tilted her face back. "Walker mentioned me? What did his high-and-mightiness say?"

Her eyes widened at his fierce tone. "He was curious about why you came with me."

"What did you tell him?"

"The truth."

Taking her arm, he led her into the bedroom. He edged around the tub as he said, "Pack your things, honey, while I wring mine out. We are getting out of here first thing in the morning."

"Caleb—"

Again he interrupted her. "We will cross the upper part of the lake and go across to Bluefields, then south along the Mosquito coast to Greytown. If we find no sign of him by then, you shall have to accept that you are not going to find him."

She stared at him for a long while, and Stephen tensed for her next protest. Then she put her arms around him and whispered, "I don't know what I would have done if you had not come with me."

"You would have gotten yourself into almost as much trouble all by yourself."

A smile lightened her face. "Probably, and you would not have had as much fun."

"That is for sure." He laughed as he leaned her back onto the lush bed. "This has been fun, honey."

As she brought him to her, he forgot the war that was threatening the city and the reason he had come to Nicaragua. He forgot everything but the pleasure he could find deep within her, for he knew how soon it might be gone.

CHAPTER FIFTEEN

The lake matched the sky. It had started raining at dawn, and Arielle would never take being dry for granted again. Only a short stretch of the shoreline was visible in the fog. The distant crash of waves sent spray into their faces. A weak wind teased her damp skirt. It swirled the fog away before its clammy caress closed around them again. She held tightly to Stephen's hand as they walked along the warped boards connecting the city to the long pier.

He peered into the distance. "It is going to be difficult finding someone to take us across the lake today."

"No ships?"

"Nothing but the Transit steamer. That will be going to the river. We need to find someone as insane as us." He pointed to a small hut by the water. "Maybe they know someone who is interested in a little extra money."

She did not answer as she stared at the storm-swept lake. Its fury frightened her. A small boat on this churning lake could be upset easily. Tightening her grip on her bag, she followed Stephen toward the stone hut. The hem of her skirt was heavy against her legs, and the sand scoured her face. She wanted to tell him to go slower but lowered her head and hurried.

They stopped before the weathered building that could have been the twin of the tavern where he had taken her to meet Charlie. Its thatched roof was as thin, and filth tainted the sand in front of the door.

When Stephen opened the door and motioned for her to enter, she did not hesitate. She wanted to escape the storm. Two men were sitting on wooden crates in the middle of the single small room. She was not sure if the place, which was filled with the stench of fish and acrid pipe smoke, was a business or a home or both. Grimy blankets were heaped in a corner, and shelves were stacked with stained tin cups and fishing equipment.

The younger man watched them warily, but the white-haired man did not look up. He puffed on his pipe while his gnarled finger deftly repaired a net.

"We need transportation across the lake," Stephen said into the silence.

"Today?" asked the younger man.

"Today."

"You cannot be serious, señor," he replied with a disdainful smile.

Arielle recognized the condescending tone she had heard from other Nicaraguans. It had infuriated her when the innkeeper used it to her. At first she had thought he treated her like that because she was a woman. Then she had heard him use the same tone with Stephen.

Pulling a few bills from his pocket, Stephen asked, "Does this look serious enough to you?"

The young man's eyes burned with greed, but he said, "The lake is upset. He makes waves too high. I do not want to end up as dinner for the sharks. My boat stays ashore today."

Nodding his head, the grizzled man took another draft

on his pipe. A swirl of noxious smoke oozed from his nostrils.

The young man said, "Papa does not go. I do not go."

Stephen's voice remained friendly as he shrugged and stuffed the money back into his pocket. "Do you know someone else who will take us?"

"In two days I shall take you." The young man licked his lips and stared at Stephen's pocket. "Cheap, señor. Come back in two days."

"No, we want to go today. Do you know someone who will take us?"

With a snort of derision the boatman tilted the box back and leaned against the wall. "I know no one that stupid, señor."

Arielle put her hand on Stephen's arm as he tensed at the insult. Arguing would gain them nothing. Stephen had been insistent that they not spend another night in Granada. When she had asked him why, he had changed the subject to their route across the isthmus, but she had heard the strain in his voice. Stephen knew something terrible was about to happen. She wondered if Henningsen's arrival might have been a warning she could not understand. When Stephen had hurried her to the lake through the rain, she was afraid the situation was deteriorating even faster than he feared.

His eyes met hers. Their flash of frustration told her she was right. "C'mon," he muttered. "We will find someone."

The men chuckled as Stephen held the door for her. Ducking her head into the storm, she shivered, although the rain was warm. More than ever she wanted to find Caleb and leave Nicaragua. She did not want to be caught in the madness when Walker and his fanatics faced the armies raised by his enemies.

"Stephen, if all the—"

"Don't jump to conclusions." His sharp retort was softened by his smile. Slipping his arm around her shoulders, he added, "We will not know what all the boatmen will do until we ask them."

She sighed. "That may take the whole day."

"What else do we have to do?"

She did not answer as they entered the next hut. As she listened to him debating in Spanish with the men inside, she wondered how long he would accept the abuse, which was barely veiled in courtesy. His arm around her was tense with unuttered rage, although his voice remained even.

From one hut to the next they went. Most times they were simply told no, but one daring lad laughed in their faces. Only Arielle's insistence kept Stephen from teaching the boy a lesson in respect. As midday passed, she grew hungry and tired and discouraged. Her legs ached, and her clothes were wet and damp against her. She wanted to sit down and rest and have something warm to eat.

"Honey, don't look so mournful," Stephen whispered. His face was covered with the greasy mist. As his arm swept her to him, she wrapped her arms around him. Her bag struck his leg, but he said nothing as he held her. Just holding him comforted her. She did not want comfort, she realized when she looked at his mouth. She wanted the danger of loving this man who would never be tamed by any woman.

"Stephen, it is insane to cross the lake today. Let's wait for the storm to end. Then we'll go."

"If we do not go soon, I shall not be able to help you. *The Ladysong* is a strict taskmistress. I have that shipment waiting for me in New York. It has to be brought here before year's end."

"But we can wait a day or two."

He shook his head. "I should have been back in Greytown a week ago. We are going to lose more time tramping through the jungle again. I cannot afford a single extra day."

"Maybe we should . . ." She looked past him.

They were no longer alone on the foggy beach. A bent man was watching them. His clothes were cleaner than most of the boatmen's. His surprisingly fine-boned hand rose in a greeting.

"Captain Lightenfield?"

"Yes."

Arielle heard suspicion in the single word. The white-haired man walked toward them. Stepping closer to Stephen, she looked from his taut face to the other man's smile.

"I take you across the lake, señor. One dollar." The white-haired man's smile grew broader. "I go to the other side of the lake today. I hear, *mi amigo,* that you wish to go also. I go in my empty boat, or I make a dollar taking you."

"And the lady?"

He tipped his battered cap in her direction. "The lady is small. I take her for free."

Stephen grinned. "You have a full boat, then. When do you leave?"

"When you are ready, señor, señorita."

Taking Arielle's hand, he said, "We are ready now."

As the man led them to a battered pier, Arielle said nothing. How strange it was that just when she had been ready to admit this quest should come to an end, they found a way to continue. This seemed too easy. Looking up at Stephen, she saw him wink. She smiled weakly as she knew his thoughts must be identical to hers. For months she had been struggling to find Caleb. She should not question help in the guise of an old man. Maybe their luck was about to take a turn for the better.

Her hope vanished when she saw the small craft he stepped into. It was no more than a *bungo.* If she had not known better, she would have said it was the same one Miguel had piloted. Its cedar sides were held in place by small brads. At the back, a roofed area covered the engine.

Water splashed around her feet when Stephen assisted Arielle into the boat. Hiding her dismay, she sat in the middle.

Stephen went back to the *chopa* to help the boatman start the steam engine. The two men bent to work on it like novitiates before a fiery-eyed god. Arielle shivered. Once she found Caleb, she must leave this horrid country. It was too easy to be fanciful here.

Once the boat was cutting through the choppy waters, sending more spray over her, Stephen came forward to sit next to her. He winked again before pulling his hat over his eyes. She smiled. So many things had changed since they had begun their journey up the Rio San Juan. Anger had turned to love and irritation to desire. Her gaze moved along the body she knew better than her own, but she submerged the urge to touch him. Yet she wanted to sit in the arc of his embrace as she leaned her head on his chest. With a sigh she knew she must let him sleep while he could.

She could not. Even though they had slept very little during their last night in Granada, for desire had urged them to make their dreams come true while they were awake, she was too nervous to think about sleeping. The boat was so tiny and the lake so huge. If the storm worsened, she feared the boat would be swamped.

A creepy sensation crawled along her. Turning toward the stern, she found the boatman staring at her. Her eyes widened when she saw how unlined his face appeared beneath his straw hat. He was younger than she had supposed, probably no more than ten years older than Stephen.

When he motioned for her to join him by the engine, she hesitated. Stephen was snoring softly. Suddenly she knew she was being silly. The boatman had been nothing but friendly. She did not want to insult him by being rude.

Arielle stretched out her arms to keep her balance on

the rocking boat as she walked toward the stern. She sat on a low board next to the man and waited for him to speak. He said nothing. The only sound was the chugging of the boat as it slipped through the fog. Finally, to break the silence, she asked, "Do you cross the lake often?"

"Yes," he answered, his full voice booming over the rumble of the engine. "This *bungo* is a good one."

"Does it have a name?"

He chuckled. "The *bungo?* No. It's nothing more than the *bungo*. Me? I am Alfonso, señorita. It is a name that has been in my family since the first light of the first day." Checking the various dials on the engine, he asked, "And you are?"

"Arielle." When he smiled, she tried to like this man who was being so generous, but she found it difficult. Something about the way his eyes strayed along her was disquieting. She tightened her shawl around herself. "Have you been working on this lake long?"

"Many, many years."

"Do you know a man named Caleb Drummond? He worked for the Accessory Transit Company."

He rubbed his bewhiskered chin. "Why are you looking for him?"

Arielle sighed. So many times she had been asked this question, and not once had she gotten the answer she needed. "He asked me to come here. We were supposed to be married."

"Supposed?" He shot a glance at Stephen and smiled before saying, "Lots of gringos work for the Transit Company. I do not know them all."

With a strained smile she accepted defeat more gracefully than when she started on the trip. She watched the fire in the boiler. "How long before we reach the other shore?"

He returned his attention to the engine. "Soon."

"Soon?" The trip on the *Director* had taken almost a whole day.

"The road which will take you east is near the northern-most point of the lake where it nears Lake Managua. No more than a short journey, señorita." He did not look at her as he adjusted a dial. "Soon."

Arielle saw Stephen stir in the tentative sunlight seeping through the thinning fog. She murmured an excuse and went to sit next to him. She wished she could explain her sudden uneasiness but said nothing when he put his arm around her shoulders. The rhythm of the waves beneath them reminded her of the days she had worked on *The Ladysong,* and she had come to admire the captain who worked as hard as his crew.

"Do you miss *The Ladysong?*" she asked softly.

Stephen stretched his long legs over the side of the *bungo.* With a smile he said, "I will be glad to be asea again, but I never guessed a proper New England schoolmarm could be so much fun."

Ignoring his teasing, she asked, "Do you think we will find Caleb on this route?"

"Look about you." He motioned at the indistinct shadows of the distant mountains. "A million trees, a million million vines. If a man wants to remain lost, he will never be found here."

"But he wants me to find him."

"I know, honey. I know." He caressed her cheek as he tipped her face toward him. Just as he was about to kiss her warm lips, he glanced toward the stern.

"What is wrong?" she whispered. She stared to turn, but he halted her as his hands tightened on her.

"Our friend is eager to see what we are doing."

"I don't think Alfonso will be upset if you kiss me." Her hand curved around his neck. "I know I will be if you don't."

He ignored her teasing. "Alfonso? Who is that?"

"Our captain. We had a short chat while you were sleeping."

"And what did you tell him?"

Arielle gasped as his hold became painful. "Nothing! What could I have told him?"

He released her, leaning his arm on the side of the boat as he stared into the gray afternoon. "Nothing," he mumbled. "Just remember this is not New England."

"I never forget that." She shivered as she stared at the jungle ahead of them. "Not for a moment."

Despite Alfonso's optimism, it was late afternoon before they reached the muddy shore. There was no dock. A dirt path led from the water. When Stephen flashed her a grin, Arielle could not help smiling. She hoped there were no bloodsuckers there.

She did not need to worry. Alfonso ran the bow up onto the soft ground. Stephen assisted Arielle out and told her to wait on solid ground. As she stood in the lengthening shadows, Stephen spoke to Alfonso. She knew he was getting advice on the best route east.

His forehead was scored with bafflement when he climbed the small hill where she was standing. When she asked what was wrong, he shook his head and looked back to where Alfonso was pushing his *bungo* back into the lake. "I am not sure, honey. When I tried to give him an extra dollar for his directions, he refused."

"He didn't want it?" If he had said that the next morning would bring snow to the tropics, she would not have been more shocked.

"Doesn't that beat all?" He tilted his panama back and wiped his face. "He said there is shelter not far east of here."

Settling her bonnet more firmly on the back of her head, she adjusted the silk ribbons under her chin. She put her hand in Stephen's as they walked along the path that was nearly overgrown with vines. Although Stephen wore a machete on his hip, he did not use it. The path was passable. He would save his strength.

She used a skipping step that enabled her to leap over the vines clogging the road and keep up with him. Knowing she resembled a giant rabbit, she was glad that Stephen did not joke with her. She glanced around at the trees and the thickening greenery and wondered if she had lost her mind when she said she didn't want to return to Greytown on the Transit packet. So many miles were ahead of them, and each would be hard won.

Night came quickly. They did not pause to make supper from the supplies in the sack Stephen carried as they followed Alfonso's directions. The place where they could spend the night shouldn't be much farther. Arielle told herself that over and over as they trudged on and on. Stars popped into the darkening sky, but their faint light offered no help. She slapped at the annoying insects as her legs ached with every step.

When Stephen stopped, she gratefully did the same. She asked, "Are we there?"

"How the hell would I know? I think your buddy Alfonso gave us the wrong directions." He glowered at the sky.

She batted away another whining mosquito and listened to the rumble of a river that was lost somewhere in the trees. "We can go on if you want," whispered Arielle, wondering if she had the strength to take even one more step. "Maybe there is something by that river."

"No," he said. "We will not find any better place to spend the night than right here. Even if we find a village, I do not know how much welcome two gringos are going to get."

Arielle sighed as her legs folded beneath her. The spongy ground was damp, but she did not care. She just wanted to sit. Stephen sat next to her. When he leaned her back on the ground, she rested her head on his shoulder. He pulled a wide swath of mosquito netting over them.

"Where did you get this?" she asked.

"I thought I would let the innkeeper think you ripped the netting from the rings over the bed during a moment of passion." He grinned as he slipped his arm beneath her. Rising to lean over her, he ran his tongue along her lips.

She moaned his name as he traced a fiery path along her neck. Slipping her fingers beneath his ragged shirt, she stroked the rough skin on his back. Each touch, each wafting of his breath against her, each sparkle in his expressive eyes, was a separate pleasure. His fingers sought beneath her heavy skirt to meander along her leg, drawing it closer to him.

When he yawned, Arielle smiled. "I hope I am not that boring already, Captain Lightenfield."

"Not in the least, honey." He teased her ear with a swift kiss. "Sleep if you can, Arielle." The murmur of his words floated through her hair. "We are safe here, and we are going to need all our energy tomorrow."

Ruffling his mustache until he pushed her hand away and grimaced, she said, "But not all for walking, I hope."

"Not all for walking," he repeated with a grin.

"Do you want supper?"

"Are you hungry?" he asked through another yawn.

"No." That was a lie. She was starved, but she doubted she had the energy to eat.

He chuckled as he nestled her closer to him. "Much, much better."

His fingers moved along her side to graze her breast. When she whispered his name with the yearning that only grew each time he touched her, he smiled. He did not kiss her. He did not speak. He just ran a single fingertip along her breast, teasing its tip through her chemisette.

Her hands clenched on his shoulders. Shivers, hot and

moist, raced through her, setting every inch of her ablaze. "Kiss me," she whispered.

"Are you sure that is what you want?"

With a groan she pushed him onto his back. She leaned across his chest and sampled his smile. "This is what I want."

"So do I, honey. So do I." His laugh drew her into an ecstasy only they could share.

Lying in his arms, Arielle stared at the stars. As exhausted as her body was, her mind chased the renewed puzzle of Caleb's disappearance. She wished she could understand this—why he wanted her to come to Nicaragua, why he had vanished from his job, why he had changed his mind about longing to come home.

She understood the fascination that had drawn the filibusters to this magnificent land. Somewhere in the tangled undergrowth Caleb waited. Somehow she would find him. Then . . . She did not know what would happen then.

Stephen would return to *The Ladysong*. She closed her eyes to shut out the image of saying farewell to him. Yet there was no place in his life for her. Tears welled into her eyes, but she would not let them fall as she drifted into an apprehensive sleep. Her nightmares were filled by monstrous demons that chased her and tried to separate her from the man she loved.

Arielle stumbled after Stephen. It seemed as if she had spent her whole life in this nightmare land. Breaks between the trees were filled with rocks and debris that threatened to slice through her boots. The sweaty stickiness of her shirt clung to her body. Slimy beads coursed along her face, tracing slick lines in the dirt.

They had reached the river the previous morning to find it impassable. Following its rushing waters past the rapids and down a treacherous descent by a cataract, they discovered gentler waters and had managed to ford it. Their wet clothes had dried slowly as they fought the cloying heat.

The night before, they had slept under the stars again. Although they were nearly too exhausted to eat, Arielle worried about the small amount of food remaining in Stephen's knapsack. They had planned to purchase food as they wandered from village to village, but they had not found a village.

When Stephen put out his hand to block her way, Arielle asked, "What is it?"

"I'm not sure."

She peered through the trees to see a half dozen huts clustered in a clearing. "A village?"

"That is what it looks like."

"Where are the people?"

"That is what I'm wondering." He handed her the machete and pulled his pistol from his belt. "Keep your eyes open. Something is wrong here."

Arielle eased through the bushes after him. Her dress ripped more when she pulled it off a bramble. When Stephen scowled at the shriek of ripping cloth, she ignored him. She was doing the best she could.

The village was deserted. When Stephen called out a greeting, no one answered. Arielle stayed close to him as they explored the huts. Dishes waited on the floors. Pallets were stacked in corners.

When they saw a rifle propped against one door, Stephen lifted it and sniffed the barrel. "It has been fired recently. The gunpowder still stinks in it."

"Do you think there was some kind of sickness?"

"No, bodies would remain." His boot tried to erase something in the dirt.

"What is that?"

"Nothing. Let's go, Arielle."

She knelt and outlined the pattern that had been dug deeply into the ground. "Doesn't this mean Old Ones?"

He jerked her to her feet. "Let's get the hell out of here. This place gives me the shivers."

"Stephen?" she gasped. "What does it mean?"

He did not pause until a clump of trees blocked the village from view. He glanced over his shoulder. "You know damn well what it means. Someone is using lies and superstitions to scare the people around here away."

"Lies?"

"There are more stories among these trees than you could imagine, honey. The most fantastic ones reach Greytown, where they are retold in exchange for a few pennies."

She persisted. "But who are the Old Ones?"

Taking the machete, he chopped into the vines ahead of them. "I am not exactly sure. They appear in the stories as devils and as angels. Gods and demons. All wise and unforgiving. Givers of pain and pleasure."

"But is there any truth in the stories?"

He turned to her, but no smile tilted his lips. "All I know is that I want to get out of this jungle before I have to find out."

CHAPTER SIXTEEN

The next day of their journey began as the last had ended. Walking into the rising sun, Arielle was glad for Stephen's help as they scrambled across the treacherous terrain. The darkness of worry weighed his lips in a perpetual frown. Hours passed while she prayed that night and the chance to rest would come soon. As the sun soared past its zenith and began its descent, they climbed a steep ridge.

Arielle did not notice Stephen had paused until she bumped into him. His steadying arm kept her on her feet as she stared at what was waiting on the other side of the hill. A gasp of astonishment wrenched her from her exhaustion.

Surrounded by the jungle on every side, the valley was naked. Ash covered rocks and stumps of trees. In the center stood a dominating mountain. From its peak, a plume of smoke climbed to merge with the clouds.

"Damn," Stephen said. "If we go around, it will take us the better of two days."

"And if we go across?"

He laughed. "And to think I once accused you of being a coward!" He sobered as he stared at the alien landscape. "We would be in real trouble if it starts erupting when we are halfway across."

As if to emphasize his warning, the ground shook under her feet. She grabbed Stephen's arm as rocks clattered down the hill.

"What is that?" she cried.

"Just a small tremor."

Her eyes widened when she saw his grim smile. Was he teasing her again? She took a deep breath. Turning back would be the smart thing to do, but she said, "We are a good distance from the cone. It cannot be more than one or two miles across the valley."

"Optimistic, aren't you, honey?" He shaded his eyes as he gauged the distance. "At least three miles and damn tough terrain."

"So what do you want to do? Go around or across?"

"How about admitting defeat and going back?"

"No!" She did not want him to guess she had been thinking the same thing.

He faced her, his lips drawn so tightly, white puckered at the corners. "I do not intend to die for your quest." He pointed to the volcano. "You do not even know if Caleb is on the other side of that monster. Crossing those wastelands is too damn risky under the best of circumstances. Without a guide and in the dark—"

"It's not dark."

"It will be before we are across." He gripped her shoulders. "Arielle, for once in your life, use your head. You have done your best."

She tugged away. "Caleb is in trouble. If I do not help him, who will?"

Arielle ignored his curses. Tightening her hold on her bag, she went down the hill. She looked back. Stephen was watching her, a frown lengthening his face. Blast him! When was he going to understand that she could not turn her back on this obligation?

She screeched as her foot slipped on the steep surface. She slid, desperately grabbing for a bush, but her fingers clutched only the air. Grass rolled in a green-brown avalanche beside her. She hooked an arm around a rock. Her body shrieked with pain, but she hung on. Dirt and pebbles pelted her, but she closed her eyes and rested her head on the stone.

Gentle hands settled on her shoulders. Raising her head, she loosened her grip to put her hand in Stephen's. He brought her slowly to her feet. She waited for his mocking jest, but he said nothing as he brushed twigs off her torn skirt. She winced when he touched new bruises.

"Hold on," he ordered as he inched down the hillside.

Arielle nodded. As he did, she dug her feet into the soft soil. Despite her efforts, her feet slipped on the layers of damp leaves. Each step resurrected odors of rot.

When they reached the floor of the valley, a tempest of ashes rose to cling like fuzz to her sweaty skin. Trying to wipe it off was futile. She just made it stick more stubbornly. When she looked at Stephen, she laughed, for even his mustache wore a furry covering.

"What is so funny?" he asked.

"You. I could not imagine you before as an old and hoary sea captain, but I can now."

He ran his fingers through his light hair, sending a cascade of ashes on her. As he helped her across the uneven ground, she was pleased his smile had returned. After two days of his dark moods, it was as if the sun had emerged to light their path.

And they would need any hint of sunshine. Strange formations created inexplicable shadows. Rock had frozen where it had been thrown or carried along on a river of lava. Everything smelled of sulfur and other hot, distasteful aromas. She grimaced as she bumped her ankle against the porous rock, scraping it. She did not complain as blood trickled along her ripped stocking. If she opened her mouth, she might admit Stephen was right . . . again.

When they edged around a cluster of rocks, which was taller than the cathedral in the central square of Granada, Arielle stared at the mountain. Molten lava oozed from a crevice high in the cone. Its reddish glow rivaled the sun, which was sinking beyond the ridge. Sparks burned eye-scorchingly bright as huge chunks of rock were tossed like jetsam.

"Look at that!" she whispered, awe silencing her.

"Quite a sight."

"Do you think the volcano will erupt?"

"You are asking the wrong man. Ask me about the sea, and I can give you an answer, but I have never needed to know much about volcanoes." He put his arm around her shoulders. "Let's keep going, honey. I want to get out of this Hades before Lucifer decides to put in an appearance."

"To collect your soul?"

He grinned. "I am not ready to relinquish it yet." He twirled her into his arms, paying no attention to the ashes flying from her skirt. With his eyes twinkling as malevolently as a demon's, he added, "I will not let him take my soul until I have had my fill of you, honey."

He captured her lips with his, which were as heated as the liquid rock sizzling and snapping in the distance. The craving for his kisses and caresses erupted through her with the power of the volcano. Since the night they had left Granada, they had done no more than mumble a good night after a chaste kiss. She wanted his arms about her as they sampled ecstasy.

"Soon," he whispered, reluctantly releasing her.

Arielle nodded and clung to that promise as she tagged after Stephen. Although he had shortened his paces, every step was more difficult than the previous one. A piece of ash had slipped into her boot. With nowhere to sit and remove the boot, she limped after Stephen across the hot ground. She vowed that she would never complain again about the insects, the heat, or the vines. Traipsing through the jungle would seem easy after this.

In the last light she saw how foolishly naive she had been. Directly in their path a crevice in the earth appeared, smoke billowing out to choke her. They would have to retrace their steps to the ridge and go around. Her heart sank. It had taken hours to get this far.

When Stephen peered through the smoke, she cried, "What are you doing?"

"It is not that wide." Coughs exploded from him. Wiping his watering eyes, he lurched back to her. He smiled. "Do you want to dance, honey, before we cross that hole?"

Arielle stared at him, then laughed as she realized she was rocking from one foot to the other to keep from being burned by the heat seeping through the ground. "You are crazy!"

"I can jump it. You can too."

"No!" Her smile vanished. "You are crazy if you think I am going to do something stupid like that."

"We do not have time to argue. It is nearly dark. We have to keep going. That means jumping this crevice."

"Stephen, I cannot jump that in this heavy skirt. If—"

"You've always done what you had to, honey."

"Stephen—"

"You have to." He held out his hand. "C'mon."

Knowing to try this was insane, she followed him closer to the chasm. He bent so his eyes were level with hers and pointed to where the opposite edge was barely visible through the smoke. She nodded, trying not to choke on the caustic fumes. Her eyes pricked with smoke and heat.

"Give me your bag," he ordered. "It is only about four

feet across. Get a running start. Just hike up your skirt and you will sail across."

"All right." When he started to turn away, she put her hand on his sleeve. She wondered how his arm could be rock steady when her fingers quivered. "Be careful."

"Always am, honey."

He motioned for her to back away. She slid her feet against the hot earth and watched him gauge the crevice. With a wave he leapt through the smoke. Her hands clenched as she waited for his shout. When she heard him call to her, she closed her eyes and whispered a prayer of gratitude. Relief became fear. Now it was her turn.

"Jump!" he called.

She stared at the steaming crevice. The lava must be close to the surface. To fall would mean being cooked alive. Stephen shouted again.

"I do not know if I can jump that far," she called back.

"You can, honey!" He held out his hands. "Trust me, Arielle."

Her fear thawed as if the fire beneath her feet had climbed to her heart. Once when Stephen spoke of trust, she had laughed. That had changed. She could trust him. She had to trust him now.

She kept her eyes on his outstretched hands, knowing they would enfold her if she could reach them. Her boots slapped the rock, blinding her in a storm of ashes. When she leapt, time slowed to a standstill. She stretched her hands toward his. She waited and waited for a thousand lifetimes as their fingers came closer. His hands caught hers, and a sob ripped through her as she clung to him.

"I told you that you could do it," he murmured into her hair as he stroked her trembling shoulders. He tilted her chin, and he smiled. "You are quite a woman, Arielle."

"I nearly was a scorched one."

"Nearly. We make a good team."

She steered his mouth to hers, wanting to touch him,

to be sure that they both had survived again. As his breath swirled in her mouth, as hot as the ground beneath her, she pressed closer. In his arms she had found safety and insanity. She wanted both.

Arielle pulled away with a scream when the ground moved under them again. Stephen grasped her hand. She lifted her skirts and ran. With a roar the ground broke in front of them. She did not pause as they jumped over it. Rocks tumbled into their path. Her side ached as she fought to breathe. The brief tropical twilight vanished. Darkness swelled up around her. Only when Stephen slowed did she realize they had reached the sanctuary of the trees.

She leaned against one, her hand clutching her heaving side. The luminous landscape behind them appeared more hellish in the darkness. Red lines marked the crevices where the blood of the earth was bubbling out.

"I do not want to do that again," she wheezed.

Stephen chuckled as he dropped his knapsack and her bag. They were covered with gray ash, which had bleached to white in the darkness. "It was fun though."

"Fun?" She shook her head in resignation. "I think you could find fun at your own funeral, Stephen."

Brushing the top of her hair, he said, "Let's put a few more miles between us and the River Styx." He added in a husky whisper, "I wish we could find a place where I could order a tub of water to wash you clean."

A surge of longing weakened her knees, but wishes were worthless when the jungle was unbroken by a village. She soon discovered that trying to walk through the darkness was dangerous. Tripping over vines and stones they could not see, they paused less than a mile into the jungle. If the mountain blew up, they would not be safe within a dozen miles.

She used the last of their bread and rice to prepare a skimpy supper. She said nothing about their desperate state. Stephen knew. Somehow they would find a way to survive. They had not come this far to give up.

They ate, and exhaustion overtook her, making each word harder to form than the one before it. When they were finished, she cleaned the dishes with broad leaves she plucked, while he made them a bed beneath the trees.

A strange feeling pricked the back of Arielle's neck. She gasped, pointing skyward, "Stephen! Look!"

"I'll be damned." His words oozed from him in awe as the moon rose.

Its cold glow was bluer than a midsummer day. The strange blue-gray light turned their faces the shade of death.

Arielle whispered, "I thought 'Once in a blue moon' meant never. I thought a blue moon was impossible."

"I had heard about this, but I never believed it." He chuckled to break the primitive wonder holding them captive.

"Do you think the volcano causes it?"

He shrugged. "Who knows? It doesn't seem dangerous, so let's go to sleep."

"Are you sure?"

"Why should we be frightened by the moon?" He laughed as he drew her to him.

She savored his kiss in the moment before she fell asleep, hoping that the morrow did not bring more surprises.

"Arielle?"

At Stephen's whisper, she mumbled, "Just a few minutes more. It cannot be morning yet." Her aching legs recalled the long miles they had walked.

"Arielle!" His voice became more urgent. "Wake up!"

"It cannot be morning." She rolled onto her back and opened her eyes. A stone-tipped spear was inches from her nose. A scream ached in her throat as her eyes followed

the shaft to the scowl far above her. Wrenching her gaze
from the strangely painted face of the nearly naked man
holding the weapon, she moved nothing but her eyes as
she looked at Stephen.

He was surrounded by more men armed with the same
type of primitive lances. One man pulled Stephen's gun
from his belt. He handed it cautiously to another man,
who slid the pistol into his loincloth. A third man grabbed
Stephen's machete and raised it.

"No!" she cried. "Stop!"

The man laughed as he tossed the knife away. She
flinched at the crash.

The spear jabbed at her. Stephen knocked the weapon
away. "Leave her alone!" he snapped. "She is unarmed."
He repeated the words in Spanish.

A man shouted back at him.

"What did he say?" Arielle asked.

Stephen shrugged. "I don't know. It's not English or
Spanish. Who the hell are they?"

Arielle did not have a chance to answer. Hands grasped
her arms and jerked her to her feet. When she stumbled
forward, arms encircled her. She bit back her screech when
she realized Stephen was holding her. She pressed against
him as the men ripped apart their packs and tossed the
contents aside. She put her hand to her breast. Against
her heart, Caleb's letter was safe . . . as long as she lived.

Stephen stepped in front of her as the men looked
eagerly at the captives. Their eyes glittered with evil anticipation.

The man who had Stephen's gun walked toward them.
He was taller than his companions and could meet Stephen's eyes evenly. His smile pulled his painted lips back
across his teeth. He poked his spear at Stephen. When
the blond man did not react, he shouted something. The
others laughed.

"Don't do anything, honey," Stephen muttered through

clenched teeth. His hand settled over hers. "Just wait and see what they want."

The man turned to her. He snapped an order.

"No! Stephen!" she shrieked when she was pulled away from him.

A half dozen spears pointed at him, and he did not move. Even in the dark she could see the fury blazing in his gray eyes. She moaned as her bonnet was ripped off. The man smiled sadistically as he motioned toward her hair.

"I do not understand," she whispered.

She heard Stephen curse when the man plucked a pin out of her hair. Slowly she drew out the last few. Her tangled hair dropped heavily along her back. Grasping a handful, he examined it. She did not dare to protest as she tried not to think what he might order her to do next. He gripped her face and tilted her head at a painful angle. When she gasped, he shoved her away. She fell to her knees.

"Arielle!" Stephen tried to push past his captors.

"I am all right," she lied. "Don't!" She put out her hand to halt him before the warriors used those deadly lances.

Another warrior pulled her to her feet. Horror clamped its cold fingers around her throat as the leader walked around her, examining her from every angle. She looked past him. When Stephen mouthed two words at her, she was sure her heart had forgotten how to beat.

Old Ones!

She wanted to shout that this was no time for joking, but she knew he was serious. These men might be the ones who had inspired the terror along the river and through the mountains.

Arielle screamed as a spear rose behind Stephen. He whirled to his attacker, but another man struck him with the butt of his spear. Stephen fell to the ground. With an exultant cry the warrior lifted the weapon to drive its tip through him.

"No!" she shrieked. "Don't kill him!"

Slowly the warrior lowered the lance to his side. An order was snapped by the man with the gun. The warrior started to lift his spear. Then, looking at Arielle, he turned away from Stephen.

Rage filled the leader's voice. As the warrior argued, pointing toward her, Arielle saw Stephen lifting his head. She started to step toward him, but her captor's massive hand settled on her arm.

Glaring at her, the leader snarled an order that needed no translation. If she moved, Stephen would die. As the men argued, lighter bands of gray brightened the eastern sky. In the thinning shadows she could see more than a score of men. Fear flashed through her when she saw ashes on the warriors' sandals. The men had tracked them from the volcano. Sickness churned in her stomach.

Stephen sat. A poke with the butt of the spear that had hit him urged him to his feet. "Have they hurt you, honey?"

"No." Arielle winced as her captor tightened his grip on her arm but added, "They have been following us. Who are they?"

He shrugged. "Old Ones, maybe, or . . ." He swore when a sharp point in his back warned him to remain silent.

The leader shouted. A shove propelled Arielle toward Stephen. She grabbed his hand and drew his arm around her. Raising her chin, she met the leader's fury with quiet defiance. She was not going to let them kill Stephen, and she would not die without a fight.

Her aching legs protested each step as they left the clearing. The bare trickle of sunshine offered little light, and she stumbled on the vines clogging the path. When they turned north and west, she wanted to weep tears of discouragement. So hard she and Stephen had struggled to come this far, and now they were being herded back toward Lake Nicaragua.

When her hand was squeezed, she looked up at Stephen. His gray eyes were twin storms of fury, but he whispered, "Don't worry, honey. This is just a side trip."

She struggled to maintain the pace set by their captors past the fallen trees and rocks covered with greenery, but she started to falter. She clung tighter and tighter to Stephen's hand as she fought to lift her feet until she could go no farther. Stephen tugged on her, but she shook her head. The man behind her pushed her forward a few steps, but she planted her feet. He shouted to the leader, who shrieked an order.

Exhaustion gave her courage. She said, as if to a dim-witted child, "If you do not have the decency to cut a path for me, I am not going any farther."

Arielle heard stifled laughter, but she did not look at Stephen. She was not sure what he found funny about this horrible situation.

A man advanced on her. He pulled a knife from the woven belt of his loincloth. Too tired to care, she stared at the blade that was longer than her forearm. No one spoke as the leader glared at her.

Grumbling, the man pushed past her and began to chop the vines. When a hand settled on her shoulder, she did not turn. Stephen's pleasure at her small victory would add to the fear twisting her stomach. Maybe he did not realize what she was discovering.

She was not sure why, but the men acceded to her demands. The leader wanted Stephen dead, but her protest had negated his orders. Why would they listen to her? Terror stroked her with its evil caress. She wanted nothing to do with these men or whatever they planned for her or Stephen.

When the leader followed the man clearing away the vines, she did not wait for the inevitable shove forward.

She gripped Stephen's hand and wondered how much longer they would listen to her. A single misstep, and both she and Stephen might die.

Arielle lost track of time as they followed a path only the leader could see. She kept hoping he would signal for a halt, but they continued in silence. The hushed waters of a river sounded in the distance. Defeat crushed her as she wondered if it was the same river she and Stephen had crossed. Rain dripped from the sky in an endless drizzle. She lost any idea how long they had been walking. It could have been hours or years.

A shout tore Arielle from her lethargy. She looked about in fear. She was grabbed away from Stephen. He launched himself past the man holding her and propelled her to the ground. Pain slapped her. She heard a scream.

"Don't move," Stephen whispered.

"I—I ca-cannot breathe," she called in desperation. "Please, Stephen!"

He moved slightly, but he refused to let her rise. Dampness seeped into her clothes. A man did not stop shrieking. She cried out when Stephen was yanked away. Hands forced her onto her back. A lance pressed its needle-sharp tip between her breasts. When she started to move, it jabbed her, ripping her chemisette. She sagged against the earth, unable to see where Stephen was.

Fingers lifted her skirt and ran along her leg. She screamed, "Stephen!"

"Don't move, honey," he shouted. "Just—" His words ended in a puff of pain.

The leader squatted next to her. Grasping her left arm, he examined it. He stretched across the unmoving lance to do the same with her other arm. When he reached for the buttons on her chemisette, she knocked his hand away.

"Don't touch me!" she spat out.

As if she had not spoken, he loosened the buttons on her collar.

"Stop!"

He batted her hands aside and growled something. The lance pricked her again, and she sagged against the ground. When his fingers moved along her neck and shoulders, she saw the cold shimmer in his eyes. He was enjoying forcing her to submit to his barbaric rites.

When he rose, she hastily redid her collar buttons. He chortled at her modesty. Another man made a comment, and their captors roared with appreciative laughter. A flush heated her cheeks, and she tried again to sit.

The leader snapped a single word. Ignoring him, she reached up to push away the spear. He smiled coldly and snapped his fingers. Another man appeared. He held out his hands.

Arielle screamed in mindless terror. A snake! Its fangs shone in the dim light. She clawed the ground to escape. She screamed again when he pushed it closer to her.

Stephen shouted, "It is dead, Arielle! They just want to be sure you were not bitten."

Blinking hard, she tried to clear the fear from her eyes as she looked at the leader's smile. He had wanted to terrify her. She watched his painted face twist with a smile as the dead creature was tossed away. His fingers touched her hair, which was tangled with leaves.

"No!" she cried. "Leave me alone!"

"Don't fight him, Arielle," Stephen called. "Don't make him kill you."

The leader's ebony eyes twinkled as his hand moved across her cheek in a tight spiral. The other men fell to their knees and repeated the low words he spoke. They did not see Stephen lock eyes with her captor. She held her breath as neither man moved. Their hatred hung between them as thick as a fog over the lake.

Another scream shattered the silence. Arielle leapt to her feet. The leader grasped her arm. She tried to tug away. With a malicious chuckle he whirled her to look in the other direction.

She pressed her hand to her mouth as she saw a man writhing on the ground. One of his legs had swollen to twice the size of the other. The leader gave a terse command and shoved Arielle toward Stephen. He drew a knife. She choked as he emotionlessly drew the knife across the wounded man's throat. Blood spurted everywhere. She hid her face against Stephen's chest.

"I am going to be sick," she whispered.

"They did the only humane thing. He would have died anyhow."

"And will they kill us so humanely?"

He stroked her back. "I don't think we have to worry about that. They want us alive."

"For what? To torture us? To make us slaves? To—"

He drew her closer. "Don't panic. Save your strength for when we can escape."

"Can we?" She searched his face to see if he was telling her the truth.

"We are going to try." A corner of his mouth tilted in a hint of his roguish smile. "Just be patient, honey."

Arielle almost laughed. Patience? She didn't have any. If she had, she would have been willing to wait in Concord—Greytown—or Granada—for Caleb to come to her. Then they would be safe. Now they might become, as Stephen had warned her from the beginning, just another lost legend swallowed by the jungle.

CHAPTER SEVENTEEN

Arielle stared at the nameless river. Storm clouds obscured the sun, so she had no idea in which direction they were traveling. Two days had passed since their capture by these strange warriors. They had journeyed deeper and deeper into the jungle. After the first day she and Stephen had been kept separated. She was constantly surrounded by five or six warriors.

She checked over her shoulder. Stephen appeared out of the vine-tangled bushes. Although the leader had made no more threats to either of them, she knew he had not changed his mind. He wanted Stephen dead and . . . She still had no idea what they intended to do with her.

When she was shoved forward, she fought to keep her precarious perch on the bank. Groping at the web of vines, she stared at the water cascading over the boulders. She stumbled forward, praying the journey would be over and fearing what awaited them at its end.

The familiar terror settled on her. An explosion between the leader and Stephen was inevitable. She could see that when Stephen's gray eyes met the leader's raven ones. The leader wanted vengeance on Stephen for daring to ignore his orders.

A moan of despair slipped from her lips as she saw the leader step onto one of the rocks at the edge of the river. He intended for them to cross the wide expanse. She shook her head as she looked at the roiling water. The rapids on the Rio San Juan had been like this, and she nearly had drowned there.

"No," she whispered, "I can't."

Stephen shoved past the two largest warriors to put his hand on her arm. The tatters of his shirt slapped her as he growled a warning to the men who tried to push him away from her. "Can't you imbeciles see she is scared?" He lowered his voice. "Honey, you are going to have to try."

"I don't know if I can." She closed her eyes, which burned with tired tears.

He brushed her hair back from her face and drew her head down onto his shoulder as he called to the leader. He spoke in English but added the primitive sign language he used on the few occasions he had to speak to their captors. "Arielle cannot cross. She does not know how to swim."

The leader pointed to the opposite bank.

"No," Stephen argued. "The water is too fast. She cannot cross."

The leader shrieked an order. The warriors grasped Stephen's arms. He swung at them. Arielle grabbed on to a tree when her feet slipped again. He was dragged away from her.

"Don't hurt him!" When she tried to follow, the leader caught her and pulled her back. She screamed, and her arms flailed as she fought to keep her balance on the edge of the bank.

Laughter battered her ears. She clutched the leader's

wrist with both hands. Gritting her teeth, she vowed she would not be the only one to die in the mad waters if he shoved her in.

Stephen ripped his arm out of one man's grip and struck the other. The man dropped with a groan. He whirled, shouting Arielle's name, but paused as he faced a half dozen spears. He raised his fists to knock them aside, then froze when his eyes met hers. Viciously he cursed as the leader laughed.

"Arielle, hold on!"

"What do you think I am doing?" she called back, hysterical laughter bitter in her throat.

Stephen's eyes burned with impotent rage as the warriors herded him toward the river. The leader drew her back upon the bank and released her. Wrapping her arms around herself, she turned her back on him to watch Stephen. The leader strode past her and jumped down from the bank.

Stephen was shoved after him. He slid. Her scream brought an answering shout that he was safe. When she saw Stephen standing on the rocks not far from the leader, she tried to guess what the men were saying to each other in the rapidly improvised sign language. Their broad motions announced their loathing for each other.

"Arielle," Stephen called, "he assures me you will be safe."

"And you believe him?" she cried.

"We don't have much choice."

Her shoulders sagged as she was led toward where Stephen waited. The furious water foamed about the rocks, but a zigzag path of boulders led to the opposite shore. Stephen ignored the spears poking at him. He reached up and put his hands on her waist. Carefully he lifted her down to the first rock. His hands encircled her face.

"Honey, you will be all right. You can do this."

She wanted to choke back that she didn't want to do it,

but, when he gave her a crooked grin, she smiled back. "This will be fun, right?"

"Right." He took her hand to help her to the next rock.

The shaft of a spear struck his arm, knocking him away from her. He dropped to one knee. His hand reached for his belt, then clenched with fury as the leader snapped an order. Two men leapt down between Arielle and the other men. When he rose, blood stained the ragged knee of his trousers. He rubbed his arm.

"It's not broken," he said before she could speak the dread washing over her as fiercely as the water over the rocks.

Arielle's captors motioned for her to follow as the men started across the rocks. She watched where the man in front of her walked and tried to put her feet exactly where he had his. Water splashed over her boots and soaked the hem of her skirt. She held her arms out to keep her balance. With Stephen's encouragement she moved forward. All she could hear was her frantic heartbeat and the crash of the water. Keeping her eyes on the rocks, she concentrated on each step. When the man in front of her jumped to a stone that was farther from the next, she hesitated. The gap was not as wide as the chasm on the volcanic plain. Taking a deep breath, she leapt.

Her boots fought for a foothold, but the rock was slick. She heard shouts. She shrieked Stephen's name. Arms reached for her as she fell. Water closed over her, sucking her down. Thrashing, she tried to fight her way to the surface. She had to breathe. Her hands broke the water, and she forced her face upward. She swallowed more water than air.

The swift current spun her. She was thrown against a sharp rock. Water cascaded down her throat as she screamed. From her ripped fingers blood flowed into the water. She clawed her way up the rock until her head was above water. She gulped fresh air. A wave slapped her face.

Strands of hair blinded her, and jagged shards of pain sliced through her from where her shoulder had struck the rock.

Arguing voices drifted toward her over the roar of the water, but she leaned on the stone and thought only about her good fortune. She was still alive!

An arm reached around her waist and tugged on her. She shook her head as she stared at one of the warriors. He floated so close to her that his breath was hot on her cheeks. She was not going to let go of this rock. It was the only thing keeping her from drowning.

The warrior tied a rope around her waist. When he tapped on her cheek and motioned with his head toward the rocks where Stephen stood with the others, she shook her head vehemently. He plucked her fingers from the rock. She moaned in horror as the current tugged against her skirt. When she tried to hold on to the boulder, he slapped her fingers away. He twisted her head.

Arielle gasped when she saw that the other end of the rope was being held by the men standing on the stones. The man wrapped his arm around her waist and let the others pull both of them toward the rock bridge. Arielle winced as she struck another boulder. When she heard what was undeniably a curse from the man holding her, she longed to smile vindictively, but she had no strength.

Every muscle ached when she was lifted out of the water. She was deposited into waiting arms. Familiar arms, she realized with a sigh of relief.

"Are you all right?" Stephen asked as he had so often since they'd been captured.

"I thought you said this would be fun." She leaned her head on his shoulder as the rope was untied. Water ran along her back from her hair, and her drenched skirt flapped heavily against Stephen's legs.

"It is. Just not for us."

She had not thought she could smile when she had

come so close to death, but she did. Stephen's bizarre
sense of humor was the only thing between her and panic.
She needed its warmth to cocoon her from the terror
around her.

Stephen lurched forward to a sharp order. She gasped
when her aching shoulder was shoved into his chest.

"You bastards!" he snarled.

The leader blinked but pointed for them to continue
across the river. He chortled his aggravating laugh when
Stephen did not place Arielle back on her feet.

"I am all right," she whispered. She was certain the
leader understood both Spanish and English. She didn't
care why they continued their mumbo jumbo.

"I will not drop you."

She smiled weakly. "I know." Truthfully she wanted to
stay in his arms. With her head on his shoulder, she savored
the sensation of his strong muscles moving against her as
he stepped from stone to stone. Only when they reached
the far shore did he set her on the ground.

He held out his hand to her. Arielle started to put her
left hand in it, then winced as her scraped fingers burned.
She tried to ignore the pain as she took his hand with her
right one. Every inch of her ached. Her scraped face was
wet with water and blood. When Stephen smiled at her,
she saw the sympathy in his eyes. A few scratches would
be the least of her worries if those spears were turned on
them.

The leader maintained the rapid pace. With the trees
more thinly spaced on this side of the water, Arielle found
walking a bit easier. She watched for the shadows that
signaled the coming of night. Along her left hand the
scorching pain was climbing to merge with the throbbing
in her shoulder. She did not know how much farther she
could go.

The leader called for a stop when they reached a clearing

that seemed no different from any other they had passed. Dropping to sit, Arielle stared at her sore palm numbly.

When Stephen brought over the food doled out to them in one bowl, he asked, "Honey, are you hurt?"

She shook her head. "I just scraped my hand. I am going to look like a patchwork quilt by the time we get to wherever we are going."

"Did you get hurt in the river?"

"Yes! I told him I could not do it!" Tears bubbled into her eyes. "I could have drowned."

"But you didn't." He set the bowl on the ground as he knelt beside her. Carefully he lifted her hand. It was crisscrossed with scratches and lines of dried blood. He ignored them as she had, for both of them were covered with a grotesque pattern of scrapes and bruises. Folding her fingers between his, he said, "Stay strong, Arielle. It is the only way we can survive this."

"I wish I knew who they are."

"They are pretending to be Old Ones." He picked up their food bowl. He swept out the bugs in it and held it up to her. As she dipped her fingers into the mush, he said, "Their costumes and the way they have their faces painted match the descriptions of the Old Ones. But they are not phantoms." Rubbing his knuckles, he smiled grimly. "That was living flesh I hit."

Arielle grimaced at the bitter taste of the food. She had no idea what it might be, but her hunger warned her not to be fussy. "I do not care what they are. I just wish I knew why they stalked us through the jungle and took us prisoner."

"I don't."

"You don't?" she asked, startled.

He shook his head. "We are going to find out soon enough. Right now I am just glad to be inside my skin." His eyes twinkled with mischief. "I would rather be inside your skin, honey."

Warmth rushed over her, sweeping aside the cold of fear. She put her fingers on the soft tawny hair on his arm. "I need you to hold me tonight, Stephen. Last night I was so scared, I could not sleep. I thought they were going to kill you."

"I did too." He chuckled and leaned her against him as he stretched out on the damp ground. "We shall find a way out of this somehow. We have managed to escape everything else in this jungle."

"And then what?"

His eyes widened at her soft question, but Arielle had to ask it. She loved him. He wanted her in his arms and his bed, but not once had he spoken to her of love. If he had to choose between his ship and her, she was not sure which he would choose. She wanted it to be her.

For a long while, he was silent. The mumbles of their captors drifted to them, but she thought only of why Stephen was not answering her.

"Arielle," he said, "I know what you want me to say, but this is the wrong time. I could make you every promise your heart yearns to hear. Then you would think I am sure our captors are going to kill us. I could tell you how my life is on the sea, meeting each day with a zest for adventure, and you would be certain that I do not want you as part of it."

"Do you?"

"Ask me when I am sure there is going to be a tomorrow to share with you." His voice lightened. "Get some sleep, honey. Don't think about our friends tonight."

She sighed. Badgering Stephen would be a waste of time, and she truly did not want him to fill her head with platitudes and promises that he couldn't keep. She must, as she had from the moment she first had faced him aboard *The Ladysong,* think only of the joy of this moment. But there was nothing joyous about it.

Stroking his cheek, she whispered, "I'm so scared."

"You would be a fool not to be."

She smiled. "Captain Lightenfield, are you afraid?"

His chuckle was too low to reach their captors. "These men are lunatics. Only another crazy man would be unafraid of them."

"You haven't answered my question."

"Does that mean you think I am insane?" His mouth near her ear warmed her with the caress of his breath.

From his eyebrows, which were the best barometer of his feelings, her fingers swept along his cheek. She sighed with the craving for his lips on hers. When she guided his mouth to hers, she sensed his desperation.

"Stephen," she whispered, "do you think they will let us live?"

"They have so far. Let's hope they do not change their minds."

An impatient foot against her side woke Arielle. When she didn't open her eyes, the foot kicked harder. She heard a shout and Stephen cursing. Opening her eyes, she gasped as a body fell toward her. She rolled out of the way and jumped to her feet.

One of the warriors lay motionless on the ground where she had been sleeping. In a taut voice Stephen snarled, "Kick her again, and I will take off your foot."

"Stephen, look out!" she cried.

He whirled but lowered his fists when he faced his own pistol. Arielle held her breath, praying the leader would not shoot him. The leader motioned with the gun for Stephen to move away from her. When Stephen shook his head, the tall man clicked back the hammer. The sound ricocheted through the clearing.

Arielle did not move. She did not dare to breathe. With his back to her she could not see Stephen's face. She watched the leader's smile broaden as Stephen stood and stepped aside.

Her arm was seized, and she was pulled to stand next to the leader. He raised his hand, then lowered it at a rumble of dismay. Not from Stephen, she realized, but from the leader's men. The leader muttered something and went to prod the prone man with his foot. Glaring at Stephen, he stamped away. The man holding her called after him. He snapped back an answer.

Arielle inched away from her captor when he released her. Stephen's arms brought her back to him. She hid her face against his chest and surrendered to the shivers of terror that had been dammed inside her.

One of the warriors, a slight man with a bashful grin, brought two bowls to them. Stephen sniffed his. "It smells something like coffee."

"Is it safe?"

"I don't know, but we might as well drink it. I don't think we are getting anything else for breakfast."

She nodded. Lifting the bowl, she downed the acrid liquid in a single gulp. It did not lessen the emptiness in her stomach.

The leader motioned for them to stand. Wearily she rose. Stephen's arm slipped around her waist to steady her. The coffee burned in her, adding nausea to her misery. Saying nothing, she began to walk as she had for what seemed a lifetime.

The nausea ebbed and flowed until she wondered if the day was even more uncomfortably hot than usual. Heat billowed in a thick cloud. She thought she heard Stephen say something to her, but she could not focus on his words. She could not feel the pain in her hand. She could not feel the ground under her feet. Numbness climbed her limbs. Her knees wobbled, and she collapsed. Velvet nothingness swallowed her.

"Arielle!"

Stephen shoved past his guards. They shouted at him. He did not care what they threatened when Arielle was facedown on the ground. Carefully he turned her onto her back. Her eyes were closed as if she were sleeping. He held his hand to her lips. Dread washed out of him as the welcome rhythm of her breathing warmed his hand.

Someone tried to shove him aside. "Get away, you bastards! Haven't you done enough to her already?"

The leader shouted. The warriors swarmed over him. He was wrenched away from her. He swung his fist into the face of the closest man. The man fell to the ground even as Stephen struck another. Pain hammered the back of his head. He slumped to the ground beside Arielle.

He struggled to get back to his feet. His hair was grasped. As he groaned, his head was jerked back to see the leader's satisfied smile. The leader spat in his face. Weakly Stephen cursed. Another flash of pain let him escape the victorious laughter and dragged him into a dark void.

Waves of purple and yellow squares danced before Arielle's eyes. She simply watched them whirl. Slowly she began to realize there had been a time before this roundelay had begun. She searched her mind for her most recent memory. Not Concord. She had left there when she had received Caleb's letter. *The Ladysong*, Stephen Lightenfield, the jungles of Nicaragua, and the capital city of Granada flashed through her head, but she was unsure if those were real or only a part of the dream.

Fingers stroked her face. Her eyelids were sealed in place. She moaned as she tried to escape from the twirling of the squares.

Curses ached in her skull, but they did not come from her lips. Grasping on to the voice, she used it to pull herself out of the deep well of senselessness. She opened her eyes to see Stephen. His face was all wrong. One cheek was swollen out of proportion, and his eyes were sunken into black shadows. Her fingers trembled as she lifted them to see if what her bleary eyes were showing her was real.

"No, honey," came back Stephen's laughing reply as he caught her fingers and folded them gently in his hand. He added in a whisper, "Are you awake?"

"Mostly." When he smiled, then winced, she asked, "What happened to you?"

"These boys play rough. When you passed out, they wanted to keep me from checking you." Satisfaction rang in his voice, although it was distorted by his bloody lips. "I am not the only one who looks this bad. How are you?"

"I passed out?"

"My guess is that our friend put sleeping drugs in your coffee. I was foolish to trust him, but I thought he was in a hurry. Instead, we have been sitting here all day while you have slept."

Turning her head, she saw lengthening shadows spreading across the men who guarded them. Weak tears sprang into her eyes. She had hoped that memory had been just a nightmare.

When she started to sit, Stephen shook his head. "Lie still. We will be staying here tonight. You cannot travel when you are so weak you could not slap a mosquito."

She closed her eyes, glad she did not have to move. Listening to Stephen talk, she cared little what he said. It was enough that the man she loved was with her. She slipped into the soft arms of sleep on the melody of his voice.

Arielle stared at the bare back of the man in front of her. In the heat her muddy clothes had dried and cracked each time she moved. But her head was clear, as she was rested for the first time since they had left Granada.

Her eyes widened as she emerged into a huge break in

the jungle. Buildings, taller than those in Granada, rose to challenge the sky. It was like nothing she'd ever seen. She stared at a quartet of pyramids, which were separated by broad avenues. The tops were flat, but two had small towers sprouting from the apex. The one at the very center of the settlement was twice as large as the others. Smaller buildings were low and longer than *The Ladysong*.

A low whistle came from behind her. Stephen said, "I thought the pyramids were just legends."

"That is what Caleb thought too."

He grinned as he drew her closer, but disquiet clouded his eyes. "I guess we both were wrong."

"I guess we were. The Old Ones have come back to claim their city."

"Or that is what they want people to think."

The butt of a spear in her back prodded Arielle to follow the leader. She was glad Stephen continued to hold her hand. Sunlight glimmered on limestone where the jungle's attempts to reclaim the city had failed. When they came around the side of the first pyramid, she saw steps cut into the stone. Pools of stagnant water by the road gave way to fresh ones as they neared the huge pyramid. Flowers had been planted beside the water, and freshly raked gravel marked roads and pathways.

People worked near the low buildings. The men were dressed like their captors, but the women wore loose gowns that were decorated with unfamiliar symbols. They melted back into the shadows. One man sank to his knees but was hauled to his feet by others who reprimanded him in the unintelligible language.

"This is very strange," Arielle whispered.

"The people?"

She barely shook her head, not wanting to call attention to their low conversation. "They act as if they are afraid of us."

"We are different."

"We are prisoners. We should be the ones who are afraid."

Stephen did not answer as they were steered onto a path leading toward a building set in the shadow of the largest pyramid. Renewed fear swelled through her. This might be the end of their journey, and they must face what waited for them.

When she gripped Stephen's hand, he put his arm around her. She whispered, "Whatever happens, don't forget that I love you."

"I won't," he answered as softly.

Knowing that she could die before she took her next breath, she asked, "Do you love me?"

Arielle was shoved through a door before Stephen could answer. Expecting a prison cell, she gasped in astonishment. A few pieces of furniture were arranged on the long, narrow floor. The beautiful walls were embellished with intricate and alien patterns. Red and gold twisted in a baffling mélange of designs.

Arielle saw all of that in the second before her gaze was caught by a man sitting on a raised chair at the far end of the room. Everything and everyone in the room vanished as she stared in disbelief at the red-haired man leaning toward her. A smile settled on his lips as he affixed her with his dark eyes above the scar on his left cheek.

In the silence her whisper roared like a shout. "Caleb?"

CHAPTER EIGHTEEN

"Caleb, I have been looking all over Nicaragua for you. What—?" A warrior grabbed Arielle.

"Release her!" Caleb stated in an imperious tone. When the hands holding her dropped away, she took a step toward him. He held up his begemmed fingers. "That is not the way to approach a king, beloved."

"King?" She paused in confusion and stared at Caleb. Had the shadows betrayed her? How? The redhead had called her "beloved" as Caleb had before he left Concord.

"I said you must show respect!"

She heard Stephen's familiar growl of rage. When she started to turn, a hand forced her to her knees. Wincing as stones cut into her, she began to rise. A fist knocked her to the floor.

"Remember your manners, beloved," continued the voice that was Caleb's and yet was not. She had never heard such coldness in his tone.

Arielle rose to her knees. Wiping blood from her split lip, she flinched at maniacal laughter. This was not the

Caleb she had known. He wore a cloth wrapped around his waist. Strings of gems and strange amulets hung from his neck.

He thinks he is a king! The thought careened through her, as wild and insane as what was before her. Maybe it was another nightmare. When blood trickled along her chin, she knew she was only fooling herself. Until she discovered what was going on, she must play along with this weird game.

"Caleb, you sent for me?" she asked meekly.

"You may come, Arielle." When she stood, he snapped, "On your knees in my presence!"

She folded her hands. "Grant me the boon of walking."

When he looked over his shoulder, Arielle saw a shadowed man behind him. Caleb's dark eyes pierced her as he called, "Very well. Approach, beloved. I trust you shall remember this benevolence is for this one time."

"Yes," she whispered. She fought the urge to look at Stephen. Caleb had not noticed him yet, and she did not want to bring Stephen to his attention.

Her boots on the stone floor were preternaturally loud in the strange quiet. She could not deny the truth. The man on the carved wooden chair was Caleb Drummond. His unruly hair was as familiar as his round face. So many times she had seen him peering at her from around a fence. Only his dark eyes were different, for their sparkle had vanished.

He signaled for her to kneel and placed his hands on her shoulders. He kissed her cheek. "Welcome, beloved, to Cielo Azul. We have anticipated your arrival with great joy."

"What are you doing here?" Searching his face for a sign of the man she had known, she asked, "Why did you leave the Transit Company? What—?"

"Your questions will be answered. Until then, welcome

to paradise." Raising his hands, he shouted, "Rejoice at the arrival of my beloved!"

All the men were on their knees, their heads pressed to the floor. Arielle's breath burned over her heart when she saw two lances against Stephen's back to force him to his knees. Layers of questions filled her mind. Caleb's eyes glittered too brightly as he exulted in Spanish. Several times, she heard *esposa*, which she knew meant wife.

When he pointed at Stephen, he demanded in English, "Who is this untutored one?"

Arielle gasped as the leader explained in unaccented English that they had discovered Stephen with her. His gaze rested on her for a moment. His expression did not change, but she knew he was amused by her shock.

Caleb did not notice. "Dispose of him as you should have before."

"No, Caleb!" she cried, jumping to her feet.

A murmur rumbled through the room. She stepped back, but Caleb's hand on her shoulder forced her to her knees again. "Do not deny your king his wishes, woman. The man will not be killed until we determine if he has a use." With a wave of his hand he repeated his order.

"Be careful!" shouted Stephen as he was dragged from the room.

Arielle whispered, "Stay safe."

Caleb took her fingers and placed them on his palm. Like a trap, his fingers closed around them. A tug told her she was to follow. Silently she obeyed. Stephen's safety depended on her continued cooperation.

He led her into a beautiful room. Cushions surrounded a low table, where food was arranged in ceramic bowls decorated with the same symbols as on the walls. From a skylight overhead, the sun filtered in to warm the room. Four men entered to stand silently against the walls.

When he seated her on a cushion, Caleb asked if she

was hungry. She nodded. Shock had frozen her mind. She had to think more clearly.

Arielle reached out to touch the scar on his face as he sat next to her. The bull had gored Caleb's cheek in the same spot. This had to be Caleb Drummond, but that made everything more puzzling. She had to get some answers. Cautiously, she asked, "What will you do with Stephen?"

"Stephen?" He selected an orange section and offered it to her. When her fingers trembled with fear, he laughed coldly. "Your companion dares much to be in the company of my beloved."

The orange spurted as she clenched her hand. "Please, Caleb, do not hurt him."

He shrugged indifferently. "You were to come alone. I sent explicit directions."

Arielle withdrew the tattered letter from her bodice and offered it to him. "This is all I received. We nearly had given up hope of finding you when we met . . ."

He snatched the note from her. With a chuckle he tossed it onto the nearby brazier. The paper burst into flame. Shivering, she wondered if she could have guessed he was insane if she had seen the whole letter. No, Caleb was not crazy. Something or someone had caused this change.

"So little it said, but you came." He crossed his arms on his bare chest and smiled. "Yet did you have a choice? My will brought you to me."

"I came because you needed me. Why are you here?"

He imprisoned her hands beneath his. Her eyes widened. His hands were soft. They always had been as coarse as rigging from his hard work. "So many questions! You have not changed, have you, beloved?" He stroked her cheek. "Neither have you lost your beauty."

She pulled away and lowered her eyes. She had to find a way to reach Caleb, *her Caleb,* not this stranger. When he tugged on her hand, she looked at him. She must be obedient until Stephen was safe.

She stared at his vacuous smile. "Caleb, we must leave. This is not our world."

He patted her hand. "I have found a paradise for us to share. We shall grow old here with our children."

"Children?" She drew her feet under her. What signal Caleb made she did not see, but a lance poked her back. She sat on the pillows again. "Caleb, I did not come here to marry you."

"You are my betrothed." He stroked her dirty hair.

"I was! Things have changed."

"I was not a king. I could offer you only a boring little house in that boring little town."

"When I agreed to marry you, I did not know what love is."

He laughed. "I shall teach you."

Grasping her elbow, he jerked her to him and leaned her back on the pillows. His mouth lowered toward hers, and she cried out. The sound was muted when his lips crushed hers. She tried to push him away. What was so sweet with Stephen was wrong with Caleb. He grasped her arms and pinned her to the pillows. Her struggles were futile.

"You are my beloved Arielle." He clamped his mouth over hers.

She could not squirm from beneath him. The bare skin beneath her torn shirt rubbed against his chest. She wanted to scream for help, but no one would come. The guards would allow nobody in. The thought of witnesses gave her renewed strength. When she twisted her face away, triumphant laughter filled the room. Not Caleb's voice, but another.

She cringed when she saw the silhouette of a giant eagle standing in the arch. A man stepped into the room. The bird shape was an illusion created by a feathered cloak and a headdress shaped like a beak.

"Surely it is a day for rejoicing, my king," announced the man in his sonorous voice.

Arielle blurted out in horror and disbelief, "Alfonso! You are the boatman on the lake!"

Laughing, Alfonso brought her to her feet. He put his hand against her cheek, tilting her face one way and then the other. That he was dressed like this warned her that the machinations that had brought her to Caleb had been more intricate than she had guessed.

"Why are you doing this?" she asked.

His smile broadened. "As I foretold, my king, your bride is here on the night when the moon is full again."

"Of course I am!" she shouted, her frustration becoming rage. "Your men made certain of that. I do not—"

"Be silent!" ordered Caleb. As if ashamed of her, he added, "She always has been a volatile creature."

Arielle wanted to brush the slimy caress of Alfonso's gaze off her. Although he did not raise his voice, she recognized its threat. "Knowing your benevolence to her traveling companion, she will do exactly as you wish, my king."

She clamped her lips closed. She would not let them torture Stephen. Her life without him would be as flavorless as it had been before she had met him.

Alfonso said with a smile, "You might yet save Lightenfield's life."

"Why should I believe you? You have poisoned Caleb's mind with lies! He never would—"

"Silence!" Caleb's hand swung back. Pain thundered through her head, and she fell against the pillows. Through the ringing in her ears she heard him snarl, "Never speak to the High One like that. To him as to me, you are subservient. Be stupid again, and you will die as horribly as your traveling companion."

"My king," Alfonso said, "she is a child in the way of the light. Give her to me. I shall teach her as I taught you with the magic potions."

"No, Caleb!"

"She is yours, High One." Caleb's eyes were empty as he pushed her toward Alfonso. "The poor thing fails to understand the honor we do her.

"Go!" snapped Caleb.

Alfonso said, "If I may return later, there is a matter that requires your attention."

"Go!"

Arielle saw the narrowing of Alfonso's eyes. Whatever held the boatman to Caleb, it was not loyalty. When she met Alfonso's gaze, she knew that continuing to look for Caleb had not led to this disaster. If they had stayed in Granada, Alfonso would have arranged for her to be brought to this palace of horrors. She simply had made it easier for him.

The guards stepped away as Alfonso forced her into the hallway. A warrior grasped Arielle's arm and pulled her away from the room. A shiver ached along her bruised body as she heard another crescendo of deranged laughter.

Stephen sat against the wall of his cell and watched water roll along the opposite wall. If he did not escape soon, there would be no hurry. Simon had orders to take *The Ladysong* north by the end of October even if her captain had not returned. Slamming his fist on the stone floor, he swore.

How was he to guess Arielle would find Drummond? He grinned wryly. No hints of a cult had filtered out of the jungle. Only tales of the Old Ones, which he had dismissed as legends.

His smile fell into a scowl. Drummond had called Arielle "beloved" more than once. Drummond must believe that she would docilely marry him. Jealousy throbbed through him, consuming him like a cancer as he tried not to think of Arielle in Drummond's bed.

The longing to make love with her ached in him. So many wasted nights of sleeping on the jungle floor when all he could think of was pulling her against him and tasting the luscious warmth of her skin. The sweet lushness of her breasts, the firmness of her slender legs, the tantalizing flavors of every inch of her. The echo of her soft sighs whispered in his ears like a siren luring a sailor to the rocky shore. His body tightened with the craving that was a torment.

With a sigh he closed his eyes and leaned his head against the earthen wall. Until he could find a way out of there, he couldn't do a damn thing about Drummond's plans.

Death had haunted him since he had become master of *The Ladysong,* but never had it seemed so assured as now. When he had left Charleston, he had not listened to the warnings not to follow in the footsteps of his carefree father. Instead of staying home to enjoy his wealth, his father had sailed with his ship on its final voyage. Somewhere in the mid-Atlantic, the ship rotted on the sea bottom. Since his cousin Elmer had left for an adventure in California, Stephen had not returned home. His aunt's recriminations were a reminder that his cousin had died trying to emulate him.

He wondered if anyone would learn what had happened to them. His mouth twisted. He would suffer less than Arielle. Her charming Caleb wanted her as his queen. Stephen tapped his drawn-up knee and waited for the inevitable.

His indifference vanished when he heard a scream. Arielle! Stephen grasped the bars in the door. He pressed his face against the rust. When Arielle shrieked again, he hammered on the door. "Leave her alone, you bastards!"

He heard only silence. It was more terrifying than another scream. Then he heard footfalls. He pressed against the wall. An iron key clanked in the lock. As the door opened, he tensed to jump to his feet.

"Arielle!" he gasped.

She was shoved at him so forcefully, they were knocked to the floor. He leapt to rush their captors. He managed to strike one, but the others attacked him. Pain enveloped him as he was beaten with methodical fervor. He was dropped next to Arielle. The door closed as he crawled to her.

"Honey, don't cry." He bit back an oath as his lip cracked again and blood gushed from it. "Once we are out of here, I shall—"

"We'll never escape. They have toyed with us since the beginning." She leaned her cheek against his chest but pulled away with a moan.

"Who did this?" He touched her bruises gently.

"Caleb."

"Caleb?"

She wrung her hands. "I think he has been drugged. He struck me for daring to speak out against Alfonso."

"Alfonso?" He shook his head, wishing just one thing she said would make sense. "What in hell is he doing here?"

She dabbed her chemisette sleeve against his mouth. When he winced, she explained, finishing with, "Alfonso plans to set up Caleb as his puppet to rule Nicaragua when President Walker is ousted."

"With you as his queen?" The words were distasteful.

"Alfonso has convinced Caleb that he will be a god."

A key rattled in the lock. He waved her to silence. He squatted, ready to meet the next assault as the door opened. He swore under his breath when he saw Alfonso in his grandest glory. The boatman scowled and looked past him.

"Forgive me, my queen," Alfonso purred. "My orders were misunderstood. This place is not meant for you but for those who are to be granted the highest honor of dying for the Old Ones."

"Let Captain Lightenfield leave." When she stood, Stephen could believe Arielle was soon to be a queen. Her regal dignity was not lessened by her tattered clothes. "I will stay to do as you wish if you release him."

"Arielle, don't be stupid!" Stephen shouted.

Alfonso laughed. "And deny him the chance to exult with the highest?"

"You do not need him. I shall do as you ask. He—"

"Don't beg, Arielle," Stephen said. Putting his hands on the wall, he tried to convince his battered head to stop spinning. "Don't worry, Arielle. The Old Ones he blasphemes will repay him with death." When he started to repeat the words in Spanish, Alfonso shouted.

Arielle cried a warning as a lance rose over Stephen's head. He dropped to the floor. "Stephen!" she cried. She ran to him, but another spear blocked her way. She was herded toward the door and Alfonso. "Damn all of you!"

Alfonso's mouth straightened with rage. He barked orders, which sent the warriors scurrying like frightened kittens. She did not protest as her guards pulled her out of the prison. She feared both she and Stephen had underestimated the power Alfonso wielded.

The moon was rising over the trees as Arielle emerged from the palace. Other shadows solidified into human form as the residents of the city followed the flaming torches lining the main road leading to the central pyramid.

Filmy robes flowed around her legs. With her hair loose behind her, the breeze brushed it into a dark cloud. She heard the strange rhythm of drums and fought to keep from walking to their tempo. She must hold on to her last moments of freedom before she was forced to marry a man she once had dreamed of having as her husband.

Caleb smiled as he led her to the base of the pyramid.

In the shadow of the stairs leading up to the sky, his pale robes were closed with a golden belt that matched hers. She adjusted the shoulders of her gown, for the neckline was cut too low across her breasts. His gaze burned her naked skin.

Alfonso appeared from the dusk. "My king, we await the arrival of one more." He turned as guards escorted another person to the pyramid.

Terror cut through Arielle. When she started to move, Caleb took her arm.

"Remember yourself, beloved," he warned.

"Caleb, don't do this!" Stephen was separated from her by only a few feet of gravel. She must save him. "Caleb, listen to me!"

She watched helplessly. At least, Stephen was still alive. Relief became horror as Caleb took her right hand and Alfonso her left and forced her up the stairs. She counted until the chanting and smoky braziers invaded her head. It felt light as she continued up the steps.

At the top they turned to face the city. Alfonso's voice boomed across the night. Only Arielle watched as the guards brought Stephen to the apex. If she could speak to him—even for a moment . . .

Alfonso drew her to the very edge. She shivered, trying not to look down. He began to intone words she could not understand.

A quick signal brought a man forward. He held out a large package. Alfonso unwrapped it with reverence. When something glittered, Arielle's gasp echoed those from the ground. A master artisan had embedded gold with precious stones to create a crown with the serpentine pattern that was repeated throughout the palace.

Alfonso held it over her. His voice careened through her aching head as he bellowed a question. An answering shout echoed off the stone.

She nearly collapsed under the weight of the crown.

Locking her knees, she did not move as Alfonso signaled again. Stephen was led toward them. The chants gained a feverish pace.

"Nice bonnet," he whispered nearly soundlessly.

His irreverence shattered the panic choking her. She smiled, but turned to watch Alfonso. Over his head he held a long knife. Again the chanting escalated. Caleb continued to stare straight ahead. When Alfonso pressed the hilt into her hand, she raised her eyes from the stone blade to the high priest's insane smile.

"You are the queen, the bringer of life to the light. Choose your mate, my queen."

"Pardon me?" If the circumstances had not been so absurd, she would have laughed at her question. "I thought I was supposed to marry Caleb. What—?"

"Choose your mate, my queen." Gripping her wrist, he turned it so the knife was visible to those below. "Only one man can be your king. The other must die. Who shall live? Caleb Drummond or Stephen Lightenfield?"

"I cannot condemn one to die!"

"Then you wish me to choose for you?"

She shook her head. The headpiece tumbled to her feet. When the priest reached for it, Stephen signaled to her. In disbelief she watched while his lips moved. "Choose me to die." He scowled to emphasize the words. His face became emotionless when Alfonso placed the headdress on her hair.

Arielle struggled with her fear. Stephen must have some plan. She had to give him a chance to try it. Softly she said, "My king shall be the one you named your king."

"As I foretold," intoned Alfonso, "so shall it be."

Stephen was forced to his knees, his head pulled back roughly. From beneath his cloak the high priest pulled out a jeweled amulet. He rocked it in front of Stephen's eyes.

"It is my place to bring you to the light." Alfonso's voice

matched the movement of the jewel. "To the light. The light. The bringer of life. The bringer of peace."

Arielle gasped. A lance against her spine silenced her.

"Speak, Stephen Lightenfield," crooned Alfonso. "Tell me who possesses your heart."

In a voice that was nothing like his normal one, he said, "My heart belongs to the light."

"No, not Stephen too," Arielle moaned.

"Rise." When Stephen obeyed, Alfonso shot a victorious smile at her. "Walk to the table."

Like a puppet, Stephen followed his commands. Horror strangled Arielle as he reclined on the stone. When Alfonso motioned for her to be brought, she shook her head.

"I will not kill him!"

She was pushed next to the table. A hand over her fingers pinned the knife in her fingers. She listened to Alfonso's raving. Lowering her gaze to Stephen, she smiled as she saw his slow wink.

A laugh paralyzed her. She looked at Alfonso. Her smile had betrayed them. As she took a breath to scream, a hand gagged her. Stephen made no attempt to rise as guards surged forward to secure him.

The priest whispered as the ropes lashed Stephen to the table, "Did you think I would be fooled, Lightenfield?"

"It was worth a chance, wasn't it?"

"I shall enjoy watching our queen cut your beating heart from your chest."

"Do not make Arielle do that!"

Snapping his fingers, Alfonso accepted a bowl. He held it out to Arielle. "Your choice, my queen. You may drink it to free you from the memory of what will happen when you sacrifice this unbeliever to the light, or you may give it to Lightenfield. I warn you that there is enough for only one."

"Drink it, honey. My pain will be short-lived." Stephen smiled at his inadvertent jest.

She gazed at the dark liquid then at Caleb's blank face. If she swallowed it, she would be like him. She did not want to think what Alfonso could force her to do then. She saw sympathy in Stephen's eyes. His suffering would end within minutes. Hers would continue as long as she and Caleb remained the fake priest's pawns.

Alfonso turned to order the guards from the top of the temple and raised his arms to shout to his followers. Arielle set the bowl on the table and pushed past Caleb. Slowly she crept toward the priest. She raised the crown.

Something must have warned Alfonso. He whirled, his rage drilling her. The feathers of his cloak billowed out as if they still possessed life. "You fool! You could have been a queen. Now you shall die."

Arielle leapt aside as he rushed toward her. She threw the crown at him.

He screamed and teetered on the edge. He shrieked as he fell. She cringed, covering her face with her hands.

"Arielle! This isn't the time for hysterics!" Stephen shouted.

She spun. Caleb held the knife in his hand and was raising it over Stephen's chest. She grasped his wrist. The knife struck the edge of the table before rebounding against his thigh. He groaned, and she wrestled the knife from his fingers. Ignoring him, she cut the ropes holding Stephen in place.

He slid off and snatched the knife from her. He grasped her arm as she was about to kneel next to Caleb.

"Stephen, I must see to Caleb," she cried. "He is—"

"We are all going to be dead if you do not play the queen, honey."

"Me?" she squeaked.

He shoved her forward as soldiers poured over the top of the pyramid. "You are their queen! Order them to stop."

She raised her trembling hands. "Halt!" When Stephen whispered the command in Spanish, she repeated it.

The men faltered. Their high priest lay dead at the base of the temple and their bloody king leaned against the altar. Only their queen remained on her feet. When she repeated her command, they sank to their knees.

"This man will translate my words." The men exchanged an uneasy glance as she pointed to Stephen. "Go, and bury the high one with all due ceremony from the temple of the priests." Stephen raised an eyebrow as she improvised, but she hurried on. "Mourn for seven days. Then return here. Answers will be given to you then."

The warriors bowed. When they went down to tell the others, she silently thanked Alfonso, who had stolen their wills. She turned to Caleb, sinking to her knees to check him.

"We have to leave before they return," Stephen said. "How is he?"

"Bad."

Caleb was covered with a layer of perspiration, but his skin was clammy. Even if she had known what Alfonso used to control him, the treatment must be the same. Deprivation of the horrible drug.

"There is a hospital in Granada," Arielle said.

"There must be one in Bluefields." When she regarded him in amazement, he continued. "If we go back, we may be walking into a war."

Tears filled her eyes. "I will not let Caleb die just so we can protect our skins."

He gripped her arms. "Dammit, Arielle! Why can't you think with your head just once?"

"He saved my life—"

"And you have saved his."

"So I can leave him here to die?"

He rose with a sigh. "All right, Arielle. We can drag him to the lake on a litter. It is only a few miles from here.

We will have no trouble reaching Granada from there."
Suddenly he smiled. "They will be expecting the gringos
to be leaving, not sneaking back in. We can get Caleb
patched up and take the *Director*." He drew her to her feet
and twisted his fingers into her hair. In the moment before
his mouth caressed hers, he whispered, "This had better
be fun, honey."

CHAPTER NINETEEN

The city slept, enshrouded in the tropical darkness. Arielle wanted to ask how much longer it would take to get to the hotel, but she needed all her strength to help Caleb. No one stopped them from entering Granada. The campfires of the armies of Walker's enemies edged the city like a virulent crown, but they had been able to sneak into the city.

Any signs of the carefree life had vanished. The plazas were deserted although it was not yet midnight. No glimmer of light or lilt of music broke the night. Doors were chained shut, and boards had been nailed over windows. As she helped Stephen support Caleb along the empty streets, their footfalls seemed too loud.

Stephen whispered, "Arielle, can you hold him by yourself?"

She nodded and clenched her teeth. Caleb could not stand alone. Denied Alfonso's drugs, he had shrunk into himself to become an unspeaking husk.

When Stephen vanished into the shadows, Arielle

scanned the street. A shadow crept toward her, and she
tensed. A scrawny dog peeked out of an alley. Seeing her,
it ran in the other direction. Otherwise, the street was
deserted. She wondered how many *norteamericanos*
remained in Granada. Her lips tightened. None of President Walker's fanatical filibusters would leave without a
fight.

"Arielle?"

At the low whisper she saw Stephen moving toward her.
He motioned with his head toward an open door. "This
house is empty. We should be safe here."

"I thought . . ." She sighed as he took Caleb's weight
from her aching shoulders.

His chuckle sounded as exhausted as she felt. "The
Hotel Granada must be overflowing with Walker's syco-
phants. We will be better off if we remain anonymous. In
the morning we can get to the *Director* and get the hell out
of here."

Arielle helped Stephen lift Caleb's rubbery legs over the
threshold. They stumbled across the uneven stone floor.
Gratefully she lowered Caleb to a pile of discarded sacks
in a corner. She pulled one of them over him.

When she looked up, Stephen was gone. She put her
hand on the knife in the belt of the silly outfit she still
wore. Tugging at the shoulder, which slipped along her
arm, she wished Stephen had let her delay in the temple
city long enough to change out of this ceremonial gown.
The fine material was tattered by their journey, and it
offered her little modesty.

"How is he doing?" Stephen asked as he returned from
the other room with a broken chair and some scraps. He
piled it on the simple hearth and lit a fire.

"I don't know. He has not said a thing since we left
Cielo Azul." She knelt to check the bandage on Caleb's
leg. The blood had dried to crack across it. Putting her

hand on his cool cheek, she wondered if he ever would open his eyes again.

Stephen drew her to her feet. "You have to let him heal by himself, honey."

"I want to help him."

"I know you do." His broad hands framed her face as he said in a husky whisper, "And I want you. It is been too long since I last made love with you."

"A thousand years ago."

Bending, he placed his mouth against the curve of her neck. She shivered at the potent yearning searing her and stroked the assertive angle of his unshaven cheek. When he grinned, she tugged on a strand of his hair that brushed the back of his collar.

"You look awful," she teased.

"Truthfully, honey, you've looked better yourself."

"What a thing to say to the woman who saved your life!"

He bowed before her. "Forgive me, Queen Arielle."

"No!" she whispered. "Don't ever joke about that." She looked at Caleb, who could have been a statue. If Alfonso had had his way, she would have been as much of a prisoner of his drugs as Caleb was.

"Never again." He turned her to meet his lips. Gently, then more persuasively, he explored her mouth.

She ceded all her thoughts to desire. She wanted to forget everything but the glories of his touch. As her hands moved along his ripped shirt, she teased his tongue with her own. Against her mouth his lips tilted in a smile. His fingers flitted across her, each touch eliciting a flame of yearning.

A groan intruded like a slap. Arielle pulled away and went to kneel by Caleb. As her body craved Stephen's touch, her heart hurt for Caleb's suffering.

"It is all right," she whispered. "Caleb, we are free. It is over. He cannot hurt us again."

Caleb's arm thrashed out, knocking her aside. Pain shot

up her elbow as she struck the floor. She scrambled back to him as he screeched. She caught his hand before it could hit her again. He jerked away, and her arm was wrenched from wrist to shoulder.

"Caleb, it is Arielle! Listen to me."

"Honey, he cannot understand you."

When Stephen put his hands on her shoulders and drew her away, she began to cry. Everything she had dreamed of was dying around her. The man she had promised to marry had betrayed her for his own dreams, and she feared the one she loved would do the same as soon as they escaped from Granada.

"Hush, Arielle," he whispered. "We will get out of this somehow. Then we'll go back to *The Ladysong*. She is waiting for us."

"For us?" She raised her head and met his gaze steadily. "Or for you?"

"Aren't you going back to Boston?"

"Then what?"

He shrugged. "It is up to you, honey."

More tears blinded her. She did not want to hear the truth, but she must. Acting as if she did not care if he left her tomorrow or the day after was a lie she could not continue. She loved Stephen, and she wanted him to be a part of her life forever.

"Do you love me?" she whispered.

She bit her lip when he turned away. In disbelief, she watched him stand, grab his hat, and stride toward the door. He vanished into the night. Closing her eyes, she put her hands over her mouth to silence her sobs. She must let Caleb sleep. She must be strong . . . for Caleb. Ironic laughter battered at her lips. She had succeeded in her quest but lost the one thing she wanted more than her next breath.

Hands covered her shoulders. With a gasp Arielle looked

up to see Stephen's unshaven face. She opened her mouth, but he put his finger to it.

"Don't," he murmured. "Just listen, then tell me what it is about Arielle Gardiner that makes me act like a fool. I came along for the fun, but you have demanded more from me. You want me to be your hero, guarding your heart, trusting you with mine." His gray eyes grew darker with his strong emotions as his hand curved along her cheek. "I am no hero, honey."

"I love you, Stephen, whether you are a hero or not."

"If you knew why—"

As he had, she placed her finger against his lips. "Hold me, Stephen. Hold me and love me while you can."

He reached for the golden belt holding her gown in place, then looked at the man lying in the sacks. Standing, he brought Arielle to her feet. He led her into the other room. As he closed the door, she opened shutters on the lone window to let moonlight flow across the floor.

Arielle smiled when Stephen pulled a thin pallet from a rickety bed frame. He set it in the middle of the river of moonlight. Sitting on the edge, he held his hands up to her. She pulled out the few pins left in her hair and released it in a chocolate wave.

Taking her hands, he drew her down beside him. He smiled as he lowered her onto the dirty mattress. When he did not kiss her, she whispered, "Are you having second thoughts?"

With a soft laugh he leaned on one elbow next to her. "Second and third and hundredth. Nothing is on my mind more than you."

Her lips found his ear, and he shivered against her with the longing they could restrain no more. He answered her with his lips over hers. The gentleness vanished into the desire that demanded she become one with it. Her fingers slid along the firm line of his neck, then combed up into his hair, which was as coarse as unrefined silk. He allowed no mysteries to hide within her mouth, setting each slippery shadow alight with his tongue until she moaned against her lips.

Raising his mouth from hers, he held her gaze as he reached again for the gold belt. She closed her eyes when he bent forward to tease her neck with flicks of his tongue along the loosening material. Her body ached to be close to him, sharing each breath in a glorious storm of delight.

The gown fell away to reveal her curves. Her breath exploded into a sweet flame when he drew her to her feet, his hands roving along her waist. A single tug of the knot at her hip sent the fabric floating to her feet like discarded petals. Quivering, she gasped when he pulled her tight to the rough texture of his clothes.

"My Arielle," he whispered in the moment before he claimed her lips again.

Savoring them for only a moment, he blazed a fiery path along her throat and across her breasts. Her hands clenched on the thin material of his shirt, for she was afraid she would collapse as the tantalizing playfulness of his tongue flitted across a tip. Need roiled within her as she strengthened her knees so she could reach for his shirt's buttons. The few remaining fell away easily before her fervor.

With a frayed laugh he stood. She watched in fascination while he stripped off his clothes. The strong sinews revealed his potent masculinity, drawing her eyes to each leonine motion of his body as he knelt.

When he reclined next to her, the thin mattress conformed to them both. Lying on her side, her legs entwined with his strong ones, she ran a single fingertip across the sternly sculptured planes of his face. His mustache had lost its scratchiness to become more pliable than his skin. Teasing a line along his lip, she laughed lightly when he glowered even as he was chuckling. He pushed her hand away.

"Tickling my mustache was not the pleasure I had in mind," he murmured.

"And what did you imagine?"

He pushed her onto her back. She grew warm when she saw the unfettered passion in his eyes. When he placed his mouth near her ear, she shivered. His breath scorched her skin and tingled to the very tips of her toes.

"I imagined tasting every inch of you until you wanted me as much as I want you."

"I do want you for today and forever," she murmured, each word an effort as she tried to maintain her thoughts amid the siege of rapture.

"For today and forever."

Her smile vanished, for the beguiling sensations of his skin against her were too glorious for such a tepid expression. Letting her fingers seek pleasure along him, she explored his virile lines, each touch augmenting the wild tempest whirling within her. She swayed against him in a feverish quest for a way to sate the escalating need.

When she heard his sharp gasp, she raised her eyes to meet his. In them glowed the longing engulfing her in its fierce, frantic power. His uneven laugh was her only warning before he abruptly pulled her over him. With slow enticement his hands slipped along her back to settle on her hips. He pressed them to his, smiling when she sighed at the swell of longing coursing through her. Giving her no chance to relish in his masculine firmness against her, he raised her above him.

She choked out his name when his mouth moved along her breast again. Letting his fantasies, honed by nights of sleeplessness, guide him, he feasted on the delights waiting on her naked skin. She gripped the mattress, for her body refused to remain still. Each motion brushed her against him, sparking an explosion that threatened to detonate within her.

Again he leaned her back, holding her with his lips as

his fingers moved along her legs in a sinuous spiral. A cry erupted from her when he sought the moist flame within her. With her body no longer hers to govern, she matched his probing caress as he lifted himself over her.

Gently he brought them together, the savage need imprisoning them. Wrapping her arms around his shoulders, she brought his mouth over hers so their breaths mingled, straining with the force of ecstasy. Splendor seared through her, the flames devouring her as their souls became a single heartbeat. The implosion surged through her until she could contain the love no longer. Dazzling luminescence surrounded her to sweep her into the very heart of the storm, the lightning melding her heart to heart with the man she loved.

"The *Director*'s gone." Stephen threw his broken panama on the floor. "It doesn't look as if it is coming back until Walker loses Granada to his enemies."

Arielle stuck the last hairpin in the curtain she had made from the dress that would have been her wedding gown. Smoothing the skirt and garish blouse that Stephen had found for her somewhere, she sat on the edge of the hearth. "What do we do now?"

"It will be harder sneaking out of Granada than it was to sneak in." His eyes, which were shadowed by the remnants of his bruises, looked past her. "How is Drummond?"

"He will not be able to walk on his own." She rubbed her hands together. "He did not sleep much last night."

Stephen sat next to her and rested his arm on her shoulder. "Neither did I, honey." Tipping her mouth toward his, he whispered, "I want you so badly I cannot think of anything else."

"We need a doctor." She saw astonishment in his eyes as she drew away, but she must think of Caleb now. And of her own heart, which would be broken when Stephen abandoned her to return to his free life on the sea.

"There aren't any."

"None?"

Standing, he grumbled, "The few that were here have been drafted to work for Walker's bully boys."

"Then we will have to nurse him back to health."

"This is not going to be the most restful place."

She rose and picked up a bucket she had found in the back of the house. "I had better get some more water. Cold compresses seem to help."

Stephen pulled out an antiquated pistol from beneath his ragged shirt. "Here, Arielle. You may need this. I know you are not used to this kind of gun, but just aim and pull back on the trigger. Then run like hell."

"Where did you get this?" She turned the wooden gun over in her hands.

He patted his side. "Someone was stupid enough to trade two of them for the gold in your belt. The gun has a single shot, so use it well."

"Keep an eye on Caleb."

Stephen nodded as she walked out. He had better things to do than play nursemaid to Drummond. If the fool had not gotten himself mixed up in that stupid cult, they all could have been long gone from Granada by then. Stephen cursed under his breath. Everything he had done since he left *The Ladysong* would be for naught if he did not get out of Granada soon. He did not plan to die for Walker's perverted ambition.

He shoved aside the curtain and sat on the floor beside Drummond. Reaching for the damp cloth on Drummond's forehead, he was startled to see dark eyes regarding him with a semblance of sanity.

"Who are you?" came the breathless whisper.

"Stephen Lightenfield."

"Lightenfield?" he asked. "I thought you looked familiar. What have you been sent to—?"

Stephen interrupted sharply, "I came with Arielle to find you."

Pain contorted his full mouth. "With Arielle? You?"

"She needed help."

"And you brought her here?" A laugh strained his cracked lips. "What did Alfonso pay you to arrange that?"

"He was *your* ally," Stephen said stiffly. "Not mine, but your fun is over, Drummond. Your friend Alfonso is dead. Arielle killed him."

Drummond's hands clenched at his sides. "She killed him? Damn the both of you, Lightenfield! I had found a paradise, and you have taken it away."

"Go back."

"I will." He struggled to sit, then collapsed back on the sacks. "And I will take Arielle with me. I will not leave her with you. She deserves better than you."

Stephen almost laughed as he heard Drummond repeat what he once had told Arielle himself. The familiar longing resonated through him. A drunk Arielle had offered herself to him that night. He wanted her tonight. He was not going to let Drummond lure her back to that dead city.

Drummond continued. "She will replace Luisa."

"Luisa?"

"My wife . . . my late wife, who died bearing my child." His smile grew predatory. "When she died, I told Alfonso about Arielle. I needed a queen. What better one than my fiancée? I knew she would never forget her promise to marry me."

"Even though you forgot yours to her?"

He shrugged. "Now I shall have her. Don't try to stop me, Lightenfield."

Stephen said quietly, "I will not let you take her back to that place."

Drummond's smile broadened. "She will go. She has

never forgotten that she owes me her life." He scratched the scar on his cheek and chuckled. "Dear, loyal Arielle. What an innocent fool she is!"

"So you did not save her life on purpose?"

"What do I look like? Some sort of dim-witted hero? She was playing in the field. I thought it would be funny to scare her by setting the bull on her. I pushed her aside at the last minute. She escaped. I almost did not." His lips clenched. "She owes me for all that pain."

"She owes you nothing."

His eyes narrowed. "Tell her any of this, Lightenfield, and I shall deny every word. Which one of us do you think she will believe?"

"Do you think she will believe you after you had her drugged so you could abduct her?"

Drummond's smile became a sneer. "She's believed all these years that I saved her life."

An explosion resounded through the city. The house quivered. Thatch trickled onto Stephen's head.

"That is artillery," Drummond shouted. "Where are we?"

"Granada."

He laughed mirthlessly. "You came back here? How could you be so damn foolish?"

Rifles fired. Screams raced along the street. Panic stole Drummond's smile. He turned to flee.

"Are you going without Arielle?" Stephen called to his back.

"I shall find her and—"

"Will *you* believe that her first child is yours when it may be mine?"

The redhead whirled, his face contorted with fury. "She would not—"

Stephen had no chance to tell Drummond how wrong he was. A bomb exploded not far away. It propelled him from his feet. Drummond, too, he saw as he raised his head. He struggled to his knees. A fist knocked him to the floor.

With a smile he jumped up, hitting Drummond squarely on the chin. Drummond collapsed to the ground just as another mortar detonated.

Stephen rubbed his knuckles. That had felt good. He hoped it would not be his last pleasure before his death.

Leaving Drummond lying there, Stephen raced out of the house and into the small plaza. A stream of panicked people blocked his way, but he waded through them, shouting Arielle's name. More artillery detonated throughout the city. He put his arms over his head as flowerpots crashed to the street.

Smoke blinded him. He choked, pressing his ripped sleeve to his mouth. Slender fingers touched his arm. He blinked to see Arielle's colorless face.

"Come on." He steered her through the crush toward the house. "Drummond woke up."

"How is he?"

He almost told her the truth. As another explosion ripped through the air, he knew he did not have time to waste. She would find out for herself soon enough how blind she had been about the man she had vowed to wed. Her hero! He almost laughed. Drummond wanted her only so he could proclaim himself a god.

"We have to get out of here," she cried when he did not answer.

"Too late. We have to find a hole to hide in."

Another blast followed them into the house. Screams were shrill in the street. Stephen said nothing as Arielle ignored them to go to where her fiancé was rising to his feet. Happiness glowed in her eyes as she put her arms around Drummond. The redhead smiled triumphantly at him.

Stephen turned away. What else did he expect, when he had not told her the truth?

"No," he heard her say. "It is not the allies. President Walker has fled and left Henningsen to raze the city. The filibusters are blowing up Granada."

"Henningsen?" Stephen asked.

Arielle looked from Caleb's strained face to Stephen's. She never had seen him so emotionless, but she knew his strongest passions were boiling behind that mask. Standing between the two men, she said, "Maybe this is why the president was so excited to hear he had arrived."

Stephen checked the pistol in his belt. She was not sure why he hesitated before asking, "Are you with us, Drummond?"

"It is my fault you are here." When he held out his hand and smiled at her, Arielle handed him her gun. He put his arms around her shoulders and squeezed gently. "I will see you get out, Arielle. I have not had a chance to play your hero in a long time."

Arielle flinched at his unwitting choice of words. She glanced at Stephen, but his back was to her. So many things she wanted to tell him. She could not now. Going to him, she put her fingers on his arm. "Can we escape?"

"I don't think we have any choice. We go, or," he added, looking past her to Caleb, "we die."

CHAPTER TWENTY

Arielle tried to keep up with the pace Stephen set along the street. Glancing over her shoulder, she saw Caleb following. Refugees clogged the plaza. The screams of children mixed with the screeches of hysterical horses. No order existed among the overloaded wagons. Everyone cringed as another cloud of smoke and a ball of fire rose into the morning air.

"They are trying to clear a path to the lake," muttered Stephen as he paused by a wagon. Although she could not understand what he said to the driver, she guessed he was negotiating for a ride.

Suddenly he jerked Arielle back. "Keep going," he ordered.

"What is it?"

"The woman in the back of that wagon looks as if she's got cholera."

Fear caressed her with icy fingers. She had heard whispers at the pump in the center of the plaza that the filibusters had brought the sickness back from Rivas. "We cannot stay here."

"We are not going to." He grabbed her hand and shouted, "Drummond, this way!"

Panicked voices followed them as they inched along an alley. Arielle cringed at another explosion. Smoke clung to her sweaty body, but she did not slow. They had to find a place to hide.

"Lightenfield, the lake is this way." Caleb took Arielle's arm. "You are going the wrong way."

"Why go to the lake? The ships are gone."

"The jungle?"

"Three gringos will not get past the allies." Stephen's lips twisted in a sarcastic smile. "They would kill you and me in short order, but think what they would do to Arielle."

Sure she was in the midst of a tug-of-war, Arielle whispered, "Don't argue. Let's just find a place to hide." She moaned as more buildings erupted.

Stephen brushed dirt from her face. "Henningsen is working his way toward the lake. We can cut across to where he is. Maybe they have a way out." He looked at Caleb, who nodded reluctantly.

When they came out on another street, it was piled with abandoned wagons. Sunlight mixed with the smoke from the fired buildings. Each step became a victory and every breath a miracle.

Suddenly Stephen shouted. He pressed her against a wall. An artillery canister screamed overhead. It exploded only a few streets away. Debris flew around them. She cowered, hiding her face against his chest.

He kicked open a wooden door in the wall. "Go!" he ordered.

"Caleb—" She stared in horror at her fiancé. He was lying in his own blood.

Stephen did not hesitate. He propelled her through the door. With a curse he added, "I will get him. Go!"

She tripped through the ruined garden. Its house had crumbled, but a small lean-to still stood. More artillery soared overhead. The concussion dropped her to the ground, but she rose to run toward the lean-to. Crouching on the damp earth, she watched Stephen and Caleb lurch toward her.

Settling Caleb on the ground, Stephen put his hand on the flimsy wall and gasped for breath. "Is he alive?"

Arielle put her hand over Caleb's lips. His breathing was shallow and fast. "Yes." She pressed her skirt against the wound on his shoulder to stanch the blood. "It doesn't look too bad."

"Stay here."

"Where are you going?" she cried as she leapt to her feet. Banging her head on the low roof, she ignored Stephen's grin. "Don't leave! If something happened—"

He kissed her quickly. "I am too mean to be killed by a minié ball, and I can watch out for the artillery. We have to know what's going on. We cannot stay in the middle of this much longer." He pressed the second gun in her hand. "Drummond cannot use this now. I hope you will not need to."

When he skulked across the garden and disappeared, she sat next to Caleb. Her ears rang with each explosion, but she did not flinch. Slowly the sun crossed the smoky sky. She balanced the heavy pistol on her lap. The artillery was intermittent, but the pop of rifles was coming closer. Fear tricked her eyes, and she raised the pistol, only to discover she had seen nothing but a branch moving in the breeze. How long had Stephen been gone? Too long.

Caleb opened his eyes and groaned. She put her fingers over his mouth and cautioned him to silence.

"Lightenfield?" he whispered.

"He went to find our best route out of here." Arielle shivered as Caleb sat with another moan. "He has been gone for hours."

"Don't worry about him. His type always lands on his feet."

"His type?" Arielle asked tightly, startled by the insult.

Instead of answering, Caleb said, "I did not think you would make a fool of yourself over a slick one like Lightenfield."

"Stephen isn't—He is—"

He laughed coldly when she faltered. "You know damn well what kind of man he is, Arielle. He will—"

Snatching the gun from her hands, he raised it at a shadow moving through the darkness.

"Arielle?"

"That is Stephen," she said at the whisper. When he kept the pistol aimed at the man crossing the garden, she cried, "Caleb, it is Stephen!"

She gripped his wrist, but he shook her off. His mouth twisted into a satisfied grin as he pulled back on the hammer. Stephen froze only an arm's length from the lean-to.

"Caleb, you owe him your life," she whispered. "I could not have found you without Stephen."

Slowly he released the hammer. With a laugh he shoved the pistol into his gold belt. He sat back and crossed his arms over his chest. For a moment Arielle saw the haughty king who had ruled over Cielo Azul.

"What in hell are you trying to prove?" Stephen dropped next to Arielle, but his words were for the other man. "Don't we have enough trouble without killing each other?"

"I want you to stay away from Arielle," Caleb snarled. "She is too decent to be mixed up with you, Lightenfield."

"We are all going to be very good friends before this is over," he answered. "We are cut off from the lake, and my conscience, although I know you doubt such a thing exists, Arielle, would not allow me to leave a helpless little thing like you here."

"Helpless?" she shot out. "I remember saving your useless hide more than once since we began this. If you—" She saw laughter in his eyes. A warmth spread through her. As long as Stephen teased her, she could believe they were going to survive this.

When he put his arm around her shoulders, she leaned her head on his shoulder, not caring now what Caleb thought. She needed the solace of Stephen's arms when he said, "I got delayed trying to skirt the party. Henningsen's men found a cache of liquor, so they are having a premature victory celebration."

"They are getting drunk *now?*" she asked.

"They are insane. They like overwhelming odds. I guess the allies are not enough for them. They have to be drunk too."

Caleb's voice struck her as he snapped, "So what great idea to get us killed do you have now, Lightenfield?"

His answer was lost in another explosion. Arielle buried her face in Stephen's chest. This was madness!

"Go to sleep if you can," Stephen suggested. "We cannot wander around in the dark." Following his own advice, he tipped his ruined hat over his face and rested back against the wall.

Arielle looked at Caleb and saw his fury, but she did not move. With death lurking in every shadow, she would not be hypocritical. She might have promised to marry Caleb, but she would sleep beside Stephen tonight. Maybe for the last time.

Arielle started awake from her half-doze when a shriek shredded the night. Arms closed around her, holding her to the ground that was still vibrating with shock waves.

"That one was close," she whispered.

Stephen nodded as he watched the flames climb in a false dawn. "One of the buildings off the central plaza,

I would guess." He cursed beneath the roar of another detonation. As the noise rumbled across the lake, duller thuds of artillery echoed through the ravaged city.

"Should we leave?"

"Not yet. Henningsen must have convinced a few to remain sober enough to fight. Until we gauge his route, we are better off here."

She rubbed her burning eyes, then asked, "Caleb? Where is Caleb?"

The other side of the lean-to was empty. Stephen pulled his pistol from his belt and took her arm. "Let's go, honey. I have no idea what Drummond has planned, and I am not staying here to find out."

"He would not abandon me to—"

He twisted her face to meet his narrowed eyes. "How do you know what he might do? He has betrayed you once already."

"Betrayed me?"

Stephen did not answer as he drew her out of the low building and across the garden. The wounded sky burned against the silhouettes of the mountains surrounding the lake.

Suddenly he pushed her back into the lean-to. Her heart pounded with fear. She heard a click in a lull of artillery. She scanned the darkness. A form appeared directly in front of her. The long shadow of a rifle pointed at them. A scream solidified in her throat.

"Who is there?" called a slurred voice.

"O'Neal, is that you?" Stephen answered as he put his thumb on the hammer of his pistol. With his arm keeping Arielle in the shadows, he waited for a reply. She heard him counting slowly and knew if he did not get the answer he wanted, he would fire.

"Lightenfield? What in hell are you doing here?" Arielle gasped as she saw the blood splashed liberally over O'Neal. He had discarded his coat, and his scarlet-covered feet were bare. "Henningsen is rounding up our allies. We are going to show these Guatemalans they can't push us around. Who is with you?"

"Arielle Gardiner."

Somehow O'Neal managed to give her a drunken bow. "Miss Gardiner, I thought you had left Granada."

"I did," she answered dryly. "Mr. O'Neal, have you seen Caleb Drummond?"

"Are you still looking for him?"

"We found him, but he has disappeared again."

He arched a brow. "Damn inconvenient of him." O'Neal motioned toward the gate.

"How many does Henningsen have?"

They slipped along the deserted street as O'Neal said, "Not quite four hundred. Only about two hundred men are fit for duty. We have wounded as well as women and youngsters." He hefted his rifle as they edged around a corner. "That is why Henningsen sent us to find all the Americans. We need every man. Are you with us, Lightenfield?"

"At this point I have little choice. The Guatemalans seem to have us cut off."

O'Neal chuckled. "There are fewer of the devils to regroup against us. I led a group of Rifles to avenge my brother's murder this morning. We showed the bastards. The ones we did not shoot, we rode down as if they were wheat before the wind. If Henningsen had not called us back, we could have cleared a path straight to the lake and President Walker." He laughed with malevolent pleasure. "Soon every street will be flushed with the blood of our enemies."

Arielle bit her lip to quiet her heaving stomach. Stumbling behind them, she realized the sun was rising to bring another day of fighting and dying. As the dawn swept aside the shadows, she stared about in horror.

Rubble was pockmarked with bullets and artillery. No

trees stood higher than a man's head. Sickness devoured her as she stared at the heaps of bodies contorted in death. She cringed, closing her eyes.

A gentle kiss urged Arielle to open her eyes. Stephen gave her a wry smile.

"How are you feeling, honey?"

"Lousy."

He chuckled as she leaned against him. The crash of gunfire brought a cry of despair. When Stephen hushed her gently, she looked at him.

"Henningsen has seven guns and a quartet of mortars. They are not going to give up until every last one of them is dead," he said grimly.

"Caleb?"

"O'Neal is going to find him and sign him up to be a filibuster." He laughed shortly. "Maybe he will find someone else to shoot." He pointed toward the broken wall beneath the pall of smoke. "We still cannot reach the lake. So we are going to have to wait for your hero to lead the way through."

Arielle did not defend Caleb. She could not forgive his cruel joke. Then she realized it might not have been a joke. He might have killed Stephen.

Throughout the long day others straggled into the shelter. The hollow-eyed refugees cringed at the renewed fighting. When the filibusters invaded their haven, a tall man with hair as blond as Stephen's called for everyone's attention. Arielle knew he must be Major General Charles Henningsen when he told them they must move to a safer place. He seemed unaware of the blood coursing from his forehead.

Henningsen smiled as he said, "The Guatemalans are holed up in the Guadaloupe Cathedral near the wharf. They gathered there after we blew their comrades to hell." Enthusiastic cheers met his words. "Tomorrow we storm the cathedral. We will take it as our own. Using it as a base for the noncombatants and wounded, we will find our way to the lake from there. At sunrise we attack."

He turned to confer with his officers. The others realized they were dismissed.

Shivering, Arielle looked up at Stephen when he stood. He had been oddly silent. He whispered he would be back soon.

She nodded, knowing he could not sit and do nothing as the sun vanished into the sea behind them. Pulling up her knees, she leaned her face on them. She did not want to think of the morning, when they intended to commit mass suicide. Looking skyward, she wanted to reach out and stop the moon. If she could keep dawn from coming, perhaps they would be rescued before the drums called them to death.

Fire cascaded into the morning. Screams from terrified children were louder than the orders shouted by their elders.

Stephen put his hand on Arielle's shoulder as he peered over the stone wall. "Be ready to run. They're getting ready to assault the church."

"Should we flee?"

"Where?"

He helped her to her feet. With the wall between them and the plaza, they were safe from Guatemalan sharpshooters. "Honey, I want you to stay here as long as it is safe."

"Me? Where are you going?"

A smile quirked his lips. "I have been conscripted."

"No!" she exclaimed. Gripping his forearms, she cried, "Stephen, this is not your fight!"

"It is now." His arms encircled her waist and brought her the half-step into his embrace. He kissed the tip of her nose. "Don't worry, honey. I do not intend to let Henningsen talk me into doing something silly."

"Stephen . . ."

His mouth covered hers. As her arms swept up his back, sobs rattled in her chest. She might never see him alive again.

In her ear he murmured, "Stay here, so I know you are safe. Don't be foolish like O'Neal or Childs."

"Childs? Rutledge?"

"Childs was with Captain Hesse when they attacked the cathedral yesterday," he said tonelessly. "A score of men are missing, either captured or dead. It does not matter, because the Guatemalans do not want prisoners."

She hid her face in her hands but had no tears left. All sorrow had been wrung from her.

He peeled her fingers from her face. "Dammit, Arielle, forget about him. Think about your life! I want you to stay here. Don't be a hero."

"If—"

His grip on her arms tightened until she gasped. "Arielle Gardiner, for once in your life, obey an order. Will you stay here?"

"Yes." As he turned to go to where the men were congregating, she added, "Stephen, I love you."

He smiled, the tension leaving his face. Again he was the carefree Captain Lightenfield, eager to find excitement in the jungle. Taking her hand, he raised it to his lips. "Remember that I kissed you there."

"Why?"

"Because as soon as I can, I plan to kiss every bit of you. That is my starting place." He pressed his mouth hungrily against hers. "If you forget where I was, then I must start over."

"I shall forget so you must start over," she whispered.

He grinned. "I was hoping you would, honey."

Arielle watched him walk into the clump of filibusters. She sank to the ground as Henningsen quickly dispersed his men. Three crews surrounded the artillery. Sixty men primed their rifles and waited for Henningsen's order to rout their enemies.

Artillery shattered the uneasy peace and sent the few remaining birds spiraling skyward. She put her hands over her ears. A trembling hand touched her arm. Opening her eyes, she held out her arms to the little boy whose dirty face was crisscrossed by the paths of his tears. He propelled himself into her arms. She held him close.

Suddenly the firing stopped. Orders were shrieked in the ear-aching silence. Arielle leapt to her feet. She took the child's hand and ran around the broken wall to see everyone racing toward the Guadaloupe Cathedral. What were they doing?

"Go! To the church."

She whirled. "Stephen!"

He scooped up the little boy. "The church is abandoned, but the allies must be close. Henningsen wants us all inside."

She ran after him. The sun burned her, and she ignored the corpses. Coolness welcomed her into the church.

Stephen steered them through the crowd until he found a spot near a windowless wall. Motioning for her to sit, he put the little boy on her lap. With a grin he asked, "Who is your friend?"

"I'm not sure. We did not have time to exchange names." She smoothed the child's flaxen hair and leaned his cheek against her chest. "Is Caleb here?"

He shrugged. "Who knows? If he is still alive, he is."

"I should—"

Putting his hands on her shoulders, he said, "You saved his life once. You do not owe him anything else."

"I know, but he was my friend, Stephen."

"Was?" He didn't give her a chance to answer. "Stay here, honey. I will be back when I can." He grinned sheepishly. "I have been put in charge of the men guarding the front of the cathedral."

"You?"

"Why are you so surprised, honey? Didn't you think I could command on land as well as at sea?"

She ran her fingers along the scorched leg of his trousers. He must have been standing very close to the artillery. Stephen Lightenfield would do nothing halfheartedly. "Be careful."

Arielle silently held the weeping child. Although she should be looking for his mother, she remained by the wall. As others passed her, looking for loved ones, seeking an answer to the destruction of their hopes, she wished she could push back time to when they had been safe.

"Young lady?"

Glancing up, Arielle saw a smile on a woman's care-lined face. "Yes?"

"I am Mrs. Bingham. You are?"

"Arielle Gardiner. This young man has not told me his name yet."

"Come with me, Miss Gardiner." Mrs. Bingham held out her hand to the child. "We are gathering in a room near the back so we are not in the soldiers' way."

Arielle listened as Mrs. Bingham assured her they soon would be rescued by President Walker. All they needed to do was rest so they could cheer on the victorious filibusters. Arielle wished she could share her optimism.

Holding the little boy's hand, she stepped over the women and youngsters occupying the floor of the small room. When the child tugged, she released him to run to a woman who held out her arms. The child's mother flashed Arielle a smile.

At a commotion Arielle looked across the room, which was lit by the windows set high in the wall. Francine Childs was glancing about the room with disdain, her pose announcing that the war was being waged only to discomfort her. She demanded, "Who is in charge? I cannot stay here."

Everyone froze at her outburst.

Tersely Arielle ordered, "Be quiet, Francine."

"What are you doing here?" she asked with a sneer. "I thought you and your lover had run off into the jungle."

"Be quiet," she repeated. "Your husband is among the missing. If you cannot mourn for him, then respect the wishes of the others who have lost as much as you."

Francine sniffed inelegantly. "My dear Miss Gardiner, what right do you have to be here? You and your cowardly Captain Lightenfield hold no position in our city."

"No one holds anything but this crumbling building! What you had is gone."

"Miss Gardiner is correct," chimed in another woman whose eyes were red from weeping. "Mrs. Childs, my husband was with yours and Captain Hesse. They may be dead, but my husband would have wanted me to bear the hardships as if I were he."

When Francine started to argue with the woman, Arielle walked away. She did not want to listen to the pettiness. Finding a place to sit, she stared at the design in the stained glass window. The reds and greens played across her face as the sun climbed over the cathedral.

Surely Walker would send troops to help those here. The president must rescue the ones who had proven their loyalty. He must, or they all would be martyrs to a dying cause.

During the first three days the refugees crowded into the cathedral, Arielle saw more of Mrs. Bingham than Stephen. Mrs. Bingham asked her to help with nursing. The first case of cholera had appeared before sunset the second day. Within hours the small sick room was full. With more than three hundred people crowded into the building, they had little room for the wounded and ill. Friends and strangers suffered together.

Arielle spent hours on her knees, trying to get water down the parched throats, hoping they could save these tortured souls, praying no one else sickened. Neither wish was answered.

Occasionally she passed Stephen in a hallway, for he seldom was able to leave his post, where he supervised the sentries. When he did, she was busy running errands for the tireless Mrs. Bingham. Each brief meeting gave her strength to carry her to the next.

Arielle was shocked when Stephen came into the sickroom. "Stephen, you should not be here," she admonished him.

He drew her to her feet. "I have to talk with you." He led her to a corner. There was no privacy in the church, but, near the dying, nobody would heed their conversation. Neither of them looked at the mutilated bodies clinging to life as fiercely as they had fought the allies.

Arielle wanted to ask a thousand questions, but when she saw his serious expression, she shivered. The twinkle had vanished from his eye. Even when he faced death at the hands of Alfonso's cult, she had seen it.

His hands stroked her shoulders. "Henningsen asked for a volunteer to carry a message out to the lake to Walker out on the *Virgen*."

She understood instantly. Others might fall victim to cholera, but Stephen Lightenfield feared dying of boredom. "When do you leave?"

"Now."

"All right."

He whispered, "Arielle, I love you. I wanted you to know that before . . . before I left." He did not need to say more. She knew, as he did, that no one else had survived crossing the plaza.

"I love you, Stephen." There were other things she wanted to say. Secrets of her soul she yearned to share with this man who possessed her heart. She wished they had had time to create memories that reached back through years instead of weeks.

When he pressed his mouth against hers, she wanted its heat imprinted on her forever. She could not breathe, for he held her tightly. Her fingers moved along his back as tears burned her throat. Releasing her, he caressed her cheek.

"See you soon, honey."

She nodded, afraid to speak. If she opened her mouth, her grief would spill out. His fingers slipped from hers, and he walked past the pallets.

A pang tore through her heart as the door closed at the far end of the room. "Oh, Stephen," she whispered, "why did you have to be a hero this time?"

CHAPTER TWENTY-ONE

Caleb Drummond was dying. As she sat by his side and watched cholera suck life from him, Arielle knew that. She had seen so many others die in the past week. With little food in the church, they were surviving on a stew of mule and horse meat. More would sicken when even that was gone.

She reached past Caleb to a basin. Taking out a rag, she put it on his head. She shivered as she heard the continuous patter of gunshot beyond the walls.

He struggled to speak. "Lightenfield—"

"Stephen is gone."

"Good. Stay away from him, Arielle. Promise me that."

She shook her head. "No. I will promise you almost anything else, but not that. I love Stephen."

"Fool . . ." He shuddered.

"He loves me too."

"And you believe that?" A weak smile pulled at his lips. "Where is he?"

"He has gone for help."

Arielle was not sure if he was laughing or coughing. She reached for a cup of water, but he turned his head from her. Tears cascaded from her eyes when she heard him mutter, "Good riddance."

An hour later Arielle rose. She had watched his chest labor for every breath until he gave up. No grief haunted her. She had lost the Caleb she had known when he left Concord. This hard man who could not forgive her for loving Stephen had been a stranger.

The brief rest Arielle had that night was the last she had for days. With a vengeance the epidemic spread. She spent every hour working with Mrs. Bingham, Reverend Hastings, and Christian Foner.

The filibuster she had met at President Walker's ball had been wounded. As soon as he was well enough to walk, his bed had been given to someone sicker. He remained to assist the nurses. At first he had been shattered by each death but swiftly learned the necessary apathy.

When he limped toward her, she asked, "How is Mrs. Bingham's daughter?"

His face grew longer. "I don't think she'll make it until morning. Another Bingham child was brought in just an hour ago."

"Another?" Renewed pain sliced through her. Two nights before, Mrs. Bingham had been stricken. Tired by the long hours she had worked, Mrs. Bingham had died before anyone could help her. Already one of the Bingham children had died. If they remained in the cathedral much longer, none of them would emerge alive.

Someone had to do something, and it would be she if no one else would help.

General Henningsen had taken the priest's office for

his own. Bravely she knocked on the door. If she did not do this now, she feared she would lose the courage to confront him. When the door opened, she recoiled in astonishment to see General Henningsen. She had been sure an aide would answer.

"May I take a moment of your time?" she asked quietly.

"Miss Gardiner, isn't it?"

"Yes, sir."

"Come in." He pointed toward a chair, but she shook her head.

"I don't want to keep you." She wrung her hands, which were reddened from the many times she had washed them in the brackish water from the cistern. "Sir, I know you're busy, but I wondered if you had received any word from Captain Lightenfield."

"Captain Lightenfield?"

Hysterical laughter taunted her. This was like the most incredible of Stephen's jokes. The man who denounced William Walker had been willing to risk his life to bring help to the filibusters. The man who had said he was crossing the isthmus for fun had shunted it all aside for a deadly adventure. But this was no joke. No matter how much she might wish otherwise, this was no joke.

Before she could explain, the general rubbed his finger beneath his mustache. "Stephen Lightenfield ... yes." When he paused, she hoped she would not have to wait as long for him to speak as she did his president. He nodded to himself, then said, "There has been no word of his success in reaching the lake or the *Virgen*."

"Oh." She should say something else, but her brain refused to work.

"Of course that means little," he added. "We've had no communication with President Walker since our supply lines were cut by Zavala's Guatemalans."

"You needn't cushion the truth to spare my feelings,"

she said when his kindness freed her from her horror. "I appreciate your kindness, General, but Stephen was well aware of the risks."

"Captain Lightenfield is a brave man. A true hero."

"Yes," she answered. Bidding him a good day, she backed out of the office. She was afraid if she turned, the mask hiding her grief would crack.

She hurried across the church. When she reached the back door, she saw filibusters gouging holes in the sand and pouring molten lead and scrap metal into them. They were making ammunition. The war was far from finished.

Arielle turned away. The war was over for her, because it had claimed both men she had dared to trust with her heart. Finding a dark corner within the shadow of the confessional, she drew her knees up and folded her arms on them. Laying her head on them, she let tears fall.

"Stephen," she whispered as if speaking his name could bring him back to her. "Don't be dead. I need you to hold me. I need you now. I'm so scared."

Sobs burst from her. She was tired of being brave. She was tired of dreaming of his arms around her and his body warm and rough against her. She was tired of being haunted by the thought that Stephen's body might lie now in the sun, unburied.

"Arielle?"

Hope leapt in her heart. Was Stephen calling to her? She pushed herself away from the door and saw Mrs. Langley, who now was in charge of the sickroom.

Mrs. Langley held out a bucket. "Can you bring us some water?"

Arielle nodded. The well was in the courtyard, but, with the soldiers out there, she should be safe.

"I looked for you," Mrs. Langley said. "I thought you might want to be there when Mrs. Childs joined her husband in heaven."

She closed her eyes as she sighed. She had not even

known that Francine was among those taken ill with the horrible sickness. Death was destroying Walker's dreams of an empire.

Taking the bucket, she went out into the sunset that was staining the courtyard stones with a light as red as the blood spilled beyond these walls. She edged around the soldiers and went to the well by the shattered wall. Walker's order to raze Granada had left his enemies little cover, but it was an exquisite torture to know that help waited only a short distance away. She could see the lake beyond the maze of Walker's enemies.

Her stomach grumbled. They were starving within the cathedral. What little food they had was being saved for anyone who survived the cholera.

She set the bucket on the well and began to turn the handle to bring up water. Greasy sweat oozed down her back. A motion caught her eye, and she reached for her pistol. She released her breath slowly when she realized it was only smoke from the allies' distant campfires. With a sigh she kept turning the handle.

She heard a pebble strike a rock. She spun to the right. Horror froze her as she saw a flitting shadow, then another. Behind her, men shouted. She whirled to run. Her eyes widened as the door was slammed closed. She heard the bar fall.

They had left her out here to die!

Pressing against the wall in the thin shadows, she pulled out her pistol. One shot. It had only one shot.

Stephen's voice echoed in her mind, warning her not to use the gun until she had no other choice.

She stuck the gun through a chink in the wall. Blindly she pulled back on the hammer.

The gun knocked her back. She could not see, because acrid gunsmoke hung in the hot air. Suddenly a form burst from the curtain of smoke. With a scream she lifted the pistol to use it like a club. She was shoved to the ground as balls whizzed overhead. Shards of stone cut into her. She looked up.

"Stephen?" This must be a dream—a nightmare that had come to taunt her. Or was she dead? She put her hand out, but he raised his rifle and fired over the wall.

"What are you doing out here?" he demanded as he reloaded.

"What are *you* doing here?"

"I got tired of playing the hero for Walker, so I thought I would come to see how you are doing."

"Not well."

With a low laugh he captured her lips, which had ached for his kisses. Melting into his embrace, she prayed this sweetness was real.

As quickly as he had swept her into his arms, he released her. He drew her away from the well. The stern set of his jaw warned her not to protest. Leading her into the shadow of a half-wall, he looked back to be sure they had not been followed.

She shrieked as something moved toward them. Stephen pressed his hand over her mouth as another man appeared out of the deepening dusk.

"Will you be quiet, Arielle?" Stephen whispered. "You are going to alert everyone within a mile with your screeches." He lifted his hand away.

"You could have warned me that you were not alone."

"Preston Crane is here with a contingent of Commodore Vanderbilt's men. He thought it would be fun to see what was happening in Granada, so I offered to show him." With a wry grin he added, "*This*, as you may have guessed, Preston, is Arielle Gardiner."

He bowed his balding head. "My pleasure, Miss Gardiner. Now that you have found her, Stephen, let's get the hell out of here."

"You are right. We do not want to be here when the Guatemalans attack the cathedral tonight."

"You came back for me?" Arielle whispered.

"I told I would, didn't I?" He smiled. "I try not to break too many promises either."

Mr. Crane cleared his throat. "We should leave. Colonel Waters has been given orders to rescue those in the church. We don't want to get caught in the cross fire." He backed away to let Stephen take the lead. As if they were about to enter an opera house instead of a battlefield, he graciously motioned for Arielle to go next. He drew a pistol as he followed.

Although she had seen the lake from the courtyard, no other landmarks told Arielle where they were going. Granada had been destroyed.

When Stephen dropped to his knees and pulled her to the ground, she put her hand against his back and was not surprised that his breathing remained slow and steady. Her heart throbbed with terror as someone walked toward them.

Stephen exploded from his hiding place. The flash of his pistol against the man's head dropped the soldier to the ground. Signaling to them, he began to run along the alley.

Arielle hurried to catch up. Stephen held her hand as they turned toward the lake. Night settled around them.

"There," whispered Stephen when they paused in the rubble. "Walker's new recruits must have come ashore at sunset."

Mr. Crane cursed.

Stephen's laugh no longer astonished Arielle. He loved a challenge even if their lives were what they were gambling. "Ready, honey?"

"I might be if you tell me what we are doing."

Mr. Crane chuckled, but Stephen warned, "Now, now, no nastiness when I'm acting as your dashing knight in shining armor. We are going for a moonlight cruise on Lake Nicaragua."

Running through the sand, they stayed close to what remained of the fishing huts. The skin prickled along Arielle's back, but no gunfire came as she struggled to match the men's long strides.

Stephen put his arm around her. Her breath rasped in her ears. She feared it would betray them. He stopped at the water's edge and helped her into a *bungo*. The men pushed it into the water. They climbed in and dipped the oars into the waves. She looked behind her, but had nothing to say in farewell to Granada.

Arielle sat in the saloon of the small steamboat chugging toward the Rio San Juan. She had changed from her ragged, sweaty clothes into a silken wrapper that was waiting in the stateroom Stephen had escorted her to.

Stephen and Mr. Crane lingered over their after-dinner brandy while she continued to eat. Neither man commented on her appetite. They must know that the food in the cathedral was almost gone. Between bites she answered their questions.

"Henningsen is a better soldier than Walker deserves," stated Stephen as he leaned back and gazed across the room. "Of course, it doesn't matter. Walker's done. None too soon."

"Do you want me to take your report to the Commodore, Stephen?" Taking a sip, he smiled at Stephen.

Arielle waited for Stephen's answer. It was time for the truth.

His gray eyes met hers. "No, I can finish my report on *The Ladysong*."

"Write it, you mean," retorted Mr. Crane.

"You know I hate reports."

Mr. Crane refilled his glass. "You'll get no sympathy from me. This was all your idea, so you have the honor of reporting to Vanderbilt." With a grin he poured more brandy into Stephen's glass. "You are fortunate it turned out as it did. The Commodore had a fit when he heard you had sent Roach Walden to California. For a while no one dared to mention your name around the Commodore."

"Is that so?" Pushing back his chair, Stephen stood and held out his hand to Arielle. "Honey, why don't we take a walk on the deck?"

"Yes," she answered. She dared say no more, for she was unsure what would happen if she allowed her questions to spill from her lips.

Fresh air enveloped her as they stepped onto the narrow deck. Arielle listened to the contented steam engine and the whisper of the sidewheels churning the water.

"I heard that Drummond died of cholera," Stephen said quietly.

She nodded, no longer surprised that he knew things he should not. "He gained consciousness for only a few minutes at the end and wanted me to promise to have nothing more to do with you."

Stephen laughed without humor. "That is no surprise. Did he say anything else?"

"Not much." She paused and faced him. "What are you afraid he told me? The truth?"

"About him?" He shook his head. "He would never have told you that."

"What truth about him?"

He hesitated, then folded his arms on the railing. "Let the past die with the dead."

Although she wanted to ask him what he was talking about, she nodded. "So what is the truth about you?"

"The truth is I work for Commodore Cornelius Vanderbilt."

"That I guessed. If you came to Nicaragua regularly, you must work for either President Walker or the Commodore. What do you do beside look for fun and adventure?"

"Spy."

"Spy?" she repeated.

With a chuckle he said, "There are nicer words for it, but that's what I do."

"I don't believe it."

Putting his hands on her shoulders, he massaged her tight muscles. "Honey, believe it. The Commodore was furious when Walker's government stole the Accessory Transit Company. I had my own reasons for wanting to help destroy Walker." He paused, then sighed. "My cousin Elmer got mixed up with Walker in his campaign to annex Baja California. Walker came back to try again. Elmer didn't."

Arielle put her hand against his chest, wanting to ease the pain she never had guessed he hid.

"When we first came to Granada," he went on, "when you thought I had abandoned you, I was on the lake trying to discover if the crews of the Transit Company's boats were loyal to Walker."

"So you used me?"

He brushed back her hair that the breeze sent drifting over her face. "Honey, I did not want to use you, but you have to admit that your need to find Drummond was a welcome excuse to go to Granada."

"You and Roach Walden could have found another excuse."

When she pushed past him to walk toward her cabin, he said nothing until she put her hand on the doorknob. His larger hand covered hers and kept her from turning it as his finger tilted her face toward him.

"Roach betrayed me. I couldn't trust him again."

"So you decided to use me instead?"

His lips tightened beneath his mustache. "I helped you too, honey. You wouldn't have gotten five feet out of Greytown without my assistance."

"I remember your help!" she snapped. "Leeches, rapids, mosquitoes." Her eyes widened. "You did not want to get on the river packet because you were afraid someone would recognize you and tell me the truth?"

"There was that." He grinned.

"So you made me suffer in the mud and the heat!"

"But you got to Granada, didn't you?"

Grudgingly she said, "Yes."

"When we reached Granada, your quest enabled me to gain access to people I might not have been able to meet otherwise. Now you can understand why I couldn't risk meeting Walker. He might have recognized me."

"At least, you are finally being honest." Her heart cramped. Caleb had pushed her away at the end, and Stephen never had let her near. Why had she been such a fool?

"While I am, let me tell you something else. Arielle, I really do love you."

She stared at him. "You really love me?"

He turned the knob and opened the door. "I fought hard to resist you, honey. I never thought I would want a woman complicating my life, but that was because I had never met a woman like you. Say you'll marry me. In Greytown or New York or Concord or here or wherever."

"So are you my brave hero now? Rescuing me and expecting to win my hand in reward?" She smiled as joy bubbled through her.

With a laugh he grasped her at the knees and tipped her over his shoulder. He kicked the door closed and dropped her on the bed. Leaning over her, he pinned her to the pillows with the caress of his lips. As his fingers reached for the sash at her waist, he murmured, "I must be brave if I am willing to spend my life with you."

"Brave or stupid?"

"Just incredibly in love with you. Say you'll marry me, Arielle."

"It could be fun," she whispered as she drew him closer. "Always, honey."

She did not answer as his kisses burned away memories of terror. With a laugh she drew him closer, knowing that he would never be reluctant to love her.

AUTHOR'S NOTE

I hope you enjoyed reading *Her Only Hero*. Much of the background story—the tale of William Walker and his filibusters and Commodore Vanderbilt's determination to destroy him—is true. The filibusters were defeated in Nicaragua when most of them were too sick or too wounded to fight. They left Nicaragua, and many, including Walker, returned to the United States. Walker tried twice more to build himself an empire in Central America. He was hanged in 1860 by the Hondurans.

My next Zebra Splendor romance will be *Anything for You*, which is scheduled to be on sale in April 2000. In a logging camp, a woman can hide her past—or so Gypsy Elliott thinks until it comes stalking her. Now she must hide it—and her heart—from Adam Lassiter, who may be there to help her, or destroy the haven she has found.

I enjoy hearing from my readers. You can contact me by E-mail at:

jaferg@erols.com

Or write to me at:

Jo Ann Ferguson
VFRW
PO Box 350
Wayne, PA 19087-0350

Visit my Web site at:
www.joannferguson.com

Happy reading!

BOOK YOUR PLACE ON OUR WEBSITE AND MAKE THE READING CONNECTION!

We've created a customized website just for our very special readers, where you can get the inside scoop on everything that's going on with Zebra, Pinnacle and Kensington books.

When you come online, you'll have the exciting opportunity to:

- View covers of upcoming books
- Read sample chapters
- Learn about our future publishing schedule (listed by publication month *and author*)
- Find out when your favorite authors will be visiting a city near you
- Search for and order backlist books from our online catalog
- Check out author bios and background information
- Send e-mail to your favorite authors
- Meet the Kensington staff online
- Join us in weekly chats with authors, readers and other guests
- Get writing guidelines
- AND MUCH MORE!

**Visit our website at
http://www.zebrabooks.com**

Put a Little Romance in Your Life With
Janelle Taylor